SCOTTISH
TRADITIONAL TALES

Edited by

Alan Bruford

and

Donald A. MacDonald

BIRLINN

This edition published in 2003 by
Birlinn Limited
West Newington House
10 Newington Road
Edinburgh EH9 1QS

www.birlinn.co.uk

Reprinted 2011

First published in 1994 by Polygon, Edinburgh

ISBN 978 1 841 58264 1

Printed and bound by CPI Antony Rowe, Chippenham, Wiltshire

CONTENTS

Tales with an asterisk have been translated from Gaelic; if the storyteller's name has a dagger, the tale has been taken from a manuscript rather than a tape-recorded source. Some titles have been supplied by the collector or editor rather than the storyteller: if this is known to be so the title is bracketed in the Notes.

CONTENTS

CONTENTS

Alan Bruford

INTRODUCTION

TRADITIONAL STORYTELLING

All over the world traditional tales used to be told at the fireside, or whatever marked the centre of a family's life, until their place came to be taken in developed societies by books, newspapers, the radio and most recently television. They are still told in pubs and clubs, lounges and waiting-rooms, on trains or boats or anywhere that people meet, though most of us may not think of jokes, shaggy-dog stories, tall tales, contemporary legends or ghost stories as 'folktales', certainly not as anything like 'fairy-tales'. All the same, they are, and they can be just as old. For instance, ten or twelve years ago, Bob, one of the servitors who kept the door at the School of Scottish Studies – the research and teaching department of the University of Edinburgh where Donald A. MacDonald and I work and whose archives are the source of all the stories in this book – told me a story he had heard from a comedian in an Edinburgh club. It was about two Irish twins called Pat and Mike who had been put in different classes at the same school. Pat was just a bit too clever, and his teacher decided to take him down a peg. He set him three questions to answer: 'How deep is the sea?' 'How heavy is the moon?' and 'What am I thinking?' If he couldn't bring him the right answers after school next Monday, he wouldn't be allowed on the class excursion.

Next Monday the boy turned up, and the teacher asked him: 'How far is it to the bottom of the sea?'

'A stone's throw.'

'I suppose I can't argue with that. Well, how heavy is the moon?'

'It must be a hundredweight.'

'How do you make that out?'

'Well, there are four quarters in it, aren't there?'

'That's very clever, but answer me this. What am I thinking?'

'You're thinking I'm Pat, but I'm his brother Mike.'

Like any story told from memory, that story has details that I put in myself when I could not remember what Bob said, and some of them may come from similar versions I have read,[1] but it went something like that. Basically it is the same story as 'The King's Three Questions' (No. 30 below), a version of which was first written down in Egypt in the ninth century AD, about the same time that the tale we know as 'Cinderella' was first written down in China, as a story told by southern barbarians about a girl who lived in a cave and was helped by a magic fish.[2]

In 1976 Dr Ann Silver wrote to *The Scots Magazine* about a story she remembered from her childhood in Ayrshire; the magazine printed her letter under the heading 'An Ayrshire Tale'.[3]

My great grandmother who was born in Mauchline about 1835 taught my mother a story which is known in the family as 'start to your strunterfers'. We have never met anyone else who has heard of it nor have we seen a written version. The gist of the story is this: One day the Mistress of the house went into the kitchen and asked the Cook how she referred to the Master. The Cook said: 'The Master or the Maister or Himself or anything you please, m'em.' The Mistress then said, 'In future you will call him the Master above all Masters,' to which the Cook answered 'Very good, m'em.'

(This dialogue is then repeated, the Cook being given words for the Master's trousers (strunterfers), the Mistress (Lady Peerapolemaddam), the kitchen range (Vengeance), the cat (Old Calgravatus), the river (The River above all Rivers) and the house (The Castle of St. Mungo).)

That night as the Cook was sitting by the kitchen range a coal fell out on the cat. The Cook ran to the bottom of the stairs and called to the Master: 'Master above all Masters, start to your strunterfers, waken Lady

Peerapolemaddam, for Vengeance has seized Old Calgravatus and unless assistance be procured from the River above all Rivers, the Castle of St. Mungo is *doomed.*'

Can anyone tell me if this is a well-established Ayrshire story, and whether it is written down anywhere? I would love to know how to spell these extraordinary words.

The editor of the magazine, Maurice Fleming, asked if I could help, and I was able to say that though it had never before been written down in this form (the words are spelt here as Dr Silver wrote them) the story is again an international folktale type, No. 1562A 'The Barn is Burning' in the Aarne-Thompson (AT) index, which lists versions from Russia, Lithuania, Czechoslovakia, France, Italy, Spain, Chile, the Caribbean and the USA, as well as Scotland, England, Ireland and Wales. In 1936 most of the versions in English, Scots, Irish and Welsh were analysed in the journal *Folklore* by Kenneth Jackson, later Professor of Celtic at the University of Edinburgh,[4] who deduced that the story had first been made up in the late Middle Ages to make fun of laymen who pretended to know more Church Latin than they really did. So the water may be called 'Pondolorum' (with a Latin ending) in one version and 'Absolution' (which washes away sin in Catholic belief) in another, and similarly the fire may be called 'Hot Cockalorum' or 'Fire Evangelist' – 'Vengeance' is probably corrupted from this phrase, in the same way as 'send reinforcements' is said to have changed to 'send three and fourpence' by being passed from soldier to soldier in the trenches, though here the result is an improvement: 'Vengeance has seized Old Calgravatus' is the most impressive way I know of saying 'the cat's on fire'. As for Old Calgravatus himself, he seems to bear a mediaeval name for a wonderful cat that has only survived otherwise, as far as I know, in the Gaelic of South Uist, as Cugrabhat, or Gugtrabhad, the king of the cats in story No. 12 below.

Jackson had only found two versions from Scotland, one with just the words of the cook's message in Robert Chambers' *Popular Rhymes of Scotland* from the beginning of the last century, the other published by the great folklorist from the north-east of Scotland, the Revd Walter Gregor, in the 1880s; we had just printed a third tale No. 37 below. After Dr Silver's letter and my note on it appeared in *The Scots Magazine*, a Stirlingshire woman sent a version of the story to the magazine, a Lanarkshire man sent one to me, and a Canadian woman sent one she had heard as a child as 'a recording of what was called simply a Scottish story', so the score was doubled, and we got an English version from a woman near York.[5] If any reader who has heard the story, other than from a book, would like to send their version in, we might easily double the score for Scotland again.

That story was heard by Dr Silver in childhood, and Bob's story was about schoolboys, but neither of them was designed to be told only to children. This is a popular misconception about folktales or at least 'fairy-tales'. Very few traditional tales are meant only for children: the first eight in this book are the only stories in it that would normally have been told to children under the age of eight or nine: the rest were intended for adults. Storytelling, in communities where it was a regular entertainment, was generally something that happened in the late evenings, when small children would have been in bed; older ones might be allowed to listen but could well drop off to sleep and leave the really adult stories to be told to an adult audience last thing at night. Many of the best traditional storytellers started to pick up the stories they told around the age of nine or ten, and many of these were 'fairy-tales' or international 'wonder-tales' on the lines of 'Jack and the Beanstalk' or 'Beauty and the Beast', which were not generally thought of as being only for children. In some societies, including most African tribes and the travelling people of Scotland, all stories were believed to have an educational function as well as being entertaining, so they were directed particularly at adolescents, who might pick up hints from them, at least on how to face the wider world with confidence and optimism: but they would also be appreciated by older people who had heard them before.

It may be more important to remember that where fireside storytelling flourished mainly in post-mediaeval Europe, among working people in the country, it was not generally used to entertain people who were there just to listen, like the audience at a play or a modern storytelling festival. Certainly people would sometimes travel some distance to hear a particularly famous narrator or story, but in Scotland most stories were heard either in the home or at furthest in the township's 'ceilidh house', and, apart from younger children, most members of the audience would be making or mending something as they listened. Walter Gregor, describing 'evenings in the farm kitchen' when he was a boy in Highland Banffshire over 150 years ago,[6] emphasised that 'all were busy. One of the women might be knitting, another making, and another mending, some article of dress. Of the men, one might be making candles from bog-fir – *cleavin can'les* – another manufacturing harrow-tynes of wood, a third sawing brogues, and a fourth weaving with the *cleeck* a pair of mittens.' Apart from this last, the men's occupations were typical of these wooded uplands, and the slivers of bog-fir used to light the room are a local speciality. In coastal communities men might be mending fishing-nets or making creels, or anyone of either sex might be baiting small-lines to go out next morning. Women might also be carding or spinning wool, and Gregor mentions that neighbours might visit the family, '*geein thim a forenicht*. On such occasions it was no unusual thing for the young women to carry with them their spinning-wheels on their shoulders, and their wool or flax under their arms.'[7] On the larger farms men might be mending harness or polishing horse-brasses for a show, or twisting ropes of straw, rushes, heather, bent-grass or hair for use about the farm, and in the woodless Northern Isles weaving these in turn into baskets, mats and nets. Even the storyteller might be employed in this way: from the niece of Angus MacLellan from South Uist, well-represented in this collection, we recorded a hilarious account of MacLellan winding heather rope as he told stories (interspersed with songs) throughout a winter's evening 'till eleven o'clock, and you couldn't see him at last for the heather rope all round him – coiled round his chair'.[8] However, Donald Alasdair Johnson's father, a generation earlier in the same island, was able to insist on the spinning-wheels and wool-cards being silenced while he performed:[9] he was evidently a star who could attract a dozen visitors to his croft kitchen, and not every ceilidh house would have been so strictly run.

Apart from the home fireside there were plenty of other places where long stories might be told in rural Victorian Scotland: at the camp firesides where travelling people met; by the kiln fires of big water-mills, which were often gathering-places on winter evenings; on a journey, where stories could 'shorten the road', as the Irish saying has it; or on board a fishing-boat waiting to 'tide its lines' (A. T. Cluness called his book of Shetland tales *Told Round the Peat Fire*, but included a chapter with a description and a fine example of the way in which *haaf* (great-line) fishermen's stories had time to digress into 'episodes, sometimes in themselves containing episodes, and ever returning to the main theme only to diverge again'[10]). However, even in Gregor's youth, stories (mingled with songs and ballads) could not begin until any children at school had 'prepared their lessons' by learning passages by heart from books. When it began, 'the story was for the most of the supernatural': short and often frightening tales of local fairies, witches and warlocks from the examples he gives, which drove the children to cling to their parents as the fire burned lower 'with the eyes now fearfully turned to the doors, and now to the chimney, and now to this corner, whence issued the smallest noise, and now to the next, in dread of seeing some of the uncanny brood.'[11] Many people in the second half of this century have told us how as children they were frightened to go home in the dark after an evening listening to stories in a neighbour's house. Other longer traditional tales are not mentioned in Gregor's account, though he mentions tales of pirates and polar seas, and the wars between England and Scotland (very likely based on chapbooks) and bawdy tales 'told without the least conception that there was any indecency in them'. Elsewhere he refers to *quarterers*, 'a class of respectable beggars' who were given lodgings in return for the news they carried, and sometimes their skill in music, medicine or repairs; chapmen or pedlars who stayed the night; and travelling tailors, who used to live in their customers' houses while they made up garments for them from cloth woven by a local weaver out of the householder's own homespun wool and flax.[12]

The visiting tailor or cobbler is often mentioned in stories (see Nos. 69a and 87b, and cf. 28) and might well tell stories himself as he sat cross-legged at his sewing: so might quarterers, as well as bringing news; so might chapmen, as well as selling chapbooks and ballad sheets.

The accounts of Highland storytelling from around the same time which John Francis Campbell 'of Islay' published in the introduction to his *Popular Tales of the West Highlands* paint a similar scene, but the work element is less emphasised and many of the stories told are different: Hector MacLean[13] wrote that people in 'the Islands of Barra . . . appear to be fondest of those tales which describe exceedingly rapid changes of place in very short portions of time' – heroic or romantic adventure tales, not local legends, and ones which drew from the audience every reaction from loud laughter to 'almost shedding tears'. That part of the Gaelic-speaking Highlands would not have had to wait for stories till after the school homework or, as happened at least once a week in most Lowland farm kitchens by the end of the century, the reading of the local newspaper; but MacLean claimed that in Protestant North Uist and Harris 'these tales are nearly gone, and this I believe to be owing partly to reading, which in a manner supplies a substitute for them, partly to bigoted religious ideas, and partly to narrow utilitarian views'. In fact 'these tales' can only be the long hero-tales, for many folktales, and not only local legends, survived in North Uist to be recorded a century or more after MacLean wrote in 1860, and even from Lewis, where the early nineteenth-century evangelists had perhaps the greatest impact: there are in this book late twentieth-century recordings of international tale-types and even a version of a religious *exemplum* well-known in Catholic Ireland (No. 49 below). But Hector Urquhart from Poolewe[14] confirmed that in Wester Ross by 1859 there were no longer the gatherings of young and old there had been on winter nights when he was a boy, to listen to stories from travelling tailors, shoemakers or other visitors known for their 'store of tales', or for the company to set each other riddles or discuss the Fenian heroes. 'The minister came to the village in 1830, and the schoolmaster soon followed, who put a stop in our village to such gatherings; and in their place we were supplied with heavier tasks than listening to the old shoemaker's fairy tales.' In 1859 he could find few of the old storytellers or their stories left – but again, the *céilidh* (in its original sense, a visit to a neighbour's house which might include singing, storytelling, riddles, card-playing or just conversation) was not totally stamped out anywhere that Gaelic was spoken, and we have been able to include stories from twentieth-century Wester Ross.

The Gaelic-speaking parts of the Highlands and Islands are one place where only now the new electronic media, the drift away from the crofts and a general decline in sociability between neighbours have apparently finally put a stop to ceilidhing. Though in Barra or South Uist today we know of nobody who knows long hero-tales from oral tradition, there are one or two elsewhere, and there should still be a handful of Gaels who have learned traditional tales of some sort in their traditional context living into the twenty-first century. The only other part of Scotland where anything like ceilidhing remained a regular part of social life in the twentieth century was Shetland, where the habit of calling 'in aboot da nyht' for a chat, a game of cards, some fiddle-tunes or songs or stories was well-established in the long winter evenings. Men could use the pretext of 'guising' for visits around Hallowe'en and the '24 Nights of Yule' and in practice such visiting took place at any time from the end of October until February. Women still met to work together at wool-cardings or spinnings (bringing their spinning-wheels as Gregor de-scribed, and with luck getting them carried home by their boyfriends), right up till the 1930s, and 'makkins' where they would knit for the host family, went on at least until the Second World War: these meetings lasted usually from early afternoon till eleven at night, ending with supper and a dance, and must surely have aided the passing on of stories as well as songs.[15] But most stories were probably told in much the same circumstances as Gregor describes, and the same sort predominated: local legends, often about named people from the past century or two, as often as not with an element of witchcraft or the supernatural in them.

In Orkney the occasions for storytelling seem to have diminished earlier, but James Henderson (born 1903) gave us a vivid second-hand description of how it was a hundred years ago:[16] 'I've heard my mother sayin aboot the nights' – the echo of the Shetland term may be more than a coincidence – 'in some ways it was almost like a ceilidh . . . She remembered the neighbours used to come in: her mother would be sitting spinning and her father sitting makin these straw bands, and men would com in, women would com in – well, they all worked, they would be knitting or doing something. And say, one old fella would tell a story of his days in the Nor-Wast' – with the Hudson's Bay Company in Canada – 'another fella his time at the whalin; so-and-so he always sang a certain song, ye see . . . They all had their bits they did,' and the stories of many sorts which James himself remembered must have been told there alongside the old men's reminiscences.

On the Scots-speaking mainland funny stories and anecdotes of local characters, ghost stories and brief accounts of local events – persecuted Covenanters, illicit distilling, murdered packmen, shipwrecks – can still be picked up in many places, but the longer and more magical tales have come to be thought of usually as something you read in books. There was one group of people, however, who kept up regular fireside gatherings to tell stories well into this century. They used to be known as 'tinkers', from tin-smithing, a skilled trade which most of their men could practise (until it was rendered redundant by the introduction of plastic containers in the past fifty years), but this name was also used by many non-tinkers as a byword for dirt and dishonesty and all those qualities people like to associate with groups who are recognisably different from themselves. As a result they now prefer to be called 'travelling people' or 'travellers' – but the latter form at least is confusing: it is also used by English Romanies, who likewise want to avoid the associations of 'gypsies' or 'gippoes', and can be applied to commercial travellers (sales representatives) or tramps and other wanderers, and now to the urban drop-outs who call themselves 'New Age Travellers' – all groups whom Scottish travellers may either tolerate or view as rivals, but few of whom they would consider as in any way related to themselves. For precision I have therefore often replaced 'travellers' by 'cairds', a Scots form of their Gaelic name (meaning craftsmen), which for most people is less likely to carry derogatory implications than 'tinkers' or 'tinks', and is respected at least as a family name.

Whatever you call them, the cairds did travel and until this century, when the law requiring them to send their children to school for at least a hundred days in the year made many families spend the winters in houses, they camped by the roads they travelled on, the farms they worked on or the rivers they fished for mussels with freshwater pearls. At the camp fires in the evenings, especially where more than one family was camped together, there was too little light to work late except in high summer, or to read if anyone could (around the turn of the century a few children taken as we would now say 'into care', because the authorities felt their parents could not provide for them, had been taught to read at 'industrial schools' and found their families again after they left). The only possible amusement was to tell stories, sing, ask riddles or simply talk around the fire – and anyone who has camped with Scouts or Guides, on military service or a walking holiday with friends, will probably recognise the situation. If there was little or nothing to eat, at least a story might take the young ones' minds off it. Mothers told bedtime stories in the dark tents, and during the day, when the men might all be off working in the tattie fields and the women hawking round the houses, an old man, left in charge of the children too old for their mothers to carry and too young to go to work, might tell them long stories from a repertoire amassed over a lifetime. Moreover, in lonelier parts of the country a family of cairds might be lodged in a crofter's barn and asked into the house for a bite to eat, and to exchange news, stories or songs, or mend a sprained ankle or a leaky pot, just like Gregor's quarterers.[17] In this way many stories that settled speakers of Scots – even of Gaelic in some mainland areas – had lost were kept alive by the cairds, like the unwanted children some of them adopted from country girls in trouble. Their hunger for new stories was such that they acquired many that came originally from books or magazines, read or retold to them by country people or the few cairds who had learned to read, and often improved the stories in the telling; they also invented a good many for themselves on traditional models, though only their older tales have been included in this book.

INTRODUCTION

FUNCTIONS AND CLASSIFICATIONS OF TRADITIONAL TALES

This collection is intended to give good examples from unpublished sources of all the main kinds of older stories told in various parts of Scotland in the past fifty years, since tape recording made it fairly easy to take them down as they were told, without forcing the storytellers to slow down for dictation or stop every few minutes while discs or wax cylinders were changed on the recording machinery. Few of them have been taken down in the sort of traditional context described above, since, as explained, the ways of life that included such storytelling gatherings for settled people were lost or declining early this century. However, it is worth describing in some detail the proper habitat of the creature, so to speak — the conditions for which the stories were developed. Likewise, the Notes which follow the stories include brief sketches of the storytellers, as far as we know them, as well as the histories of the stories themselves, as far as we know *them*. However, this is designed to be a representative collection for students of the folktale from Scotland and elsewhere as well as enjoyable reading for non-scholars. The Notes, and sometimes the stories themselves, will be easier to understand if you read what follows, which includes some definitions and a very potted history of folk narrative research in Scotland and elsewhere: I will try to keep it brief and not too technical.

Storytellers themselves, in most European cultures, seldom have any clearly defined terms for the different kinds of old stories they tell: these are created by scholars, usually by narrowing down the definition of words that originally just meant 'story'. For instance, 'myth' comes from the ancient Greek for a word, or anything spoken, hence a story of any kind. Some of what we still call the 'Greek myths' are tales of magic much like modern 'fairy-tales', some are historical legends about the ancestors of various noble lines, some are fables about the origins of creatures, landmarks or constellations. Gods or other supernatural beings played a part in many of them, but by no means all. It was only when philosophers like Plato started to complain, just like some critics of modern television, that the stories which tragedians were using in their plays provided plenty of dramatic situations but not often good examples of moral behaviour, that the term 'myth' began to be restricted to stories about gods, right and wrong, life and death – beliefs which mean a lot to people. 'Fable', from a Latin word meaning something spoken, has come to be used particularly for parables with a moral whose central characters are animals or inanimate objects. Yet the adjectives from these words, 'mythical' and 'fabulous', have nothing to do with morals or fundamental beliefs: they are used for imaginary things in stories you are *not* expected to believe.

Modern scholarly study of traditional tales began in Germany in 1811, with the publication of the collection *Kinder- und Hausmärchen* by the brothers Jakob and Wilhelm Grimm. Their title means something like 'Children's and Household Tales', though we usually know the collection as 'Grimm's Fairy-Tales'. Since the helpful 'fairies' in such stories are quite unlike the generally dangerous fairies in many fairy legends, like Nos. 64–78 below for example, most folklorists prefer to avoid using the term 'fairy-tale' to refer to *all* such stories, and it is a bit of a problem to know how otherwise to translate the word *Märchen*. The heart of this genre of traditional tales is the body of 'tales of magic' or 'international wonder-tales', many of which are known all over Europe and the countries colonised from Europe, and often in Asia, too, though less often in Africa or Oceania: stories like 'Cinderella' or 'Jack and the Beanstalk', which are often set in a vaguely defined country or like 'The Green Man of Knowledge' in the Land of Enchantment, and happened 'once upon a time, long ago'. However, the German word *Märchen* is usually also extended to other tales with a similar or wider distribution, covered by the Aarne-Thompson index mentioned above, which do not involve magic as such, though they generally include some element which involves the suspension of disbelief: thus the category encompasses animal fables (where animals talk and behave like people), religious tales (with miracles instead of magic), what are called 'romantic tales' or 'novellas' (which like early novels usually involve incredible luck or coincidences), and various sorts of comic tales and trickster tales (which generally depend on incredible stupidity or credulity on the part of some characters, or sometimes the audience). Some English-speaking scholars simply render *Märchen* as 'folktales', but this sounds like a term for all traditional tales – we prefer the latter as the general term simply because it avoids the implication that these stories are only told by 'the folk', a Victorian concept originally synonymous with 'the peasantry'. The essence of *Märchen* as distinguished by the Grimms from their other main category, *Sagen*, is that they do not need to be believed to be literally true, though they may be symbolically true like parables, and so I suggest that the best English term may be 'fictional folktales', or 'fictions' for short, though I may use the well-established German term too. Some storytellers are convinced that their fictional folktales must have happened somewhere, at some time, and some tell them as something that happened in their own neighbourhood, but the audience does not have to believe this: the enjoyable way to listen (or read) is to suspend disbelief and relax in sheer escapism, but you can also listen to such stories as parables illustrating a moral message. Many cultures, including African tribes and Scottish cairds, insist that all these tales have a moral and play an important part in educating children. The Grimms thought that they were 'worn-down myths', once full of significant messages.

Max Lüthi, an authority on central European *Märchen*, points out that they are best told, remembered and picked up by other storytellers with the plot of the story unencumbered by detail. The action is what matters. Descriptions of people, places or things, unless some detail has to be included to make sense of the plot, are brief, and tend to take the form of the single striking epithet – 'golden apple', 'iron castle', 'dress of starlight'. This helps to put the wonder into wonder-tales, but the storyteller does not dwell on the detail, and though the audience may be struck by it the first time it is mentioned, the next time they can take it for granted and concentrate on the new action. Repetition, where the same thing happens, typically three times with a difference in the last – the youngest son kills the giant who has killed his two brothers, but the fight is described in almost the same words used for the two earlier battles, right up to the last minute – is perfectly acceptable: it is almost as easy to remember as a single episode, but makes the story longer. Dialogue can be reported as fully or as briefly as the narrator likes, unless it is a spell, command or explanation that is essential to the plot. Characters and places seldom have proper names at all, and from end to end of the story are referred to simply as 'the prince', 'the old man', 'the giant', 'the fox', 'the palace', 'the dark forest'. If the hero of a Lowland Scots fictional folktale has a name, it is likely to be Jack (sometimes pronounced Jeck or Jake, but very rarely Jock), the minimal name which typifies the common man, used throughout the English-speaking world for this character, as Hans may be used in German stories and Jean in French ones. Occasionally a hero, villain or magic object may have a more elaborate name – The Green Man of Knowledge, The Speaking Bird of Paradise, say: if so, the whole story will probably be called by that name. All this applies to Lowland Scots and most European *Märchen*, but not necessarily to Scottish Gaelic or Irish Gaelic ones: this will be explained below.

The other basic genre of traditional tales which the Grimms defined was the subject of their later book *Deutsche Sagen*, which translates fairly easily as 'German Legends'. Legends to the folklorist are not as closely tied to historical characters or national events as they are in the common usage of the word, and include a lot of stories of supernatural contacts which happened to someone or other in a particular place, or just in the neighbourhood. *Sagen* are, or were when they flourished, believed to be true according to the Grimms' definition, and may be remembered not just because they are enjoyable stories or have a moral message, like *Märchen*, but also because they belong to the neighbourhood or even to the family – so a legend that doesn't make all that much sense may still be preserved as part of its teller's heritage.

So-called 'modern (urban, contemporary) legends' are largely to do with wonderful, or horrible, happenings in present-day surroundings, like the woman who tried to dry her miniature poodle in the microwave oven and blew it up. Some of the effect again depends on at least a tincture of truth – they tend to be told as something that actually happened to a friend of a friend, or was in the paper, like the one about the local couple who went to a specialist restaurant in Hong Kong and asked the waiter to look after their dog. That one has been traced back as far as one of Thackeray's novels,[18] and quite a few 'modern' legends have very old roots: many of them can be collected almost anywhere in the world. Many types of *Sagen* too, though the word is sometimes translated as 'local legends', can be found all over Europe if not the whole world; in other cases what can be recognised as the same legend is associated with different places in the same country. They could perhaps be called localised legends, but the national catalogue of them most often used for comparison between different countries is the Norwegian one published in 1958 and compiled by Reidar Christiansen, who called it *The Migratory Legends*, and that is as good a term as any. Nearly all the legends in this book are migratory types.

There are other stories in tradition which cannot be classed as either fictions or legends: some are borrowed from books or the oral literary traditions of earlier times, some are the myths of a religion, though in modern societies most myths have 'worn down' to supernatural legends. Some have very precise forms with little point to the plot of the story: what matters is that they are repeated accurately word for word – chain tales like 'The Old Woman and Her Pig', 'Henny Penny' or just 'The House that Jack Built', endless tales, shaggy-dog stories and so forth. And then there are stories based on the teller's personal experience or life story, or something heard from the person who experienced it and maybe beginning to sound a bit like a migratory legend, but still a bit more shapeless: at that stage folklorists tend to use the term 'memorate', coined between the Wars by the Swedish folklorist Carl von Sydow.

At the other end of the scale are stories that come from literature. Apart from the recent borrowings by Lowland cairds already mentioned, the top rank of the Gaelic storyteller's repertoire is occupied by long hero-tales derived from the secular literature of the mediaeval aristocracy of Ireland and the Highlands and Western Isles. The most admired are those belonging to the Fenian Cycle of tales about Fionn mac Cumhaill (traditionally anglicised as 'Finn Mac Cool') and his followers the Fenians (*An Fhéinn* in Scottish Gaelic), after whom all hero-tales are called *fianaíocht* in Irish. A parallel cycle of late mediaeval ballads was the basis of James Macpherson's eighteenth-century *Ossian*, a set of gloomy prose epics claimed to be translated from Gaelic poetry written by Fionn's son Oisean in Scotland in the third century AD. The Fenians are a legendary war-band based, according to the latest theories, on the teenage noblemen of pagan Ireland who trained for war in the woods and hills on the borders of each petty kingdom. Accordingly they are represented bot' as outlaws living by hunting like Robin Hood's men, and as the standing army of Cormac, king of Ireland, who defend his country against invaders, though some of their hardest struggles are with supernatural adversaries. The Fenian tales and other tales of battle and magic with heroes from pagan or Dark Age Ireland or imaginary lands overseas – rarely from Scotland – were evidently written for reading aloud in the halls of chieftains, but in parts of the south of Ireland were still being copied and read aloud in farm kitchens well into the nineteenth century. In Scotland one or two manuscripts of such tales survived and could be read in South Uist after 1800, but the stories must in general have passed into oral tradition a century or two earlier.[19]

The result was not only that many of these hero-tales themselves have been told in Scotland and Ireland in this century, but that they have influenced the telling of other tales of adventure and magic in Gaelic. For one thing, there are far more names in Gaelic *Märchen* than in Scots or most European ones. There is a whole stock of names for the countries they are set in, ranging from France (as in No. 16 below) or Greece to Lochlann (approximately Norway) and totally fictional kingdoms like Sorcha – variously identified by eighteenth- and nineteenth-century antiquaries as Portugal, Sweden, China or Ardnamurchan, but more probably derived from a Latin name for the province of Syria assimilated to a Gaelic word for 'bright'. The heroes and villains are often kings' sons from such domains (see Nos. 17 and 18 below, told by storytellers from South Uist, but in which many names come from a general stock rather than the manuscript sources of these particular tale-types). In tales of battle or transformation the heroes and heroines are more likely to be of royal or noble blood than woodcutters' children. The most frequent hero in Scottish Gaelic tales is not Jack the widow's son but the son of the king of Ireland. This reveals both where the tales came from and their aristocratic bias, acceptable to crofters who could mostly claim, if not kinship, at least a hereditary attachment to the line of one chief or another. In Gaelic the brief descriptions of most European *Märchen* may be replaced by strings of alliterative adjectives, or whole stereotyped accounts of recurrent happenings such as fights, journeys or hunts, known in English as 'runs', derived from similar set-pieces in manuscript stories. The written runs are designed both to sound good and to impress with their learning: with oral transmission the archaic alliterative words may degenerate into nonsense, but often a verse-like rhyme and rhythm develops in compensation, which may make them sound even more impressive.

Before looking at folktale collection in Scotland and folk narrative scholarship, we should define some other terms that will be used in the Notes. *Tale-types* are plot summaries created by scholars, but it is surprising how close many oral versions are to the theoretical basic type: the type catalogues most often used in the Notes are the Aarne-Thompson *Types of the Folktale* (referred to as AT, with a type-number) for *Märchen*; the Irish national version of this by Seán Ó Súilleabháin and Reidar Christiansen, *Types of the Irish Folktale* (TIF); Ernest Baughman's *Types and Motif Index of the Folktales of England and North America* (TMI) – this includes some Scots tales, but there is still no published index for all Scotland; and Christiansen's *Migratory Legends* (ML). (Full details of all these publications are given in the select Bibliography.) We will call a single storyteller's way of telling a particular type a *version* (if it has been recorded more than once, the different recordings may be described as *tellings*) and a group of versions sharing features not listed in the catalogue a *variant*.[20] One sort of variant or sub-type is an *ecotype* (a term borrowed from botany by von Sydow), which is restricted to one language, country or district. We would normally describe a story or type as being made up of *episodes* and *motifs*. 'Episodes' are substantial parts of a story which might be told on their own; 'motifs' in our usage are short self-contained elements of the narrative. The term 'motif' has been used by others to cover any detail of a story, such as a description ('Fairies dressed in green') or a name ('Heroine called Snow White'), and Stith Thompson's *Motif Index of Folk Literature* MI unfortunately uses it in this sense, which is one reason why we have hardly bothered to refer to it (the other is its use of quite different numbers for 'dwarfs fear the cross', 'fairies fear cross', 'ghosts . . .', 'troll . . .', 'witch . . .' etc., which all express one idea). 'Motif' to us is a structural element of narrative, and it does not matter whether it is the crowing of a grouse-cock that lays the Devil, as in tale No. 60a below, or that of a crofter's cock that stops his house being burned by a fireball, as in No. 62b: the motif is the same, and the points that differ would be referred to as *details*.

THE STRUCTURE OF THIS COLLECTION

This collection is not an anthology from earlier books, like most collections of Scottish folktales published between 1910 and 1980, but a representative selection from the archives of the School of Scottish Studies, mainly from tape-recordings made since the School started work in 1951, but also using manuscripts written for us or given to us, which include one or two outstanding survivals from the last century. We have chosen to limit the selection to versions of recurrent types, many of which have been collected in other countries and nearly all told in several parts of Scotland: in some cases we have given two or three variants of one tale-type, or closely related parallels, to emphasise the fact that there is no 'correct' version of any traditional tale, and many of them have different forms in Scots and Gaelic. In just two sections of the book, 'Origin and Didactic Legends and Robbers', 'Archers and Clan Feuds', the stories are too closely tied to places to be recurrent types, but even they include recurrent motifs. Several classes of similar historical legends have been passed over for lack of space: they include stories about clearances and evictions, the Press-Gang, disasters such as shipwrecks, murders and massacres, and more acceptable crimes such as poaching, smuggling and illicit distilling. These too may include migratory motifs, but there simply was not space for them in this book, nor have we attempted to include 'modern legends'. We hope a later volume may redress the balance. Non-recurrent types omitted include several kinds of comic tales and local anecdotes, and serious stories about second sight and the Evil Eye, which are based on widely-held beliefs but told as true experience. We have also had to leave out many of the longer tales told by travelling people, which may use the conventions of international *Märchen* and even episodes that are known from particular tale-types, but cannot be assigned to any existing Aarne Thompson type or compared with anything recorded from another Scottish storyteller. Many of these, however, have recently been published, notably those of Duncan Williamson and Stanley Robertson, who can tell hundreds of these very individual tales. Since we do not want to take away anything from the living which Duncan and Stanley are managing to make between live storytelling and their publications, we have included only one story of the many they have recorded for the School's archives, and recommend their own books (and the *Tocher* features where they first appeared) for the rest.[21] Similarly we would have liked to give more stories from that superb travelling storyteller in the traditional mode, the late Betsy Whyte, but since a book to include versions of most of her tales is planned soon, we have only used two here.

The first half of the book contains fictional folktales, beginning with Children's Tales, stories often told to children (though not all of them may seem very suitable for that!) and going on to Fortune Tales, wonder-tales in which the hero or heroine either sets out to seek his or her fortune or makes it in spite of earlier misfortune. There follow Hero Tales, mostly with Gaelic literary roots, in which the hero really is brave and strong, not just lucky, and Trickster Tales – originally a term used by anthropologists for a category of tales from North America, but perfectly applicable to stories nearer home – in which the central character is not necessarily a hero to be admired at all, but is clever enough to outwit others. The pleasure in European trickster tales comes largely from the type of people who are duped: rich men, misers, bad neighbours, grasping employers, clergymen and anybody who might usually be envied by the poor have the tables turned on them. The outrageous crimes the characters may get away with perhaps also have a cathartic effect on those who tell and hear the stories: if you were ever tempted to wish a troublesome old relative dead, imagining a scenario where people kill their mother and try to sell her body (as in tale No. 22 below) may exorcise your wish without violence. Other Cleverness, Stupidity and Nonsense contains similar stories of cleverness and stupidity, but with less malice in them, and tall tales, whose main point is to see whether any listener might actually believe such lies. The following section, Fate, Morals and Religion, is transitional, including stories told as true and local, like legends, and one or two which are set in the timeless world of *Märchen*; they have either a Christian message or at least a clear moral, or simply demonstrate that what is ordained by Fate cannot be avoided.

The Origin and Didactic Legends which follow often seem to us as incredible as tall tales, but may have been believed at one time: certainly one of the functions of the myths of many tribal peoples is to account for the origins of creatures and landmarks. The didactic stories, with a moral for children, seem little more convincing, and the single place-name legend at the end of this section is like a great part of the learned lore of early Ireland. The tales in the next two sections, Legends of Ghosts and Evil Spirits, and Legends of Fairies and Sea-Folk, may sometimes appear to make little sense, but are nonetheless frightening for it: many of these supernatural legends may reflect long-lost, perhaps pagan beliefs about life, death, nature and the unknown, and today their lack of logic can perhaps simply be seen as an expression of the chaos scientists still acknowledge as an inevitable part of our incomprehensibly vast and complex universe. The legends in these sections cover many beliefs – widely held ones, because these are mostly migratory legends – including the cures and precautions that were used in the attempt to avert disaster, disease and want. If spirits out there did not get the blame for these misfortunes, the old woman next door might, and such beliefs, much worse for the health of the community itself, are the basis of the Legends of Witchcraft, which fortunately seldom bother with the punishment of witches as long as they are defeated, and sometimes even treat the subject, with hindsight, as a joke. Finally there are the historical legends of Robbers, Archers and Clan Feuds, some of them migratory types, nearly all from the Gaelic. The clan legends at the end could not be left out because they sum up the rest: they incorporate elements of almost everything that has gone before – fictional folktale, ancient hero tale, witchcraft, fairy lore, cunning tricks and inevitable fate – in a framework based on actual events of Highland history in the storyteller's home area, and in some ways could be said to represent the climactic peak of Gaelic storytelling.

FOLKTALE COLLECTION IN SCOTLAND

The first evidence we have for traditional tales being told in Scotland is in *The Complaynt of Scotland*, a nationalist tract published in Paris in 1550, probably by Robert Wedderburn, a cleric from Dundee. In between urging resistance to English oppression, the author inserts a pastoral scene in which a company of Scottish shepherds pass a long summer's evening, apparently telling every story, singing every song and dancing every dance that he could think of. The stories listed include the Canterbury Tales, (John Barbour's) *Bruce*, Greek myths and Arthurian romances, but also such titles as 'The Red Etin' (a word for a giant) and 'The Well at the World's End',[22] which reappear among the 'Fireside Nursery Stories' included in the third and later editions of the *Popular Rhymes of Scotland* (*PRS*), published by Robert Chambers nearly three centuries later. Chambers gives Scots texts of the stories (mostly in prose though he includes some wholly in verse) as they might have been 'told by the fireside, in cottage and in nursery, by the old women, time out of mind the vehicles for such traditions'. These were probably not taken down from dictation but remembered and reconstituted years later, like the three stories which the ballad collector Charles Kirkpatrick Sharpe wrote down as he heard them 'at the knee of Nurse Jenny, at his father's house of Hoddam in Dumfriesshire, about the year 1784'. Most of the stories seem to have been sent to Chambers in manuscript: he sometimes names the writer, sometimes just the county, sometimes he says nothing of the source. His version of 'The Red Etin' seems to have been rewritten in Scots from a manuscript collection offered for publication by the ballad collector and publisher Peter Buchan from Peterhead, in which all the stories are presented in a stilted English not unlike that of chapbooks such as Buchan printed and sold, though he said the tales were 'taken down from the recitation of several old people in the *North Countrie*'[23]. Buchan's 'Red Etin' begins:

> Near the burgh of Auchtermuchty in Fife, lived two poor widows who were unable to pay the rent of the small plot of ground allotted them by the farmer whose sub-tenants they were. This being the case, the landlord insisted on their putting away their sons to some employment, that they might the better be able to pay their rents, as they were grown up, and able to do something for themselves and their mothers. These old women, though loath to part with their sons, having no alternative left to them, to part they must. Their situation having been communicated to each of the sons separately, these young men determined to push their fortune in some distant country.

For this Chambers has:

> There were ance twa widows that lived ilk ane on a small bit o'ground, which they rented from a farmer. Ane o' them had twa sons, and the other had ane; and by and by it was time for the wife that had twa sons to send them away to spouss their fortune.

He has perhaps over-simplified the situation to make a 'nursery' story, actually changing the relationship of the two widows' three sons, and 'spouss' (espouse) seems to be his own romantic false etymology for the usual Scots phrase 'push their fortune' – but who could prefer Buchan's long-winded wording?

There are fourteen stories in Buchan's collection and seventeen prose tales (some in two or three versions) in Chambers' section, and these thirty (allowing for the overlap) are almost all the *Märchen* published from

Lowland Scotland for over a century after 1841: Walter Gregor printed two or three from the North-East, and a few others appeared in various periodicals from the Northern Isles and Galloway, but it was generally felt (as in England) that fireside storytelling had been wiped out by general literacy. It was only in the 1950s that Hamish Henderson, helped by Maurice Fleming and others, started to record stories as well as songs from cairds in Perthshire and Aberdeenshire, and sometimes further north, which showed that fictional folktales were still flourishing among the travelling people. The vast size of some cairds' repertoires was not really revealed until a second wave of collection, led by postgraduate students including Linda Williamson, Sheila Douglas and Barbara McDermitt, began in the 1970s.

Meanwhile hundreds of *Märchen* had been written down and latterly recorded on disc, wire and tape in Scottish Gaelic. Chambers was inspired largely by the example of Sir Walter Scott, but Gaelic collection goes back in a clear line to the work of Scott's correspondents, the Brothers Grimm. They inspired the Norwegian collection of fictional folktales (*eventyr*) by Asbjørnsen and Moe; this was translated as *Popular Tales from the Norse* by Sir George Dasent and published in Edinburgh early in 1859;[24] Dasent's friend John Francis Campbell must have seen the translations as they were being made, for he was immediately reminded of the Gaelic tales he had heard as a small boy in Islay from his father's piper John Campbell, 'my nurse' as he called him, among others, and realised that as good a collection could be made in the Highlands: by April 1859 he already had several people working for him taking down stories. Campbell's father had been forced to sell his Islay estate to pay his creditors some years before, but his son is always called 'Campbell of Islay'. He was trained as a lawyer, based in London, held such positions as Secretary to the Commissioners for Northern Lights, and had many interests beside folktales: he travelled widely in Scandinavia and elsewhere and published books on his travels and various scientific subjects. He was also a valued friend of the Duke of Argyll. He could speak and write Gaelic, but could not take down whole tales from dictation, and for this he employed half a dozen collectors, including an Islay schoolmaster and gamekeepers on the Argyll estates, who went all over the West Highlands and Islands in 1859–60 writing stories for him. Only part of the resultant collection was included or summarised in the four volumes of his *Popular Tales of the West Highlands* (*PTWH*), and there are hundreds of stories in the National Library of Scotland still awaiting publication.[25] The English translations in the book, which are Campbell's own work, try too hard to give the literal meaning of idioms or the sound of words and do not appeal to many readers, but his comparative notes and his insistence on giving the storyteller's words as exactly as they could be got down on paper are far ahead of most folklorists of his time.

Campbell's publication aroused a new enthusiasm for the collection of Gaelic folklore, especially tales, and between 1880 and 1910 a number of important books were published, mainly by ministers such as those who contributed to *Waifs and Strays of Celtic Tradition* (*WRS*), under the general editorship of the Duke of Argyll's brother Lord Archibald Campbell,[26] one of the founders of An Comunn Gàidhealach and the Mòd. Several Gaelic journals which appeared at the same period, such as *Transactions of the Gaelic Society of Inverness, The Celtic Magazine, The Celtic Review*, and *An Gàidheal*, were also full of stories. Some collectors, like the exciseman Alexander Carmichael, a late recruit to Campbell of Islay's helpers, Father Allan MacDonald, priest in the island of Eriskay, or Lady Evelyn Stewart-Murray, a daughter of the Duke of Atholl, published only in the journals or not at all, though they took down many stories along with other Gaelic lore,[27] and there are enough Gaelic folktales lying unread in their manuscripts to provide a lifetime's work for a dozen researchers.

After 1914 it seems to have been assumed that every story worth collecting had been collected, until the independent researchers John Lorne Campbell and K. C. Craig began to publish Gaelic tales (often only in one language) in the 1930s and 40s.[28] Dr Campbell was the first to use wire and tape recordings to take down a natural text rather than a dictated one. Soon after, Calum Maclean was sent to his native Hebrides to collect for the Irish Folklore Commission, recording mainly tales, as he had done in Ireland, on an Ediphone cylinder recorder and reusing the scraped wax cylinders when the text had been transcribed. Some disc recordings were also made by Edinburgh University's Phonetics Department shortly before the University set up the School of Scottish Studies in 1951; Calum Maclean became the School's first researcher and recorded hundreds of tales, now on tape, throughout the Highlands, and in Shetland and the Borders, before his untimely death in 1960.[29] Other fieldworkers from the School's staff, postgraduate students and some volunteer contributors to the archives have helped to record most of the stories in this book. Again, though a good number of stories have appeared in the School's journals in the past thirty-five years, hundreds more are lying untouched in the archives.

Most of the published collections of traditional tales from Scotland covered by the sketch above have concentrated on international wonder-tales and other longer stories. The legends are quite different; most of them are scattered through guide-books, local histories and reminiscences, nearly all retold in the author's own words, sometimes at great length (as in Wilson's *Tales of the Borders*),[30] sometimes just briefly mentioned in passing. A few appeared before 1950 in something more like the storyteller's own words (though often they are a reconstruction) beside the wonder-tales in books and journals,[31] but content rather than language tends to be what matters to the writer. The legends are among the thousands of tales in unpublished manuscripts, notably the Dewar manuscripts of clan legends at Inveraray Castle.[32]

FOLK NARRATIVE SCHOLARSHIP

This book is intended to be enjoyed as a representative sample of texts of Scottish traditional tales, but it may be as well to mention that folktale scholarship (which again has tended to concentrate mainly on fictional folktales, especially international wonder-tales) today indignantly repudiates the suggestion that texts as such are worth studying for their own sake: it is necessary instead to look for a deeper meaning beneath the surface of the story. This approach began with the Grimms' 'worn-down myth' idea, which was taken to ridiculous extremes by nineteenth-century scholars who saw every story as a 'solar myth', a metaphor for the workings of nature, heavenly bodies, the weather, the seasons and so on. Andrew Lang ridiculed this school by 'proving' Max Müller, its leader, by his own methods to be a solar myth himself, but Lang championed the equally romantic, if slightly more convincing, theory that myths and folktales embodied the principles of pagan rituals. After an interval of fifty years, the search for meaning has now become fashionable again, with the difference that apart from some cosmologists who are still looking for symbolism and ritual behind narrative plots, most analysts now base their approaches on the psychology of Freud or Jung, look for binary oppositions in the style of anthropologist Claude Lévi-Strauss or threefold classifications after Dumézil, unearth traces of the class struggle or the battle between the sexes, or pursue the quest for national or community identity. The most publicised are those who psychoanalyse Greek myths or the stories from Grimm and Charles Perrault (author of 'The Sleeping Beauty', 'Red Riding Hood' and 'Bluebeard'), that so many Westerners know, but the most interesting are those who take the trouble to ask active storytellers why they themselves choose to tell particular stories in a particular way.

Earlier this century, in the fifty or so years between the ages of "meaning", stories were studied in their own right, as enjoyable texts which had a history and travelled. A nineteenth-century suggestion that all European tales (and the Indo-European group of languages) originated in India was followed by the development of the very successful Finnish 'historic-geographic method' of study, which sought to establish tale-types and by comparing all available texts discover where they had originally come from and how they had spread and taken on different forms ('redactions' or 'ecotypes') in different countries. A great deal of hard work went into these studies, based mainly on the Aarne-Thompson type index, but by the 1960s they were being criticised for the superficial criteria used to define tales and motifs, for over-simple ideas about the ways tales were diffused, and above all for concentrating on published

Märchen texts, which might, for example, have been thoroughly collected in Lithuania while those in Iran had hardly been touched. The critics turned to genre analysis, paying more attention to neglected types of narrative such as legend and folk epic, and to 'structuralism', following the first English translation of Vladimir Propp's analysis of Russian wonder tales.[33] In fact Propp's binary, cause-and-effect system of constuction proved difficult to apply to other sorts of stories, and his greatest achievement seems to me the definition of the 'donor' – the essential character in wonder tales who helps the hero by giving him advice or a magical object, whether he gives it to the hero as a reward for his kindness in sharing his bannock with him or the hero takes it from him as a ransom and then kills him.

Another frequent reaction in the 1960s and 70s was to turn from text to context, studying the occasions when stories were told and the purposes their telling served. This involved a more anthropological, synchronic approach to living traditions of storytelling, rather than studying the history of 'dead' texts. Good collectors for the past century had found out all they could about the people from whom they recorded stories, and this practice now gained the praise it deserved. Apart from studying the narrators' repertoires, how they used them and why they and their hearers liked them, researchers studied all elements of storytelling technique, not only words but gestures, asides to the audience, tones of voice for different characters, and every trick of the trade used in this very dramatic art-form that modern audio and video-recording could capture. Some reacted so far against the study of texts that they denied the validity of the concept of a tale-type, and insisted that any telling of any story must be studied as a unique happening in as much detail as possible. This extreme approach fortunately did not last long, but the interest in storytellers and their audiences has continued, and now includes not only the study of many sorts of live performance other than the telling of wonder-tales, but attempts to reconstruct the personalities of past storytellers and the methods of the collectors who took down and edited their tales.

It is now possible, therefore, to look at any rendering of any traditional tale from many points of view – structure, style, context, function, meaning and so on. It is also still valuable to compare obviously related tales either from these points of view or more traditionally to discover how they may be related historically and geographically. Applying the Finnish method to AT 922, the story with which we began, for instance, tells us that this story probably reached the Gaelic Highlands from France or Spain by the mediaeval wine-trade route, while the version told by Scots-speaking cairds came across the North Sea.[34] The transmission of traditional tales from one person to another is after all what distinguishes them from novels or television plays. We have been particularly interested in two aspects of transmission: the way in which written and oral sources can combine to make an orally delivered story – there are plenty of examples of this below – and the process of remembering a story. The latter is certainly not usually a matter of memorising words, like learning a part in a play; it has generally been assumed to involve learning a framework which is fleshed out with words in each performance, perhaps drawing on a stock of verbal clichés for descriptions and dialogue. But this reflects a method some of us have learned at school: it is not necessarily the way a person will tell someone else the story of a film they have seen, or the way a storyteller who can hardly read remembers stories. Most people who hear or read a story form some sort of image of characters or scenes in their mind's eye, and may complain that a film of a novel they have read is not at all like the way they see it. Scottish traditional storytellers have told us that they use such pictures to help them to recall and re-tell their stories, and that they would not be able to do this without them.[35] This has, of course, significant implications for the study of structure, style, meaning, and so on.

SOURCES, EDITING AND NOTES

Most of the stories in this book have been transcribed from tape-recordings in the Sound Archive of the School of Scottish Studies (SA): in this case the Notes acknowledge the storyteller, the fieldworker who made the recording, the transcriber and (if the story was told in Gaelic) the translator, unless the last two functions were carried out by us. If so, most of the Gaelic stories were transcribed by Donald Archie MacDonald (DAM), though a few began as transcriptions by me (AJB), which were then revised by D. A. MacDonald; mostly the translation was started by the same person who made the transcription, but all translations in their final forms have involved the collaboration of both editors, and we have also revised those made by other people. All stories in Scots (including Shetlandic, and English) were either transcribed or revised, with consultation of the original tapes, by me. We have not included the Gaelic texts of any tale in this collection because we feel few of our readers would have any use for them, but a separate publication is a possibility, and many of them have already appeared beside the translations in the School's journals *Scottish Studies* (*SS*) and *Tocher* (*T*). These references are also given in the Notes. Outside these journals, none of the stories in this book has been fully published before except for ten Scots ones which appeared in my collection *The Green Man of Knowledge and Other Scots Traditional Tales* (*GMK*), now out of print, and the Gaelic texts of two which appeared in Peter Morrison's *Ugam agus Bhuam* (*UAB*), edited by D. A. MacDonald. However, a large part of this book consists of stories which were privately printed under the same title in 1974 by the School of Scottish Studies as a textbook for the then course in Oral Literature and Popular Tradition, the predecessor of Scottish Ethnology 1. This was out of print within ten years, by which time it had been turned down for full publication by several Scottish publishers, but in more enlightened times this revised and enlarged version has been accepted.

Unlike the earlier version, this book also includes some stories from manuscript and typescript collections deposited in the School, the oldest dating from 1891. In these cases the collector and storyteller are acknowledged with a note of the history of the collection: Scots texts are reproduced in the manuscript form, Gaelic ones have been translated by us. The tale-types to be used were selected, with a textbook for teaching traditional narrative in mind, by me, and I chose the Scots examples, but most of the Gaelic texts were found by D. A. MacDonald. The Notes were written by me, and include a very brief biographical sketch or assessment of each storyteller if possible, supplied by the fieldworkers, D. A. MacDonald and myself. Living storytellers, and relatives of those now dead (sadly, the vast majority), if they could be traced have kindly given permission for their stories to be used. We are grateful to them and the fieldworkers for their contribution, and hope this book will be to the credit of all the storytellers; many fine ones, like Brucie Henderson and Jamesie Laurenson from Shetland, have had to be left out because few of their tales were recurrent types, but we hope this will be remedied in future collections.

The translations from Gaelic are intended to give the flavour rather than the literal meaning of the storytellers' words, though they keep as closely as possible to the sentence structure of the original. Occasionally a 'he says' or the like, used by most oral storytellers as a sort of punctuation in the flow of dialogue and a constant reminder that one of the characters is speaking, may be omitted silently. However, in both transcriptions from Scots and translations from Gaelic ellipses (. . .) are regularly used, to indicate not just a pause but the omission of some words, either because they could not be understood, or more often because they are part of the hesitation and repetition that the ear accepts in speech but the eye may find disturbing in reading: the storytellers would not have wanted their 'ers' and 'ums' and mumblings printed, but we leave the ellipses to show that the narrative does come from an imperfect oral original. Where we have been uncertain of a word or phrase, or have had to supply one to make the meaning clear, it is in square brackets. The transcriptions from Scots likewise try to indicate the flavour, showing characteristic features of the accent and dialect with a spelling which suggests the standard English form of a word if there is one. So 'maet' transposes the vowels of 'meat', though 'mait' would indicate the sound more closely. 'Hey' sounds like 'high', rather than 'hey'. In Orkney and Shetland dialect $\ddot{O}$ and $\ddot{U}$ are pronounced much as in German, and $\ddot{a}$ indicates something closer to short e than a standard British a. Vowel changes are the main dialect indicators, though different parts of Shetland use 'quite' for 'white' or 'white' for 'quite', and sometimes I hear an intermediate form which I have written as in old

INTRODUCTION

Scots 'quhite'. The spellings of the Scots Style Sheet, which dispense with apostrophes in common forms (o', wi', a', an', -in' etc.) are often followed, but apostrophes at the beginning of words (as in ' 'at' for 'that') are kept for clarity, and we write 'oot' for 'out' when we hear that, because in such words both the Scots and the English forms are used side by side by many Scottish speakers. We expect readers to understand the fairly standard, elementary Scots forms which most storytellers use, and sometimes build on top of them ('aafae' = 'awfy' = 'awfully'). Remember that in Scots it is correct to use such forms as a singular verb with a plural subject ('his dogs is forgotten'), while in Orkney and Shetland 'is' rather than 'has' forms the perfect tense ('they *were* all hed to clear oot'). All Scots dialects also use 'they were' to mean 'there was' and 'they are' or 'there' for 'there is'. '-ed' often becomes '-it' and may be swallowed by a preceding *t* in words like 'start', meaning 'started'. David Murison's *The Guid Scots Tongue* (Edinburgh, 1977) is a good introduction to the regular features of the language many of which (such as *thu are* for 'thou art') might seem like mistakes to most Scots today. More unusual words and phrases are explained in the notes, along with, for instance, Gaelic names when the meaning is of importance to the story.

CHILDREN'S TALES

THE OLD MAN WITH THE EAR OF CORN

THIS WAS AN OLD MAN who was going along this high-road, and he found an ear of corn on the high-road. There was a house close by there, and he brought it into this house and asked them if they would keep the ear of corn for him until he came back at a year and a day's end.

He came back at a year and a day's end and asked for his ear of corn. They told him that the hen had eaten it.

'Keep the hen itself for me until I come at a year and a day's end.' He came back at a year and a day's end and asked for the hen. They told him that the cow had eaten the hen.

'Well, keep the cow itself until I come at a year and a day's end.' He came at a year and a day's end. There was no cow to be had. She had broken her bones on the ice when a girl was taking her out to get a drink – it was freezing.

'Well, keep the girl herself for me until I come at a year and a day's end.' He came at a year and a day's end and got the girl. He put her in a sack with a string round its mouth, and out he went. But the day was warm and the girl was heavy, and he thought he would go into the hotel to ask them if he could get a drink. But somebody came along and saw that the girl was in the bag. They let out the girl, and they put stones in the bag. He came out and picked up the bag, and the girl was heavier than ever. The day was warm and he was getting really tired. Anyway he came to this loch, and he heaved the bag and the girl and the stones and the whole lot of it into the loch, because he couldn't be bothered carrying them any further.

1b   *Kate Dix*

THE OLD MAN WITH THE GRAIN OF BARLEY

DID YOU EVER HEAR about the story of the Old Man with the Grain of Barley? Anyway he was a bachelor. He lived with his mother. And apparently he failed to get a wife anywhere in the world and he made up his mind that one way or another he would get a wife. So he went and wrapped up a grain of barley in his handkerchief and off he went with it. He walked miles over mountain and moor but it was when night came that he saw a small light far away at the bottom of a glen. But though it seemed far from him it didn't take long to reach and he knocked at the door. He asked if he could get shelter for the night. Oh, they said, yes, he could come in. And there was a woman at the door and he said to her: 'Now keep this grain of barley for me. See that no harm comes to it till morning.'

He went to bed and when he got up in the morning and the poor woman was giving him the grain of barley it fell and the hen ate it.

'Oh if you've been the death of my grain, it's the living hen for me.'

And away he went with the hen. And he carried on through the moor again until night came and he saw another light. When he reached the light he knocked at the door and he asked if he could get shelter and they said he could. And he asked them to see to it now that no harm came to the hen till morning came, and he took it away with him.

When he got up in the morning and the woman was giving him the hen it slipped from her hands and the cow stood on it, and killed it. 'Oh if you've been on the death of my hen it's the living cow for me.'

Away he went with the cow over the mountain and moor till night came and he saw a small light in the glen again. He made for it . . . and a beautiful girl came to the door, and he said to her: 'Well now, mind and take good care of the cow so that no harm comes to it till morning.'

The poor girl was thinking in the morning when she got up that the cow had better have a drink. However it was snowing a blizzard and the girl let the cow out, and it slipped and dislocated a hip joint and they had to kill it.

'Oh well,' said the man, 'if you've been the death of my cow, it's the living girl for me.'

He took the girl home with him, and he had got a wife at last, and they say that they had a great wedding.

I don't know whether that's true or not.

THE GREY GOAT

WELL, I WILL NOW TELL you the story of the Grey Goat as I remember it.

One day the Grey Goat was going to the strand to get shellfish for her family and she left at home the three Grey-Speckled Kids and the Grey-Headed Billy and the Billy-Boy. And when she was going, she warned them that they must never open the door to anyone who came to the house until she came home. And she was going to put a mark on herself when she went; that mark was that she was going to tie two threads round her foot, a red thread and a blue thread, and if anyone came to the door they were to ask him to put his foot in under the door and unless they saw this red thread and blue thread on the foot that came in under the door, it would not be her.

'And you will say to anyone who comes – "There was a red thread and a blue thread round our mother's foot".'

And unless this was on the foot that came in under the door, the door was not to be opened.

But, anyway, the Fox came. He put his foot in under the door and asked that the door should be opened. He said: 'Here is your mother back again.'

And it was then they said to him: 'Put in your foot under the door, and we will know if it is our mother.'

And he put his foot in under the door and there was no thread or anything round his foot. And they said:

'O, that is not our mother at all. There was a red thread and a blue thread round our mother's foot.'

Anyway, the Fox went away and he went to the weaver's midden and he got a bit of red thread and blue thread and he tied that round his foot.

He went back to the house of the Grey Goat and he knocked at the door and he said that their mother was back now from the strand. And they said to him: 'Put your foot in under the door and we will know if it is our own mother.'

And he put in his foot under the door and sure enough there was a red thread and a blue thread round his foot.

The poor creatures inside opened the door and the Fox got in and in the twinkling of an eye he ate all of them up, the three Grey-Speckled Kids and the Grey-Headed Billy and the Billy-Boy.

But not long after, the poor Grey Goat came back from the strand and came home and there was no sign of any of her family. And she was overcome: she didn't know what to do. And she went to look for them and she went first to the house of the Gull and she climbed up to the chimney and the Gull called from inside:

'Who is that on the top of my shaggy, raggy little hut who will not let out the smoke of my little hearth while I am cooking my little bannock?'

'Here am I, the Grey Goat, worn out searching for my kids.'

'By the earth beneath you, and by the sky above you and by yonder sun passing by,' said the Gull, 'I have never seen your kids.'

She went then to the house of the Crow and she climbed up to the top of the chimney again and the Crow called from inside:

'Who is that on the top of my shaggy, raggy little hut who will not let out the smoke of my little hearth while I am cooking my little bannock?'

'Here am I, the Grey Goat, worn out looking for my kids.'

'By the earth beneath you and by the sky above you and by yonder sun passing by, I have never seen your kids,' said the Crow.

She went away then and went to the house of the Raven and she climbed to the top of the Raven's house, up to the chimney again, and the Raven called from inside:

'Rochdada, rochdada,' said the Raven, 'who is that on the top of my shaggy, raggy little hut who will not let out the smoke of my little hearth while I am cooking my little bannock?'

'Here am I, the Grey Goat, worn out looking for my kids.'

'By the earth beneath you and by the sky above you and by yonder sun passing by, I have never seen your kids.'

Now, she did not know on earth which way she should turn, and she went to the house of the Fox. Anyway, the Fox took her inside and he had a great fine fire on and he was feeling very pleased with himself, and they were very friendly to each other, he and the Grey Goat, and he stretched himself in front of the fire and she began to stroke his head with her hand [sic] and the Fox fell asleep.

And the Grey Goat saw – she saw an old stump of a little rusty knife somewhere and she jumped up and seized this and she slit open his belly and out of the belly of the Fox leaped the three Grey-Speckled Kids and the Grey-Headed Billy and the Billy-Boy as much alive as they ever were, and she and they made off home and they lived happily ever afterwards. And I parted from them.

_____

THE FOX AND THE WOLF
AND THE BUTTER

Long, long ago, when all creatures spoke Gaelic, the Fox and the Wolf were living together. They used to go around together to gather food for themselves, and one of these days they were beachcombing – just as people do here when the wind is right – to see what had come ashore. And what should they find among the tidewrack but a cask of butter.

O, they were delighted and they brought it up and they said to each other:

'We'll hide it now till we get to take it home.'

And they carried it up and dug a hole for it and buried it, and they went home. And next morning when they woke up the Fox said to the Wolf:

'I'm going away today.'

'Where are you going?' said the Wolf.

'I'm going,' said he, 'to a christening.'

'O yes,' said the other. 'Very well then.'

And the Fox went off and he was away for most of the day and when he got back the Wolf said to him:

'Well, you're back.'

'Yes,' said he.

'What name did you call the young one?' said the Wolf.

'We called him Mu Bheul ["About the Mouth"],' said he.

'O yes,' said the Wolf. And nothing more was said about it.

Next morning when they woke up again, the Fox said again:

'I'm going away again today,' said he.

'Where are you going today?' said the Wolf.

'I'm going to a christening,' said he.

'O yes,' said the Wolf.

And the Fox went off, and a good part of the day was past before he got back and the Wolf asked him:

'What name did you call the young one today?'

'We called him Mu Leth ["About Half"],' said he.

'I see,' said the Wolf.

And nothing more was said about it, but they settled down for the night and went to sleep and next morning when they woke up, it was the very same story with the Fox.

'I'm going away again today.'

'Are you?' said the Wolf.

'Yes,' said he.

'Where are you going today?' said the Wolf.

'I'm going to a christening,' said he.

'O yes,' said the Wolf.

And the Fox went off, and late in the evening he came back, licking his chops, and the Wolf said to him:

'What name did you call the young one today?'

'We called him Sgrìobadh a' Mhàis ["Scraping the Bottom"],' said he.

'O yes,' said the Wolf, all unsuspecting.

And no more was said about it and they went to bed that night and when they got up in the morning the Fox said:

'Isn't it time now that we went to see about the cask we hid the other day?'

'O yes indeed,' said the other. 'We'd better go. It's time we got it home.'

And they set off and they came to the hole where it had been hidden, and they uncovered the cask, and when the cask was opened there was not a scraping left on the bottom of it.

Man, man, wasn't this awful! The Fox – he was terribly puzzled that there was nothing left in the cask, and the Wolf didn't know what to say, he was so puzzled.

'Well,' said the Fox, 'this is terribly queer. Not a soul knew about this cask except you and I. Now,' said he, 'this is a terribly queer business and it must be one or other of us, and this is my verdict on the matter,' said he.

If I ate the butter and it was I
Chiorram chiotam, chiorram chatam, chiorram chiù,
But if you ate the butter and it was you,
A galling plague on your grey belly in the dust.

There was no great harm in the curse that the Fox laid on himself but there was plenty of venom in the curse he laid on the Wolf.

3b   *Tom Tulloch*

THE CATS AND THE CHRISTENING

. . . THE MOST O ALL THE Shetlan stories, they might seem silly, but they usually sarved a purpose, and this story 'at was telled aboot the cats and the christenin emphansised the need fir . . . wän person to be truthful an honest an upright wi the ither person.

But this parteeclar stoary geed on to say 'at this two cats wis very, very friendly an very paully, and they güd every wey together, and they wir wän night 'at they succeeded in stealin a jar o butter. And they hoided it, but they didna hae time to brotch the jar that night, but they wid laeve it to some ither more convenient time. So they wir wän night a while efter yon 'at wän o the cats said 'at they were been invitit til a christenin. So shö güd, an shö wis awey fir a good long while, an when shö cam back again her paul axed her whit wis all gone on at the christenin, an shö of coorse hed a graet description o the christenin. And then the cat axed hir what they were caa't this young kitling, an shö said 'at they wir caa'd hir Well-Concealed.

So two or three nights efter yon this saem cat was been invitit til anither christenin. An the saem procedure wis fallowed, an when the cat cam back ageen the ither cat axed hir quhat they caa'd this kitlin? Noo she said it wis Top-Aff.

So two or three nights efter this ageen then shö wis invitit til anither christenin! An when shö cam back ageen th'ither cat enquired whät wis the neem o the new arrival, and this time it was Half-Dön.

An than the . . . cat 'at wis aalways sittin at hom wis beginnin to get a bit suspeecious aboot this. So the ither cat was invitit til a still farther christening. But the cat 'at wis aalways sittin at hom, shö shadowed her this night. An then shö discovered 'at shö wis teen the jar o butter oot o the oreeginal concealment place, an shö wis oapened it an shö wis lickit ir aeten nearly the whoale lot o it. An when the cat 'at wis aalways sittin at hom saw 'at shö wis been preyed upon, then shö got in a graet fury, and they jumpit in a fight, and they hed a moast lood-an-lawless fight, and they wir never freends no more whät wis efter o their lifes!

(. . . 'Well-Concealed' wis the first een: that wis meant to say 'at shö wis teen the jar oot o the first hoidin-place and shö wis pitten it on . . . anither hidin-place. And then 'Top-Aff' shö wis gotten the top off o the jar; and then 'Well-Begun', shö wis gotten . . . into the butter an gotten it well startit,* an 'Half-Dön', that wis half-dön. But of coorse

* Tom typically emphasises the ad-lib element, and in fact adds a name in the explanation afterwards which he didn't put into the story.

accordin to the imagination o the story-teller an the paetience o the bairn 'at they were tellin it til, it could ha' gone on almost indefinitely wi different neems . . .)

4   *Tom Tulloch*

THE BOY AND THE BRÜNI

THIS BOY ARRIVED hom fae the schül wän nyht, an his fokk telled him to go to the hill and 'can the kye': this meant to say 'at he had to go to the hill an see if the kye was all ryht and coont them, an if they were turn't them fir hom, that he was to turn them back to the hill an select a good piece o pasturage fir them tö aet upon atil it wis time to tak them hom an put i the byre. So . . . his mither baekit him a brüni an pat in his poaket an sent him to the hill to look to the kye, to 'can them'. An he güd to the hill an he fand the kye all ryht an he turn't them up and lookit efter them an then he t'owt 'at he wid set him doon an aet his brüni. And this parteeclar nyht he wis fund the kye pretty near the Erne's Knowe, an it was ipo the Erne's Knowe 'at he'd set him doon to aet his brüni. An when he was takin the brüni oot o his poaket, the brüni haippen't to slip oot o his haund, an he row't doon the side o the knowe. And the boy t'owt 'at this wad be a very good game fir him to hae a bit o playfer wi the brüni afore he ett him, an he row'd him up an row'd him doon the knowe different times. But they were wän o the times 'at he row't the brüni doon the knowe, 'at he disappeared oot o his syht in amang a big clump o heather. And the boy wisna wantin to loss his brüni, and he was also curious to keen whar the brüni wis gone til.

So he pairtit the heather an he oagit in . . . amang it to see if he could find an retrieve his brüni. But when he oapen't up the heather, he cam upon a graet big gully o a holl leadin into the hill, an he oagit into this gully, and the farther he cam in, the bigger the gully turn't. And finally he laundit in atil a graet big cave, and they were nobody in i the cave aless a graet big owld wife, an he noaticed 'at shö wis blinnd an couldna see him.

So he güd some wey aboot the cave an he hoided him to see what wis goin to go on yondroo. An shö wis preparin eenormious diet o maet ipae the table. An he wätched all this moves o hirs, and efter a while he haerd a graet skraufling in yon same wey 'at he wis come in, an the first 'at appear't in i the cave was a giant, an he was come back fae his day's hontin cairryin all his booty. An he set doon his booty an he set him in to the table and he stairted to aet upon his denner. But all the time 'at he was aetin he was aye liftin his heid an snoffin aroont the cave, and then aut the latest he says,

> 'Fee faw fam,
> I feel the smell o an earthly man,
> But be he livin or be he deid
> I'se hae his heid wi my sopper breid!'

But he güd on wi his denner until he was feenished, an when he was feenished his denner he rase op an he startit to search the cave, an he fand the boy.

An he took him oot an exaemined him, but he t'owt that he wisna warth t' aet *that* nyht. An he tell't the wife 'at shö wis to take the boy an binnd him to the stoop o the mill, an shö wis to feed him op wi milk an meal until the boy's wrist turned as big as whit *his* peerie finger wis, and then he wid be fit fir aetin. So day efter day the wife fed ipae the boy, an the giant älways güd oot till his hontin. But occasionally the giant exaemin't the boy to see what wey his condeetion was gettin on, an wän moarnin he pronounced 'at the boy would be fit fir aetin that nyht.

So when the giant was gone the owld wife got on a graet caudereen of wäter upon a huge fire, an efter a while shö said to the boy 'at he was bidden to com an clim op ipae her shooder to see if this wäter wis boilin. But the boy, although he wisna certain, he hed his suspeecions o what was goin to tak place, an he said that he kent naething aboot whether wäter was boilin or no, an although shö couldna see, shö would . . . hae mair sense aboot that as him, and the best 'at shö could do was to clim op ipae *his* shooder. And so, to allay his suspeecions shö fell in wi yon plän, and he croopled him doon, an shö climmed op ipae his shooder to see whadder the waater wis boilin or no. An didn't the boy plomp her in i this caudereen o boilin wäter? An he boiled upon her an better boiled upon her till he t'owt 'at the giant would be comin hom, and then he laid her op ipo the table. An he lookit aroont the cave, an he fand twa 'r three peerie stons an he oagit up ipo some ledge op i the röf o the cave.

An efter a while the giant cam in, an he set him doon to the table, an he startit t' aet oot o the owld wife. An he ett, but every noo an ageen he was ay sayin, 'Tyoch, tyoch, tyoch!' But finally he feenished this denner, an he was kind o exhaustit, pairtly be what he was aeten and pairtly be . . . his day's hontin. An he drew this chair to the table and he laid back ower his heid, and he fell soond asleep, an he startit to snore an his mooth fell oapen. And the boy oot o the röf o the cave, he slippit doon yon peerie stons, and they güd ryht in the giant's t'rot an they shoakit him an he died.

An when the boy wis awaur 'at the giant was deid, he cam doon oot o his hoidie-holl i the röf o the cave, and he gaidered op the best o the giant's gold an silver an booty 'at he wis collected, an he made hom til his owen fokk wi hit. An needless to say they all lived in plenty and happiness ever efter!

THE WEE BIRD

THE STORY'S ABOUT A little girl. It was one fine day, her mother sent her for a joog of milk to the dairy. So she says, 'Can I take ma skippin-rope with me?'

Her mother was awful bad, says, 'No, ye can't,' she says.

'But I won't spill the milk, Mummy, I promise.'

'Well,' her mother says, 'ye can take the skippin-rope, but if ye spill the milk, I'll kill you.'

So the little girl takes the skippin-rope, an on the way goin, she's skippin with it, an she gits the milk, an she's skippin away, comin back, the milk in the jug, an the jug falls an breaks, so she looks fir anither jug. So this kind old lady comes along, says, 'I've got a jug, jist the neighbour of the one you broke.' She gies it to the little girl, an the little girl goes back fir more milk. So when she goes back fir more milk, she doesn't skip on the way comin home, she folds the rope up an then carries it in her hand.

When she comes home, her mummy says, 'Well, did ye get the milk?'

She says, 'Yes, Mummy.'

She says, 'Let me see the jug,' an she looked at the jug, she says, 'This isn't my jug.' She says, 'This is a different jug.'

She says, 'No, it's no, Mummy,' she says, 'that's the same jug as ye give me.'

She says, 'No, it's not. It's a different jug,' she says. 'My jug had a blue stripe on the top. This one has a red.'

So her mummy killed her, an baked her in a pie. But then her father comes in. He asked where the little girl wes, an the woman said, 'She'll likely be out playin.'

Says, 'Well, hurry up an shout her for her dinner.'

She says, 'Ach! Let the child play.' So she gives the man his dinner, an when he eats hauf-way through the pie, he sees this finger in it, an it had a little silver ring on it, an he looks at it an says, 'Why! This is my daughter's ring,' he says. 'What did ye do to her?'

She says, 'Well, I told her that if she broke my jug, I wad kill her, so I've killed her.'

'Now,' he says, 'look at what ye've went an done.' Says, 'I've a good mind to kill you.' Says, 'No,' he says, 'I'll let ye live.'

The two sons cam in an they were lookin fir thir sister, an the father told them whit had happened. So they startit to cry.

But then, Christmas came, an this wee little bird wes always peeping through the window. So when the boys put crumbs an things out to the window, the little bird ett it. Bit then it wes Christmas night, time fir to get the presents, then a voice cam doon the chimney: 'Brother, brother, look up, look up, look up an see what I've got.' So when the brother looked up, she dropped down a bagful of toys and sweets.

Then she said it again, an the other brother looked up, an she dropped don anither bag full of toys an sweets.

Then she says, 'Father, father, look up, look up, an see what I've got.' So when the father looked up, she dropped the father a new suit an a letter, an on the envelope it said, 'Don't open this letter until two hours after Christmas night.'

So she shouted, 'Mother, mother, look up, look up an see what I've got,' an when the mother looked up, she dropped a stone, an hit the mother on the head. Killed her.

So when the two hours came, the father opened up the letter, an he read it, he says, 'Dear Father, this is your little daughter. The spell is broken. Once I have killed my mother, I shall come back to you on New Year's Eve.'

So New Year's Eve come, an they're waitin an waitin, waitin fir the daughter to come. Bit she didn't come, an then, three minutes before midnight, a knock came on the window. They open't the window, the little bird came in, says, 'I'm home, Father.'

The father says, 'Why!' he says, 'You're the little bird now!'

She says, 'I know, but if you take my mother's ring pinkie, pinkie of the right hand,' she says, 'I'll come back tae a girl.'

So he goes away to where the mother was buried an takes the right pinkie, where still the ring wes, the same as on her. He took it, an the little girl changed back from a bird into a girl. When she took the ring, she says, 'My mother weren't really bad, it wes jist that the Devil was inside her,' she says, 'bit now that she's gone,' she says, 'she'll be in Heaven.' An she took the ring that wes on her own pinkie, she put the two in a box, an they all lived happily iver after.

6   *Jeannie Durie*

LIVER AND LIGHTS

ONCE UPON A TIME there was a miller, and one night after he and his wife had gone to bed, his wife took an awfu greening for liver and lights, and she would not be content till her husband got up and went to the town, a little way off, to buy some.

The miller was very unwilling to go for he was warm and comfortable in bed and it was still dark and very cold outside, but still as he was a good-natured man and liked to please his wife he set out. 'It is so dark and so early in the morning that I shall have to wait a long time before the shops are open in the town, besides the long way I shall have to tramp: I'll just go in here and see if I can't get liver and lights nearer home.' So he went into the churchyard, and he howkit up a dead body from a newly made grave, and cut out the liver and lights from the poor corpse and carried them home to his wife, and she not knowing where they came from, and having a greening upon her, she boilt them and she eated them, and was never a bit the wiser, while as for the miller you may be sure he held his tongue.

One night soon after, however, when it was dark, the miller went out to grind some corn and his wife was left alone in the house, and bye and bye she heard something come to the door, and then she saw the something come thrawing through the keyhole and it came up to her and said: 'Is Mungo at hame?'

'No,' said she, 'he's at the mill grinding the corn and he winna be back till it's a' ground!'

Then she looked at 'It' and said: 'What wye's yere e'en sae how?'

And 'It' answered: 'Because the worms have howkit them oot ere now.'

Then she said: 'And what wye's yere feet sae braid?'

And 'It' answered: 'Because I've traivelled, mair than e'er I rade!'

And then she looked at 'It' again and said: 'What wye's yere puddens trailing oot ahint ye?'

And then with a terrible shriek 'It' sprang on her crying: 'Auch ye thief, ye've ate the wyte o't,' and just tore her to pieces.

FORTUNE TALES

SILLY JACK AND THE
LORD'S DAUGHTER

THIS STORY THAT I'M goin to tell you, Isaac, is the story that my grandfather used to tell me an all the rest o the bairns aroon the fireside on a lang simmer's nicht to keep us quiet and to pass the time by. My grandfather's name was William Stewart, and he died about sixteen years ago.

Now, this story that I'm to tell you is about the old wumman that lived on the other side of [? Kinnevie] Hill and had the three sons. She'd one called James, John and Silly Jack. Well, but we'll start the story . . .

One son wes called James, John and Jack. Of course Jack wes supposed to be silly, and he wes the youngest of the family. But they were very poor and very hard up, and had very little to eat at times.

So one mornin James says til his mother, he says, 'Mother,' he says, 'bake me a bannock,' he says, 'and rost me a collop,' he says, 'I'm off to push ma fortune.'

She says, 'Well,' she says, 'will I bake you a big bannock with a curse, or a wee bannock wi a blessin?'

He says, 'Ach,' he says, 'mither,' he says, 'bake me a big bannock,' he says, 'wi a curse.' (Course he wes real greedy.) But whatever, his mither bakit him the bannock wi the curse; so she gave it til him, so the next day he went off to push his fortune.

So anyway an another, when he goes away, she says, 'Curse ye, curse ye, wherever ye go!' (Ye see? He jist took too much fae them and left them real hungry.) Whatever, he goes on the rodd and on the rodd, anyway or another with rests fir the wee birds but none for poor James. But he walks and walks and walks till he's tired an weariet an very, very thristy. So he sits down beside a nice little green wal fir tae take a bit of his bannock an a bit of his collop, and . . . he knew thit when he wes sittin at this wal he wad get a rest, he wad also get a drink. (Ye see? Out of this fresh spring wal.)

So he's eatin the bannock an he's eatin the collop, an suddenly up jumps a little man, an he said to James, he said, 'James, wad ye give me the crumbs,' he says, 'that faas fae yir mooth?'

So he said, 'Get oot o ma road,' he says, 'A havenae got enough for masel,' he says. 'Ah need aa ma crumbs to masel. A've nane to spare tae you.' So he wouldnae gie the wee mannie the crumbs that fell fae his mooth.

Whatever, he wes finished, an when he geed to take the drink out o the wal, which was a bonny great spring-wal before that, he discovert, insteid of the bonny fresh water that wes in it, it wes aa full of puddocks' spewins. (Ye see?) So he couldnae drink it. So he wes chokin off fir a drink.

So he gets up and he goes on the rodd again. So he traivels and traivels fir days, and finally he come til a big castel. So . . . When he came to the castel he went to the front door, an he askit if they could give him a job to do, or any work round about the place. So when the fitman went in to see . . . this great rich lord, he said that there wes a man at the front door an he wantit to see if he could give him a job, that he wad do anything.

So he said, 'Yes,' he says, 'fetch him in,' he says. So of course the fitman, he took him in, and he says, 'Yes,' he says, 'A'll give ye a job,' he says, 'I have three tasks that I want done.' He said, 'Could you do this three tasks fir me?' (Ye see?)

So he says, 'Well, I dinnae ken,' he says, 'bit A'll try.'

'Well,' he says, 'in,' he says, 'that wuid,' he says, 'a mile or two from here,' he says . . . 'lives a giant,' he says, 'the giant with the three heads. And,' he says, 'if you can kill that giant fir me,' he says, 'that'll be one of yir tasks. But,' he says, 'if you can do the three tasks,' he says,

'A'll give you my daughter to marry,' he says, 'which is very beautiful, an a lovely castel tae yirself,' he says, 'an three bushels of gold.'

Well, James, he stays at the castel all night and he feeds on the best, an had a good feather bed to lie down upon, an has the best of everything an the best of attention. So in the mornin he gits up an he goes away, gets a nice horse an he's mountit on his horse now, an a good sword an everything, an he goes to kill the giant with the three heads.

So, when he comes to this wuid, he wes jist nearin the place where the giant lived, when suddenly there were three roars just like three roars of thunder, an the very trees in this forest shook wi the roars that this giant gied. (Ye see.) And he said, the giant says,

'Vee, vye, vum!
I feel the smell of an English man.
Let him be dead, or let him be alive,
A'll crunge his bonns to meal.'

Poor James, he wes terrified to death when he hears this. But whatever, he faces up to the giant and he fought the giant bravely, but James was not a match for this giant, and the giant killed poor James, instead of James killin him. (Ye see.) So when the great lord found out that James wes killed, he ordert his head to be cut off, and he put it on the gate of his castel.

Now a year an a day passes. So John says til his mother, he says, 'Mother, it's a year and a day since ma brother James went away,' he says. So he says, 'I think I'll go an push my fortune too,' he says, 'as thir not enough to eat here,' he says, 'for the three of us. So I'll go away.' So, like James, John wes greedy too. So he says til his mither, he says, 'Bake me a bannock,' he says; 'an rost me a collop.'

She says, 'Will I bake you a big bannock with a curse, or a wee bannockie wi a blessin?'

'Ach,' he says, 'bake me the big bannock,' he says, 'wi the curse.'

So the next day he goes away to push his fortune too. So he comes to this wee wallie. It wes full o the bonny spring waater. An he sits down to eat a bit of his bannock an a bit of his collop.

So, just as he wes sittin eatin it, up jumps the wee hairy mannie again – little mannock – and he says, 'Oh,' he says, 'John,' he says, 'gie me the crumbs,' he says, 'thit faas fae yir mooth.'

'Get oot o ma road,' he says, 'A'm sairly needin the crumbs tae masel,' he says, 'it's nae fir aa 'at A hev,' he says, 'and A need every crumb tae masel.' So he couldnae spare the wee mannie a crumb either.

But, when he ett his bit bannock and ett his collop, when he geed tae take a drink, the wee wallie wes full of puddocks' spewins tae – he couldnae get a drink. So he had to get up an git on the road too, frichtit, weary an tired.

So he traivels fir days an days upon the rodd, couldnae get work at nothing, but finally *he* lands at this great lord's castel, an *he* goes tae the front door, an *he* asks for somethin tae do. So the fitman said – told the lord, and he said, 'Fetch him in.' So he fetches in John. So John asked him if he could give him any work or anything to do. So he says, 'Yes,' he says, 'there's three tasks that I would like done. An if you can do this three tasks,' he says, 'I'll give ye my beautiful daughter to marry, an three bushels of gold, and a castel fir yerself to live in.'

So John was game to try. So he told him the first task 'at had to be done was to kill this giant wi the three heids 'at lived intae the forest a mile or two away from the castel.

So the next mornin, he gits up after havin a good night's rest and everything thit he wantit an plenty to eat, an he gits up, and he mountit a beautiful horse, an . . . good sword, an he goes to face this giant wi the three heids. So when he comes into this wuid where this giant wes bidin, the same thing happens . . . the giant gives three roars 'at was like three roars of thunder, and he roar't the same thing:

> 'Vee, vye, vum!
> I feel the smell of an English man.
> Let him be dead,' he says, 'or let him be alive,
> A'll crunge his bonns to meal.'

Now, poor John, he was frighten't, but still . . . he was goin to face the giant, because it was a big temptation, the money and this beautiful young wummin to marry. So he bravely went in, an he fought the giant, but the giant killed poor John, and when the great lord knew thit John wes killed, he took *he's* head off; an he put it at the other side of the gate.

But a year an a day passes, an poor Silly Jack now . . . this is all that the old wummin had left. He says, 'God!' he says, 'Mither,' he says, 'it's a year 'n a day,' he says, 'since my brither John went away,' he says, 'and,' he says, 'I wad like to ging an push my fortune tae,' he says, 'but I dinnae like to leave you, Mither, an it's nae fir aa thit you hiv,' he says. 'Thir nae much,' he says, 'aboot this place, thir nae much to eat. Bit whatever,' he says, 'if I ging awa,' he says, 'Mither,' he says, 'it'll leave,' he says, 'mair fir you,' he says, 'fir tac cat,' he says. 'And,' he says, 'A'll ging awa,' he says, 'and A'll try my best. An if I can mak onything,' he says, 'through time,' he says, 'A'll send fir you. A'll get you,' he says. 'And then,' he says, 'A'll tak ye tae bide wi me an A'll maybe be able to look eftir ye,' he says, 'when ye're owld an done.'

'Well, well, laddie,' she says, 'it's aa right,' she says, 'you ging and try an push yir fortune,' she says, 'and look eftir yirsel, fir we've never got no word,' she says, 'from James or John,' she says. 'They've niver come back to let us know whether they got on or not.'

So poor Jack says tae his mither, 'Well,' he says, 'Mither, bake me a bannock,' he says, 'and rost me a collop.'

She says, 'Well, Jack,' she says, 'dae ye want a big bannock with a curse or a wee bannockie wi a blessin?'

'Och, Goad help us!' he says, 'Mither, ye havenae very much . . . A'm nae greedy,' he says, 'I wouldna like to think,' he says, 'A left you,' he says, 'wi little. Naw, naw,' he says, 'bake me . . . a wee bannockie,' he says, 'wi a blessin, an rost me a wee collopie.'

So, the next day he sets oot to push his fortune, an when he goes away, his poor auld mither wes broken-hertit ootowre her youngest son, and of course she wad kent she wes gaen to miss him, and she said, 'Well, bless ye, bless ye wherever ye go.' So away he went to push his fortune.

So he gaes on the rodd and on the rodd, there wes rest fir the wee birds, but none fir poor Jack. He wes hungry, tire't and wearied. But he comes to this wee wallie, and he sits doon. He saa it wes bonny waater, and he says, 'A'll get a fine, clean, refreshin drink here, when I eat a wee bit o ma bannock an a bit o ma collop.' Soon as when he sits doon, eatin his bit of bannock, and eatin his bit o collop, up jump't this wee mannie. An he says, 'Oh, Jack,' he says, 'wad ye gie me the crumbs,' he says, 'at faas fae yir mooth?'

'Goad bliss us!' he says, 'it's nae much to gie naebody,' he says, 'the crumbs that faas fae their mooth. Sit up beside me,' he says, 'wee mannie, an,' he says, 'A'll gie you a bit of ma bannock an a bit of my collop.' And of course he liftit up the wee mannie, set him doon beside him, an the two o them ate a bit o the collop and a bit o the bannock. It wesnae much, bit nivertheless he share't it. So the wee mannie disappears now fir a whilie. So whan Jack lookit, insteid o watter intae the wal, as whit he saa at first, it wes the bonniest wine that iver he saa in his life, rich, very, very rich – the wal wes full o wine. So, Jack bent doon, an jist took his two hans an cupped them thegether, and drunk his bellyful o this wine an it refreshed him in many ways.

So Jack wes goin to go away when the wee mannie appears again. So he says, 'Jack,' he says, 'here's a sword tae ye,' he says, 'take it and fasten it on ye,' he says, 'and when,' he says, 'when you're tired and weariet,' he says, 'just put your hand upon your sword,' he says, 'and wish. An whitever ye wish for,' he says, 'you'll get it.' (Ye see.) So of course Jack lauched at him, an first he didnae believe it, and he's put it roon his middle – he faistened it roon his middle, this sword, an he put it on. 'Now,' he says, 'that sword'll protect ye wherever ye go, though ye go tae other side o the world,' he says, 'it'll pirtect ye. Just anything ye want,' he says, 'put yir hand upon yir sword an wish,' he says, 'an whitever ye wish fir,' he says, 'ye'll get it.' So Jack wesnae believin it, bit he faisten't it on him, an away he goes, on the rodd.

Bit Jack gaes on fir days and days, he's tired an he's weariet, an, aw, he wes jist feelin aa wrang. And he sits doon, an he wes really hungry. He had nothing now. And jist as he wes restin, his hand accidentally went on til his sword, and he thought nothing of it. Bit he wes that hungry he couldnae stick it nae langer, and he says, 'Aw, A wish, A wish,' he says, 'that I had something tae eat.' Nae sooner did Jack say that, whan up jumpit a table afront him: up in front of Jack jumpit a table. And on this table was everything thit the finest gentleman could sit down til an eat an drink, wine of every kind. Jack rubbit his eyes, he couldnae believe it. Then he remember't his haund was on the sword. And he also remember't what the wee mannie said til him. And he said, 'God bless me!' he says, 'it is true,' he says, 'A didnae believe it at first. Bit there,' he says, 'it is true. It's happen't. A wished fir something tae eat,' he says, 'an A've got the best of everything.' So he sat down an he fillt his belly. So after he was . . . his belly wes full, he took a good rest, and then he says, 'Now, I've a long road to go on,' he says, so he put his hand upon his sword, 'I wish,' he says, 'that I had one o the finest horses,' he says, 'that ever,' he says, 'a man,' he says, 'throw't his legs over.' (See?) And there appeared the loveliest cray horse that ever he saw in his life, ready fir tae jump on. So Jack jumpit on this horse's back, an he set off.

But he come tae this castel, and he ties up his horse at the gate, an he goes right to the front door, an he asks if they could give him anything to eat. So this great lord told the fitman, 'Take him in,' he says, 'I want to see him.' So he takes him in, and he says to Jack, 'Jack,' he says, 'I can give ye something to do. I'll give ye three tasks to do, and if you can do this three tasks,' he says, 'fir me, I'll give you my beautiful daughter to marry,' he says, 'and three bushels of gold, an,' he says, 'a fine castel to live in. And,' he says, – 'but ye've thir three tasks,' he says, 'of course. One is,' he says, 'to kill the giant wi the three heads, and the other one,' he says, 'is,' he says, 'to kill the fiery dragon that guards,' he says, 'the house thit my daughter,' he says, 'is intil. She's guardit there,' he says, 'with a monstrous snake also,' he says, 'which,' he says, 'is a witch. And,' he says, 'she's keeping my daughter,' he says, 'a prisoner in this house, and,' he says, 'ye've the fiery dragon to kill as well as the giant, and also,' he says, 'this monstrous snake. And then,' he says, 'when ye do that three tasks,' he says, 'you can free my daughter. And,' he says, 'you can get her to marry,' he says. 'She's the beautifullest wumman in the land. And,' he says, 'the three bushels of gold, an,' he says, 'this castel to live in.' So this wes a big temptation to Jack.

So of course he has a good night's rest, he feeds on the best of everything, and in the mornin he rises up fine, refresh't an feelin good. So he mounts his horse, and of course he goes away, and he comes to this wuid and the same thing happens. The giant gied three roars, gulders as my grandfather used to cry it, three gulders. And the very wuid shook. An he says,

'Vee, vye, vum!
I feel the smell of an English man.
Let him be dead,' he says, 'or let him be alive,
A'll crunge his bonns tae meal.'

Bit Jack wes brave, and he had faith now, in his sword, he knew his sword would carry him through. So he put his hand upon his sword, and he asked his sword to protect him, and he faces up tae the giant as the giant comes til 'm fir tae kill him. His sword jumpit from his side, out of its scabbart, his sword jumpit out, an his sword fought the giant an it – they fought an fought an fought, his sword and the giant – remember it wes his sword that wes fightin – and his sword first cut off one of the giant's heads, then he cut off the next head off the giant, then the next head, an the giant wes lyin dead now.

So of course Jack took the three heads and he put them intil a graet big bag-thing, an he carries them down to this lord's house – this lord's castel, should I say? And when the lord saw this, he wes pleased. So that night he had a graet feast. He wes highly pleased that this giant wes killed . . . as they were all terrified of this giant. Through time he would have destroy't them all, you see.

So next mornin Jack rises up. He wes feelin fine again. He mounted his cray, an he went to do his other task. But just as he came to this big mountain where the fiery dragon was, had guardit a way through this mountains, to where this young wumman wes hidden into this – I don't know, wes't a cave, or – it wes a cave or som'n like that, but made like a house – and he came to this fiery dragon, and it meets him as he's comin, an the flemms of fire wes flyin from its mouth, bit Jack – Jack wes frightened when he saw it – but he put his hand upon his sword, and he says, 'Pirtect me,' he says, 'fir God's sake, protect me!' But just as the fiery dragon wes comin, his sword jumpit out from its scabbart and hit fought the fiery dragon. So thit wes a fierce, a very, very fierce battle. But the fiery dragon was killed. So Jack took home parts of it to let the lord see that it wes killed. So that night they had a graet feast. The lord was very well pleased as it wes now – Jack wes gettin nearer to savin his lovely daughter.

So the next mornin Jack gets up feelin good, an he mountit his cray again, an off he went fur tae meet now the monstrous snake thit guardit the cave, which was turnt intil a place like a house, thit held this beautiful young lady. So Jack cam near it. An when Jack was comin near – it wes a fierce brute wi two heads upon it – it tried to attack Jack. Jack was frighten't again, very frightened, as this wes a monstrous brute. And he put his hand on his sword, an he says, 'Fir God's sake,' he says, 'protect me!' Just as he said that, his sword jumpit out of its scabbart and it met the snake as it riz in mid-air. And they fought and fought and fought for ages, maybe about an hour, but whitever, the sword killed the snake.

And now Jack could go freely into this place, and free this young wumman thit wes hidden in there. And he did go intae the cave, an here was this beautiful young wumman . . . livin intil a thing like a trance – she wes intil a thing like a trance. Bit Jack got til her, an he took her til hersel. So she didnae remember anything, why she'd come to be there or what happened. She wes actually under the spell of a bad witch. You see, the snake actually wes the witch 'at guardit the place where she wes hidden. So Jack took her and he put her on his horse's back along with hisself. So he took her right back til her father.

So this great lord wes that pleased, they wir nothing too good fir Jack. So he says, 'Now,' he says, 'you did your three tasks, and,' he says, 'you've won my beautiful daughter. And the three bushels of gold,' he says, 'and the castel to live in.' So he says, 'You an my daughter can be marriet now, any time.'

So Jack marriet the beautiful lady an got his castel to live in. So he went an fetched to the castel his poor old mother, thit wes dressed in rags and had very, very little tae eat. So he took her home an made her like a lady, and she lived in the castel with Jack till she died.

So, ye see, it wis nut the poor simple son thit wis really supposed to be silly, thit *wis* silly. The simple son thit could 'live't on little fir the sake o helpin his poor mither, and he gain't everything, where the ither two brithers, that *wis* greedy and only live't fir theirsel, lost their lifes an got their heids put at each side o the lord's gate of his castel.

So that's the story as we used to get tell't it whan ma grandfather told it til us children.

8   *Elizabeth MacKinnon*
          Annie Johnston

THE TALE OF THE BROWN CALF

ONCE UPON A TIME there was a nobleman, and he married a beautiful, elegant woman who had no equal in the country. When she put on her finery he thought she was as beautiful as the bright summer sun, and one to be envied by every woman in the place. Her husband was so proud of her that he thought nothing on earth was beautiful enough for her, and he gave her a dress of starlight, a dress of the down of birds and a dress of moss cotton. He also gave her a gold shoe and a silver shoe, and a comb which left one side of her head gold and one side silver when she combed her hair. They had three daughters, and they were as happy as the day is long.

At last it came about that the lady died, and melancholy and grief fell upon the nobleman. He bound himself by oaths and vows that he would never marry another woman but the one whom his wife's golden shoe would fit. He gathered together every woman in the country, young and old, and he tried the gold shoe on every one of them, but it fitted none of them. In the end he brought in his own three daughters to the room to try the shoe on them. He tried it on the eldest daughter, but it would not go over the tips of her toes. He tried it on the second daughter, but it would not go on her big toe. He tried it on the youngest, and her foot was as if it had grown inside it. He was bound by oaths and vows, and he had to marry his own daughter.

She was quite prostrated when she heard that she must do this. She took to her bed in sorrow, saying to herself that she would rather death itself than yield to her father's will. Night came, and she was on her own in the dark room, when she heard something moving under her window. She looked out, and what was there but a brown calf.

'There are you, poor lassie,' said the brown calf, 'sad and sorrowful, and here am I to help you. Make ready and prepare to go along with me. Your mother's chest is in the corner of the room, with all her finery in it. Bring it with you and come outside, and I shall carry you to a place where you will be free from your father's vows.'

When the girl heard this, she gathered up her own belongings and her mother's chest, and she was out through the window in a flash. She put the chest on the brown calf's back and sat beside it herself, and they made off.

The brown calf travelled and travelled for three days and three nights over mountain, hill and moor, till they came close to a fine big city with a king's castle right in the middle of it. The brown calf halted on a little green hillock near the town and said, 'Now, you must come down from my back here and lift down the chest, and we'll bury it in this hillock. You must go in to the king's castle and ask for work there, and don't refuse any work that they give you to do.'

The girl did as the calf asked her, and she got work in the king's scullery, where she stayed from dawn to dusk washing the pots and dishes.

One day word went round the town that the king's son was going to hold a grand glittering gathering, and every girl in the town got an invitation. The night of the great gathering came, and what a fuss the young women of the town made as they got themselves ready to go to the palace. After all the guests had assembled, the girl was on her own in the scullery, when she heard something moving under the window, and who was there but the brown calf. 'Why are you not at the gathering tonight?' said he.

'Because,' she replied, 'I never got an invitation. I'm only the poor servant-girl who works in the scullery.'

'You come with me,' said he, 'and I'll take you to the gathering.'

She went with the brown calf, and they got to the hillock where the chest was buried. They dug up the chest and the brown calf took out the dress of birds' down which had belonged to her mother, and he put it on the girl, together with the gold shoe and the silver shoe, and when she had combed her head with the comb which left one side of it gold and one silver, there was none in the hall who could surpass her.

'Now,' said the brown calf, 'go into the ballroom, and I warrant you no-one to match you will set foot on the floor tonight. And when you are tired of dancing, come out, and I'll be waiting for you.'

The girl went in, and when she did every eye below the roof of the building stood still to gaze on her beauty. The king's son himself came to ask the favour of a dance with her, and he never let her quit the floor all night. A little before the gathering was due to finish, she took her chance while no-one was looking, and slipped out without anyone noticing. The brown calf was waiting for her at the main door. He carried her off to the hillock where the chest was hidden, the fine clothes were put back in the chest and it was buried where it had been before, and the girl was back in her rags in the scullery when the ball broke up.

The king's son was vexed that he had lost sight of her, because he had fallen so deeply in love with her that he would get neither sleep by night nor peace by day until he saw her again. He sent out a proclamation that he would hold another great gathering the next evening, and he wanted everyone who had been at the first gathering to come to the second one. It was rumoured that the king's son had fallen in love with one of the girls, and every girl hoped and wished that it was herself.

The servant in the scullery was washing and scraping the pots as usual when she heard something moving under the window, and who was there but the brown calf. "Here, here," said he, "get ready and let's go to the gathering."

She was willing enough – she jumped at the chance to go with him. everything happened that night as it had happened the night before. The calf dressed her in the dress of moss cotton and the other fineries that were in the chest, and he carried her to the hall, and she went in to the ball with the rest of the company. There were plenty of beautiful young maidens to be seen there, but none of them was as beautiful as she.

The dancing began, and the king's son was as attentive to her as ever, and he was quite determined to find out before the night ended who she was or where she came from, and then he would offer her his heart. But she managed to slip off when his attention was distracted. The brown calf was waiting at the door, and he did as he had done before, and when the clothes had been put back in the chest, he brought her back to the scullery, and there was no sign for the king's son where to seek or search for her.

Thereupon the king's son vowed and swore that another night would not pass before he found her, and he sent out the same proclamation for the third night. Everything happened as it had happened on the previous nights. The brown calf came for her and took her to the green hillock where the chest was hidden, and this night he dressed her in the dress like starlight and all the other fineries she had worn the other nights.

The king's son had warned the doorkeepers to be on their guard, and if they saw her leaving, to lay hold of her. Everything happened as before. The king's son had not an eye for anyone but her, but she found a chance to slip away when the ball was coming to an end. The doorkeeper was on his guard, and he tried to catch hold of her, but for all that he only got hold of the heel of the golden shoe, and when the king's son came up to him, he had only the golden shoe. The brown calf helped her as usual, and she was in the scullery as usual by the time the ball finished.

Now the king's son had the golden shoe, but he had no idea whose it was. He decided to summon the girls who had been at the ball the night before, and marry the one the golden shoe fitted. That was what he did, but the golden shoe wouldn't fit any of them.

The hen-wife had a daughter, and the mother cut off the tips of her toes and the backs of her heels and sent her up to the palace with the rest, and when the shoe was tried on her it went on with a squeeze. The king's son said that he would marry her according to his promise, though he was certain that this was not the girl he wanted. How proud the hen-wife was when the king's son came to fetch her daughter and carried her off on a white steed to marry her.

They had not gone far along their way when a little bird came and sat between the ears of the horse and began to sing. When the king's son listened, this is what he heard:

> Nipped foot, clipped foot
> Behind you on the horse;
> You'll find the one the gold shoe fits
> Sad and sorrowful in the scullery.

He listened for no more. He leapt off the steed, seized the hen-wife's daughter by the foot and pulled the shoe off it – and the shoe was full of blood, and the foot wanting the tips of the toes and the back of the heel. He went back to the hen-wife's house with the girl and left her with her mother, and leaving there he spurred his horse to a gallop until he reached the scullery where he found the girl he was looking for. He tried the shoe on her and it seemed as though it had been made for her foot. She had to marry him without further delay. The wedding feast was already laid out in the king's palace, and the marriage was arranged for the next day.

That night the brown calf came to her window and said to her: 'You won't see me again: I leave you my blessing. You are wondering who I am. I am your own dear mother who has entered into the form of the brown calf to save you from your father's vows, and turned into the bird to deliver the king's son from the hen-wife's wiles. You have no more need of my help, and you will be happy with the king's son. You can get your mother's chest from the green hillock and bring it home, and my blessing will follow you and your beloved as long as you live.'

They were married, and they held a merry, mirthful wedding but they never gave a morsel of it to me.

---

9   *Andrew Stewart*

THE THREE FEATHERS

Well, ONCE UPON A TIME there was a king and this king wis gettin up in years, he wid be away nearly the borders o eighty year auld, ye see, and he took very ill, an he wis in bed. So his doctor come tae see him and . . . he soundit oot the old king lyin in bed, an everything – he come doon, he's asked for the oldest brother tae come, ye see, so he spoke tae the oldest brother, and he says tae the oldest brother, he says: 'Yer father hasnae very long tae live,' he says, 'the best o his days is bye, an,' he says, 'Ah wouldn't be a bit surprised,' says the doctor, 'if ye come up some mornin an find him lyin dead in his bed,' ye see?

So, of coorse, it wid come as a blow tae the oldest brother, and here, the oldest brother sent for the other two brothers, ye see, sent for Jeck and the other two brothers, see? So when the two brothers come up, there wis one o this brothers like, ye understand, they cried him 'Silly Jeck', he wis awfae saft an silly, ye know, he widnae dae nothing. He wis a humbug tae the castle; he'd done nothin for the father – in fact he wasnae on the list o gettin onything left when the father died at aw. That wis jist the way o't, ye see. He wis a bad laddie. So anyway, here the three sons is stan'in, the oldest brother tellt them that the father wis goin tae die and something wid have tae be done, and 'at he was goin to be king, ye see. So the good adviser said: 'Well,' he says, 'before the father dies,' he says, 'he told me that the one that would get the best table-cover, the best an the dearest table-cover that could be found in the country, would get the castle and be king,' ye see?

'Well,' says the oldest brother,' he says, 'what are we goin to do,' he says, 'have we tae go an push wir fortune?'

'No,' says the good adviser,' he says, 'your father gave us three feathers,' he says, 'here they're here,' he says, 'out of an eagle's wing,' an he says, 'each o yese got tae take a feather each an go to the top tower o the castle, and throw yer feather up in the air,' he says, 'an whatever wey the feather went, flutter't, that wis the way ye had tae go an push yer fortune for the table-cover.'

So right enough they aa agreed, ye see, an Jeck wi his guttery boots an everything on – the other yins wis dressed in gaads, ye know, and swords at their side, an Jeck jist ploo'ed the fields an scraped the pots doon in the kitchen an everything, cleaned the pots, but Jack wis up wi his guttery boots along wi the rest o the brothers, ye see, an they threw the feathers up, ye see, the two brothers, an one o the feathers went away be the north, the oldest brother's. 'Well,' he says, 'brothers,' he says, 'see the way my feather went,' he says, 'away be the north,' he says, 'Ah suppose that'll have to be the way Ah'll have to go an look for the table-cover.' The other second oldest brother threw the feather up, and hit went away be the south. 'Ah well,' he says, 'Ah think,' he says, 'Ah'll have tae go be the south.' So poor Jeck, they looked at Jeck, an they werena gaen tae pey any attention tae Jeck, ye see, but Jeck threw his feather up an it swirl't roon aboot an it went doon at the back o the castle, in the back-yaird o the castle, ye see? Aw the brothers startit laughin at him: 'Ha! ha! ha! ha!' They were makin a fool of Jack, ye see, because his feather went doon at the back o the castle. So Jack gien his shooders a shrug like that an he walks doon the stairs, intae the kitchen.

Noo the two brothers, they got a year an a day to get a good table-cover. So Jack never bothered goin to see aboot his table-cover or nothing, ye see, aboot his feather, rather, or nothing, ye see, so he'd jist aboot a couple o days tae go when the year an the day wis up and Jack's up one day lyin in his bed and he says: 'Ma God!' he says, 'Ah should go an hae a look at ma feather tae,' he says, 'Ah've never seen where it wis gettin.' It wis a warm kind o afternoon. He says: 'Ah'll go for the fun o the thing,' he says, 'an see where ma feather went.' So for curiosity Jeck went roon the back o the castle, an went roond the back o the castle, an he wydit through nettles an thistles an he heard a thing goin. 'Hoo-hoo, o-ho-ho-ho,' greetin. Jack looks doon at his feet an here there wis a big green frog sittin, a green puddick, sittin on top o a flagstane, an the tears wis comin out o its een. An Jack looks doon an says: 'Whit's wrang wi ye, frog?'

'Oh Jeck, ye didnae gie us much time tae go on tae get ye a table-cover, did ye? Ye should hae been here long ago. You were supposed tae follow yer feather the same as ony ither body.'

But Jeck says: 'I didnae ken,' he says, 'I thocht . . . when the feather went doon at the back o the castle Ah jist had tae stay at the castle.'

'Oh well, ye cannae help it noo,' said the frog, he says, 'Ye'd better come away doon. Luft that flagstane,' he says. There wis a ring, an iron ring in the flagstane. (Ye know whit a flagstane is? It's a square big stone that's in the ground an ye can lift it up, ye see.) An this big iron ring wis in this flagstane, an Jack wis a big strong lump o a fella, he lifts the stane up aboot half a turn aff the grun, ye see, an there wis trap stairs goin doon. Jack went doon the trap stairs, an the puddick hopped doon the stairs like 'at, an tellt Jack tae mind his feet.

Jeck went in. He says: 'Well, Ah never seen frogs,' he says, 'haen a place like this before.' A big long passage an 'lectric lights burnin an everything an frogs goin past him, hoppin past him, an the smell o the meat an', nice smell o reshturant an everything was something terrible, ye see. Took Jack into a lovely place like a parlour, an here when Jack went in he sut doon on this stool, an the frogs aw speakin tae him, ye see, an one frog jumpit on tap o Jack's knee, an Jack's clappin the wee frog like this, an it's lookin up wi its wee golden eyes, up at Jack's face, an Jack's clappin the wee frog, pattin him on top o the back, an it's lookin up at him an laughin at him in his face.

'Well Jack,' he says, 'you better go now,' he says, 'ye havenae much time, yer brothers'll be comin home tomorrow,' he says, 'we'll hae tae get ye a table-cover.' So Jack thocht tae hissel, where wis a . . . puddicks goin tae get him a table-cover, frogs, ye see, goin tae get a table-cover tae him. But anyway, they come wi a broon paper.

'Now,' he says, 'Jack,' he says, 'there is a broon paper parcel,' he says, 'an there's a cover in there,' he says. 'Right enough,' he says, 'yer brothers will have good table-covers, but,' he says, 'the like o this,' he says, 'is no in the country.' He says, 'Don't open it up,' he says, 'till you throw it on your father's bed, an when you throw it on your father's bed,' he says, 'jist tell him tae have a look at that.' See?

Jack said, 'Aa right.'

'Haste up noo, Jack.'

He could hae done wi lookin at the table-cover, but he stuck it 'neath his airm an he bid the wee frogs farewell, an he come up, pit the flagstane doon, an back intae the kitchen. So one o the maids says tae him, 'What hae ye got 'neath yer airm, Jeck?' Jack's pitten it up on a shelf, ye see, oot the road.

'Och,' he says, 'it's ma table-cover,' and aw the weemen start laughin, 'Ha-ha-ha-ha-ha, silly Jeck gettin a table-cover in his father's castle. You've some hopes o bein king, Jack.' An they never peyed nae attention tae Jack, ye see, so Jack jist never heedit, he's suppin soup wi a spoon, liftin the ladle an suppin, drinkin a ladle oot at a pot, drinkin the soup an everything, ye see.

When he looks up the road, up the great drive, an here comin down is the two brothers comin gallopin their brae steeds, an the medals on their breist an the golden swords, they were glutterin, an here they're comin at an awful speed down the drive, ye see. 'Here's ma two brothers comin,' an he ran oot the door an he welcomed his two brothers, ye see, an they widnae heed Jack.

'Get oot o ma road,' one o them said. 'Get oot o ma road, eediot,' he says, 'you get oot o the road.' An they stepped up, ye see, an opened the door an went up tae see their father. So the father said, 'There no time the now, sons' – they were greedy, they wantit tae get made king, ye see . . . 'Wait,' he says, 'until yese get yer dinner, boys,' he says, 'an then come up an . . . Ah'll see yer table-covers. Ah'll have tae get the good advisers in, ye see.' (The good advisers was men. There wis three o them an they pickit whatever wan wis the best, ye see, same as solicitors an things in this days nowadays, ye see.)

So anyway, the two brothers efter they got their feast an everything, their dinner, an come right up, ye see, an here the good advisers – rung the bells, an here the good advisers come up, red coats on them an they're stan'in beside them. Well, the father, the two sons felt awfy sorry for the old king because he wis gettin very weak an forlorn lookin. He wis ready for tae die any time. 'Well, sons,' he says. 'Well, sons, did yese get the table-covers?'

'Yes,' says the oldest son, 'father,' he says, 'have a look at this table-cover.' An he throwed it ower on the bed an they all came an liftit the table-cover, an he examined the table-cover an it was a lovely, definitely, a lovely silk that ye never seen the like o this table-cover, heavy. Ah couldnae explain whit kind o table-cover this wis.

'Yes,' he says, 'son,' he says, 'it definitely is a good table-cover,' he says, 'an it'll take a bit o beatin. Have you got a table-cover?' he says tae the second youngest son.

'Well,' he says, 'father, there's a table-cover,' he says, 'Ah don't know if it's as good as ma brother's or no,' he says, 'but have a look at that table-cover.' An they looked at the table-cover. Well, the one wis as good as the other. The good advisers couldnae guess which o them wis the best.

'Aw but,' says, 'hold on,' says one – there wis wan o the good advisers likit Jack, ye see. He says, 'Hold on,' he says, 'where's Jack?'

'Aw,' says the other good advisers, 'what dae we want with Jack?' he says.

'Aw, but he's supposed tae be here,' he says, 'and see if he's got a table-cover,' the oldest yin said . . . tae the other good advisers. He says, 'Ye're supposed tae be here,' ye see?

So anyway, here now . . . they shouts for Jack an Jack come up the stairs, in his guttery boots as usual, an he's got the broon parcel 'neath his airm. So the two brothers looked at Jeck wi the green [sic] parcel 'neath his airm, ye see, an he says, 'Have you got a table-cover,' he says, 'son?' the old king said.

'Yes, father,' he said, 'did ma brothers get the table-covers?'

'Aye,' he said, 'there they're there.'

'Well,' says Jack, he says, he says, 'They're definitely nice table-covers, but,' he says, 'if Ah couldnae get a better table-cover,' he says, 'than what ma two brothers got,' he says, 'in yer ain castle, father,' he says, 'Ah wadnae go searchin, Ah widnae go,' he says, 'seekin ma fortune,' he says, 'the distance they've went,' he says. 'tae look for table-covers,' he says.

So the men start laughin at Jack as usual: 'Ha-ha-ha-ha! nonsense, Jack,' an the old king says, 'Ah told ye not tae send for him, he's daft,' ye see.

'Well,' he says, 'have a look at that table-cover, father,' so here the father took the scissors and opened the string, an took out . . . Well, what met their eyes was something terrible. It wis lined with diamonds and rubies, this table-cover. One diamond alone would ha' bought the two table-covers that the brothers had, ye see?

'Aye, aye,' says the good adviser, he says, 'that is a table-cover an a table-cover in time,' he says. 'Where did ye get it, son? Did ye steal it from some great castle?'

'No father,' he says, 'I got this,' he says, 'in yer own castle.'

'It can't be true,' says the king, he says: 'I've never had a table-cover like that in ma life.'

But tae make a long story short, the two brothers wouldnae agree. They said, 'Naw, naw, naw, father,' he says, 'that's not fair,' he says, 'We'll have tae . . . have another chance,' ye see. 'We'll have tae have another chance,' an here they wouldn't let Jack be king. 'Aw right,' says Jack, he says, 'it's all the same tae me,' he says, 'if yese want a chance,' he says, 'again,' he says, 'very good,' he says, 'it's aa the same tae me.'

So the father says, 'Well, if yese want anither chance,' he says, 'Ah tell ye what Ah want yese tae bring back this time,' he says, 'an Ah'll give the three of yese a year an a day again,' he says, 'seein that Ah'm keepin up in health,' he says, 'Ah'll give yese another chance. Them 'at'll go an bring back the best ring,' he says, ' 'll get my whole kingdom,' he says, ye see, 'when Ah die.'

Well, fair enough. The three brothers went an got their feathers again and went tae the top of the tower. The oldest brother threw his feather up an it went away be the east. 'Aw well,' he says, 'it'll have tae be me away for east.' The other brother threw a feather up – the second youngest brother, an it went away be the south. 'Aw well,' says the other brother, he says, 'Ah'll go away be the south.' Jack threw his feather up, but they didnae lauch this time. It swirl't roon aboot like that an it went doon the back o the castle in amongst the nettles an the thistles. So they looked, the two brothers looked at each other but they never said a word. They jist went doon the stair an Jack follae't them the big tower, ye see, doon the steps. (Stone steps in them days in the old castles.) And the two brothers bid farewell, mountit their horses and they're away for all they can gallop in each direction, waved tae each other wi their hands an away they went. Ye could see them goin ower the horizon, see?

Jack never bother't, ye see. He went down an he's two or three month in the hoose an oot he went roon. An he seen the same thing happen't again, he went roond the back o the castle an here's the frog sittin on tap o the flagstane. 'Aye,' he says, 'Jack, ye're back quicker this time,' he says. 'What did ye think of the table-cover?'

'Och,' he says, 'it wid hae bought ma faither's castle althegither, right oot be the root.'

'Aye,' he says, 'Ah tellt ye it wis a good table-cover,' he says. 'Now,' he says, 'Ah'll have tae get ye a ring,' says the frog. 'Ye better come away doon an see the rest o the family,' ye see? Lifts the flagstane up an Jeck went doon the steps, ye see, an intae this big parlour place an he's sittin down, the 'lectric lights is burnin, an this wee frog jumped on tap o his knee an he's aye clappin this wee frog, ye see, on tap o his knee, clappin the wee frog, an it's croakin up in his face wi its wee golden eyes, ye see. Well, when the time come when Jack got – they gien him a good meal, ye know, no frogs' meat or onythin like that, it wis good meat they gien him on dishes, this frogs hoppin aboot the place an gien him a nice feed, ye see, an they gies him this wee box – it wis a velvet box, black, did ye ever see wee black velvet boxes? He says, 'There it is, Jack,' he says, 'an the like of that ring,' he says, 'is not in the country,' he says. 'Take it tae yer father an let him see that.'

So Jack stuck it in his waistcoat pocket – an auld waistcoat he had on, ye see, an he's oot, an he's cleanin – but he wis forgettin aboot the year an the day – it passed quicker, ye see. Here's the two brothers comin doon the avenue on their great horses, galloping. Jumped aff an said, 'Did ye get . . .' They wantit tae ken if Jack got a ring.

Jack says, 'Look,' he says, 'dinnae bother me,' says Jack, he says. 'Go up an see the aul man,' he says, 'instead o goin lookin for rings,' he said. 'Ah've never seen as much nonsense as this in ma life.' He says, 'Why can they no let you be king,' he says, 'onywey, ye're the oldest,' he says, ' 'stead o cairryin on like this?'

'Oh,' he says, 'what's tae be done is tae be done, Jack,' so away they went, up tae see their father. The good advisers wis there. And they showed the rings tae their father, an the father's lookin at the two rings, an judgin the rings, oh, they were lovely rings, no mistake about it, they were lovely rings, ye see, diamonds an everything on them. Here they come – Jack come up the stair again an he wabbles in an he's lookin at them arguin aboot the rings and Jack says, 'Look, father,' he says, 'have a look at that ring.' Jack never seen the ring, and the father opened the wee box and what met his eyes, it hurtit the good advisers' an the old king's eyes, it hurted them. There wis a stone, a diamond stone, sittin in it would have bought the whole castle an the land right about it, ye see?

So anyway, here the brothers widnae be pleased at this. 'Naw, naw, naw, this is nae use, father,' he says, 'give us another chance,' he says. 'The third time's a charm,' he says, 'give us another chance.'

'But,' says the father, he says, 'Jack won twice,' he says, 'it's no fair,' an this good adviser, the old man 'at liked Jack said, 'No, no, Jack'll have to be king; he won twice.'

'No, no, father, gie us another chance,' he says, so the brothers says, 'Ah'll tell ye, father, let us get a good wife,' he says, 'tae fit the ring an them that gets the nicest bride tae fit the ring'll get the king's castle. How will that do, Jack?'

Jack says, 'Fair enough tae me.' But Jack got feart noo because he mindit it wis puddicks he wis amongst. Where would he get a wife from amongst a lot o wee puddicks, frogs an things, ye see? Same thing again, up tae the tap o the tower an threw off their feathers, and one feather went away one road and the other feather went away the other road, but Jack's feather went roon tae the back o the castle. 'Aw,' says Jack, 'Ah'm no goin back. That's it finished now, Jack.' Jack says, 'Ah'm lowsed.' He says, 'Ah'm no goin tae tak nae wee frog for a wife,' ye see?

So anyway, Jack waited tae the year wis up, an jist for the fun o the thing, he says, 'Ah'll go roond the back o the castle,' he says, 'an see what's goin 'ae happen.' Roon he went tae the back o the castle and here's three or four frogs sittin greetin, and the wee frog that sut on his knee, hit wis greetin, the tears runnin out o its een, an it wis jist like a man playin pibroch, 'Hee-haw, hee-haw', an aa the frogs is greetin, ye see, an here all danced wi glee, and this wee frog come an met him an looked up in his face and climbed up his leg, this wee tottie frog, an he lifted the flagstane an they hoppit doon, ye see.

'Well Jack,' he says, the old frog says to Jack, he says, 'Ah wis thinkin,' he says, 'Jack, ye widnae come,' he says. 'Ye were frightened,' he says, 'we couldnae get ye a wife, didn't ye [sic] Jack?'

'Yes,' says Jack, 'tae be truthful wi ye,' he says, 'I thought,' he says, 'a frog,' he says, 'widnae do me for a wife.'

'Well,' says the old man, efter they gied him somethin tae eat, he says, 'How wid ye like Susan for a wife?' An this wis the wee frog that wis on his knee, an he wis clappin it.

Jack says, 'That wee frog,' he says, 'how could that make a wife tae me?'

'Yes, Jack,' he says, 'that is yer wife,' he says, 'an a woman,' he says, 'a wife,' he says, 'yer brothers,' he says, 'will have pretty women back wi them,' he says, 'but nothing like Susan.'

So anyway, here, they says, 'Go out,' to Jack. 'Go out for an hour,' he says, 'round the back,' he says, 'an intae the kitchen,' he says, 'and take a cup o tea an come back out again,' he says; 'we'll have everything ready for ye.' Jack went roond noo an he's feared, he didn't know what wis gonnae tae happen, an he's taken a cup o tea, but he's back roond.

Here when he come roon at the back o the castle beside the trees, there wis a great big cab sittin, lined wi gold, an the wee frog, it wis the frog, was the loveliest princess ever ye seen in yer life. She wis dressed in silk, ye could see through the silk that wis on her – she wis jist a walkin spirit, a lovely angel she looked like, an when Jack seen her, he says, wi his guttery boots an everything, he wouldn't go near her. So this old king, it wis an old king, a fat frog wi a big belly, green, an he says, 'There is yer bride, there's Susan,' he says, 'How dae ye like the look o her, Jack?'

Jack rubbed his eyes like that . . . He says, 'Look,' he says, 'I couldnae take a lady like that,' he says, he says, 'it's impossible . . . Look at the mess Ah'm in.'

'Oh but,' says the puddicks, they says, 'we'll soon pit that right,' says the old frog, and he says, 'jist turn three times roon aboot,' an Jeck turned three times: an as he's turnin roon aboot his claes wis changin, an there he's turned the beautifullest king ye ever seen in yer life – a prince, medals an a gold sword – ye never seen the like o it in yer life, an this cab wi six grey horses in it and footmen an everything on the back o the cab, an here when she seen Jack she come an put her airms roon Jack's neck, an Jack kissed her, ye see, an they went intae the cab.

Now they drove oot – this wis the year an a day up now, ye see, this was the [? term's day] – but when they come roon here they're comin drivin up the road, but the two brothers wis up before Jack, an . . . they sees the cab comin up the drive, an the two brothers looked oot the windae, an 'Aw, call out the guard,' they said, an here's the guard out and the old king got up oot o his bed, he's lookin through the windae, opened the big sash curtains back, an he says, 'Ah told ye,' he says, 'Jack stole the ring an stole the table-cover. This is the king come,' he says, 'tae . . . claim his goods,' he says, 'that Jack stole.'

Well anyway, here, what happens but the two brothers cam oot an they says, 'Oh,' they says, 'Ah told ye, father, not tae take Jack,' but here when Jack stepped oot o the cab an they seen Jack, Jack waved up tae the windae, his father, 'Hi Dad!' he says, an he shouts tae his father. The father looked doon an he rubbed his een an he says, 'Is that you, Jack?'

Jack says, 'Yes, father, it's me,' he says, 'an here is ma wife. Ah'm comin up tae see ye.'

Well, when the two brothers seen Jack's wife they went an took their two wifes an they pit them intae the lavatories an locked the door. Haud them oot o the road, intae the lavatories they pit them. 'Get away oot o here, shoo, get oot o here, get oot o here! Oh, Jack's wife,' he says, 'we wouldn't be shamed wi youse women!' An the two lassies that the two oldest brothers had, started tae cry, ye see, they shoved them intae the lavatories. 'Go in there,' he says, 'oot o the road,' he says, 'until I get ye a horse,' he says, 'that ye can gallop away.'

An when Jack come up an . . . when the father an the good advisers seen this lovely princess, the like wis never in the country, they made Jack king, and the bells were ringin for the feast an Jack was the king; an he wis good to aw the poor folk aw roon the country, folk 'at the owld king used tae be good to, Jack wis three times better tae them an they loved Jack for ever after, an Jack lived happy, an he's king noo on the tap o Keelymabrook, away up in the hills. That's the end o ma story.

THE GREEN MAN OF KNOWLEDGE

W<small>ELL, THIS IS A STORY</small> aboot an old lady – an auld woman – she bred pigs. She wes a widow-woman, an she'd a son cried Jack. An this son wes jist a nitwit, he'd nae sense, they said – so they said, onywey – an he used to sit at the fireside amongst the ashes. Aye, he'd a big auld hairy Hielan collie-dog. An this collie-dog wes aa he look't at an mindit; him an his dog used to sit, an play cards wi the dog – an I couldnae say the dog played back, like – he played cards wi his dog. An that's aa he did, the lee-lang day.

But Jack, he comes to the age of twenty-one. An on his twenty-oneth birthday, . . . he rises fae the fireside an streetches hissel – an he's a man weel over six fit. An his breekies he was wearin fin he did streetch hissel went up to abeen his knees. An his jaicket an schuil-buits . . . he wes a giant o a man, compared to the clothes he wore. He was aye sittin humphed up.

He says, 'Mither,' he says, 'you feed awa at your pigs, Jack's awa to push his fortune.'

'Ah,' she says, 'feel Jack, dinnae gae 'wa noo, 'cause ye'll jist get lost, an ye ken ye've niver been past the gate o the place there aa your life, Jack. Jist bide far ye are.'

So: 'Ah, but mither,' he says, 'I'm gaun awa to push my fortune, an nothing 'll dee me but I'm gaun to push my fortune.'

'No, no, Jack, awa an play wi yir doggie.'

He says, 'No, I'm gaun to push my fortune.'

She says, 'Weel, Jack, dinna wander awa.' But Jack niver bothers,

mither or nothing else – he hauds awa, whenever she turns her back. An
. . . he opens the gate an walks oot – and whenever he opened that gate,
he's in anither world. He didnae know where he wes, because he'd niver
been oot o the fairmyard in his life. An he walks doon the road. So – if
everything be true, this'll be nae lies – there were a crossroads, an on
wan o the signposts it says: 'To the Land of Enchantment.' So Jack says,
'Here's for it.'

So he hauds doon the road to the Land of Enchantment onywey. And
in the Land of Enchantment – I must tell ye this, because you'll understand what I tell yeze! – everything spoke: animals, birds, everything
spoke. So he's comin on, an he's feelin gey hungry, Jack. He's a gey lump
o a lad, an he liked his meat, and he was feelin hungry. So he says, 'Lord,
I weisht I asked my mither for a bannock or something to take on the
road wi me, 'cause it's gey hungry, gaun awa.'

He's comin on, an he looks – an did ye ever see a horse-troch, aa kin'
o grown wi moss? – an a lovely troch it wis, at the road side. An Jack
says: 'O, thank the Lord, I'll get a drink onywey, it'll quench the hunger
for a bittie – ma thirst tae.' So – there a wee robin sittin on the edge o
the water – the edge o the troch, ye ken – so he bends doon his heid an
takes a drink.

The robin says, 'Hullo, Jack.'

He says, 'Lord, bi God, it's a bird speakin! Whit are ye speakin for?'
he says. 'I never heard a bird speak in ma life.'

'Oh,' he says, 'Jack, ye're in the Land of Enchantment – everything
an everybody can speak.'

'Oh, but' – he says – 'nae a bird!' He says: 'If I didnae see't wi my
ain een, I wouldnae believe.'

'Oh yes, Jack, I can talk.'

He says, 'Fit wey d'ye ken ma name?'

'Oh,' he says, 'Jack, we knew ye were comin – we'd been waitin on
ye for twenty-one year, Jack.'

'Lord, ye'd a gey wait, had ye no?'

But – he has a drink o water – he says, 'Ye ken fit I could dae wi,'
he says, 'birdie,' he says, 'I could dae wi a richt feed o meat.'

'Oh, well, Jack,' he says, 'jist follae me.'

So it trittles awa, doon the road a bit, an here's a lovely thackit cot at the roadside, an an old woman as if she'd the age o a hunder, an she's rockin back an forrit in an aul rockin chair. So she says, 'Come in, Jack.' She says, 'Go in an get your supper, Jack.'

So when Jack comes in, here's a lovely table set, an a plate o porridge an milk an some tea, an so on, cakes an biscuits – nae it, scones, an things like that – there wisna ony cakes at that time, scones was . . . home-made fancy at that time on aa. An a lovely young girl. An she was supplied wi the food, d'ye see?

So he sits doon, an has a plate o this porridge, an it tasted lovely, he never tasted anything finer in his life. (When ye're hungry, onything tastes fine). An he had some tea – no, I'm gaun through my story: I made a mistake in that story . . . there were nae tea; it was home-brewed ale. . . . He'd a mug o this home-brewed ale, an some scones, oatcakes, things like that.

So she says, 'Jack, would you like to lie down?'

An he says, 'I wouldnae care,' he says, 'I'm feelin gey weary,' he says, 'an things, an I could dee wi a lie-doon.'

She says, 'Come up here, Jack.' An she takes him up, an there the loveliest feather bed that ever you seen in your life, a richt bed. And so Jack jist lies doon, an sinks in, an faas quite asleep.

So he's lyin, but he waukens through the night, an he's lyin on a sheepskin an three peats. He says, 'My God, ma bed's changed quick! Lord,' he says, 'a queer bed.' But he faas awa again – Jack didnae worry, he wis used to lyin in ashes onywey. He faas awa again, but he waukens in the mornin, an he's lying in this lovely bed again. He says, 'My God, this is a queer country.' He says, 'It's jist nae like ma mither's place at aa.'

But he jumps ootowre his bed, an he gaes doon, an the breakfast's waitin for him again. So . . . the young girl says: 'Go out, an my grandmother'll gie ye some advice, Jack. In the land you're in, all 'e advice you can get, you take, Jack, 'cause you'll need it, see?'

So Jack says, 'Aye, I aye tak advice, lassie.' He says: 'It's nae doin ony hairm.'

So he gaes oot tae the door, he says, 'Weel, Grannie, how are ye keepin?'

'Och,' she says, 'fine, Jack.' She says, 'Jack, I'm gaun to give ye some advice. When you go along this road today, Jack, never talk to anybody first. Wait tae they talk to you first.'

He says: 'Weel, whatever ye say, Grannie.'

So he says good-bye, he hauds on his wey, but when he's gone . . . doon a bit o the road, the young girl cries efter him, an gies him some sangwiches to carry on with – ye ken, scones an butter, an things like that. So he carries them wi him, ye see?

But, to mak a lang story short an a short story lang, he hauds on the road. An he's ho the road, hey the road, doon this road, ye see? But he's walkin, an he hears the bells o a village, like a church-bell ringin awa; it wis helluva sweet-like music, ye ken – he hears awa in a hollow, ye wad think; it wis bonny-like. So he comes on ower the ridge, an he looks doon in a den, an here's a lovely village. So, . . . the most of the scones . . . that he got, he ate them, and there was a small bit o . . . a somethin got up in a piece o cloth, ye ken – an he opens it up, an here's a gold piece. Either a geeny, or a . . . what kin it was I dinna ken, but a gold piece, that's aa that I ken. An he takes it oot, looks at it, pits it in his pocket, an gaes on tae the village.

So he looks, an here's a inn. He says, 'I'll gang in here,' he says, 'for some home-brewed ale an scones,' he says (he wes feelin hungry again). So he gaes in, an he orders home-brewed ale an scones, an he eats a gey hillock, at least a platefae. An has a richt drink.

So he looks ower in a corner, an there three men playin cards, an they're aa playin cards jist, neither speakin, movin, or anything else, jist playin cards. An there a man dressed fae the [? paws o] his taes tae the heid . . . his heid in green. An oh . . . a very cunnin-lookin man – mebbe he's a man aboot fifty, but what a cunnin face. Jist by the face, ye would ken he was very clever – that man had brains.

So Jack gings ower til 'im an says, 'Can I get a game?'

He says, 'Have ye money?'

Jack says, 'Weel, I hinna a lot o money, but I've money' (he had change o this gold piece). An he says, 'I'd like a game.'

He says, 'Can you play at cards? We don't play,' he says, 'with men that cannot play at cards.'

'Oh,' he says, 'I've practised a bittie in my day' – twenty-one year he'd practised – he says, 'I've practised a bittie o it in my day,' but he sits doon, an he starts to play at cards. An the four of them plays an plays – but Jack . . . the Green Man o Knowledge wis a good card-player, but he couldnae beat Jack, 'cause Jack had aa his life played wi his collie. He could play cards!

But aathing's comin Jack's wey, so the ither two faas oot, but Jack an the Green Man of Knowledge plays an plays an plays up tae the early 'oors o the mornin.

Sae he looks at him, an he says, 'Jack,' he says, 'ye're maybe yir mother's feel,' he says, 'but ye're too good a man for me at cards.' He says, 'Good-bye, Jack.'

He says, 'Wait a minute. Fa are ye?'

He says, 'I'm the Green Man o Knowledge.'

'Sae you're the Green Man o Knowledge?'

'Aye.'

He says, 'Far dae ye bide?'

He says, 'East o the moon and west o the stars.'

He says, 'Lord, that's a queer direction.'

He says, 'Make oot o't onythin ye like, Jack.' Sae he jist left like that.

He jist gied a kin of laugh: 'My God, he's a gey peculiar kin o lad. Och,' he says, 'a lad winna worry. I've got plenty o money now.'

But he heaps aa his . . . he has any amount o money, I couldnae value it, but he's any amount. So he pits it in bags, an he says tae the innkeeper, he says, 'Will ye keep this gold to me till I come back this wey?' he says. 'I must fin' far the Green Man o Knowledge bides.'

An the innkeeper shaks his head. He says, 'Jack, dinnae follae him,' he says. He says, 'You'll go to disaster if you follae him.'

'Ach,' Jack says, 'aabody has only oncet to die – why worry? I'll just follae him.' But Jack reckoned withoot the Green Man o Knowledge.

So he hauds on the road, the only road to walk oot o the village, in the opposite direction fra whence he come.

An he's haudin on the road, ye ken – an he started gettin tired an weary again, an he took a few gold pieces wi him, nae much, in his pocket, 'fear he would come tae ony mair inns or that, ye ken, where he could get refreshments an that. An he's haudin on the road – but he jist comes right in aboot til anither thackit hoosie, the same.

He says, 'Well, I'll go up an see this thackit hoosie,' he says, 'an they might help me onywey. I'll pay them.'

So he chaps at the door, so . . . he hears a voice: 'Come in, Jack.'

He says, 'Lord, they're weel-informed in this country,' he says, 'everybody kens my name.' So he opens the door an comes in, an says, 'I'm in.'

She says, 'Are ye hungry, Jack? I suppose you are.'

He says, 'Yes, I'm hungry.'

She says, 'Sit down, Jack.'

So he sits doon. So he gets the same meal again as he got in the ither place. An yon girl . . . If the first girl was bonnie, this girl was ten times bonnier. She was much bonnier. And if the auld woman was old, this woman was much older – she was ancient! And she was sittin, rockin awa in her chair tae. So they pits him to bed, but the same thing happens in the bed I tellt ye in the other part o the story. He goes tae his bed an rises in the mornin, and the peats was through the night . . . But he notices before he goes to bed this old woman was knittin and she was knittin just a round piece of knittin, ye ken, like crochetin, but it was knittin she wis, jist a round piece like that table there. And it was lyin on the floor when he cam in the mornin.

'Now,' she says, 'Jack, you're lookin for the Green Man o Knowledge.'

He says, 'I am.'

And she says, 'Jack, we're here to help you, because you could never manage yourself, Jack.'

He says, 'Weel,' he says, 'I'll tak aa the help I can get.'

So efter his breakfast, she says, 'Jack,' she says, 'take this piece of knittin out to the door, and lay it down and sit on't – and sit plait-leggèd, Jack, and cross your arms, and,' she says, 'whatever happens, don't look behind you.' She says, 'Don't look behind you, because if you look behind you, it's the end.' She says, 'Whatever happens, don't look behind you.'

So he sits this plait-leggèd, and folds his arms. And she says, 'Say "Away with you." And,' she says, 'whirl it three times round, when you land with it,' she says, 'and say "Home with you". And,' she says, 'that'll be all right, Jack.'

And he says, 'Weel, weel, thank ye.'

So he says, 'Away with you' – but he moves that quick the wind just leaves his body. And he's through what he doesn't know what – Hellfire, brimstone, water, everything. And he's just dying to look back! But he minds – he's a strong-willpowered man – he minds what the auld woman said. He says, 'Weel, she did nae hairm so far,' he says. 'We'll just keep lookin forrit.' So he looks forrit.

But he lands, and he was glaid to land. So he stands up, and he catches this bit o knittin, and he pits it roond his heid three times like that, ye ken, an he says, 'Away with ye' – or 'Back with ye', it wis, sure, and away it wis. So he jist comes roond the corner, he hears 'ting-ting-ting', a blacksmith on an anvil, tinkerin, an so he comes in-aboot, and here a house. And here an old woman sittin like the first, rockin, ye ken, and she was older. If age coonts in that country, she was older.

And he says, 'Ah well, well' – he goes in-aboot, and she says, 'Well, Jack, we've been waitin for you.' She says, 'Go in to the house, Jack.' So Jack goes into the house, and he gets the same meal again. The same bed, the same procedure aa through, till the mornin.

'Now,' she says, 'Jack, go round to the smiddy shop,' she says, 'and you shall see,' she says, 'my husband, and he's made something for you, Jack. And . . . do what he told you, and you won't go wrong.'

So the smith says, 'I want to talk to you, Jack,' he says. 'Now,' he says, 'you're nearin the Green Man o Knowledge. But,' he says, 'the Green Man o Knowledge has many precautions.' ([I'm] forgetting aboot them.) He says, 'There must be a river to cross – there a river to be crossed,' he says. He says, 'I can't help you cross it, Jack, and there a bridge. But,' he says, 'if you step on that bridge it'll turn to a spider's web. You'll fall through it, Jack.' He says, 'If you fall in the water, Jack, you're finished, because the water goes into boilin lava.' He says, 'You're instantly dead.' He says, 'There only one way across, Jack,' he says, 'it's his youngest daughter. He's got three daughters, Jack, and the youngest one,' he says, 'is the most powerful of the lot.' He says, 'They come down to swim, Jack, every mornin,' he says, 'at mebbe ten o'clock,' he says, 'that time o the mornin. And,' he says, 'whenever they touch water,' he says, 'they turn to swans.' He says, 'There two black swans, Jack, and a white swan. It's the white swan you must get, Jack. But if you don't trap her in the way I'm tellin you, Jack, you're finished, for she'll pull you doon. You watch where they're puttin their clothes, and pick every article up o her clothes — and if you leave a hairpin, she'll make a outfit out o it,' he says, 'don't leave nothin.' And he says, 'Jack, they cross the bridge to the side you're on,' he says, 'and go into the water,' he says, 'from that side, Jack.' He says, 'They come back and dress there, Jack.'

So he says, 'Weel, it'll likely be true. But,' he says, 'this is a gey queer affair, but,' he says, 'weel, weel, we'll try't.'

He says, 'You see that horse-shoe, Jack?' It was a very large horse-shoe. He says, 'You sit on the horse-shoe, Jack, and don't look behind, whatever you do, and say, "Away wi you!" and,' he says, 'put it round your head three times and say, "Back wi you!" '

So Jack does't, and he gings through the same again, it wis jist torture. But he lands at the banks o the river. And now, as the blacksmith telt him to hide hissel, so Jack hides hissel . . . just aside the bridge, and he sees this three lovely maidens comin ower, and they were bonnie lassies. But the littlest one was the slenderest, and the most graceful o the lot, you would have thought, you know? So they come trippin ower the bridge and undress, and into the water. And whenever they touch the water, the two oldest ones turned til a black swan, and they swum fast an away. And this youngest one undresses; and he watches where she pits her clothes, and ye ken what like Jack, I mean a fairm servant, never seen a woman in his life hardly, says, 'Lord, this is fine!' They're into the water, and they're away swimming. So he's awa up wi her claes, up every stitch o claes she had, everything, even the very ribbons, and hides them.

So the two oldest ones comes out and dresses, and across the bridge and away. And she's up and doon this side, and she says, 'Where are you, Jack?'

He says, 'I'm here.'

She says, 'My clothes, please, Jack.'

'Ah na na, I'm nae giein ye nae claes,' he says. 'I was weel warned aboot ye.'

She says, 'Jack, please, my clothes. Are you a gentleman?'

'Na na,' he says, 'I'm just Jack the Feel. I'm nae gentleman.'

She says, 'What have I to do, Jack?'

He says, 'Well,' he says. He says, 'It's a cruel thing to ask, but,' he says, 'you must help me across this river on your back.'

She says, 'Oh Jack, you'd break my slender back.'

'Ah,' he says, 'the old smith's nae feel. Ye're nae sae slender.' He says, 'Ye'll take me across the river.'

She says, 'Well Jack, step on my back, but whatever you do, on the peril of my life and your life, don't tell how ye got across.'

He says, 'Okay.'

So he jumps on her back, and she takes him across, an he steps up on the bank.

So . . . 'Now,' she says, 'Jack, he shall try his best and . . . [to ken] how ye got across, but tell him nothing.'

He says, 'Weel, weel,' he says, 'I'll tell him nothing.'

So he walks up to the hoose – noo she gaes awa an gets dressed, an runs past him awa – he jist goes straight up tae the hoose an he chaps at the door, see. So the door opens, and here's the Green Man o Knowledge, and he was flabbergasted . . . he was shocked!

So he looks at him an he says, 'My God, Jack, how did you get here?'

'Och, jist the wey ye get.'

He says, 'Jack, how did you cross the river?'

'Och, flew across.'

He says, 'You've no wings, Jack.'

'Oh, nothing's impossible. I can grow wings,' he says.

'Well, Jack, come in,' he says. He says, 'I must shake your hand,' he says. 'You're a good man.' So Jack shakes his hand – and Jack's against the waa – sae he gies Jack a push, an Jack's through a kin o drap-door affair, an he lands in a wee roomie, an there's nae so much room for a moose, never mind a big man like Jack, he gies a couple of notes.

An he looks, an there a bit dry breid, an hit blue-moulded, an water, an it says, 'Drink, an eat, an be merry.' He says, 'My God, a lad widnae be very merry on that!'

So he's sittin awa, but 'at night he hears a whisper – here's this girl that helped him. She says, 'Jack, you've won me.' She says, 'Whenever you made me take you across the river,' she says, 'you spelled me, an I love you,' she says. 'I'll love you till the day I die, an I can't do nothing else.' But she says, 'I'll help you anyway, but please, Jack, don't move foolish, 'cause he'll kill ye.' She says, 'My father, he's evil.'

She says, 'Here's some food, Jack.' So Jack gets a feed o meat, an he was one aboot loves the meat! . . . He was sittin there fair right wi hunger aboot.

So in the mornin, the place opens and Jack creeps oot. An the Green Man o Knowledge says, 'How was ye last night, Jack?'

'Ach,' Jack says, 'very comfortable, jist fine.'

He says, 'Ye wisnae fine, Jack?'

'A never slept better.'

He says, 'You're not bad to please, Jack.'

'Ach, a lad cannae be bad to please in this times.'

So he says, 'Would you like,' he says, 'Jack,' he says, 'would you like,' he says, 'to prove to me that you are a man?'

Jack says, 'Yes, I would like to prove to ye I'm a man.'

'Well,' he says, 'Jack, I'll gie ye three tasks.' He says, 'They're not hard tasks, any child could do them,' he says. He says, 'They're not hard tasks, but,' he says, 'they take doin, Jack.' He says, 'Do you see,' he says, 'that dry wal . . . well in the garden, Jack?'

He says, 'Aye, I see the dry wal.'

He says, 'I want you,' he says, 'Jack, to go down to the bottom o that wal,' he says, 'an take out my wife's engagement ring,' he says, 'which she lost there twenty year ago. Oh,' he says, 'it isn't hard to dae, Jack, I could do it.'

Jack says, 'Why d'ye nae dee it?'

He says, 'I want you to do it, Jack.'

Jack says, 'Weel, I'll try 't.' So he's claain his heid, an, 'My God!'

And he says, 'Jack, not today; tomorrow, Jack.' An he says, 'Come on tae I show you a photograph o my wife, Jack.' So Jack's standin lookin – he says, 'Aye, she's a bonnie woman' – an he gies a push again, an he's intae anither kin o a cavity, an he gies a note this time.

So the hard breid's there again, an the water, an the same fare.

So here she comes again, wi mair food for 'im. So she says, 'Jack, the task he's going to give you is near impossible – it *is* impossible, Jack,' she says. 'I shall help you to make it possible. Now,' she says, 'the well is thirty-five feet [deep] Jack. An,' she says, 'I'll make a lether . . . a ladder oot o my body from the tap o the well tae the bottom o the well.' An she says, 'If you miss one step, Jack, you'll break a bone in my body.' An she says, 'For God's sake, Jack, watch what you're doin.'

So Jack says, 'Weel. . . .' An he says, 'Whit wey will I see't?'

She says, . . . 'The well's covered in mud,' she says, 'it's a terrible well,' she says, 'but I'll make the bottom clear, an you'll see the ring shinin.'

He says, 'Weel, weel, I'll try that.'

So he comes to the wal: the Green Man o Knowledge takes him oot the next mornin, takes him to the wal – an says: 'There's the well, Jack.'

So Jack says, 'Well.' So Jack leans ower, and feels for the lether, an he feels her there, her shouthers, God! – an he takes one step . . . [? away in] plunge doon quick, kiddin he's drappin like, an he's steppin doon, steppin doon, till he comes tae the last step, an he misses – he says, 'My God, I've broke her neck! . . . Ah,' he says, 'weel, weel, we cannae help it,' so he grabs the ring, an he's hup like the haimmers o hell, an oot o the wal.

An . . . so he shows the Green Man o Knowledge it, like that. He says, 'There's the ring.'

'Oh,' he says, 'you're clever, Jack.' He says, 'Let me see 't, Jack.'

'No,' Jack says. 'That's not you who done the work.'

He says, 'Who's helpin you, Jack?'

He says, 'Nobody's helpin me.'

He says, 'Somebody's helpin you, Jack.'

Jack says, 'No!'

He says, 'Well, Jack,' he says, 'you're a clever man,' he says. 'You've deen the first task,' he says, 'but,' he says, 'the second one's harder, Jack.'

So he takes Jack back, an Jack he sits down to a lovely meal. But Jack's awa to eat his meal when the seat gaes oot ablow him an whump! away in anither cavity. He says, 'My God, I canna stand this much longer,' he says, 'it'll kill me.'

But he's sittin, an he's lookin at this hard breid again, when she comes again. 'Oh,' she says, 'Jack,' she says, 'if it had been the other step, ye'd have broke my neck.' She says, 'You broke my pinkie, Jack, and I wore dinner gloves and Father didn't notice it.' She says, 'If he had noticed it, Jack, we'd both have been dead.'

He says, 'Fit dis he plan to dee to me the morn?'

She says, 'He's got a task for ye to do, Jack. Ye've to build a castle out of pure nothing within sixty minutes.'

'Oot o nothing?' he says. 'Lord, I couldnae thack a hoose in three months,' he says, 'never mind build a castle oot o nothing.'

She says, 'Jack,' she says, 'he's goin to take ye tae a hill at the back of our castle, an ask ye to build it. And,' she says, 'it must be bigger and larger and nicer than ours. An,' she says, 'Jack, I shall do it. But,' she says, 'watch what ye're sayin, Jack, 'cause ye'll get the baith o us trapped.' See?

He says, 'Weel, weel,' but he gets oot next mornin again, an the Green Man o Knowledge says: 'How was ye last night, Jack?'

'Ah,' he says, 'I wis niver better.' He says, 'My God, ye've got richt places in this hoose. I like this hoose – this castle.'

So he says, 'Yes, Jack,' he says, 'I've a small task for ye today, Jack. Anybody could do it, but,' he says, 'I want you to do it, Jack.'

Jack says, 'What is 't?'

He says, 'I want ye to build a castle, Jack, bigger than my one and larger, and nicer in every way.' He says, 'I want ye to build it in sixty minutes.'

Jack says, 'That's a gey stiff task to gie a lad.'

'Oh, but you're Jack,' he says, 'you got here,' he says, 'you got the engagement ring, Jack, this shouldn't bother you.'

'Well,' Jack says, 'I'll try't.'

He says, 'Go on, Jack, do't.'

'Ah but,' Jack says, 'I'll be giein awa trade secrets – you go awa,' he says.

So he says, 'I cannot watch, Jack?'

'No,' Jack says, 'I canna let ye watch.' So he turns his back and leaves.

So Jack sits for aboot half-an-'oor, an he says, 'If this deem disnae hurry up, I'll be clean killed. This lad'll be back here because she's takin an aafae time. . . . Oh,' he says. 'My God, this is nae ees, she's takin too lang.' He says, 'I'll be makin tracks oot o here.' So he turns roon, an the castle's at the back o'm, he wis lyin lookin the ither wey! So he says, 'Thank God.'

But he's walkin roon it, an he's lookin ower it – an there a hole aboot the size o this hoose. He says, 'Oh,' he says, 'she's made a mistake. Oh,' he says, 'whar is she?'

An he hears a voice sayin, 'Jack, that's nae a mistake. When he comes an looks at this hole, Jack, he'll say, "What's this, what's this?" An . . . you say til him, Jack, . . . "I've left that part for you to full up", an see whit he says, Jack.'

So up comes the Green Man o Knowledge, an he says, 'My goodness, whit a lovely castle,' he says, 'Jack,' he says, 'I do gie ye credit.' He says, 'You are a clever man.' So he walks aa roon' it, an he says, 'Oh my goodness, Jack! Whit a mess! What did ye leave this hole here for?'

He says, 'That's for you to fill.'

He says, 'Jack, who's helpin ye?'

Jack says, 'Na, na, naebody's helpin me. I wis only once pals wi a collie dog,' he says, 'that's aa.'

So he says, 'Well, well, Jack.'

But the third task . . . ye ken, I canna exactly mind . . . Oh yes, the third task was to clear the ants in a wood – ay, he'd tae clear every one oot in the half an 'oor. An . . . ye know ants, there millions o it, they're uncoontable, ye can't clean ants. So . . . he takes Jack out next mornin, the same proceedins again . . . an he says: 'Ye've got to clean all this ants, Jack, I'll give ye half an hour. If you can do that, Jack, I'll give you as much money as you can carry, any o my daughters for your wife, and your freedom, Jack, an,' he says, 'my castle, if ye need it – if ye want it – I'll gie ye your freedom.'

'Well,' Jack says, 'freedom means a lot to me. I've an auld mither,' he says, 'at hame,' he says. 'She's workin with the pigs, and,' he says, 'I'd like to help her tae.' But Jack looks at this wuid, an he says, 'My God, this'll take some clearin.' But of coorse, she did the job for him again.

So he says, 'Jack, you are clever. Now,' he says, 'Jack, come to my house,' he says, and he gives Jack a lovely meal this time, an no tricks. 'Now,' he says, 'Jack,' he says, 'I've got you,' he says, 'four bags of gold here,' he says, 'an in each bag, the money's near[? uncoontable],' he says, 'and,' he says, 'you're past bein a rich man,' he says, 'Jack. You're very wealthy,' he says. An he says, 'I'll take you to the stable,' he says, 'and gie ye the pick of my . . . my horses . . . I keep all mares,' he says, 'and they are lovely horses, Jack.' An he says, 'You can have whatever horse you want.'

So Jack says, 'Weel, weel,' he says.

But Jack's pickin his gold (an the Green Man o Knowledge is walkin along in front o him), when he hears the voice o the girl again, sayin, 'Jack, take the old mule – Jack, take the old mule.'

So he says, 'Well, well,' he says.

So he gaes intae the stable, an he's stan'in, ye see, an he's lookin – an they were lovely beasts, oh, there nae doot aboot them, loveliest beasts that he'd seen. There a grey meer, an he could see the fire in her eyes – fit a lovely meer. An there anither meer, this clean black meer, an he could see the fire in her eyes. So Jack looks at them, and he looks at this wee scruffy-lookin animal o a mule, an he says, 'My goodness, fit 'm I gaunna dae wi that?' He says, 'My God, she hisnae been wrang yet,' tae hissel. 'I better take a tellin.' He says, 'My God, it's a sin to throw this gold ootowre its back.' An he looks at this meers . . . He says to the Green Man o Knowledge, 'I'd like that wee dunkey, it's fast enough for Jack.'

'Oh, my goodness, Jack,' he says, 'you wouldn't take *that*?' . . . He says, 'It would disgrace ye goin through the country, Jack.'

'Ach,' Jack says, 'I'm nae good tae disgrace, I'm nae worriet. I'll take that wee mule.'

'No, no, Jack,' he says, 'I wouldn't allow ye to take that, ye'll take one of this mares.'

So Jack's newsin awa, an he straps his gold on tap o the mule's back. An he's newsin awa, an he looks at it, an the wee mule's stan'in wi nae rein or nothing else, so he's ower his leg, an it wis nae bother, 'cause it wis only a wee thingie, just draps ower its back and he's away, an he's aff his mark an this wee mule could rin. 'Is wee donkey or mule or whatever it wis, but it's rinnin, an Jack says, 'My God, take it easy, lassie, nothing'll catch ye.'

She says, 'Jack, you don't know my people,' she says, 'they shall catch me if I don't hurry, Jack.'

'Aw, Lord, lassie, they'll never see ye – take your time, deemie, ye'll jist kill yersel hastin.'

She says, 'No, Jack, I must run, and run hard.'

Jack says, 'Take your . . . but, God,' he says, 'hurry up, there he's ahin us.' An here, they're jist at the back o his neck. An he says, 'Run harder.'

So she's rinnin, but she says, 'Jack, I haven't got the speed for him.' She says, 'Jack, look in my left ear,' she says, 'an you shall see a drop of water,' she says. 'Throw it over your shoulder, an ask for rivers, lakes and seas behint you, and a clear road in front o you.'

So he throws it ower his shouther; he says, 'Gie's lakes, seas, and . . . so on, behint me, but,' he says, 'give me a clear road in front o me.' An he looks behind – 'Aw,' he says, 'lassie, take your breath,' he says, 'there's nothing but seas, they'll never get through it,' he says, 'they'll be droon't.'

She says, 'Jack, you don't know my people.' She's rinnin harder, see? And . . . no, I was gone through my story. This meers wis her sisters, changed into meers and if you killed them, it didna mean you wouldna have to kill them necessarily again.

So he says, 'Ah, ye're safe enough, lassie, jist take your time.'

She says, 'No, Jack.' An he looks ahin him, and they're ahin him again, an the Green Man of Knowledge on tap o one o their backs, one o his daughters' backs, and they're rinnin.

So she says, 'Look in my left ear, Jack, an ye'll see a spark . . . a stone.' She says, 'Throw it over your shoulder, Jack, an wish for mountains, hills and dales behind you, and a clear road in front of you.' So he does the same again, and the same happens, so he jist tells her to take her time again, but na, she winnae listen, she jist keeps batterin on. But as sure as truth, they're just ahin him again, within any time.

So she says, 'Jack,' she says, 'I love you, and,' she says, 'I will destroy my people for you. But,' she says, 'Jack, it shall put a spell on me for a year, an you too. An,' she says, . . . 'look in my left ear an ye'll see a spark o fire.' She says, 'Throw it behind you, an ask for fire, hell an pits behind you, an a clear road in front of you.'

So he did this, an he looks roond, and he sees her people witherin in the fire, an dyin, see? Whatever happened aboot it, he seen them jist witherin awa in the fire.

So she turned intil a woman again, and he . . . jist stands on his feet . . . haudin his gold in his hands. And she says, 'Jack,' she says, 'now, because of that,' she says, 'I must leave ye for a year.' She says, 'One year from today I'll come for ye.'

'Ah,' he says, 'lassie, I'll be waiting.'

She says, 'Jack, let nobody kiss you.' She says, 'If your mother kisses you,' she says, 'if anybody kisses you,' she says, 'ye'll forget the whole affair, Jack, forget the whole proceedings. You'll remember nothing aboot where you've been or what you've done.' She says, 'Jack, don't let nobody kiss ye.'

So he says, 'Weel, weel, I'll let naebody kiss me if it's that important, but,' he says, 'I'll see ye fin ye come onywey.' He wisna gaun to worry 'cause he'd plenty o money.

So he hauds awa hame: 'God Almichty,' he says, 'I'm nae far fae hame – that's my mither's place doon there.' So he's ower the palins, an here's his auld wife's place.

'O,' she says, 'Jack, my peer loon,' an she's trying to kiss Jack.

'Na, na, mither, I want nae kissin an slaverin,' he says, 'I want naething to dee wi that. No, no, stop it.' So he would hae nae kissin. But he went intae the hoose, and here's his big collie dog, an his collie dog jumps up on his chest and gies him a big lick. That wis hit, in the instant he forgot aathing.

So Jack's plenty money, an he's . . . nae 'Feel Jack' now. He's 'Sir Jack', an this, an that – money maks aa the difference. It even maks feels gentlemen. But . . .

So Jack's bocht a big place, and he's working awa within twa-three months, an the miller's dochter's a gey wenchy deem, an he throws an eye at the miller's dochter, see, an him an the miller's dochter's engaged to get mairriet. So Jack's a business man, he's aye intae business, an gettin a lot o payin work, an that; he mebbe couldnae write his name, but he jist put his cross, an worked awa wi't like that, ye ken.

But . . . So, he wis jist gettin mairriet, a year tae the day he cam hame. So . . . the nicht o his weddin, Jack's aafae busy, an there aa the guests there, but Jack's, ye ken, aafae busy – wi his papers an things like that, I suppose, an he's in his room. So a poor tattered and torn girl – but a bonnie quyne – comes tae the back door, and asks for a job, see? So they says, 'Whit can ye dee?'

She says, 'I can cook, I can clean.' She says, 'I would like' –

An he says, 'Oh, I'll take you on at the weddin, tonight. Help us to cook an clean an aathing, and for a couple o days efter the weddin, and then ye'll have to go.'

She says, 'Yes, that'll do me fine, thank you.'

So she's washin dishes, an scrubbin awa, ye ken, an they're waitin on the preacher – but the preacher's takin a gey while, 'cause he was comin on horseback at that time, ye see, an it was a gey bit fae the . . . fae a village – an the preacher's takin a good while. An they're gettin aa impatient, the guests, ye ken; they're gettin – did ye ever see . . . gettin uncomfortable sittin – and they're aa walkin aboot newsin.

So she says, 'I believe I could smooth the guests a little, an pass away the time for them, because I can do a trick,' she says. 'I have a wooden hen and a wooden cock, and they can talk, they can pick, and,' she says, 'everything.'

'Oh,' they says, 'that's great, we'll hear it.'

So she goes ben, an ye can imagine her amongst aa this well-dressed folk wi a, mebbe an aul white torn skirt on her, gey ragged lookin an things, amongst aa this well-dressed kin o folk. An she's doon this two birds, a cock an a hen. So she scattered some corn, but Jack jist comes oot to watch yin tee, ye see. But Jack's stan'in watchin and the cock picks an looks at her, an the hen picks an looks at the cock, and the hen says to the cock, 'Do you remember me, Jack?'

An the cock looks an says, 'Remember you? No, I couldn't say I do remember you.' So the cock gaes on pickin.

She says, 'Jack, do you remember the Green Man of Knowledge?'

'The Green Man of Knowledge? Oh no, I don't remember him.' So the cock gaes on pickin.

She says, 'Jack, do you remember me, the woman you love?'

He says, 'Ah . . . no, I'm sorry, I don't know you.'

She says, 'Jack, do you remember when I killed my own people for you, Jack?'

An the cock looked an he says, 'Yes, I do remember you.'

An Jack says, 'It's you, deem! It's you, lassie, is't?' He's aye recollected the deem. So the weddin wis cancelled, and he mairriet her, an they lived happily ever after.

That's the end o my story. But there a gey lot o cuttin done, ye ken, or I'd never managed to tell it aa – in twa nichts!

LASAIR GHEUG, THE KING OF IRELAND'S DAUGHTER

THERE WAS A KING once, and he married a queen, and she had a daughter. The mother died then, and he married another queen. The queen was good to her stepdaughter. But one day the *eachrais ùrlair* came in, and she said to the queen that she was a fool to be so good to her stepdaughter 'when you know that the day the king dies, your share of his inheritance will be a small one to your stepdaughter's share'.

'What can be done about it?' said the queen. 'If my stepdaughter does well, I will get a share.'

'If you give me what I ask,' said the *eachrais ùrlair*, 'I will do something about it.'

'What would you want, old woman?' said the queen.

'I have a little saucepan, I only put it on occasionally: I want meal enough to thicken it, and butter enough to thin it, and the full of my ear of wool.'

'How much meal will thicken it?'

'The increase of seven granaries of oats in seven years.'

'How much butter will thin it?' said the queen.

'The increase of seven byres of cattle in seven years.'

'And how much wool will your ear hold?'

'The increase of seven folds of sheep in seven years.'

'You have asked much, old woman,' said the queen, 'but though it is much, you shall have it.'

'We will kill the king's greyhound bitch and leave it on the landing of the stairs, so that the king thinks that it is Lasair Gheug who has done it. We will make Lasair Gheug swear three baptismal oaths, that she will not be on foot, she will not be on horseback, and that she will not be on the green earth the day she tells of it.'

The king came home, and saw the greyhound bitch on the landing. Roared, roared, roared the king: 'Who did the deed?'

'Who do you think, but your own eldest daughter?' said the queen.

'That cannot be,' said the king, and he went to bed, and he ate not a bite, and he drank not a drop: and if day came early, the king rose earlier than that, and went to the hill to hunt.

In came the *eachrais ùrlair*. 'What did the king do to his daughter last night?' she asked.

'He did nothing at all, old woman,' said the queen. 'Go home, and never let me see you again after the rage you put the king in last night.'

'I will be bound that he will kill his daughter tonight,' said the *eachrais ùrlair*. 'We will kill the king's graceful black palfrey, and leave it on the landing of the stairs. We will make Lasair Gheug swear three baptismal oaths, that she will not be on foot, she will not be on horseback, and she will not be on the green earth the day she tells of it.'

The king came home, and saw the graceful black palfrey on the landing. Roared, roared, roared the king: 'Who did the deed?'

'Who do you think, but your own eldest daughter?' said the queen.

'That cannot be,' said the king. He went to bed, and he ate not a bite, and he drank not a drop: and if day came early, the king rose earlier than that, and went to the hill to hunt.

In came the *eachrais ùrlair*. 'What did the king do to his daughter last night?' she asked.

'He did nothing at all, old woman,' said the queen. 'Go home, and don't come here again, after the rage you put the king in last night.'

'I will be bound,' said the *eachrais ùrlair*, 'that he will kill his daughter tonight. We will kill your own son and heir,' said she, 'and leave him on the landing of the stairs. We will make Lasair Gheug swear three baptismal oaths, that she will not be on foot, she will not be on horseback, and she will not be on the green earth the day she tells of it.'

The king came home, then, and saw his son and heir on the landing. Roared, roared, roared the king: 'Who did the deed?'

'Who do you think, but your own eldest daughter?' said the queen.

'That cannot be,' said the king. He went to bed, and he ate not a bite, and he drank not a drop: and if day came early, the king rose earlier than that, and went to the hill to hunt.

In came the *eachrais ùrlair*. 'What did the king do to his daughter last night?' she asked.

'He did nothing at all, old woman,' said the queen. 'Go home, and don't come here again, after the rage you put the king in last night.'

'I will be bound,' said the *eachrais ùrlair*, 'that he will kill his daughter tonight. You must pretend that you are oppressed with ills and agues.'

Men leapt on horses and horses on men to look for the king. The king came. He asked the queen what in the seven continents of the world he could get to help her, that he would not get.

'There is something to help me,' said she, 'but what will help me you will not give me.'

'If there is something to help you,' said he, 'you shall have it.'

'Give me the heart and liver of Lasair Gheug, the king of Ireland's daughter,' said the queen.

'Well,' said the king, 'it hurts me to give you that, but you shall have that,' said the king. He went to the squinting sandy cook and asked him if he would hide his child for one night.

'I will,' said the cook. They killed a sucking pig, and they took out the heart and liver. They put its blood on Lasair Gheug's clothes. The king went home with the heart and the liver, and gave it to the queen. Then the queen was as well as she had ever been.

The king went again to the squinting sandy cook, and he asked him if he would hide his child for one night again. The cook said he would. Next day the king took with him the best horse in the stable, a peck of gold, a peck of silver, and Lasair Gheug. He came to a great forest, unbounded and unending and he was going to leave Lasair Gheug there. He cut off the end of one of her fingers.

'Does that hurt you, daughter?' he said.

'It doesn't hurt me, father,' she said, 'because it is you who did it.'

'It hurts me more,' said the king, 'to have lost the greyhound bitch.' With that he cut off another of her fingers.

'Does that hurt you, daughter?'

'It doesn't hurt me, father, because it is you who did it.'

'It hurts me more than that to have lost the graceful black palfrey.' With that he cut off another of her fingers.

'Does that hurt you, daughter?' said the king.

'It doesn't hurt me, father,' said she, 'because it is you who did it.'

'It hurts me more,' said he, 'to have lost my son and heir.' He gave her the peck of gold and the peck of silver, and he left her there. He went home, and he lay down on his bed, blind and deaf [to the world].

Lasair Gheug was frightened in the forest that wild beasts would come and eat her. The highest tree she could see in the forest, she climbed that tree. She was not there long when she saw twelve cats coming, and a one-eyed grey cat along with them. They had a cow and a cauldron, and they lit a fire at the foot of the tree she was in. They killed the cow and put it in the cauldron to cook. The steam was rising and her fingers were getting warm. They began to bleed, and drop after drop fell into the cauldron. The one-eyed grey cat told one of the other cats to go up the tree and see what was there: for king's blood or knight's blood was falling into the cauldron. The cat went up. She gave it a handful of gold and a handful of silver not to tell that she was there. But the blood would not stop. The one-eyed grey cat sent every one of them up, one after another, until all twelve had been up, and they all got a handful of gold and a handful of silver. The one-eyed grey cat climbed up himself, and he found Lasair Gheug and brought her down.

When the supper was ready, the one-eyed grey cat asked her whether she would rather have her supper with him, or with the others. She said she would rather have her supper with him, he was the one she liked the look of best. They had their supper, and then they were going to bed. The one-eyed grey cat asked her which she would rather, to go to bed with him, or to sleep with the others. She said she would rather go with him, he was the one she liked the look of best. They went to bed, and when they got up in the morning, they were in Lochlann. The one-eyed grey cat was really the king of Lochlann's son, and his twelve squires along with him. They had been bewitched by his stepmother, and now the spell was loosed.

They were married then, and Lasair Gheug had three sons. She asked the king as a favour not to have them christened.

There was a well in the king of Ireland's garden, and there was a trout in the well, and the queen used to go every year to wash in the well. She went there this time, and when she had washed, she said to the trout, 'Little trout, little trout,' said she, 'am not I,' said she, 'the most beautiful woman that ever was in Ireland?'

'Indeed and indeed then, you are not,' said the trout, 'while Lasair Gheug, the king of Ireland's daughter, is alive.'

'Is she alive still?' said the queen.

'She is, and will be in spite of you,' said the trout. 'She is in Lochlann, and has three unchristened children.'

'I will set a snare to catch her,' said the queen, 'and a net to destroy you.'

'You have tried to do that once or twice before,' said the trout, 'but you haven't managed it yet,' said he, 'and though I am here now, many is the mighty water I can be on before night comes.'

The queen went home, and she gave the king a piece of her mind for making her believe that he had given her Lasair Gheug's heart and liver, when she was alive and well in Lochlann still. She wanted the king to go with her to see Lasair Gheug, but the king would not stir, and he would not believe that she was there. She sent her twelve maids-in-waiting to Lochlann, and she gave a box to her own maid to give Lasair Gheug, and she asked her to tell her not to open it until she was with her three unchristened children.

Lasair Gheug was sitting at the window sewing. She saw her father's banner coming. In her delight she did not know whether to run out of the door or fly out of the window. They gave her the box, and she was so delighted with it that she did not wait to be with her three unchristened children. She opened the box when the others had gone home. When she opened the box, there were three grains of corn one poison grain stuck in her forehead and another in each of her palms, and she fell down cold and dead.

The king came home and found her dead. That would have beaten a wiser man than he. He was so fond of her, he would not let her be buried. He put her in a leaden coffin and kept it locked up in a room. He used to visit her early and late. He used to look twice as well when he went in as when he came out. This had been going on for a while when his companions persuaded him to marry again. He gave every key in the house to the queen, except the key of that room. She wondered what was in the room, when he looked so poorly coming out, compared with the way he was when he went in. She told one of the boys one day, if he was playing near the king, to see if he could manage to steal that key out of his pocket. The lad stole the key and gave it to his stepmother. She went in, and what was there but the king's first wife. She looked her over: she saw the poison grain in her forehead and she took a pin and picked it out. The woman in the coffin gave a sigh. She saw another one in one of her palms, and took it out. The woman sat up. She found another one in the other palm, and took it out. Then she was as well as she had ever been. She brought her out with her and put her in another room. She sent the boy with the key to meet his father coming home and put it back in his pocket without his knowledge.

The king came home. The first thing he did was to go into that room as usual. There was nothing there. He came out then to ask what had happened to the thing that had been in the room. The queen said she had never had the key of that room. She asked what had been in the room. He said it was his first wife, and with the love he had for her he would not bury her: he liked to see her, dead though she was.

'What will you give me,' said the queen, 'if I bring her alive to you?'

'I don't expect to see her alive,' said he, 'but I would be glad to see her even dead.'

The queen went then and brought her in on her arm, alive and well. He did not know whether to laugh or cry with his delight. The other

103

queen said then that she might as well go home, there was no more need for her there. Lasair Gheug said that she was not to go home: she should stay along with her, and should have food and drink as good as herself, every day as long as she lived.

At the end of this another year had gone by. The queen of Ireland went to the well to wash there again.

'Little trout, little trout,' said she, 'am not I the most beautiful woman that ever was in Ireland?'

'Indeed and indeed you are not,' said the trout, 'while Lasair Gheug, the king of Ireland's daughter, is alive.'

'Is she alive still?' said she.

'Oh yes, and she will be in spite of you,' said the trout.

'I will set a snare to catch her,' said the queen, 'and a net to destroy you.'

'You have tried to do that once or twice before,' said the trout, 'but you haven't managed it yet,' said he. 'Though I am here now, many is the mighty water I can be on before night comes.'

The queen went home then, and she got the king up and they went to visit Lasair Gheug. Lasair Gheug was sitting at the window this time, but she showed no pleasure at all at the sight of her father's banner.

When Sunday came, they went to church. She had sent people to catch a wild boar that was in the wood, and others to get faggots and sticks and stuff to make a big fire. She got the wild boar: she got on to the boar's back, went in at one door of the church and out at the other door. She called her three unchristened children to her side.

'I am not going to tell my story to anyone at all,' said she, 'but to you three unchristened children.

'When I was in my own father's kingdom in Ireland, my stepmother and the *eachrais ùrlair* killed my father's greyhound bitch and left it on the landing. They made me swear three baptismal oaths, that I would not be on foot, I would not be on horseback, and I would not be on the green earth the day I told of it. But I am on the wild boar's back. They expected that my father would kill me, but my father has not killed me yet.'

She went in at one door, and she went out at the other door, and she called her three unchristened children to her side.

'I am not going to tell my story to anyone at all,' said she, 'but to you three unchristened children.'

'When I was in my own father's kingdom in Ireland, my stepmother and the *eachrais ùrlair* killed my father's graceful black palfrey and left it on the landing. They made me swear three baptismal oaths, that I would not be on foot, I would not be on horseback, and I would not be on the green earth the day I told of it. But I am on the wild boar's back. They expected that my father would kill me, but my father has not killed me yet.'

She went in at one door, and she went out at the other door, and she called her three unchristened children to her side.

'I am not going to tell my story to anyone at all,' said she, 'but to you three unchristened children.'

'When I was in my own father's kingdom in Ireland, my stepmother and the *eachrais ùrlair* killed my eldest brother and left him on the landing. They made me swear three baptismal oaths, that I would not be on foot, I would not be on horseback, and I would not be on the green earth the day I told of it. But I am on the wild boar's back. They expected that my father would kill me, but my father has not killed me yet. Now,' said she, 'I have nothing more to tell you.'

The wild boar was set free. When they came out of the church, the queen of Ireland was seized and burned in the fire.

When the king was going home, he said to his daughter, Lasair Gheug, that she had done ill by him: he had come from home with a wife, and he was going home now without one. And Lasair Gheug said: 'It wasn't that way: you came here with a monster, but I have a woman friend, and you shall have her, and you will go home with a wife.' And they made a great, merry, mirthful, happy, hospitable, wonderful wedding: it was kept up for a year and a day. I got shoes of paper there on a glass pavement, a bit of butter on an ember, porridge in a creel, a greatcoat of chaff and a short coat of buttermilk. I hadn't gone far when I fell, and the glass pavement broke, the short coat of buttermilk spilt, the butter melted on the ember, a gust of wind came and blew away the greatcoat of chaff. All I had had was gone, and I was as poor as I was to start with. And I left them there.

12   *Donald Alasdair Johnson*

SÙIL-A-DIA AND SÙIL-A-SPORAIN

I ONCE HEARD of two men there, and they were living together in the same house, and one of them was called Sùil-a-Dia and the other Sùil-a-Sporain. And this Sùil-a-Dia, it was in God he believed, and Sùil-a-Sporain believed in nothing at all but the purse. They always went about together however, and this time a bit of an argument started between them and Sùil-a-Sporain said to Sùil-a-Dia:

'Ah, well,' said he, 'for me the purse will . . . The purse will get anything for me.'

'Oh, I don't know,' said Sùil-a-Dia. 'It will get you anything money can buy for you,' said he, 'but God will give me something more than that.'

'Oh, no He won't,' said Sùil-a-Sporain.

'Oh, yes He will,' said Sùil-a-Dia. 'Even if you put . . . Even if you were to put both my eyes out God will give me other eyes in their place.'

Well, this is what they did. They sort of fell out so badly that Sùil-a-Sporain put Sùil-a-Dia's eyes out, and he left him there. Well, anyway, here he was now, left there, and there was a house there – it was a deserted little house – and when the cats in the town were put out at night they gathered in this house, all of the cats, and there they'd be.

And, now, anyway, they were gathered in the house this night – the night that Sùil-a-Dia's eyes were put out. And the king of the cats, their commander, it was Gugtrabhad they called him and he told them, this Gugtrabhad, he told one of the other cats to take a look outside to see if the Piseag Shalach Odhar [Scruffy Dun-coloured Kitten] was coming. And it was the Piseag Shalach Odhar, it seems, who brought them news of everything that was happening in the place, anyway. And she wasn't coming, but then she arrived.

'Well,' said Gugtrabhad, 'you've got here, then.'

'Yes,' said she.

'Well, then, what did you hear today?'

O, she started telling the news, and she started telling about a well that had been discovered and that there wasn't an affliction . . . not an affliction that anyone in the world could have that it would not heal if he got a rub of that water or a drink of that water, and that even if you were to lose your sight that you would get it back if you got a rub of that water.

Well, now, what place did Sùil-a-Dia happen to come on when he set off . . . Oh, he went . . . He was just going on his hands and knees anyway – he couldn't see where he was going – but he came up against a wall and he followed the wall round till he found an opening in it, and he went in through it. And he followed the wall back round again and he came to what seemed to be a large wooden vessel like a tub, and he went and hid under the tub.

And what should this be but the very house the cats used as a meeting-place, and he was down here under the tub and he could hear the cats muttering off and on up there, and then he heard about this well that had been discovered. And she [the Piseag Shalach Odhar] told where the well was – how far it was from the house, and everything, and the road one should take to get to it. Gugtrabhad was questioning her and she was telling all about it.

But anyway, when they left off and settled down for the night he [Sùil-a-Dia] lay there dead quiet . . . till they had settled down and he was sure they were all asleep, and, when he was quite sure, he went and crawled out from under the tub and followed the wall round the way he had come till he found the door, and he went out of the house.

And he now began to work out which way he should go – at least according to the directions she had given – and he kept going, anyway, on his hands and knees like that, and every time he happened to come to a pool on the way, and got his hand in it, he would rub his eyes with the water. And, here, at last, he happened to come to the well and he dipped his hand in this water, anyway, and wiped his eyes with his hand, and no sooner had he touched them than he had his sight back again.

And he stood up then and he spent some time cleaning himself and . . . Anyway, he set off and headed for home, and it was daylight before he got there. He went in and Sùil-a-Sporain was in bed.

'You're here!' said Sùil-a-Sporain.

'O, yes,' said he, 'I'm here all right, and didn't I tell you that God would give . . . even if I lost my eyesight that I'd get it back again.'

And, 'Well, very well then,' said Sùil-a-Sporain, 'you'll go with me today and you'll put my eyes out . . . in the very same place as I put yours out.'

Anyway, this is what they did. He went next day . . . When they were ready they set off and Sùil-a-Dia put Sùil-a-Sporain's eyes out. And there he was now, left there not knowing where to go, but, here, anyway, as happened to Sùil-a-Dia, he started on his way and he came to this house, the cats' house, and they hadn't gathered there yet. And in he came . . . He managed to get in and he got under the very same tub that Sùil-a-Dia had been under – he stumbled on it, and he went and hid under it, and there he stayed.

Next, he heard a cat's mew approaching, and he heard a lot of them coming, and he heard them muttering up there at the other end of the house and . . . Then he heard Gugtrabhad telling them to take a look outside to see if the Piseag Shalach Odhar was coming – that it seemed as if she wasn't going to come at all tonight. And they were taking a look outside now and again and there was no sign of her coming, and it was some time before she came, but then she came at last.

'Well,' said Gugtrabhad, 'what kept you so long?'

'My master,' said she, 'he went off today and he hasn't got back yet, and I was waiting to see if he'd come.'

'O, I see,' said Gugtrabhad. 'Well, then, what did you hear today?'

'Whatever I heard today,' said she '. . . You're not going to hear a syllable of what I heard today till you search the house. And the news I told you here last night,' said she, '. . . There was a fellow down there listening to us, and he's healed today because of it.'

Off went a gang of the cats right through the house and they started searching here and . . . in the corners, and in every corner of the house. And back they came:

'There was nothing down there.'

'Did you try that big tub down there?' said she.

Down they went again and they started to claw away at the tub and in spite of . . . Anyway, one way or another, they managed to overturn the tub and there was Sùil-a-Sporain. The cats got to grips with him and they dragged him up to the fire.

'Right,' said Gugtrabhad, 'stroke Mac Mharais,* and take the back of the paw to him.'

They started to stroke Mac Mharais by the fire – Sùil-a-Sporain – and they began with the back of the paw and they went on like that for a while.

'Right, now,' said Gugtrabhad, 'try both back and front.'

The lads started with 'back and front' and, at last, before they stopped, there wasn't a bit of Sùil-a-Sporain left that hadn't been torn to pieces, and that was the end of poor Sùil-a-Sporain.

Well, when he got up next morning Sùil-a-Dia knew quite well that there was something wrong when he hadn't come back, and he went and found him lying dead there and torn to pieces by the cats.

---

* The storyteller does not explain why the cats called Sùil-a-Sporain by this name.

Well, he took care of him, anyway, and he carried him away from there. And then he made up his mind to set fire to this house, and one night when he thought every one of these cats had gathered in the house . . . He had got the place ready – he had put bits and pieces of things inside. The door was shut, and every hole was closed up, and he set fire to the place and the cats were burnt to death.

And that's how I left them, and poor Sùil-a-Sporain was dead.

13   *Christine Fleming*

CEANN SUIC

HERE NOW IS A STORY which I heard from Ceit Tharmoid a long time ago, regarding a certain woman and the landlord was pressing her for the rent and the poor woman hadn't money until she would finish a web that she was weaving. And everything had to be – in connection with the tweed, as you know – had to be done by hand, and he was only giving her one month to make it, and if the tweed was not ready in a month's time she would have to give him the only child that she had so that he would rear him and have him as a farm worker, and the poor woman didn't want to do this.

On her way home she sat down by a knoll and cried, and this little man came to her, and what was it but a fairy. And he said . . . he asked what was wrong. She told him, and he said to her:

'Well,' says he, 'I will make the tweed for you, but if you don't know my name in a month's time, when the tweed is ready, you must give the child to me.'

And the woman did not know what to do, but in any case she was going to lose the child if she did not do that, and she said to him that she would have the tweed made on these conditions.

The little man came and took away the wool and everything and he was making the tweed. The woman was searching everywhere to discover what his name was, or who he was, but no one knew anything about him.

However, one day . . . Now there were, apparently, two groups of fairies. One group of them were good fairies and the other evil and seemingly he was of the evil group, the one who was making the tweed. But one of the group of good fairies, he was passing . . . the place where they were – those fairies – staying, one day, and he heard them singing and singing a song and working, and this one dancing around reciting:

'Tease, card and spin.
Little does the black tweed wife know
That Ceann Suic is my name.'

This was the mouth-music he had for them, and the others dancing as they worked. And this one came. I do not remember his name, if he had a name I do not remember it, or if I heard it. But the good fairy, anyway, he came . . . he went to where the woman was and told her the situation, and when the other one came with the tweed in a month's time, the woman had the name.

Ceann Suic said to her then, 'It was not any natural man that told you that, but when I find out, and I have a good suspicion who it was, it will not remain at that, there will be a battle.'

And the poor woman heard no more about it, but the child was not taken from her, for the two groups of fairies – the good and the evil – had a battle and the good ones defeated the evil ones. They caught Ceann

Suic and killed him and ate him, and as poor Ceit Tharmoid herself said, 'They nibbled him and they nibbled him and they picked him,' and they destroyed the whole lot of them.

---

14   *Angus John MacPhail*

THE CAPTAIN OF THE BLACK SHIP

WELL, THIS BLACK SHIP, you know, it was out at the herring fishing, and they were fishing far out at sea, anyway, for herring and they got a good catch. But a dense mist fell around them and they lost their course. But, anyway, they kept on till they came in sight of land – and what land should they come in sight of but the land of the Turks – Turkey.

Well, anyway, they headed in for this land and they found a place where ships came to land and they came alongside there and got the ship safely moored. And the first thing they came across after they had landed, on the shore, was the body of a white man lying drowned on the shore. And the captain told one of the crew to go back on board, get one of the herring boxes and bring it ashore, and a shirt he would find in his cabin. And he did – and he was to bring one of the herring shovels too – and they laid this body in the herring box, wrapped in the shirt, and they buried it with . . . They dug a hole with the herring shovel and buried the man.

Then they went on up through the town to see what sort of place it was, and they came to a big hotel there – himself and the crew. I can't remember how many of a crew there were, but there was a good squad of them anyway, and the skipper asked for food for them . . . They were put into a room where this meal was to be served, and one single herring was set down on a plate in front of them and they were amazed that one herring should be set before all those people, and what they said to themselves was that they would taste the herring to see if it was any better than the herring they had themselves.

And they started to eat their meal, and when they had finished, in came the girl who was serving them, and she began to scream that the herring had been eaten. And what then but the innkeeper himself came – the hotel proprietor – and the upshot was that every man of them was to be hanged for eating the herring – the only herring they had ever seen in Turkey, and it was preserved, you know, and just set on the table. There was a notice on the table with it too, but they hadn't read it – they couldn't: it wasn't in their language – that no-one was to eat it.

Well, since he was so angry, this man, anyway, the captain began to talk to him and reason with him, and he asked him to let one member of the crew out and that they would bring him plenty of herring – that they had plenty of it on board. He kept on at him . . . He didn't want to let any of them go, but to keep them there till they were hanged or something done to them. Anyway he kept on at him and said he thought he could let at least one man go and that the others . . . all who were left, that they were good value for one herring. Anyway, he kept on at him, and at last he let one man go and this man came back as fast as he could with the herring in case the crew should be put to death. He brought a basketful of herring. Oh, then they were the finest gentlemen this man had ever seen, and they would make their fortune there with the herring. And they did.

He and the innkeeper – the hotel proprietor – were going around the town every day, while he was getting ready to sail again. But this day they were out walking and every man they met around the town had a bundle of wood on his back – a load of sticks or a load of some kind of stuff anyway. He turned to the man and asked him what was the meaning of this, people going about carrying these bundles, every single one of them.

'Oh, you see,' said he, 'a girl came ashore here, herself and her brother,' said he, 'in a boat; they had been blown off course when they were out in a small boat . . . and her brother was drowned getting ashore here,' said he, 'but the girl, she's so beautiful,' said he, 'that our king wants to marry her, but she won't marry him. And they're going to burn her. That's why everyone around here is going about with sticks – to build the fire.'

'Well,' said he, 'that's terrible. I wonder,' said he – the captain of the Black Ship, 'if there's any way of getting the girl out of the place where they're holding her?'

They had her in prison. 'Well, I don't know,' said he, 'that I might not be able to make some sort of shift at getting that for you too.'

Anyway, he told him how he could get round the man who was in charge of the prison, and how he might be able to give him the key of the room where that girl was kept . . . that he might be able to get her out. 'And,' said he, 'they're going to burn her tomorrow, or the day after . . . tomorrow,' said he.

And, anyway, he got hold of this man who had the key of the castle where she was imprisoned: he got hold of him and managed to get it out of him that he could get the girl out at such and such a time that night. And he went and got the crew and told them to get the ship ready to sail as soon as possible and to have everything in as good order as they could – they were to have her ready and he was going to come aboard with this woman and they would put to sea immediately. The crew did this: they had the ship perfectly ready.

He came. He got the girl out and got away with her and went on board and it was just a case of casting off and away out to sea. Anyway, what girl should this be but the king of Norway's daughter. She and her brother had been out in a boat and they had been blown off course and it was in Turkey they had come ashore, and that was what had happened to them.

Anyway, in the morning . . . He held out to sea and they drove the ship on as hard as she could go all night, but in the morning they had not gone far when all the ships appeared in pursuit . . . The sea was black with ships coming after them to try and catch them, but they kept driving the ship on as hard as she could go and by nightfall they were drawing away from them, try as they might, and by next morning there were very few of the ships in sight. She had left them all behind – the Black Ship. By nightfall that evening there was not a single one of them in sight: they had lost them.

They kept on and they got home with the ship, anyway, to their own place where they had been heading. And she told the skipper – the captain of the Black Ship – she told him who she was and where she had come from, the whole story, and if he would be so good – when they had been a little while at home, if he would be so good as to go with his ship to her home so that she would see her mother and father.

This was fine. He set sail . . . She didn't go with him, but she sent him with his ship, and they got to the place and told her mother and father – she was the king of Norway's daughter – that she was alive and well in that place and the whole story.

And, oh, when the news spread around the city, the best ship in the place, the best one belonging to their country, would have to go with them to fetch the girl and her father was to go with them. There was such a stir throughout the country as there had never been before; the girl was alive. They had given them up for dead, herself and her brother.

It was on a Sunday that he arrived there and he stayed there till Monday. But the ship that was to fetch the girl, the best they had, it set sail on the morning of the very day [he came]. He stayed on till Monday morning and then he set sail and made for home with the Black Ship. And the Black Ship wasn't long at sea on her way home when she passed their ship and he was home before the ship that was sent for the girl arrived, and he went home and told her that she had not done too well by him: that there was a ship, the best they had, coming to fetch her and she would have to go with them.

'It doesn't matter,' said she, 'who comes or what ship comes,' said she. 'I'm not moving from here.'

Well, the ship arrived and they came up. Her father tried to persuade her to come with them. No, she wouldn't budge from there! And, anyway, she wouldn't move unless the captain of the Black Ship came with her, wherever she might go from now on. Well, they went on at the captain of the Black Ship then to get him to come with her. They persuaded him to come along with her and they both went on board this other man's ship.

They hadn't been terribly long out at sea when they got caught in a storm. It was all sailing ships in those days and they were toiling away with this ship in the storm and at last the captain of the Black Ship had to go aloft to reef the sails or something. And when they got him aloft they hove the ship to, you know, and the sails began to lash back and forth and at last the captain of the Black Ship was hurled overboard by the lashing of the sails and then it was just a case of making off. Away they went without a look in his direction – he would be drowned, anyway.

However, they were not too far from land and he got . . . He was swimming there as strongly as he could, and he found that there was an island fairly near him, and he made for this island. And he managed to get ashore on the island, to get to land, but he was almost finished. And he dragged himself up as best he could, he dragged himself up till he got up beyond high water mark and he managed to roll some sort of stone and lay it at his head and another at his feet, and he was exhausted. He fell asleep there and he was never going to wake up again.

Well, when daylight came, you know, the sun got so hot, it was beginning to dry him – the side of him facing the sun, and he was . . . just lying there half-dead. Some time later he felt someone shaking him and telling him to get up.

'Oh, I'm not going to move from here,' said he, 'ever. I'm not going to live anyway,' said he, 'and I'm never going to move from here.'

'Oh yes you are,' said he. 'Get up. You must get up and you're coming with me.'

And he managed to get him on his feet, anyway, and he had a little boat down there in the shallows, a slim boat, and:

'Come on down with me,' said he, 'to the boat and I'll take you off the island.'

'All right then,' said he.

He brought him down and put him sitting in the stern of this little boat he had there. He turned . . . He got in himself and turned her round and put her out to sea. And the man was rowing her and he [the captain] had never seen a boat on the surface of the sea as fast as her, though he was just rowing, and where should he bring her to land but in Norway, where the ship had been going that had taken the girl away, and where they had landed.

Well, he was pretty . . . When he set him ashore there, he asked the man what he owed him.

'You don't owe me anything,' said he, 'but you'll let me have . . . The only thing I'm asking of you,' said he, 'is that you give me the first son who is born to you. Will you give him to me?'

'Oh, I will indeed,' said he, 'but I'll never have a son – ever. But if I do, you can have him. You'll get him.'

'All right, then.' And he said goodbye to him and went away.

And he [the captain] went and kept on up the road, and there was a little house beside the road there, and he went into this house beside the road and he found a little old woman inside there, and she gave the man quite a welcome since he was a shipwrecked sailor and she said . . . A son of her own had been a sailor and he had been drowned not very long before and she was very sorry for him [the captain] and what had happened to him. And he had not been very long in the house – she gave him food and dry clothes to put on – when he asked what was happening in the city there and she told him.

'Why,' said she, 'we've got tremendous news,' said she. 'Who came here last night,' said she, 'but the king's daughter who everyone thought was dead long ago. She came home alive, hale and hearty and she's to be married,' said she, 'to a great general who belongs to the place. She's to be married to this general,' said she, 'and . . .'

'I wonder,' said he, 'if we can see them?'

'Yes,' said the old woman. 'They'll be passing here in the carriage on the way to the wedding. They'll be passing by on the high road beside us here and we can see them going past.'

And he was looking round the house and what should he see on top of a dresser over there but a musical instrument that he and the princess had had on board the ship and he got up and went over and picked it up.

'Oh!' said she . . . She was over to him right away: 'Oh, leave that where it is,' said she. 'That,' said she, 'is the only thing the princess has said since she came ashore: she gave me that and told me to keep it till she came back for it, and no-one has got another word out of her but that since she came home.'

This was fine:

'Oh,' said he, 'I'm quite used to these instruments,' said he, 'and I won't do it any harm. I'm just going to have a look at it.'

Anyway, she was keeping a look-out to see if she could see the wedding carriage coming and at last it came in sight. Well, just as it was coming up to the house, he started to play this instrument and he was playing it pretty well too – as well as ever he could, I'm sure. Anyway, they heard it in the carriage and she called to the driver of the carriage to stop. He reined in the horses – it was horses in those days – he reined in the horses and she jumped down from the carriage and went into the house as fast as she could go and they went after her thinking she had gone out of her mind. But when they got through the door, there she was with her arms round this man's neck, and he was holding the instrument, and when they saw who it was . . . When this great man who was to marry her saw who it was, he went back out and climbed aboard the carriage and dashed on down to the quay in it and out over the quay and drowned himself – and the horses and the carriage.

She told her father then that there wasn't a man in the world she would marry but that man there: it was he who had saved her life. And she told them everything he had done for her. And they got married and they lived happily ever after for the rest of their lives . . .

Anyway they got married and they had not been very long married – as long as they ought to I suppose . . .! – when they had a son, and they were quite happy and getting on fine, but this day they were out for a walk and they had the little boy – in a pram I suppose, or in a barrow or something or other! Anyway they were out walking through the city with the boy when they met this handsome man on the road and he spoke to them. And when he had been talking to them for a little while:

'Well,' said he, 'now are you going to give me what you promised me? Are you going to give me your son?'

Well, he hesitated and he said he didn't know . . . And then the woman asked her husband:

'Why,' said she, 'is he asking for the boy?'

He told her then that this was the man who had taken him off this island in this boat, and that this was the only thing he had asked him for after he had brought him here and rescued him and . . .

'Yes,' said she, 'You'll get the boy then,' said she.

'Yes, you will . . .' said he. 'You can have the boy and take him away with you.'

'Well,' said he, 'since you are so good and reasonable,' said he, 'and willing to give me the boy, I'll not take him away at all,' said he. 'All I did for you,' said he, 'was in return for what you did for me when you took me from the beach and buried me in that place after I had been drowned,' said he, 'and I'm going away now and you'll never see me again.'

I think that was all there was to it.

THE THREE GOOD ADVICES

Oncet upon a time there was a man and a wumman lived in a wee cottage, away up aboot in the north of Scotland somewhere, ye see, and this mannie was a baker to trade, but the place – the village he was stayin in, the old man o the baker's shop died and this man was throwed oot o a job – there were no baker's shop there. But he stuck his place for aboot two year, and things was gettin very hard wi him, ye see. So one day he says to the wife, he says, 'I think,' he says, 'I'll go and look for a job,' he says. 'Things is gettin very tight,' he says – 'nae work comin into the hoose,' he says, 'an the two lassies at school,' he says – 'I've got to get some money.' See?

So his wife says, 'Where are ye goin a go?'

'I don't know,' he says; 'if ye jist make me up a piece,' he says, 'an gie me a blanket wi me,' he says, 'I'll march the road, and I'll try and get a job in some toon,' he says; 'I'll surely get a job somewhere, ye see. Doesnae maitter what it is.'

So anyway, in the mornin she gies him a piece an gies him a blanket – made her man as comfortable as she could for the long journey. And he bid his – waved his kiddies farewell, and kissed his wife, an off he went – sets off, ye see. So anyway, on he goes – oh, he marched on tae he was aboot six weeks on the road, tae he comes marchin intae a village. An the village – there was . . . four cross-roads in this village in the street, a cross-roads. An he comes in, an he looks up the one street and he looks doon the other street, and he's stan'in at the corner – it was kin' o well on in the night. An across the street was a baker's shop; it was shut. In the front of the baker's shop there was a stoot man stan'in, like the man o – the boss o the shop, was stan'in: an this man o the shop was watchin this other man across the street – the baker – stan'in watchin the man that was lookin for the job, ye see.

So, he comes marchin owre to the baker to ax – to ask where there was a lodgin-hoose or anything where he could sleep for the night, and the man directed him where he could get lodgins. He says, 'What are ye doin?' he says – 'ye're a stranger here,' says the man o the shop.

'Yes,' he says, 'I'm a stranger.' He says, 'I'm lookin for a job.'

He says, 'What kin' o job are ye lookin for?'

'Well,' says the man, he says, 'it's a funny thing,' he says, 'you asked me that,' he says – 'jist the same kin' o job . . . you are in . . . ,' he says. 'I'm a baker. I'm a baker to trade.'

'Well,' says the man, 'I could do wi a man for a baker – a man to bake pastries. Well,' says the man – they've come to agreement an asked the wages, and the man tellt him – 'Well,' he says, 'ye'll get your lodgins,' he says. 'And,' he says, 'I'll gie ye a good pey, and everything.'

So he was there for aboot six month, and he could make the loveliest pastries ever the man – he was aboot the best baker this man had – the boss of the baker's shop: he told him he was a good baker. And . . . he got so much wi his keep – got his food an his bed, but at the end o the year he got so much o his wages, a lump sum for goin away.

Now he was wearied for his wife and two wee lassies – see? – so he says to the man, 'I'm goin home,' he says, 'the day after tomorrow,' he says. 'I'm goin back home,' he says – 'I want to see the wife an kiddies. And,' he says, 'I'll be liftin aa my wages,' he says. 'I mightnae be back,' he says, 'I don't know what might happen me, for I've a long road to go home.'

'That's all right,' says the man, he says, 'but,' he says, 'there one thing,' he says, 'I'm goin to ask ye,' he says. 'I jist cam in to see ye, man,' he says, 'before ye were goin away up to your bed.' He says, 'Whether wad ye take your year's wages, or take three good advices?'

So the baker looked at him. He says, 'What d'ye mean, Boss?'

'Well,' he says. 'I'm only askin,' he says, 'whether wad ye take three good advices,' he says, 'or wad ye take your year's pay?'

'Well,' he says, 'ye've got me noo,' he says, 'ye see' he says, 'I cud dae wi my week's [sic] pey. An,' he says, 'wi three good advices,' he says, 'I could walk oot in the road there,' he says, 'an get killed,' he says, 'or something like that.' An he says, 'Wad ye gie me up to the morn's mornin to think it ower?'

So the man says, 'Yes, that'll do,' he says. 'If you wait till the morn's mornin,' he says.'Ye're gaun away tomorrow,' he says. 'I'll – ye can decide then which of the things ye want tae take . . . yer money or yer three advices.'

So away, thinkin in bed . . . he could hardly sleep. An he says . . . whan he cam doon for his breakfast in the mornin, the boss says, 'Well,' he says, 'George,' he says, 'did ye make up your mind what ye're goin to take,' he says, 'your money,' he says, 'there's your wages; there's your packet,' he says, 'there's a fair lump of money in it – I know you could be daein wi the money. An,' he says, 'I've got three good advices to gie ye,' he says. 'Now, have ye made up your mind which o'm ye're gonnae take?'

'Well,' says the man, 'I could dae wi the money,' he says, 'but,' he says, 'I think I've made up my mind,' he says, 'to take the three good advices.'

'Well,' he says, 'you took a wise decision,' the man says.

'Well,' he says, 'the first advice is: Never take a near-cut.' Ye see? So . . . the baker looked at the man . . . He says, 'Never go intae a hoose,' he says, 'where there's a red-heidit man, a red-heidit wumman, an a red-heidit – an auld red-heidit man, an an auld red-heidit wumman, an a red-heidit son.'

'Oh,' says the man, he says, 'I'll mind that.'

'An,' he says, 'your third advice is,' he says, 'there's a half-loaf, an don't break that half-loaf,' he says, 'tae ye break it in your wife's aperon. Get her to haud oot her apron,' he says, 'an break the half-loaf in your wife's aperon.' See?

'Very good,' says the man.

'But,' he says, 'there's your week's pey to ye,' he says, ' 'll cairry ye hame.'

So he bid the baker – bid his boss farewell, and said 'You were very good tae me,' and bid his family farewell, and away he set off for home.

In them days it was mail-coaches – there were nae motor-cars, an buses – horseback an mail-coaches. He's marchin the road back an his feet wis sore, travellin. Well, he come to a near-cut, and across this near-cut, across this fields, if he'd 'a took the near-cut it was cuttin aboot three mile off him, off his journey, see. He forgot aboot the advice, an he says, 'Well,' he says . . . 'I'm goin ower this near-cut,' he says, 'an it'll cut three mile off me.' An he says, 'my feet's sore, I'll have to go across this field.'

So he went ower the stile, and he's marchin through the field – it was a moonlight's night – an the frost was on everything. An when he's comin over the field, he hears a scream o a man, and this was burkers cuttin the packman's throat in the middle o the field, jist as he was comin owre the brae o the hill. The screams o him an the roars o him was something terrible. He backs back, an he backs back, and he run for his life tae he got on to the road, and he run doon to the road, and wi the excitement – he run doon the road– he run to a wee crofter's hoose at the side o the road, and when he ran in oot the road, there was a reid-heidit man, an an auld red-heidit wumman, an a red-heidit son. And he knew he'd done wrong. An the man says, 'What is it?' 'Ah,' . . . he says, 'I'm tired,' he says, 'I got chased there,' he says, 'an I cam in,' he says, 'to see if ye could pit me up for the night.'

'Well,' says the man, he says, 'I'll tell ye,' he says, 'ye can gie him some parritch,' he says, 'an milk there – gie him a feed.'

So he mindit on the three advices noo: he says, 'I'm goin to be murdered here the night,' he says, 'this is a burkers' hoose.' 'Well,' he says, 'listen,' he says, 'before ye gie me a wee bite of meat an that,' he says, 'and before yeze pit me in the byre,' he says, 'will yeze let me oot for a wee minute,' he says. 'I want tae do something.' See?

The man says, 'Aye, aye,' he says, 'jist gang oot there and dinnae be lang.'

And here, when he oot, he got into the reed – that's where they keep the manure – coo's manure and horse manure – he went into the reed, and he sut in the corner of the reed an he never cam back in again. And they're searchin for him up and doon, here an there, an they couldnae fin' him; they jist – they searched byre, stacks, an everything, but they hadnae an idea to ha' gone into the reed where the dung was, where he was sitting an hidin, see? He was hidin in there.

He bud there tae aboot the break o day light, and here was the mail-coach comin, wi the mail an two horses. An the man had a gun on tap o the . . . the thing, an his two dogs, an the horses comin trottin along the road. An he jumps ower an he held his hands up to the man like that an tellt the man to gie him a lift. An he still has his parcel. He got on to the mail-coach, and he tells the man goin along the road what happened.

'Well,' he says, 'if they come eftir ye,' he says, 'I'll gie them an unce o leid,' he says, 'oot o ma gun, oot o this blunderbuss I've got,' he says, 'an I'll put my dogs on them,' he says. 'Ye should watch what ye're daein, man!'

But when he got to the wife's hoose, the wife was gled to see him, and the wee lassie; she throwed her neck aroon her man [sic] and tellt him tae come in.

'God,' she says, 'you look fagged-oot,' she says, an he tellt – She says, 'Have ye got the money?'

'No,' he says, 'I've only got this, what I've got left,' he says, 'aboot three pound,' he says.

'Did ye no get nae mair than that,' she says, 'for your year's workin?'

'Naw,' he says, 'that's aa I've got,' he says, but he startit tellin her aboot the three good advices. He says, 'My first one o the good advices was no to take a near-cut through the field, an whan I went through the field,' he says, 'there was the man gettin murdered, the packman. An,' he says, 'the other yin,' he says, 'was no to gaun intae a hoose where there was a red-heidit folk. But,' he says, 'that's what I done,' he says, 'and I had tae sit in the reed aa night. An,' he says, 'ma third good advice,' he says, 'wife,' he says, 'was this wee half-loaf.' He says, 'The baker told me,' he says, 'the boss at the baker's shop told me for to haud oot your aperon, an noo,' he says, 'haud it oot, yer aperon, tae I break the half-loaf.'

An the wife held oot her apron, like that, an he broke the half-loaf. It was full of gold sovereigns. Jingle, jingle, jingle, jingle, the gold sovereigns fell intae her apron, and they lived happy ever after, an she was gled to see her man – he was near killt. So the three good advices peyed him, didn't it? That's the finish o't an that's the end o my story.

HERO TALES

THE STORY OF THE COOK

W HO WAS THERE, then, but – as the story went – this was a king, too, and this king had two sons, but he had one son by the nurse, and the queen didn't know he was the nurse's . . . she thought he was . . . one he had adopted. And this day – they were celebrating and the hen wife (as we always call her) came along: she said (she was speaking to the queen), 'You think that the inheritance is coming to you,' said she, 'to your son, but it isn't,' said she. 'The nurse's son will have the inheritance.'

'Whose son is that?' said she.

'The nurse's son,' said she.

And they were so much alike that they couldn't be told apart, and, 'Well . . .' said [the queen], 'how will I tell them apart?'

'Well, I'll tell you that,' . . . said she, 'how you can tell them apart. You raise . . .' said she – 'Call them indoors for lunch and raise your dress above your knee. And your own son will come in and bow his head, and the nurse's son will come in and take his lunch out of your hand, and not bow his head.'

Oh, she did that – she called them in for lunch, and when they came in . . . her own son came in and bowed his head, and the nurse's son came in quite forward and took his lunch.

'Oh,' said she, 'I knew well enough that it was you!' She gave him a box on the ear.

'Ah well,' said he, 'if that's the way of it,' said he, 'I won't stay here any longer.' He was going to leave, and, oh, his brother went after him and tried to hold him back. But whatever, one way or another he got him to stay that day.

But one day, this is where they were then – on the king's big green playing shinty. They had a silver ball and a gold caman, playing the ball: and there was an old man going past them there – an old old man.

'Oh, though you're a fine pair of brothers,' said he, 'one of you is going to kill the other yet.'

'Oh, bad luck to you, old man,' said they.

He [the nurse's son] got ready to go this time: 'Well,' said he, 'I won't stay here any longer then,' said he. 'I'm going.' He set off and his brother was holding him back. 'Oh, I won't turn back at all.'

He came to the gate and he gave it a slap. It was an iron gate and he turned it red. 'As long as this gate is red,' said he, 'I'll be alive, and when it turns black I'll be dead.'

He kept going and came down to the shore, and he took a little wand out of his shirt front. He made a great well-trimmed ship, with her bows to the sea and her stern to the land. [?He sailed her by all the signs and landmarks] until he came to land in the kingdom of France.

When he landed in the kingdom of France he . . . came to an old woman . . . a little black house there and an old woman in it, and she said, 'Oh, have you come, my poor lad?' said she. 'Where have you come from?' She said, 'The king . . . the cook,' said she, 'is going to be married. I should be calling him not the cook, but the king,' said she. 'He's going to marry [the king's daughter] and he's going to kill the big giants in the hills.'

'Fine,' said he.

He got up in the morning and got an axe and went up to the wood. When he got up to the wood he saw a great lady sitting beside a tree weeping.

'What's troubling you, my bonnie lass?' said he. 'A great lady like you, why should you be weeping?'

'Ah, there's many a trouble that afflicts one that can't be told,' said she.

130

'What great trouble is afflicting you?'

'There are giants coming to kill me,' said she.

'But isn't there a man who's going to save you?'

'The man who is to save me is up in that tree,' said she, 'he's so frightened.'

'Ah well,' said he, 'I'll take your part today and let who will take it tomorrow.'

'Good enough,' said she. 'If I could even get through today alone I'd be glad. There's a giant coming with two heads – one head in a flame and one head out, and eight and eighteen carlines bound to the latchets of his shoes.'

'Well,' . . . said he, 'you can start grooming my hair, then.'

'Well,' said she, 'if you fall asleep, what will wake you?'

'One clip with the scissors out of my right ear.'

'Fine,' said she.

They weren't long there when he fell asleep. When he had gone to sleep along came the great giant with one head in a flame and one head out, and eight and eighteen carlines bound to the latchets of his shoes. But whatever, she clipped his right ear with the scissors, and he got up and saw the giant and they went for each other wrestling, and here were the hard holds: it came into his mind that this was the first test of valour he had ever entered upon and that it would be a great disgrace to lose: he laid him flat on his back and cut the heads off him, and he took his tongues and eyes out . . .

And the cook came along – he came down out of the tree: 'Here, here!' said he. 'Hoist these heads on my back.' He brought the heads home and when he had brought the heads home he went in to the king with them.

'Oh, she's a hard-won wife for me,' said he.

'Oh indeed,' said the king, 'she's a hard-won wife for you.'

[The nurse's son] came home, and oh, his ear was cut where the scissors had clipped it, and the old woman asked what had done that to him. And, oh, he was putting something on his ear, and she told him: 'The cook – I shouldn't call him the cook – has won . . .'

'Did the cook get . . . ?' said he.

'Shush!' said she, 'You're not allowed to call him the cook, you must call him the king.'

But whatever, anyway or another, this day passed. To make a long story short, he went up the next day, and when he went up she [the king's daughter] was in the same place.

'Are you here before me today?'

'Oh yes,' said she, 'I'm here today too.'

And, 'How are you today?' said he.

'There's a three-headed one coming today,' said she, 'and . . . going to kill me.'

'And where's the cook today?'

He was a bit higher up the tree that day.

'Ah well,' said he, 'I'll take your part today and let who will take it tomorrow.'

'Ah well, if I can get through today I won't have any complaints.'

But whatever, he got . . . he was just lying . . . with his head on her knee, and she asked him what would waken him?

'One clip of the scissors,' said he, 'out of the little finger of my right hand.'

But anyway it wasn't long till this giant came – three heads on him . . . two heads in a flame and one head out, and eight and eighteen carlines bound to the latchets of his shoes. But whatever, they struck . . . They went for each other wrestling, and, my word, they fell upon each other there, and here were the hard holds, but it came into his mind that this was the second test of valour he had ever entered into and it would be a great disgrace to lose, and he gave him a great gay glorious lift and laid him flat on his back and cut the heads and everything off him and the tongues and the eyes out of them. He went home.

Och, the old woman at the house was in her glory, bandaging his hand: 'Ho, did you hear that the cook – the king won?'

'Oh, did the cook win?'

'Shush, you wretch!' said she, or I'll take the tongs to you. You'd better not call him the cook.'

'Oh,' says he, 'I can't help it. I'm going to call him the cook.'

There was no more said about that. Next morning it was – he went up, and when he went up: 'Are you here again today?' said he.

'I'm here,' said she.

'Ah well,' said he, 'I don't know what I can do about you,' said he, 'but I'll try to take your part today,' said he. 'Let who will take it tomorrow.'

'Oh well,' said she, 'if I could get through today there would be no more trouble, but,' said she, 'the one who's coming today,' said she, 'is really ferocious; he has four heads.'

'Ah well, it can't be helped,' said he.

'What will waken you today if you fall asleep?'

'Cutting a piece,' said he, 'the size of a half-crown out of the top of my head with the scissors.'

But anyway, there they were and he stayed until . . . he fell asleep, and along came the great giant with three heads in a flame and one out and eight and eighteen carlines bound to the latchets of his shoes. But whatever, she made a cut with the scissors in the top of his head, and he got up. Well, he was a bit afraid of him, and he said to him: 'I'll make a bargain with you,' said he. 'If I fall first,' said he, 'you let me up, and if you fall, I'll let you up.'

'Right,' said he.

But anyway, they went for each other: oh, they were up and down there – but the young fellow was forced to his knees.

'Remember you're to let me up.'

'Oh, I'll let you up,' he said. He let him up. They went for each other again, and the giant fell.

'Let me up,' said the giant.

'No I won't,' said he. 'You're done for.'

But whatever, he laid him flat then, and took home the tongues and eyes and everything – that was the last night. Oh, that night the cook's marriage was on: he had won his wife, so he said.

But anyway he [the nurse's son] went home, and the next night was the night of the betrothal and there was a great ball at the castle.

'Well,' said he, 'I'm going down to see if I can watch the ball . . .'
He went down. Och, the king . . . the cook . . . he was sitting in the
king's throne, he was in his glory, and there was a great crowd in the
castle, and he was spinning tales and everything.

He came in, the young lad. He stood quite neutral apart from the rest
. . . standing some way away: he was just a stranger. But they had
something to eat and it was a great feast they had there, plenty of drink,
and the young woman said, 'Well,' said she, 'I'm bringing out a little
game here,' said she, and the game she brought out she brought out an
ox's shank bone and laid it on the table. 'Now,' she said, 'who's going
to break that?' said she.

The cook got up and by his way of it he would be the first one to
break it, and the first blow the cook struck it, he was shaking his hand
and putting it in his mouth. 'You, it's a queer sort of a game you've
started,' said he. 'Indeed,' said he, 'so it is!'

But never mind about that. [The game] went round everyone in the
place: there was not one who could break the ox's shank.

'I can see a young lad standing over yonder,' said she. 'Couldn't he
have a try?'

'Ach,' said he, 'what's the use of me trying when everyone has had
a shot at it?' But he came over and tried it, and with the first swipe he
took at it he broke the four legs of the table and he broke the ox's shank,
and a piece of it hit the cook in the eye and he was nearly blinded.

And she looked round then: 'But who would you think, now,' said
she to her father, 'would win . . . would have killed the giants: the man
who could break the ox's shank bone,' said she, 'or the man who
couldn't?'

'Ah well,' said the king, 'I'd say it would be the man who broke the
ox's shank who'd have won . . . who'd have killed the giants.'

'Have you ever seen heads,' said she, 'without eyes or without
tongues?'

'No,' said he.

'Well, look at those heads there,' said she. 'There's not an eye or a
tongue in them.'

He went and brought out – the young lad – he brought out the eyes and the tongues.

The cook was seized and hustled out, and kicked and booted out of the place, and this young lad was married to the lady.

And they went . . . there was a grand wedding apparently, and they went to bed this night, and he – the young lad – heard something coming in by.

'What's that?' said he.

'Ach!' said she, 'pay no heed to it. It's a hunted fox.'

'Well, if he's ever been hunted before he will be tonight,' said he.

He lit out after the fox. Where he was highest the fox would be lowest, up and down until they landed at a long narrow black house and went in.

When he went in there was no sign of the fox. There was a big fire burning there and he warmed himself by this big fire. And it wasn't long after he had gone in before he heard 'knock, knock' at the door.

'Who's there?' said he.

'The speckled hen of the one night,' said she. 'She spends one night on the hills and one night here.'

'Even if you spend every night here, old woman,' said he, 'you won't spend tonight here.'

And, 'Tut!' she said. 'Let me in,' said she, 'and I'll keep you going till day with stories and verses.'

'Well, come in then,' said he.

'I'm afraid to come in, for your animals,' said she.

'Oh, the animals won't touch you.'

'But here,' said she, 'take this hair from my thing [*sic*],' said she; 'it would hold the *River George* under full sail.'

He did that: he tied up the animals, and the old woman came in, and there the hag was. The hag kept saying, 'Huit! Huit! Huit!'

'You are growing bigger, old woman.'

'My feathers and my down are fluffing up with the hot coals,' said she.

'You are growing bigger, old woman.'

'My feathers and my down are fluffing up with the hot coals.'

But in the end he and the hag began to quarrel.

'Oh,' said she, 'you'll never do to me what you've done to my three sons.'

He was quarrelling with the hag and they went for each other and the young lad fell, and evidently she broke his back and he was laid [?behind the hearth stone among the ashes] at the back of the fire.

He had called on his hound and his hawk and his horse that were born in the same night as himself: 'Why should they not be here to give me help?'

'Tighten, hair,' said she, 'don't stretch.' That was the end of that.

His brother came out and looked at the gate; he saw the gate was black.

'Ah well, well,' said he. 'My brother's dead.'

He set off and he went on and he took a wand out of his shirt front: he made a great [?well-trimmed] ship, with her bows to the sea and her stern to the land. [?He sailed her by all the signs and landmarks] until he came in to land in the kingdom of France.

When he arrived there he came to his brother's house . . . his brother's wife's house, and when he got there: 'Oh bless me,' said she – they were so like each other – 'what has kept you away all night?'

'Oh aye,' said he.

'Come to bed.'

He went in to bed, and when he went to bed he drew his sword [and laid it] between them. And, 'What's that [noise]?' said he.

'Oh, don't you know what it is?' said she. 'It's a hunted fox.'

'Well,' said he, 'if he ever got hunted before, tonight he will be.' And off he went after the fox, the same way as his brother had gone . . . until he got to the house, and he saw his brother at the back of the hearthstone with his back broken in two. But anyway, he sat down then. He was looking at his brother and his brother was dead.

'Well,' said he, 'this is terrible.'

But he heard a 'knock, knock' coming at the door.

'Who's there?' said he.

'The speckled hen of the one night,' said she. 'She spends one night on the hills and one night here.'

'If you've ever spent a night here, old woman, you won't spend tonight here.'

'Let me in,' said she, 'and I'll keep you going till day with stories and verses.'

'Come in then,' said he.

'I'm afraid to come in for your animals.'

'Don't be afraid: the animals won't touch you.'

'But here,' said she, 'take this hair from my thing,' said she: 'it would hold the *River George* under full sail.'

He took the hair and put it over the cross-beam, and he tied up his animals with something or other else. She came in then and they sat there. Och, the same thing started: 'You're growing bigger, old woman,' said he.

'My feathers and my down are fluffing up with the hot coals.'

'Is that the story you promised me, old woman?'

'Hah! My feathers and my down are fluffing up with the hot coals.'

In the end he and the hag came to blows. They were up and down there; but however he managed it, he put the hag down.

'My hound and my hawk and my horse,' said he, 'that were born in the same night as myself, to give me help!'

'Oh, let me up,' said she, 'and I'll bring alive . . . I'll give you your brother alive.'

'Where is he, then?' said he.

'You'll find the Magic Wand,' said she, 'and the Sword of All Light and the Upper Vessel and the Lower Vessel,' said she. 'It's all behind such and such a place.'

'Well,' said he, 'I'll have that when you are gone, old woman,' said he, and he killed the hag and brought alive his brother.

And he and his brother were coming home side by side, and he looked at his brother all innocently: 'I was in bed with your wife,' said he, 'last night.'

They came to blows then and in the end one of them killed the other there – the one who had been married killed the one who had just come. Well, that was the end of that: he went home and told . . .

'Oh, bless me!' said his wife. 'Are you going to stay at home at all?' she asked. 'You came in last night,' said she, 'and laid a naked sword between us.'

'Oh well,' said he, 'if I'm away every night I will be away tonight.' He went back then and . . . found the Sword of All Light and the Magic Wand and he brought his own brother alive, and they went home, and when they got back to his wife, his wife couldn't tell them apart.

'Ah well,' said she, 'I have two husbands now in place of one. But put out your hands,' said she.

He put out his hand and [the tip of] his little finger was missing, and, 'Oh, that's my husband,' said she.

Well, [his brother] married her other sister and they lived as happy as the day is long. And I don't know what has happened to them since.

CONALL GULBANN

It was a king of Ireland and he and the nobles of the kingdom went to the hill to hunt this day and what should come on but a mist and they lost their way. One would say that this was the way and another would say, 'No, this is the way.' At last every one of them was going his own way and the king was left all alone.

Then the king saw a light and, God, he made straight for the light and when he got there, there was a *brugh* of a house there and he went in. When he went inside there was no-one there but an old man and an old woman and a big red-haired girl. And the old man said: 'Oh, come on in, come on in, King of Ireland,' said he. 'A long time have I had a year and a day's provisions waiting for you,' said he. 'Sit in.'

The king sat in and indeed he was well entertained by the old man. And then came bed-time.

'Indeed,' said the old man, 'there are only two beds here,' said he. 'Would you prefer to sleep with my wife, or to sleep with the red-haired lass?'

'Oh well,' said the king, 'it is more fitting for you to sleep with your wife yourself than for me. And if there is no other place,' said he, 'I dare say I can sleep with the girl.'

God, next morning the king got up and went out of the brugh and when he turned to go back in, he found nothing there but a bare hillock. The king set off only partly dressed and when he had gone some distance he heard a shout behind him and he looked back, and who should be following him but the old man with his cap in his hand.

'Oh come back, come back, King of Ireland,' said he. 'You mustn't go away like that when the red-haired lass has borne you a son,' said he.

'What do you say?' said the king.

'The red-haired lass has borne you a son,' said he.

'That cannot be,' said the king, 'since I only came to your house last night,' said he.

'Ho ho! You think you only came there last night,' said he, 'but it is nine months since you came to my house,' said he. 'That's just the magic of the brugh,' said he.

The king went back with him and there was the red-haired lass with a baby boy.

'Well,' said the old man, 'the baby must be christened,' said he, 'and there is no priest here,' said he. 'But there was once a time when I could manage a christening myself,' said he.

The old man went and got water and he asked the king what name the child was to be called.

'Oh, call him what you like,' said the king.

'Well,' said the old man, 'the name of this place is Brugh Beinn Gulbann,' said he. 'And can we not call the lad Conall Gulbann,' said he, 'Son of the King of Ireland?'

'Well then, let it be just that,' said he . . .

'Now, you think,' said the old man, said he, 'that I'm not telling the truth,' said he, 'but this very day,' said he, 'they're going to put another king in your place,' said he. 'They've given up hope,' said he, 'that they'll ever see you again. And there's a year's walking,' said he, 'before you can get home. But I've got a pair of boots here,' said he, 'and you put them on. And before it's ten o'clock,' said he, 'you'll be back home. And when you arrive,' said he, 'there'll be no need to choose another king. And when you get home,' said he, 'all you have to do is take them off and turn them to face the known and away from the unknown,' said he, 'and I'll have them back by nightfall.'

The king went and put on the old man's boots and he could not tell whether he was travelling on the ground or through the air, so great was his speed. And when he came in sight of his house, goodness knows how many people were gathered round it. And as they met him, every single one of them would greet him and kneel before him: 'Oh, where have you been, King of Ireland, for the past nine months?'

That was when the king realised that the old man had been telling the truth. And then there was no need to choose another king in his place.

The king had three sons.

But what should happen now but that war broke out with the Turk. He was invading Christendom and he had to be stopped and every country was turning out against him. So the king of Ireland was going to go with his army against the Turk. And he sent for his eldest son to stay behind and rule the kingdom till he got back.

'I won't stay behind to rule the kingdom,' said he. 'I'd rather have one hour by the clock of the sport of war than the whole kingdom,' said he.

Then he sent for the next eldest son:

'Indeed, I won't stay,' said the next eldest, said he. 'Suppose you died,' said he, 'I wouldn't be the one to get your kingdom,' said he. 'And the one who would get it,' said he, 'let him stay or let him go. I'm going myself.'

Then he sent for the youngest son. He would not stay either.

'Oh well,' said the king, said he, 'perhaps I still have someone hidden away,' said he, 'who will stay behind to rule my kingdom, even though you won't.'

The king had a man called Sgal Gaoithe and he was as swift as the swift March wind before him and the swift March wind behind him could not catch him. And he asked him to go to Brugh Beinn Gulbann to fetch Conall. Sgal Gaoithe set off and when he got to Brugh Beinn Gulbann he told them that the king had sent him to fetch Conall. And Conall did not want to go and:

'Oh, you must go,' said his grandfather, said he. 'Your father has never asked anything of you before,' said he, 'and you must go. But be sure you don't forget your grandfather,' said he.

Conall set off with Sgal Gaoithe: and a lookout was being kept to see if they could see the lads coming, and Conall was nine rigs ahead of Sgal Gaoithe, driving a ball before him with a caman and Sgal Gaoithe following on behind. And when they arrived the king told him he had sent for him to stay and rule the kingdom till they got back – that they were off to the war.

Conall stayed. And, anyway, God, it occurred to Conall one day that he would have to go and see his grandfather. And Conall went and when he got there, what should his grandfather be doing but making a thorn broom just inside the door. And when Conall came in he swung the broom and hit him on the back of the head and left not an inch of skin on him right down to his heels.

'Oh! oh! oh!,' said Conall.

His mother cried out that the lad was ruined for life.

'Oh, he needn't worry yet,' said the old man, said he.

The old man rose and got a bottle with some stuff in it and he rubbed it on Conall's back and made his skin smooth and white.

'You,' said he, 'to stay behind to rule Ireland!' said he. 'Suppose thé king died,' said he, 'you would not be the one to get it. But,' said he, 'it wasn't ruling Ireland you should have been but at the war,' said he . . .

'I mustn't go,' said Conall, 'till the king comes back,' said he.

'What are you saying?' said his grandfather.

His grandfather went and let a snake out of a box and the snake attacked Conall and Conall was being wounded by it.

'God help us!' said he, 'Spare my life at least,' said he.

'Will you go now?' said his grandfather.

'Oh yes, if you spare my life,' said he, 'but what's the use of me going, without weapons or anything?' said he.

'Oh, I'll give you a weapon myself,' said the old man. He went through to the other room and came back with a sword, and Conall took the sword and the first time he brandished it it broke in half.

'What good is a weapon like that?' said he, said Conall.

His grandfather went through and came back with another one. Conall did the very same thing to it.

'Oh well,' said his grandfather, said he, 'I've got a sword that I had myself when I was a young lad,' said he, 'and unless it's good enough for you,' said he, 'no sword can be got for you till it is made specially for you on the anvil.'

He went through and came back with a sword and handed it to Conall. Conall took it and brandished it and the two ends of it struck together and the sword sprang back as it had been before.

'Well, the sword is fit for Conall,' said he, 'and Conall is fit for it,' said he.

'Away you go then,' said the old man, 'and put on this pair of boots of mine,' said he, 'and this is the very day,' said he, 'that the armies are to meet. And when you get there,' said he, 'you'll know your own folk,' said he, 'and you'll go in on their side,' said he.

Conall went and put on his grandfather's boots and he had been fast enough as he was, but he was much faster now. And when he appeared the two armies were just closing with each other and Conall went in on the side of his own folk.

It was then that the hero put on his battle-hard fighting gear and fit fighting gear for a hard battle it was, when he arrayed himself in silk and satin, with his smooth shirt of saffron silk, with his fringed iron shirt of mail, with his jewelled, gold-crested helmet to guard his neck and his white throat.

It was then that the hero arranged his keen, hard warlike smiter on his left side, on which there was many a blazon of lion and leopard, of griffin and striking serpent, fiery and scaly, drawn from the slender pine-green cover where it had been carefully placed, an object of admiration, and carefully [?], and it was polished and glittering, it was strong and supple, it was elegant, thrusting, fit to strike, with its blade keen, light and marvellous like a weapon of sharpness its [?] and like a weapon of [?] its edge. That was an edge that would cut an apple on water and a single shaggy hair, that would drive water from its [?frontlet] and red fire from its [?hilt]. That was the rising, falling sword that would cut nine nines as it went from him and nine nines as it came back and he would catch it again with the self-same hand. From where he attacked them in front to where he broke through at the rear, where they had been thickest they were thin, where they had been thin they were swiftly scattered and where they had been swiftly scattered they were totally slaughtered, and he left no man alive to tell the tale or spread the news – except he hid in a hole in the ground or the shelf of a crag – but one little, squinting, red-haired man with one eye and one knee and one palm, and though there were thrice ten fluent, fully-wise tongues in his head he would be busy telling of his own trouble and the trouble of the rest, and the valour of the champion. That was all he left alive on the battlefield and no-one drew a sword except himself.

'Oh, Conall, Conall,' said the king. 'Is this ruling my kingdom?'

'There's nothing wrong with your kingdom,' said Conall, 'since I left it yesterday afternoon,' said he.

Conall went and turned his grandfather's boots the other way and before very long he was back home in Brugh Beinn Gulbann.

'Well, Conall,' said his grandfather, 'how did you get on?'

'Oh, very well,' said Conall. 'Nobody there drew a sword except myself,' said he.

'Oh, didn't I know it, Conall,' said he. 'But give the lad food,' said he, turning to his mother.

Then Conall was given a meal.

'Away you go now,' said he, 'and find the most beautiful maiden on the face of the earth,' said he, 'the daughter of the king of the Province of Leinster. And her father has her on a golden throne,' said he, 'at the top of the castle. And bring her here,' said he, 'and marry her. And any time you are in a tight spot,' said he, 'just think of me and I'll be beside you,' said he.

Conall set off and kept on till he reached the king's palace and he started to walk round the king's castle. He saw the maiden through a window going round and round on the golden throne.

'Oh, my dear, how I wish you were mine!' said Conall.

'Ho, coward,' said she, 'why don't you jump up and carry me off?' said she.

Conall backed away and with his first leap he was on the window-sill and he just took her and plucked her from the golden throne and sprang out with her and put her over his shoulder and away with her. But he had not gone far when she gave one great cry.

'What's the matter now?' said he.

'Oh,' said she, 'they're coming after you,' said she, 'five hundred fine champions, five hundred full champions and five hundred mighty champions.'

'You wait there, then,' said Conall, 'till I get back,' said he.

He set her down, and Conall went back and he didn't leave a single head on a neck among them but slew them all. And he went off with her again. They had not gone far when she gave another cry, and:

'What's the matter with you now?' said he.

'Oh,' said she, 'there are as many more coming after you,' said she.

'Oh well, you stay there,' said he.

Conall went back and killed every man of them. And he kept on till he got to Ireland, and when he got to Ireland he was pretty tired and he sat down on the side of Beinn Eudain in Ireland and laid his head on her lap.

'Well,' said he, 'you must let me sleep for a while now.'

'Ah, God,' said she, 'what shall I do if anyone comes?' said she. 'How can you be wakened?'

'Take that big rock over there,' said he, 'and strike me on the chest with it, or,' said he, 'drag me by the hair down the glen and drag me up the glen again by the hair, and that will wake me.'

'Oh, I can't do that,' said she.

'Oh well, then,' said he, 'you'll just have to leave me till I wake up by myself,' said he.

Conall went to sleep — but what should she see coming but a boat with only one man in it, and it came to land and this big man came up and made straight for her.

'Ho!' said he. 'Many's the place I've travelled looking for you,' said he, 'but I've found you at last.'

'Who are you looking for?' said she.

'The daughter of the king of the Province of Leinster,' said he.

'Who's she?' said she.

'Oh, you needn't deny it,' said he. 'You carry your own marks of identity with you,' said he. 'But who is this man with you?'

'He's a brother of mine,' said she. 'I've come to give him his dinner,' said she.

'Well, you come along with me,' said he.

'Oh, I mustn't go,' said she, 'till he wakes up,' said she, 'or he won't know where I've gone.'

'How can he be wakened?' said he.

'By striking him on the chest with that big rock over there,' said she.

'Ho! A fit waking for a mighty champion,' said he.

'Or by dragging him by the hair down the glen,' said she, 'and dragging him up the glen again by the hair, and that will wake him.'

'Well, that's the easier one,' said he.

Conall had long hair and he twisted it round his fist and dragged him down the glen and then he began to drag him up against the slope, and his [Conall's] sword was jolted out of the scabbard and it was by no means free of stains – and he [the big man] looked at the sword: 'Ha! My poor fellow,' said he, 'it's no wonder you're sleepy,' said he. 'You haven't been idle since night fell if your sword is stained like that,' said he. 'And since you haven't troubled me, I shan't trouble you,' said he.

He went off with the king's daughter and left Conall sleeping. And when Conall woke up he was all alone.

He did not know what to do and he went down [to the shore] but then he thought of his grandfather. And who should be behind him but his grandfather.

'Ho, Conall,' said he, 'you may have been strong enough but you weren't clever enough,' said he. 'Why not do what I'd have done?' said he.

He took a little wand from the sleeve of his jacket and he struck a standing stone with it and turned it into a long-ship.

'Away you go now,' said he, 'and find your sweetheart.'

Conall set off with the ship and where should he come to but the kingdom of the Wild Forest. And he went straight up to the castle and demanded that the king's daughter should be sent out to him or strife and slaughter for her.

They directed him down to the House of the Tamhuisg: he would get plenty of strife and slaughter there.

Conall went straight down and there was a big, long house there with eighteen score doors and eighteen, and when Conall went in there were eighteen score and eighteen Tamhuisg there, and every one of them gave a great bellow of laughter. And Conall gave a laugh that drowned all the rest.

'What made you laugh?' said they.

'What made you laugh yourselves?' said Conall.

'The fun we're going to have killing you,' said they.

'Well, what made me laugh,' said Conall, 'was the fun I would have killing you.'

They gathered round Conall and every one of them took out a knife, and one would say: 'Let's give him the cropping of a fool and an idiot.' Another would say. 'I'll pick your eye out.' Another: 'I'll cut your nose off.'

Conall looked them over and the one with the biggest head and the thinnest shanks he could see among them, he seized him by the shanks and laid into the rest with him, till he had killed the whole lot of them.

But then he heard a shout from the rafters over his head.

'Well! Joy and success to you.'

Conall looked up: 'What sort of creature are you,' said Conall, 'up there?'

'Ho,' said he, 'I'm the Tuathanach O Drao, and I was sent down here,' said he, 'for the Tamhuisg to eat. But I was so agile and so quick,' said he, 'that I sprang up here and they couldn't get at me. And there was nothing else for me but to stay here till I fell down among them.'

'Oh, well, you can come down now,' said Conall.

The Tuathanach O Drao came down.

'Well, Conall,' said he, 'the best thing we can do is to stay here tonight,' said he. 'The town carts come here with all the scraps from the town for the Tamhuisg,' said he, 'and we can pick among it,' said he, 'and get enough to keep us going tonight.'

That was what they did. They heard the carts coming now. The drivers just tipped them outside the doors and went away. They saw no sign of the Tamhuisg or anyone else. They went out and picked out all the best bits they could find.

Next morning Conall went straight up to the castle and called for strife and slaughter again.

Conall Ceithir Cheannach, Son of the King of the Wild Forest, was not the man to sit and listen to this. He did not wait to open the door but burst his own breadth out through the wall. Out he rushed and the duel began outside between him and Conall Gulbann, till the dark, dusky clouds of night were closing in and the long languid clouds of day leaving them. And Conall Ceithir Cheannach sprang inside and left Conall Gulbann bleeding from his wounds outside.

And the Tuathanach O Drao gave a cry:

'O, Conall, Conall,' said he, 'you'll be dead. There's that man now, all healed by a fairy woman he has in there,' said he, 'and he'll be as fresh tomorrow as he was today, and you'll be dead.'

'Oh, it can't be helped,' said Conall.

'But hold on a moment,' said he. 'He's got a sister in there and she's very keen on men,' said he, 'and I'll go in,' said he, 'and you never know but I might get shelter for you tonight yet,' said he.

The Tuathanach O Drao went in and:

'Ah, what a shameful disgrace on you,' said the Tuathanach O Drao, 'that the greatest champion sun has ever shone on or wind blown on,' said he, 'who has come for love and longing and choice of you from Ireland,' said he, 'is bleeding from his wounds out there, and your own brother all healed before his feet could touch the floor.'

'Hah, you wretch!' said she. 'If he had come for love of me he would not have come like that.'

'But was it not excess of noble pride,' said the Tuathanach O Drao, 'that made him do that? Well do I know it myself,' said he.

'Go on then,' said she, 'and ask him to come in.'

The Tuathanach O Drao went out:

'Well, in you go now, Conall,' said he, 'and be sure you say something to her,' said he.

Conall went in and there was cold water for his hands and warm water for his feet and he was laid in a bed, and she got in with him herself.

And next morning when Conall rose, he went outside and called again for strife and slaughter. Out rushed Conall Ceithir Cheannach and the fight started again till the dark clouds of night were closing in. And Conall Ceithir Cheannach leapt inside and Conall Gulbann was left outside, bleeding from his wounds.

The Tuathanach O Drao gave a cry: 'Oh, alas, alas, Conall!' said he, 'you'll be dead tonight for sure,' said he. 'You never said a word to that woman last night,' said he, 'and I don't suppose it's any good me going to see her tonight.'

'Oh, it can't be helped,' said Conall.

'But hold on a moment,' said he. 'I'm so fair-spoken and so flattering and so cunning,' said he, 'you never know but I might get shelter for you yet,' said he.

The Tuathanach O Drao went in:

'What a shameful disgrace on you,' said he, 'leaving the greatest champion sun has ever shone on or wind blown on bleeding from his wounds out there and your own brother all healed before his feet could touch the floor – when he has come for love and longing and choice of you from Ireland.'

'Hah! Get out of here you cheat,' said she. 'He went and laid a naked sword between myself and him last night.'

'But was it not excess of noble pride,' said the Tuathanach O Drao, 'that made him do that? Well do I know it myself,' said he.

'Go on then,' said she, 'and tell him to come in.'

The Tuathanach O Drao went out:

'In you go now, Conall,' said he. 'Who knows but you may . . . Be sure you say something to her tonight,' said he, 'but you needn't ever go and ask a favour of her again,' said he.

Conall went in and if he had been tired last night he was really tired tonight.

But next morning when Conall rose he went straight out and called on him for the same again. Out rushed Conall Ceithir Cheannach.

'Well,' said Conall Gulbann, 'we've spent two whole days at sword-play,' said he. 'But today we'll try a grip,' said he, 'wrestling to see which of us is the better.'

'Very well,' said Conall Ceithir Cheannach.

They came to grips with each other and then it was rock, rock, and knock, knock, and when they sank in least they sank in to their knees and when they sank in most they sank in to their eyes, till the dark, dusky clouds of night were closing in and the long, languid clouds of day were leaving them. And Conall decided he was near his foes and far from his friends and he gave him a light, lively lift and threw him to earth on firm, flat flagstones and he broke an arm below and a rib above.

'Oh, let me up, Conall,' said he. 'Well do I know the purpose of your trail and your travel – looking for Ann Uchdan, Daughter of the King of the Province of Leinster, but you won't find her here,' said he. 'Macan Mór na Sorcha has her,' said he, 'and I'll go along with you myself,' said he.

Then he and Conall and the Tuathanach O Drao set out and they kept going and when they came to Macan Mór na Sorcha and he saw them coming, he went and let out a bull. And the bull came on against them and Conall Ceithir Cheannach swung his sword at the bull and cut off its head. Then he went and let out a lion, and he did the very same to it: he killed the lion. And he came out himself then, on his knees begging for mercy.

'Oho!' said he. 'Mercy is not for you, you wretch,' said he, 'but send the Daughter of the King of the Province of Leinster out here,' said he.

'Oh though I let them out . . .' said he, 'these were just beasts I used to let out when my son was coming home,' said he. 'They would give him a game till he got to the door,' said he.

'Oh, it wasn't that that made you do it,' said they, 'but you send out the king's daughter at once,' said he.

And then they took away the Daughter of the King of the Province of Leinster with them in the long-ship.

And that was when they hoisted the billowing, bannered sails to the top of the tough tall masts, so that there was no mast unbent or sail untorn, weathering the weltering, washing waves [? of the green main, the red main of Norway]: the larger sea-creature eating the smaller creature and the smaller creature doing as best she could and the little bent brown buckie that had been seven years on the sea floor, it would crack against her gunwale and squeak against her planking. So well was the hero handling her. The black eels of the boulders were coiling around the tops of her yards.

And Conall said to the Tuathanach O Drao: 'Take a look aloft now,' said he, 'to see how the ship goes.'

'Oh,' said the Tuathanach O Drao, 'she's as fast as the swift March wind before her and the swift March wind behind cannot catch her up.'

'That is no speed for my ship,' said he. 'Give her more canvas.'

They gave the ship more canvas and:

'Take a look now,' said he, 'to see what her speed is like.'

'Indeed she would split a grain of oats end-on,' said the Tuathanach O Drao.

'That is no speed for my ship,' said he. 'Give her more canvas.'

They gave the ship more canvas and:

'Take a look aloft now,' said Conall.

'Oh,' said he, 'she's as fast now as the fancy of flighty women,' said he.

'Oh, well,' said Conall, 'that's fast enough,' said he.

Conall got to Ireland with the king's daughter and he married her. And I left them there all safe and sound.

ALTERNATIVE ENDING:

Conall and the Tuathanach O Drao and Conall Ceithir Cheannach set out and they kept going till they reached the Kingdom of Sorcha. And when they got there, she [the Daughter of the King of the Province of Leinster] was alone in there and her fingers were wet with tears. And Conall asked her where Macan Mór na Sorcha was.

'Ah, he's hunting in the hill,' said she.

'Will it be long till he gets back from there?' said he.

'Oh no,' said she, 'but there's a battle chain at the door there: if there was anyone who could shake it,' said she, 'he would hear it anywhere in the hill,' said she.

Conall went straight out and seized the chain and what a shake he gave it; and he had never heard a peal of thunder louder than that.

He [Macan Mór na Sorcha] heard it in the hill and: 'Aha!' said he, 'someone must have come in pursuit of the Daughter of the King of the Province of Leinster,' said he. 'It's time I was making for home.'

When he was getting close to the house – and they felt the house quaking – Conall Ceithir Cheannach rose and went out: it was he who went to fight him and he killed Macan Mór na Sorcha.

And then they went off with the Daughter of the King of the Province of Leinster in the long-ship.

THE MAN IN THE CASSOCK

Have you heard of the day when it pleased Murchadh mac Brian and Dunnchadh mac Brian and Tig Sionna mac Brian and Brian Borghaidh mac Cionadaigh and Cionadaigh himself along with them, to go hunting to the slopes of Beinn Gulbann in Ireland?

And the great company went off to the deer forest for the chase and Murchadh mac Brian stayed behind on the hunting-knoll. And what should Murchadh mac Brian see passing by but a stag with one golden antler and one silver antler and a white, red-eared hound in full cry on the heels of the stag. And he was so delighted with the stag and the hound that he set out after them to catch them. And a dense cloud of mist fell around him . . . And from the Strath of Eadrabhagh to the River of Eadrabhagh the stag made a leap and the hound made a leap and Murchadh mac Brian made the third leap and there was none in the whole of Ireland who could have made it after them. And with the mist falling around him, he had no idea what had become of the stag or the hound. And he was left standing there.

But then he heard the stroke of an axe up above him and he said to himself that there never was the stroke of an axe without someone behind it to strike it, and he went up in the direction where he had heard the sound of the stroke. And there he found a man with a black cassock, a squared staff, a string of bone beads and a string of bronze beads, and he was getting ready a bundle of firewood.

And Murchadh mac Brian greeted him with gentle words, with the gentleness of a maiden, with eloquent discourse, and the man in the cassock answered him with like words, if they were no better they were no worse, [asking] what man was he and where had he come from, what was his dwelling-place and where did he wish to get to?

'Nothing,' said Murchadh mac Brian, 'but just one of the warriors of Murchadh mac Brian.'

'Which one are you,' said the Man in the Cassock, 'of the warriors of Murchadh mac Brian, for that man does not have a single warrior but I have a name for him?'

'Oh,' said the other, 'I'm just one of the warriors of Murchadh mac Brian.'

'My good warrior,' said the Man in the Cassock, 'how well it would become you to do an ill deed, and how well you would excuse yourself!'

And the Man in the Cassock went and took out a rope from the folds of the cassock and he laid it out nine-fold on the moor and began to get the load ready. And Murchadh mac Brian was watching him and though Murchadh mac Brian was a champion himself he was appalled when he saw the size of the load the Man in the Cassock was making. And then when the Man in the Cassock had the load ready and tied up:

'My good warrior,' said he to Murchadh mac Brian, 'don't think ill of me because I'm going to carry this load, for it would have been easy enough for me to have got man after man and woman after woman to come here to fetch this bundle of firewood, but none of them could have taken in one load, as I can, as much as would keep the fires going in Gleann Eillt for a year and a day, but come here now,' said he, 'and lift this load on to my back.'

Murchadh mac Brian went over and put his hands under the load, but he could not raise it a hair's-breadth off the ground.

'Why,' said the Man in the Cassock, 'are you not lifting the load?'

'Indeed, I have reason enough for it,' said Murchadh mac Brian. 'I have never seen many but yourself who wanted a load lifted on to their backs who would not give some little bit of help, and you're giving me none at all.'

'My good warrior,' said the other, 'how well it would become you to do an ill deed, and how well you would excuse yourself!'

And, as he said it, he just swept the load up on to his shoulder, and the load did not touch Murchadh mac Brian in the passing but with the wind that came from it, it drove Murchadh mac Brian up to the knees into hard, clay ground on the other side of him. And he got up in a hurry before the Man in the Cassock could see him.

'Now,' said the Man in the Cassock to Murchadh mac Brian, 'keep pace with me and keep me in conversation.'

'That's easy enough for me,' said Murchadh mac Brian, 'for here am I light and empty-handed, and there are you with your own big load on your back.'

And off they went. And when Murchadh mac Brian ran at speed and at full speed, he could catch the swift March wind in front of him and the swift March wind behind could not catch him. But he could not keep near or anywhere near the Man in the Cassock.

'Why,' said the Man in the Cassock, 'are you not keeping pace with me and keeping me in conversation?'

'Indeed,' said Murchadh mac Brian, 'I've just caught two black-cock that were passing on the wing and I can't keep up with you.'

'Ha-ha!' said the Man in the Cassock. 'How am I to know that you didn't find them dead!'

'Ha-hai!' said Murchadh mac Brian. 'They can still bear witness to it. The blood is warm in their bodies.'

'My good warrior,' said the other, 'how well it would become you to do an ill deed and how well you would excuse yourself!'

And then, when they reached Gleann Eillt and the Man in the Cassock threw down his load, it seemed to Murchadh mac Brian that he could as easily see the lowest stone in the castle gateway shaking as the highest stone, as the whole place rang when the man threw down his load. Now the door was so wide that they went in shoulder to shoulder.

And the Man in the Cassock went straight on into a room and Murchadh mac Brian went straight on after him. And the Man in the Cassock sat down in a decorated golden chair on one side of the table that was ready laid there, and there was a silver chair on the other side and Murchadh mac Brian went and sat down in it.

And then the man . . . the Man in the Cassock struck a bell that stood on the table and a sturdy, black-haired man came in carrying a drinking horn.

'Give the drink to the guest,' said the Man in the Cassock.

'Indeed I won't,' said the man, 'I'll give it to you.'

'Oh,' said the Man in the Cassock, 'give it to him first.'

'No,' said the man, 'I'll give it to you.'

'And what reason have you not to give it to him?'

'This,' said the man: 'it's not his drink that's in my hand, it's not his roof that's over my head, it's not his food that's in my belly, and it's not his clothes that are on my back – and since all of these are yours, you shall have the drink first.'

'Oh, well,' said the Man in the Cassock, 'won't you give it to him for my sake?'

'Indeed, if I don't do it for you,' said the man, 'I don't know who else I would do it for' – and with that he handed the drinking horn to Murchadh mac Brian.

And Murchadh mac Brian took it, and he decided that caution was best, so he just drank half of it, and he set it back on the table in front of the Man in the Cassock. And the Man in the Cassock went and took a razor-edged dagger of a knife that would split a swallow flying over water on the darkest night of the year, and as much of the horn as was empty he cut off and set it on the table beside him.

'My good warrior,' said he then to Murchadh mac Brian, 'do not think ill of me for doing that for it is a taboo among my taboos, laid on me by the nurse who fostered me, never to raise a half-empty vessel to my lips. And I can put that piece back on the horn for you so perfectly that neither you nor anyone else could tell that it had ever been cut off.'

And the Man in the Cassock took up the vessel and drank all that was in it, and then he took the piece he had cut off and placed it on top, and it was as whole as ever it had been.

And what did Murchadh mac Brian see then, leashed at the side of the room, but the stag and the hound he himself had been chasing. And at the same time a company of women came forward to set food on the table before them, and [there was one of them and] it seemed to Murchadh mac Brian that as the moon is outshone by the sun, the stars by the planets, like quenched charcoal in the forge of a smith, so was the appearance of all the women in the world compared to her, with her beauty. And he set a steady gaze on her, and the Man in the Cassock was watching him.

'Why,' said the Man in the Cassock to Murchadh mac Brian, 'are you staring at that red-lipped woman at the table?'

'Indeed,' said Murchadh mac Brian, 'it's just that I would be ashamed if I didn't recognise her when I saw her again.'

'Ha-ha, my good warrior!' said the Man in the Cassock. 'How well you know how to do an ill deed and how well you would excuse yourself! But, Murchadh mac Brian,' said he, 'even though the food is on the table, if you would listen to my story, it was through that woman, and that stag and hound over there, that I suffered trials such as no one of my people ever suffered before me and I hope never will after me.

'A year ago,' said he, 'I was at the place where you saw me today getting ready the bundle of firewood, and the Gruagach of the Stag and the Hound that are over there came up to me with another in pursuit.

' "For the love of God," said she to me, "save my life and my stag and my hound are yours."

'I was so delighted,' said he, 'with the stag and the hound that I went to meet the Gruagach who was after her. And there were nine red tufts of hair growing out of the top of his head, and the bristles growing from each of these tufts were more numerous than those on a farrow cow on a hillside on a May day. And I twisted the three [sic] red tufts of hair round my fist, and I twisted the head off the neck and the neck from its roots, and the weakest of the nine red tufts of hair did not break.

'But before very long, the Gruagach of the Stag and the Hound came up to me again and said:

' "For the love of God," said she, "save my life again and my stag and my hound are yours."

' "Your stag and your hound," said I, "are my prize already."

'But then I said to myself that it would be an ill thing for me to let her be killed this time after saving her before, and I went to meet the Gruagach who was after her. But, Murchadh mac Brian, taking the head off that Gruagach was nothing more to me than a clump of withered dockens you would pluck from the ground on a harvest field, on a hillside.

But before very long, a third Gruagach came.

' "For the love of God," said the Gruagach of the Stag and the Hound, "save my life and my stag and my hound are yours."

'I was getting so weary of the whole business,' said the Man in the Cassock, 'that I went straight off to meet the Gruagach who was coming.

' "Oh for pity's sake," said the Gruagach of the Stag and the Hound, "don't touch that Gruagach, for that one's my own brother."

' "Indeed, to be sure," said I, "he's not behaving in a very brotherly fashion to you."

' "Oh," said the Gruagach of the Stag and the Hound, "what we have come for is to seek a judgement from you, and we were not prepared to accept any other judgement but the judgement of a man in a black cassock, a squared staff, a string of bone beads and a string of bronze beads, just like you."

' "And what," said I, "was the trouble between you?"

' "This," said she. "It's not that he hasn't land of his own and plenty of it, which he has won by the might of his own great strong hand, and," said she, "such land as I have, my father had it, and my grandfather, and my great-grandfather before me, and now he wants to take that land from me and to have it for himself along with all he has already."

'Oh, but,' said the Man in the Cassock [sic], 'this is my judgement for you,' said he, 'let him be content with the land he has, and if it so happens that he loses it by violence, or loses part of it, then you will let him have half of yours.

'Oh, this pleased them very well, both of them – "but you must come and see that it is properly settled between us" [they said].

'We went,' said he, 'and set off, and when we reached the sea we took out our water-helmets, and we had not been travelling very long on the sea when we came upon the Machaire Mìn Sgàthach. And wherever we looked, when we went ashore there, there were men coming on foot to meet us and men on horseback, with their hats off. I asked the Gruagach of the Stag and the Hound what was the reason for all these people coming to meet us.

' "Oh, just you wait a little," said she, "and I'll tell you that."

' "Indeed," said I, "I want to hurry and get home tonight yet."

'But I waited till she came and caught up with me and,

' "What you have there, then," said she, "is this: I have one daughter, and all the men you see there," said she, "they are going to kill each other and the survivor will have the girl." '

And who should this really be but the Gruagach of the Tiobart, who had come to get him [the Man in the Cassock] by a ruse, for she knew very well that if he was in the company he would win the girl.

' "Indeed, truly," said I to them, "I could suggest a better way of settling it than that if they would take it from me."

' "What way is that?" they all said.

' "This," said I: "to run a race, and the fastest runner to have the girl and no life would be lost."

'And this pleased all of them. And we went,' said the Man in the Cassock, 'and started the race, and I was back long before they had got half way, and I had won the girl.

'And we went back home to the Tiobart that night, myself and the girl, and the Gruagach of the Stag and the Hound, and their family. But, Murchadh mac Brian,' said he, 'when the food was on the table, a knock was heard at the door, and there was no second knock when the door was smashed in in splinters there on to the floor and that woman there was taken out from my side.

' "You're out now," said the man who had taken her out, "and there is not one in the four far-flung quarters of the world who can get her back inside, unless the Feamanach Mór Fabhsach should come, a man without mildness or meekness or mercy, without love of God or fear of man, and even if that man did come it would be no easy task for him to get you tonight."

' "Oh," said the Gruagach of the Stag and the Hound, "where," said she, "is there a man of that description under this roof and let him follow and truly, indeed, if there is such a one, I'd rather have him for a son-in-law than some fellow I wouldn't know where to find to get her back."

'I took it,' said the Man in the Cassock, 'that she was referring to me, and though I was not quite ready to go, I rose from the table and girded up my black cassock above my buttocks and took my squared staff in my hand, my bronze beads round my neck and my bone beads above my brow, and off I went. And when I was catching up fast with the man who had taken the woman, I called to him,

' "What daughter of the mighty and most pompous one do we have here?"

' "What you are," said he answering back, "is a man set for short shrift."

' "Put down the maiden," said I, "or you'll have to fight for her."

' "You can have as much of a fight for her as you like," said that man, "but you won't get the maiden tonight."

'And he hurled the spear he was carrying at me,' said the Man in the Cassock, 'and it went past like a red flash into the sky beyond me. But I went and hurled my own spear at him and struck him in the upper part of the chest and he fell, and I rushed over to him and killed him, and I took the woman home to the Tiobart that night. And if they had had food or drink to get in the Tiobart, they had finished it before I got back.

'But the next night then, Murchadh mac Brian, when the food was on the table, a knock was heard at the door, and there was no second knock when the door was smashed in in splinters on to the floor and that woman there was taken out from my side.

' "You're out now," said the man who had taken her out, "and there is not one in the four far-flung quarters of the world who can get you back inside, unless the Feamanach Mór Fabhsach should come, a man without mildness or meekness or mercy, without love of God or fear of man, and even if that one did come it would be no easy task for him to get you tonight."

' "Oh," said the Gruagach of the Tiobart, "where is there a man of that description," said she, "under this roof, and truly indeed, if there is such a one, I'd rather have him for a son-in-law than some fellow I wouldn't know where to find to get her back."

'I took it that she was referring to me tonight again,' said the Man in the Cassock, 'and I said to myself that I would not let her get so far from home as I had last night, and I was already prepared and off I went. And as I was catching up with them I called to them, asking what [?infant] of the mighty and most powerful one we had here.

' "What you are," said the other man, "is a man set for short shrift."

' "You put the maiden down," said I, "or you'll have to fight for her."

" 'Ho! You can have as much of a fight as you like for her,' said he answering back, 'but you won't get the maiden tonight.'

"He hurled the spear he was carrying at me," said the Man in the Cassock, "and it went like a red flash into the sky beyond me. And I went and made a cast at him with my own spear and struck him in the upper part of his chest and he fell, and I rushed over to him and killed him. And I took the woman home with me at the Tiobart, and if they had had food or drink to get in the Tioabart, they had finished it before I got there.

"And the third night, Murchadh mac Brian," said he, "when the food was on the table, a knock was heard at the door, and there was no second knock when the door was smashed in in splinters on to the floor and that woman there was taken out from my side.

" 'You're out now,' said the man who had taken her out, 'and there is not one in the four far-flung quarters of the world who can get you back inside, unless the Feamanach Mór Fabhsach should come, a man without mildness or meakness or mercy, without love of God or fear of man, and even if that one did come, it would be no easy task for him to get you tonight.'

"I took it to be my business," said the Man in the Cassock, " and I set off close after him, for I said to myself that I would not let him get so far from the house tonight. And as I was catching up with him and the woman, I called to them asking what [? infant] of the mighty and most powerful one we had here.

" 'What you are,' said that man answering back, 'is a man set for short shrift.'

" 'You put the maiden down,' said I, 'or you 'll have to fight for her.'

' "Oh, you can have as much of a fight as you like for her," said he "but you won't get the maiden tonight."

'He hurled the spear he was carrying at me,' said the Man in the Cassock, 'and it struck me on the bronze beads that were above my brow and I went down on one knee. But I leapt to my feet and I made a cast at him with my own spear and struck him in the upper part of the chest, and I rushed over to him and killed him.

'And I said to myself that night, good as the Tiobart was, that I had had enough of it. And I went and got the Gruagach of the Stag and the Hound to go with me and she and I and the woman went back home. And when we reached the sea, we took out our water-helmets and we were not long on the journey.

'And when we got home, I was sent to sleep that night in a long, bare barn, with none beside me. And a voice came to the window to tell me that I had three days of hunting and sport to put in before I could get wedding or marriage.

' "So be it," said I answering back, "but if there were any more you would not live to tell the tale!"

' "Indeed your share of the enchantment of this island would be none the less for that," said the man who was outside. "If I didn't lay these *geasa* on you, someone else would."

'Anyway, I got up next morning,' said the Man in the Cassock, 'and I went to the deer forest, and I hunted a great, gay, heroic hunt,' said he, 'such as had never, I thought, been hunted in Ireland before. And I made full haste to get back home, but if I did, when I got home there was no sign of the woman. I asked the Gruagach of the Stag and the Hound where she was.

' "Indeed," said she, "after you went off to the deer forest, three harpers came here. And since you were not at home yourself for them to kill, and since they found the woman at home, they made off with her."

'Oh, disaster and destruction and deep-sorrow upon me,' said the Man in the Cassock [*sic*]. 'Where can I find her now?

'But when I had got ready,' said he, 'I set out,' he said, 'and I went down to the shore and launched the long ship.

'And I set her stem to the sea and her stern to the shore.
I raised the dappled, flapping sails against the tall, tough masts
So that there was no mast unbent nor sail untorn
Weathering the white wallowing ocean.
Splashing of the sea-pool's shore was music to soothe me to sleep:
Screaming of sea-gulls, coiling of eels,
The greater whale eating the lesser whale
And the lesser whale doing as best it could,
The bent brown buckies of the deep rattling in on to her bottom
     boards
So surely was I steering her,
I was steersman in the stern, pilot in the prow:
I would loose the rope that was fast in her
And make fast the rope that was loose in her.

'But as I passed a great long desert island there, what did I see but the three harpers, and one of them was sitting on either side of the woman giving her kiss and kiss about, and the third one was standing playing music. But, Murchadh mac Brian,' said he, 'there was not a finger among my fingers that I did not gnaw, for fear I should fall asleep at the sweetness of the music that man was making.

'And at the same time, I was edging, edging the ship in to the island to see if I could get within striking distance. And when I got near,' said he, 'to the two who were sitting one on either side of her, I drew my squared staff that never left a stroke half-finished in a single place where it was ever struck, and as much as was below the knees of the two who were sitting one on either side of her – the woman – I cut it off. And wherever in the world the third one fled to, I didn't bother to follow him when I got the woman. And I took her back to the boat with me and went back home with her.

'And that night I was sent to sleep again,' said he, 'in a long, bare barn, and a voice came to the window calling to me that I had two days of hunting and sport to put in before I could get wedding or marriage.

' "Indeed, so be it," said I, "and if there were any more, you would not live to tell the tale!"

' "Your share of the enchantment of the island would be none the less for that," said the man who was outside. "If I didn't lay these *geasa* on you, someone else would."

'Anyway, I went next morning to the deer forest,' said the Man in the Cassock, 'and I hunted a great, gay, heroic hunt,' said he, 'such as had never before, I thought, been hunted in Ireland. And I made full haste to get back home, but if I did, when I got home I could find no sign of the woman. And I asked the Gruagach of the Stag and the Hound where she was.

' "Indeed," said she, "little do I care where that same woman is."

'I took her answer so badly,' said the Man in the Cassock, 'that I said to myself that she deserved to be killed for it, but then I said to myself that if I killed her, I would never find out where the woman had gone. And after a little while,

' "Well," said the Gruagach of the Stag and the Hound, "who came here but three great giants when you had gone to the deer forest. And since you were not at home for them to kill, and they happened upon the woman, they made off with her."

' "Hu-hu-hai!" said I. "Well do I know where to go and look for her this time, and sore, sore, were the straits into which these same three got me once before."

'But anyway,' said he, 'next day I got myself ready and set out and I reached the castle of the giants, for I knew the place well enough. And when I got there the place was terribly quiet. There was not a soul to be seen about the place at all. I kept going in at doors and I couldn't see anybody: then I would come back out. But, this time, I was coming out of a door,' said he, 'and when I was just in the doorway I felt myself being tugged at from behind. But, Murchadh mac Brian,' said he, 'I think that though the lowest foundation stone in the castle had been tied to me

I would have carried it off with me, such was the jerk with which I took myself out when I felt myself being tugged at from behind.

'But then I said to myself that it was a pretty feeble tug and that I would have a look to see what had done it and I peered closely inside, and there behind the door there was a man lying bound, and who was that but Macan Liathach Lochlann.

'And he implored me for pity's sake to untie him and he would follow me every step I made forever after, to help me in any way he could, and he said that the giants were out fishing at the moment, and that they were going to kill him when they got home in the evening – and he implored me to untie him. And I went,' said he, 'and untied him, and wherever in the world he may have fled to, I never saw another sight of him.

'But I kept going in at doors and I couldn't see anybody, but this time I went into a room,' said he, 'and the woman I was looking for was there, sitting on a decorated golden throne and the decorated golden throne was going round and round by itself . . . and one moment she would be weeping and the next moment she would be laughing.

' "What," said I, "is the cause of your joy . . . and the cause of your sorrow the next moment?"

' "Indeed," said she, "that is no small thing. I am overjoyed at seeing you . . ."

' "Why are you overjoyed [*sic*]* at seeing me?" said I . . .

' "Because your head is the first thing I shall be offered tonight."

' "Oh, indeed, they won't get my head, anyway," said I.

' "Oh, they will," said she. "Goodness knows what can stop it. That lot," said she, "are away fishing just now, and even if we make off, you and I, we shall have to pass the very point where they are fishing. And the only way I can see we would be safe: we're very lucky that they've left their water-helmets at home, and if we could get them burnt before we go, they would have no means of following us. And," said she, "you'd better go out and start getting the fires going, for," said she, "we'll have to make a separate fire for each one of them. As for putting them in the

---

* Storyteller was confused at this point owing to breakdowns in recording.

one fire, all of them, they would just become seven times as good as they were before."

'And I went out,' said the Man in the Cassock, 'and I began to get the fires built, and, now, there was a Cailleach Earra-ro-ghlas there on guard to see that she stayed inside, but she would slip out now and again without the hag noticing her and she would build two fires to my one.

'And when we had the fires ready, we threw the water-helmets into them – one to each fire – and when they were burnt to cinders, the ashes were scattered to the winds. And the woman and I set out then, and we put to sea.

'And when we were passing the point where the giants were fishing they cast their three black lines after the boat, and they caught her right in the stern. But, Murchadh mac Brian,' said he, 'if my ship was fast leaving the shore, she was seven times faster going back to them!

' "Consider now," said the woman to me; "though their three black lines are bewitched, the gunwale of your ship is not. Why not let them have the piece of the gunwale that they have hooked and put a piece of your cassock in its place?"

'I went,' said he, 'and struck a blow with the squared staff that never left a stroke half-finished in a single place where it was ever struck, and as much of the gunwale of the ship as was caught on their three black lines, I let them have, and they fell sprawling in the sea. And I went and put a piece of the cassock in its place and off we went.

' "Never mind," said they, "we won't be long catching you when we get our water-helmets."

'But then they heard the Cailleach Earra-ro-ghlas calling the giants home, for she had discovered that the woman was missing, and the names she called them by were Siobar Bheul-dubh and Corran Caiflidh and Cairgeil Cosgail. And the giants went home to get their water-helmets and go in pursuit of the Man in the Cassock [sic] to take the woman from him. And when they got home they found the water-helmets burnt, and there was not a cow in calf, or a sheep in lamb, or a woman in child, or a mare in foal, within seven miles distance of the castle gate, but they miscarried with every wailing howl that they gave lamenting for their water-helmets.

'And I took the woman home that time,' said the Man in the Cassock, 'and that night I was sent to sleep again in a long, bare barn. And a voice came,' said he, 'to the window calling to me that I had a day of hunting and sport to put in before I could get wedding or marriage.

' "So be it," said I, answering back, "but if there were any more you would not live to tell the tale!"

' "Your share of the enchantment of the island would be none the less for that," said the man who was outside. "If I didn't lay these *geasa* on you, someone else would."

'Anyway, I rose very early next morning,' said the Man in the Cassock, 'and I set out. And I hunted a great, gay, heroic hunt, such as had never, I thought, been hunted in Ireland before. And I made full haste to get back home, but if I did, when I got home I could find no sign of the woman. I asked the Gruagach of the Stag and the Hound where she was.

' "Indeed," said she, "after you went off to the deer forest, the Macan Òg of Greece came back. And since you were not at home yourself for him to kill, and since he found the woman at home, he made off with her, but he would not go to the deer forest to look for you."

' "Oh yes," said I. It couldn't be helped. But next morning I got ready,' said he, 'and I launched the long ship.

'And I set her stem to the sea and her stern to the shore.

'And my course was no crooked one,' said he, 'but I sailed straight to Greece. And when I went ashore.

'I put my hand on the prow of the ship and dragged her seven times her own length on to green grass where wind would not snatch at her and where sun would not blister her and where no little guttersnipe from the city could get near her to mock her or make sport of her till I got back to her again.

'And I went on in through the country and I had not gone far when I met a herdsman looking after a herd of cattle.

' "What news have you, herdsman?" said I . . .

' "You have given me nothing to make it worth my while telling it."

' "Have I not, my good lad?"

' "No, you haven't," said he.

'I went and put my hand in my pocket and gave him a handful of gold and a handful of silver.

' "Indeed, may good luck and blessings be your lot," said the herdsman, "and may success attend you, and your descendants after you. And there is a wedding feast and a great marriage tonight in the City of Athens for the Macan Òg of Greece and the daughter of the Gruagach of the Tiobart, and oaths have been sworn that if they see a man with a black cassock, a squared staff, a string of bone beads and a string of bronze beads approaching within seven miles of the city gate, he will be dead long before he reaches it."

' "Truly, indeed, my good lad," said I, "you are not without news."

' "I am not," said he.

' "Here you are," said I. "Here is another handful of gold and silver for you, and you take off your clothes and I shall put them on, and I shall take my clothes off and you shall put them on."

'And we did that,' said the Man in the Cassock. 'We exchanged clothes. But, Murchadh mac Brian,' said he, 'if you had seen me with the little herdsman's clothes not covering my thighs and my clothes on the little herdsman, trailing two or three yards along the ground behind him! But, anyway, I set off,' said he, 'and I reached,' said he, 'the king's palace . . . or near it. And I saw a pretty little house,' said he, 'a little way from the castle, and I went and made straight for it, and when I went in there was no one there but an old woman sitting by a fire – a pretty little fire too, and she gave a shout of laughter when she saw me at the door.

' "Why," said she, "are you not up at the big house up yonder with the other poor folk who are there, to get your share of the feast?"

' "Why," said I, "are you not up at the big house yourself along with the poor folk who are there, to get your share of the feast?"

' "Oh," said she, "I'm nothing," said she, "but a poor old woman who can't walk or get very far, and my share will be brought here to me."

' "Oh well," said I, "if my share isn't going to be brought to me, I'd better go and get it where it is."

'And I went straight out of the house and right on up. And,' said he, 'there was a big table laid there outside the main door and the poor folk of the kingdom were seated on either side of it. And they had had their fill of food and drink, every one of them. And what was going on when I got there was this: they were scattering money amongst them, and they were catching it.

'But I didn't care about the money,' said the Man in the Cassock. 'I said to myself that if I lived long enough I could easily have plenty of money, and I made for the food, for I was badly in need of it – and I started on the food and the drink.

'And when I began to feel the drink, every now and then I would pick up one of the men who were sitting nearer the house than me and I would set him down on the seat on my other side. And in this way I was getting much nearer to the main door. And before I was finished,' said he, 'I was right beside the door-post. And then,' said he, 'I just waited there to see if I could see the door being opened a chink – but I couldn't.

'But at long last,' said he, 'I saw it being opened a chink and I leapt to my feet and set my shoulder to the door and started to push it open. And the men inside started to push it shut, but, Murchadh mac Brian,' said he, 'I think it would have been easier for them to push out the lowest foundation-stone in the castle gate, than to push my shoulder away from the door when I had it against it.

'And the Macan Òg of Greece called out when he heard the disturbance around the door, asking what was the trouble down there. They told him it was just one of the poor folk trying to get in.

' "Ho! Let him in," said the Macan Òg of Greece. "He must be just a poor man who has been used to company."

'And they let me in,' said the Man in the Cassock, 'and I went humbly down to the far end of the house where no-one was sitting. And I had not been there very long,' said he, 'when a shambling, ill-mannered young man came up and stood in front of me. And he danced a reel there,' said he, 'looking at me. And when he had finished, he swung his fist and hit me on the forehead, but, Murchadh mac Brian,' said he, 'if he was quick to hit me with his fist, he was seven times quicker stuffing it in his mouth . . . for where had he hit me but on the bronze beads above my brow.

169

' "Oh, oh," said he, "I'm hurt! If he ever walked the world or the earth," said he, "you've got him right in here on the floor — a man with a black cassock, a squared staff, a string of bone beads and a string of bronze beads."

'But, Murchadh mac Brian,' said he – the Man in the Cassock – 'when I heard myself being described, I felt around all over the place and found an old red rusted sword that had not struck a blow for goodness knows how long, and I did not leave a head on a neck there except the Macan Òg of Greece and his father and mother and that woman there.

'And the Macan Òg of Greece was glad enough then to spend whatever he had left after paying for the wedding, to pay for a wedding for me. And he did it, too.

'And I brought the woman back home,' said he, 'next day, and a wedding and a great marriage were held for me here, again,' said he. 'And now you know it all,' said he, 'what hardships I suffered because of that woman you see there.'

And however long or short a time Murchadh mac Brian stayed with him after that, he went on his way and said farewell to the Man in the Cassock and the woman and the Gruagach of the Stag and the Hound. And . . . he got back to the hunting-knoll where he had first met them. And he waited there some time before the hunters came back from the deer forest, such was the power of the magic that had been worked on them.

And Murchadh mac Brian and his men went home together then. And I parted from them.

THE STORY OF OSSIAN

OH WELL, OSSIAN, that was in the days of the Féinn, as they used to say, and there were three brothers and they lived in three bothies, as they called it at that time, three shieling bothies. And Ossian was the eldest brother.

This happened one stormy night. A crow came in to . . . a black crow, to the youngest one, the youngest brother, and the crow asked, she asked him if she could get a night's lodging, and the youngest one, the youngest brother, said to it, 'Oh, get out of here, Black Crow, or I'll knock off your head with my finger.'

Then the crow went in to the second brother, and asked him if she could have a night's lodging with him, and the youngest [*sic*] brother said to it, 'Oh, get out of here, Black Crow, or I'll knock off your head with my finger.'

But then she came to Ossian's house, and Ossian said, when she came in and asked Ossian if she could have a night's lodgings, oh, said Ossian, she was welcome to a night's lodgings. [? After that,] Ossian, he was cooking his meal, 'Och well,' said she to him, 'when you've given me a night's lodging I dare say I can get my supper.'

'Och, for all you'll eat,' said Ossian, 'that's all right. You're welcome.'

Now the crow ate her share of the meal from the table, ate her fill, and then bedtime came and Ossian went to bed, and when he got up in the morning and looked, there was a woman there as beautiful as he had ever seen. And Ossian said to her, 'How do you come to be such a beautiful woman today when you came in last night as a crow?'

'Oh well,' said the woman to him, 'I've been enchanted, and till someone like you would take me in and give me a bed and food I would have to be a crow. But now,' said she, 'I'm your wife as long as we both live, unless you cast up at me in any quarrel the shape in which I arrived here, and if you do that to me,' said she, 'I'll go off as a crow again.'

'Oh well,' said Ossian, 'that's all right. And I won't mention that to you ever again.'

Now when morning came and his brothers, his two brothers came in, he was getting ready for when the Féinn left for the hills [to hunt], and when they came in and saw the woman, then they were kicking themselves for not taking her in. But she was Ossian's now.

And now, many years passed now and Ossian and his wife were together, and this day he was going to the hills and he said – it was stag-hounds they had for the deer and to bring down the deer – and Ossian said to her, 'Now,' said he, 'this bitch should have puppies today,' and Ossian told her: 'Put a string round the neck of the first puppy.' And his wife did that when the bitch had her first puppy: she put a string round its neck. And there came . . . Ossian hadn't been long gone and the bitch hadn't long had her puppies when a man came to the door. He knocked at the door and he asked the woman if the bitch had had her puppies, and she said yes.

'Well,' said he, 'I want the first puppy.'

The woman went in and brought out one of the puppies, but she didn't bring out the firstborn. She brought out one of them and gave it to him. He took the puppy and took hold of its ear and lifted it and shook it, and the puppy started to yelp and, 'Oh,' said he, 'that wasn't the first puppy.'

But she brought him [all of them] until she had brought him the last of them, and she had to . . . she wasn't going to give him the one . . . the first puppy, but he told her that if she didn't give him the first puppy he would cut off her head. Then with fear and everything she went and gave him the puppy, and he took hold of this puppy's ear and he shook it, and shook it, and shook it. Though he shook it for ever it wouldn't make a sound. And he put the puppy under his arm and went on his way.

Then Ossian came back, hurrying home from the hill, and he asked where the puppies were. Now when the first puppy had gone his wife had put a string on another one. And Ossian did just the same as the man who came to the door had done: he started shaking them by the ear, and when he shook them and they whimpered until he . . .

'Well,' said she – she told him that – that a man had come to the door, and that he had been going to cut off her head unless she gave him the puppy

Oh, then Ossian lost the head and he said to her, 'Oh, you black crow,' said he, 'who would have expected any better from you?' And as soon as he said that she turned into a crow and went out, and Ossian rushed after her. And Ossian followed her and followed her, but at last the crow settled on a rock. And Ossian came up with her and begged her to forgive him and come back. 'Come back.'

'Oh,' said she, 'I can never go back again. I told you the first morning you saw me that if you cast up to me the shape in which I arrived that I couldn't leave – that I couldn't stay, that I would have to leave.' And, 'But here,' said she, 'here's a ring for you, and put the ring on your finger, and as long as you have this ring you will live. But whatever you do don't give away the ring. Keep the ring on your finger.'

Then Ossian came back to his shieling, and he was there [until he was] an old man. And he wasn't able to do much. And then another man came along whom they called Para Naomh-cléireach [Patrick Holyclerk – i.e. St. Patrick], and he was writing books about the story of Ossian, about places Ossian knew. And Ossian was there – he was in bed: he wasn't able to get out of bed. And this day Para Naomh-cléireach came in and he had a deer and he asked Ossian, 'Did you ever get a deer among your Féinn that was as big as that?'

Ossian was blind and he was deaf, and Ossian said to him, 'Lay it [?its leg] on the palm of my hand.'

He laid it on the palm of his hand and Ossian balanced it up and down, and Ossian said to him, 'Hah,' said Ossian, 'many a time have I seen the leg of a fledgling blackbird bigger than that.'

And with the rage that Ossian put Para Naomh-cléireach into he went back to his house, and the books he was writing with Ossian's help, he started – he was throwing them into the fire. And he had a little girl, and the child started – she was taking some of the books out of the fire again and keeping them.

Ach, now Ossian had a lad who used to work for him, and he said to the lad, 'Can you,' said he, 'carry me outside?'

'Oh yes,' said the boy. Then the lad carried him outside.

'Now,' said Ossian, 'we're going to such and such a place in the moor.'

They got to this place anyhow. There was a birch wood and rushes. And Ossian said to the lad, 'What can you see?'

'Oh, I can see a birch wood,' said the lad, 'and rushes . . . they're tall rushes.'

'Well, just you make for the birch wood and the rushes,' said Ossian. When they reached the rushes Ossian said to him, 'Can you see the biggest clump of rushes?'

'Yes,' said the lad.

'Well, climb up it, and when you get to the top of it' – the rushes would come away. And the boy did that, and when the rushes came away and the turf with them he asked the lad, 'What can you see?'

'Oh, I can see,' said he, 'dogs here as fine as I have ever seen and there's one yellow one,' said he, 'among them there and I've never seen anything more beautiful than her.'

'Ah, poor Biorach a' Bhuidheag ["The Sharp Yellow One"],' said Ossian, 'the most prized dog the Féinn ever had. Let her out.' And Biorach a' Bhuidheag came out, and when she came out she just about ate up Ossian, she was so pleased to see him.

'Now,' Ossian told him, 'make a hole in the ground.' The lad made a hole in the ground, and, 'Have you made the hole?' said Ossian.

'Yes.'

'Well, put your head down into it.' The lad put his head down into the hole. 'Now,' said Ossian to him, 'keep your head in the hole.' And Ossian let out one yell – 'Halloo!' – and the cliffs and the hills, they just about shattered in pieces at Ossian's cry. And he said to the lad, 'Raise your head and see what you can see.'

'Oh,' said the lad, 'I can see,' said he, 'deer,' said he. 'I've never seen anything . . . quite as big as them.'

'Ach,' said Ossian to him, 'the . . . ?' said he. 'Let them pass. Put down your head again.'

The lad put down his head again then, and Ossian let out another cry, and he told the lad to lift his head, and, 'Oh,' said the lad, 'I can't lift my head. It . . . it's been just about split in pieces by you.'

'Och, lift it up. Raise your head.'

The lad lifted his head then, and when he had lifted his head: 'Oh,' said the lad, 'if the first lot were big, I've never seen anything,' said he, 'bigger than this, and there's one enormous one at the head of them.'

'Och well,' said Ossian, 'perhaps that will do all right. Let go Biorach a' Bhuidheag.' Biorach a' Bhuidheag went after the deer, and Ossian gave a shout, 'Has she caught it?'

'Oh yes,' said the lad, 'she has it down.' She brought down the stag then.

'Now,' said Ossian to the lad, 'take the deer and kindle a fire and cook the deer in its entrails. And give it to me.'

The lad did as Ossian told him. He made the fire and roasted the deer in . . . its entrails. And when he was looking to see if the meat was cooked, ready to give to Ossian; he took a little bit of it and put it in his mouth, and then Ossian ate the food just as it was. And when he had eaten the food Ossian grew strong, and he could see. He had his sight again and he wasn't deaf. 'Now,' said he to the lad, 'I'm as good as I used to be.'

'But there's one thing,' said he – the lad to him. 'I can see a little mark on one of your eyes.'

'Yes,' he answered, 'you took a little bit of the deer before you gave it to me, and that's what put the mark on my eye. But never mind,' said he to the lad, 'I'm fit enough again now. Now,' said he to the lad, 'I expect you're wanting something to eat?'

And he took a bow and arrow and went down to the birch wood, and shot a blackbird, and the lad who was along with Ossian, he ate all he could of the blackbird, and Ossian took the blackbird's leg home with him. And he came to Para Naomh-cléireach and went to his door, and there was a table standing in the middle of the room, and he threw the leg of the fledgling blackbird on to the table, and when he threw it on to the table the four legs of the table broke under it with the weight of the leg. 'Now,' said he to him, 'were those lies I told you now?'

But now, when he [Para Naomh-cléireach] saw the fragments of the papers and the books there . . . these books, then he started gathering them up and putting them together and . . . , until he had made up as much as he could of them again, but he didn't get half as many books as he had had.

But now time passed and Ossian, he took to his bed again. Well, there wasn't any food that could do him any good. And one day he gave a shout to the lad who stayed with him: 'Carry me out,' said he, 'to the burn.' The lad took him out to the burn, and he brought soap and a towel with him too. And the boy was washing Ossian in the burn. And as he was washing him he took the ring off his finger and laid it on a stone. And when he laid the ring on a stone a crow came along and picked up the ring and went off with it.

And Ossian felt something happening to him, as if death were approaching, and he said to the lad, 'Is the ring . . . ?'

'No,' said the lad, 'the . . . a crow carried it off.'

'Oh, I can believe it did that,' said he.

'Oh well,' said the lad . . .

Said he to the lad, 'You have seen something no living person but yourself has seen, and you shall not tell what you've seen to anyone again.' And as the boy was washing him he put his hand on the back of this boy's neck and broke his neck, and the lad fell into the burn, dead.

And Ossian came home to his shieling and . . . he never got up again. He died. And as far as I know that's the end of the story – that finishes the story – the story of Ossian.

THE PRINCESS AND THE PUPS

W ELL IT WIS THIS YOUNG king an queen, ye see, an they were as happy as happy could be, they'd everything to make life happy fir them, an a bonnie wee princess an everything, and they were livin just fine. But in a country miles an hundreds o miles awa, there wis this big giant, and he took a notion to this bairn, ye see: he'd haerd aboot this folk, and haerd aboot this wee princess, and he came and stole the bairn awa. Now this young king and queen they were haertbroken aboot their bairn, an thocht they would never get it back, the size o this man. Noo, he says to his queen, he says, 'You content yirsel an,' he says, 'by hook or by crook I'll get the bairn back,' he says, 'tae ye.'

An she was greetin an cairryin on an she says, 'You'll gang awaa an maybe you'll never come back tae.'

He says, 'A'll come back, dinna you worry.' He says, 'You try an content yirsel tae I come back.' So away he goes in saerch o his bairn, an he's hey tae the road and ho tae the road, through hills an dales an every place. An as he wis gaen awaa, there's an aald man goin alang the road, an he walked alang the road wi this aald man fir a bit, an they met anither man on the road, a younger kin o man. They were aa traivellin on thegither, but nane o them kent wha he wis, ye see, he wis jist anither man tae them, lookin for work, an they thocht he wis lookin for work tae. An he says to this yin, 'Whit do you dae?'

He says, 'A mak boats,' he says, 'A'm a boatbuilder.' He says, 'That's what I dae,' he says, 'an A'm jist lookin for work.'

He says, 'Will you come wi me,' he says, 'an A'll maybe get ye something tae dae.'

He says, 'Aa rycht then.' But the other aald man, he left them, an he went awaa some other wey. But they twa, they kept marchin on and on, an danderin on an on, an jist a drink o water here an there an sometimes they'd beg a wee bit breid tae theirsels in some hoose and some fairmer would let them lie in their barn, an they kept goin on an on an on. And as they were walkin on they met anither man, an he wis lookin for work tae. An this young king says tae him, 'Whit dae ye dae?'

He says, 'Oh me,' he says, 'dinnae ask me whit . . . I dae,' he says. 'I shouldnae be nae company for naebody.'

He says, 'Whit wey that?'

He says, 'Well, tae tell ye the truth,' he says, 'aa ma life,' he says, 'A've jist lived wi thievin an roguin,' he says. 'There's naebody in the world 'll thieve an steal better 'n me,' he says. 'A've had tae dae it tae keep mysel livin.'

'Ah,' the keeng says tae him, 'but there's aye room for everybody in this world,' he said, 'an we micht find something for you tae dae an aa. You come wi me tae,' he says, 'A've an idea A micht find something for you tae dae an aa.' He says, 'An ye're good at it?'

He says, 'Oh, the world's best.' He says, 'There nobody 'll hear me or see me,' he says: 'I could steal onything.'

So as they went alang, he proved he wis as good as his word, fir he used tae go oot an in tae places an chore gaanies [steal chickens] an eggs an things, an kept them livin as they were gaan alang the road. Noo they're walkin alang an they seen this ither man: he wis lookin fir work tae. (They were aa – nae work tae be gotten, ye see, or nae money or nothin.) An the keeng says, 'What dae you dae?'

He says, 'Well, I wis a marksman,' he said, 'actually earn't ma livin as a marksman,' he said. 'You can set up any target,' he says, 'up tae a . . . two hundred yards,' he says, 'an A'll hit it dead on, supposin it's no the size of a midge.'

He says, 'Oh well,' he says, 'there bound tae be something that you can dae an aa,' he says, 'you come alang wi me.' So on they goes an on

they goes tae they came tae this big sea that they had – the king kent he
hid tae cross this sea tae get tae whar this giant wis, ye see? So when he
came tae the sea he says, 'Well, boatman,' he says, 'it's your turn,' he
says. 'We need a boat.'

So this boatman, he went away an he got the ither yin that wis the
thief tae kill twa big ox fir him, an he got the skins an he made a smashin
boat fir him. An they got intae the boat an away they go, across the water
and across the water an across the water, tae they came tae the land 'at
this big giant lived in. An when they got there, they come ashore and
walked tae they come near this big castle whar the giant lived. Now this
young keeng said tae this yin that wis the thief, he says, 'You,' he says,
'A've tae depend on now.' He says, 'You go up tae that huge castel,' he
says, 'and see if ye can see hycht or hair o a wee young infant lassie,' he
says, 'a wee princess: it's my bairn 'at they stole, an,' he says, 'A want
her back. An,' he says, 'ye'll come back an tell me if ye see or hear
onything aboot her.'

So this yin, he did that. He wis the world's best at doin things withoot
onybody seein or hearin him. So up he went, an back he come tae the
young king and he says, 'Oh aye,' he says, 'there's a wee young princess
there – at least,' he says, 'there's a young infant there, a wee lassie. An,'
he says, 'she lies –' he says, 'this huge giant,' he says, 'keeps this wee
princess in the palm o his hand, and his hand's a cradle fir her. An there
she sleeps, an there he keeps her,' he says, 'but she's all right: he looks
efter her an 's good tae her aa rycht. An,' he says, 'he's lyin sleepin wi
this bairn in he's hand. But,' he says, 'there's a huge bitch,' he says, 'a
great big dog, an,' he says, 'hid's guardin the princess. An,' he says, 'this
dog has two puppies,' he says, 'an the puppies is like mountains.'

'Well,' this young prince [sic] says, 'dae you think,' he says, 'that you
could get the princess?'

'Oh, fine that,' he says, 'there never wis dogs, giants or nothin else –'
He says, 'I telt you I wis the best thief in the world.'

'Well,' he says, 'you go an get the princess back tae me,' he says,
'but A'll tell ye whit tae dae. When ye tak the princess,' he says, 'you
tak the twa pups an aa. D'ye think ye'd manage tae dae that?'

He says, 'Oh aye, I think A'll manage tae dae that.' So he goes up tae this huge castel, an in he goes, an he dis manage tae tak the wean and the two pups, an he brings them back tae the young king.

The king says, 'That's fine,' he says, 'we'll mak wir wey back tae the sea as fast as we can, an try 'n get awaa before the giant waakens up.' So they made their way back tae the sea, an they got intae the boat an they're away in the boat.

Ah, but this giant he waakent up – missed the princess ootae his hand, an missed the dogs – the pups. An he says tae this big dog, 'Efter them as quick as you can,' he says, 'an bring back the princess tae me!'

So this dog's away an it's through the water and through the water an through the water an through the water efter this boat, and through the water till it was almost catchin up on the boat. And this young king, he said tae one o the men, 'Throw one o the puppies intae the water!' So they throwed the puppy intae the water. Now when this dog cam up tae its pup, hit stopped an it got its pup by the neck an it swam all the road back, right away back tae whar the giant wis, wi its pup, an it put its pup on the bank.

An the giant says, 'Whit are ye daein back?'

He [sic] says, 'A come back wi ma pup.'

He says, 'I didnae tell ye tae bring a pup,' he says, 'it was the princess A telt ye to bring back.'

'Ah, but,' he says, 'A hed tae get ma pup.'

He says, 'Well, get, this time, an get the princess.'

So this dog's through the water an through the water and through the water again: hit had . . . hundreds o miles this time tae swim before it neared the boat. And the young king said tae this thief, 'Throw the ither pup intae the water!' So he throwed the ither pup oot intae the water, an when the dog wis come tae its pup – there's nothing 'at would make it pass its pup, it was jist like ony ither mother – it stopped an got its pup by the neck an it swam away back tae whar it come fae wi its pup again.

An the giant says, 'Whit's this ye've got?'

He [sic] says, 'Ma pup.'

He says, 'Is *that* whit A telt ye tae get? It wis the princess, wisn't it?'

'Oh well,' he says, 'A cannae help you, princess or nothin else,' he says: 'A'm too tire't fir tae go back.'

He says, 'Get back!'

He says, 'A cannae,' he says, 'A'm fair done.'

'Well,' the giant says, 'A'll jist hae tae go masel.' And he wis that big 'at he could wyde intae the sea, an he widd an widd an widd through this sea efter this young king an the princess an this ither men. And he . . . widd an widd an widd, an he was catchin up on them almost, spoolin an wydin through this water – some bits he swim an some bits he jist wydit – an this wis approachin the boat. An this young king he says, 'Marksman,' he says, 'it's your turn!' (Ye see, this giant – there wis a spot on he's – palm o he's hand there that wis jist like my skin or yours, but the rest o him wis like crocodile skin, a knife wouldnae even penetrate it.) So he says, 'Marksman,' he says, 'the thief telt ye whar the princess lay, whar this spot is, where the giant can be killt through there.' He says, 'Now it's your turn,' he says, 'to prove yir worth.'

So this marksman, as the giant got nearer, he aimed his bow and he's arra, an he jist waited till the giant's hand come up wi this mark on it, an he fired an got him right on the spot. An the giant jist waver't like that an aa the strength went oot o him, an he jist crept caaany an caaany an canny back through this water until it was too much for him an he jist went under, an that wis the end o him, wi this marksman, whar he shot him in the right spot. An that is the story!

TRICKSTER TALES

THE HISTORY OF KITTY ILL-PRETTS

THERE ONCE WAS A poor woman who had three daughters. I do not know the name of the two elder ones but the name of the youngest was Kitty. At last the poor woman fell ill, and as she knew she was dying she called her daughters to her to say 'Goodbye'. She was so poor she had nothing to leave them but an 'auld pat' and an 'auld pan' and half a bannock and her blessing. So to the eldest she gave the 'auld pat' and to the second she gave the 'auld pan', while all that poor Kitty got was half a bannock and her blessing. She also told them all to go, after she was dead, to the king's palace to look for work.

So after the mother was dead the three daughters set off to the palace, but the elder ones were jealous of Kitty because she was very clever and they did not wish her to go with them, so when Kitty followed after them they always turned and 'staned her hame' as if she had been a dog. However Kitty would not be turned back, but went on too to the palace to look for work.

When they got there, the king himself came out to see them, and he said to the eldest daughter: 'What can you do?' and she replied: 'I can shape, and I can shoo [sew] and money a braw thing I can do.'

Then he said to the second daughter: 'And what can you do?' and she replied: 'I can bake and I can brew and money a braw thing I can do.'

At last he came to Kitty and said as before: 'What can you do?' and she said: 'Oh, I can do all these things and a great many more besides. I can turn the moon into a cream cheese, and take the stars out of the sky.'

So they were all taken in to the palace and given work to do and very soon the king found out that Kitty was far cleverer than her sisters.

So one day he came to her and said: 'Kitty, I wish you would help me to get some thing which I want very much. There is a giant who lives near here, across the Brig o' ae Hair, who has a most wonderful sword called the Sword of Light, which shines so brightly that if you have it you can see your way in the dark without any lantern. Now if I had that sword I should be quite happy, and if you will get it for me I will marry my eldest son to your eldest sister.'

Of course this was a very difficult and dangerous task to undertake but Kitty, who had forgiven her sisters for their unkindness to her, determined to try what she could do. So she filled her apron with salt and set off across the narrow Brig o' ae Hair and arrived at the giant's house when it was dark. First of all she peeped in at the window and there she saw the giant stirring a great pot of porridge, which was on the kitchen fire, and as he stirred it he always kept tasting it and tasting it to see if it was just as he liked it. So when Kitty saw that, she climbed on to the roof of the giant's house and coming to the top of the kitchen chimney she threw a great handful of salt from her apron down the chimney into the pot of porridge. Next time the giant tasted it he felt the difference and said: 'It's ower saut, it's ower saut,' but still he went on stirring and still Kitty went on throwing down handfuls of salt, but he always kept repeating: 'It's ower saut, it's ower saut.' At last the giant ordered his servant to go to the well and get some water to put into the porridge and as it was very dark he told him to take with him the Sword of Light that he might see where he was going. So the servant took a pitcher and the Sword of Light and set off for the well.

Then down from the roof Kitty jumped and came softly behind the servant, and just as he stooped down to draw some water from the well, Kitty gave him a great push and down he fell into the water, while Kitty seized the Sword of Light and ran off with it as hard as she could. By and by the giant began to wonder why his servant was so long in coming back, and going to the door to look out there he saw Kitty running away with his precious sword. Off went the giant as hard as he could go to try and catch Kitty, and he ran and she ran, but he could not follow her for his weight would have broken the bridge down.

So Kitty got safe home and gave the king the Sword of Light, and he married his eldest son to her eldest sister as he had promised, and for a time the king seemed quite satisfied.

But by and by he became discontented again and he came to Kitty once more and said: 'Kitty, I wish you would help me again, for that same giant has a most beautiful horse in his stable, with a saddle all hung round with silver bells, and I can't be happy for thinking about that horse and wishing that it was mine. Now if you will only get that horse for me with its beautiful saddle, I will marry my second son to your second sister.'

'Well,' said Kitty, 'I'll try.'

This time she filled her apron with straw, and off she set for the Brig o' ae Hair once more. When she got to the giant's house she went to his stable and there she saw the beautiful horse and its beautiful saddle all covered with silver bells. So she went round the horse and round the horse stuffing every bell with straw to keep it from tinkling. At last when she thought they were all stuffed she got up on the horse and rode away as fast as she could to the Brig o' ae Hair. But unfortunately she had missed one bell, and as soon as she began to move the bell began to tinkle, and out rushed the giant to see who was meddling with his beautiful horse. Kitty, however, had got a good start and though the giant ran very fast she got to the Brig o' ae Hair and got across before the giant could catch her. So the king got the beautiful horse with its beautiful saddle all covered with silver bells, and he married his second son to Kitty's sister as he had promised.

After this the king seemed quite contented for a long time, but at last he came again to Kitty and said: 'Kitty, I can't be happy till I get one thing more. The giant has a beautiful bed cover all covered with precious stones. If you will help me once more and get the beautiful bed cover, I'll marry you myself.'

So Kitty said she would do what she could and again she set off for the giant's house.

This time she went right into the house and upstairs into the giant's bedroom where she crept under the bed with the beautiful bed cover and hid herself.

By and by the giant and his wife went to bed and soon fell asleep and then Kitty stretched out her hand from under the bed and gave the bed cover a great pull. This wakened the giant, who thought it must have been his wife who had disturbed him and he gave her a great shove saying angrily: 'Bide still, bide still.' The poor wife said quite meekly: 'It's no me, it's no me,' but I don't think he believed her. Kitty waited till they were asleep again, and then gave the cover another great pull; you see it was so covered with jewels that it was heavy and difficult to move. Again the giant roared out: 'Bide still, bide still,' and again the poor wife said, half crying: 'It's no me, it's no me.'

Then Kitty stayed quite still till the giant and his wife fell asleep again, and then she gave the cover such a great pull that it came off altogether and this time the giant waked right up and jumped out of bed to see who it was that was making all the disturbance.

He soon found Kitty under the bed, and dragging her out by the hair of her head, said: 'Now Kitty if you were me and I was you, what would you do to me?' You see he was such a stupid man that though he was so big, he had to ask Kitty to help him to think how he might punish her.

'Oh!' said Kitty, 'I'll tell you what I would do. I would make a big bowl of porridge and I would mak ye sup porridge till it cam oot o' your eyes and your mouth and your nose and your lugs, and then I would tie ye up in a sack, and I would go to the forest to cut down a tree, and bring it home and beat upon the sack with it, till ye were dead.'

'Well,' said the giant, 'that is just what I will do to you.'

So he made a great bowl of porridge and gave Kitty a spoon to sup it with, and waited to see how long it would be before the porridge came out of her nose, her eyes and her ears. But after a time he got tired of watching Kitty and turned away to look at something else and then Kitty quickly threw some of the porridge over her face, so that the stupid giant thought that she had eaten so much that it was really coming out of her eyes and her nose as she had said. So then he took Kitty and put her in a sack and tied the mouth of the sack with string, so that she could not get out, and went away into the forest to cut down a tree to beat her with.

But Kitty had a knife in her pocket, and when the giant was gone, she cut a hole in the sack and crept out. Then she caught the giant's wife and his children and his servants, and his cows and his pigs and his cocks and his hens, and his dogs and his cat, and put them all into the bag and tied it up again. After that she seized the beautiful bed cover and ran off with it to the Brig o' ae Hair.

By and by the giant came home with the tree he had cut in the forest, and seeing the bag where he had left it began to beat it thinking that Kitty was still there.

Then began such a noise; the wife screamed, the children cried, the servants roared, while the cows lowed, the pigs squealed, the ducks quacked, the hens cackled, the dog barked and the cat mewed, and they all cried out: 'It's me, it's me, it's me.'

The stupid giant just said: 'Weel do I ken it's you', and went on beating all the time.

At last everything was quiet, and he opened the bag, and then what a surprise he got when he saw what was there! You can fancy what a rage the giant was in now. He just put on his seven league boots and ran after Kitty as hard as he could but she had got such a good start that when he got to the Brig o' ae Hair, there was Kitty sitting on the bank of the river on the other side, quite safe.

'Oh, Kitty,' said the stupid giant, 'tell me how I can get over to you,' and Kitty answered: 'I'll tell you what you must do. Go and get a rope and fasten a stone on to the end of it, and your purse to the middle of it, and throw the end to me and I'll pull you over the river.'

So the giant went and got the rope, and a stone and his purse and fastened them just as Kitty had told him, and then threw the end of the rope with the stone on it, across the river to Kitty, and held on to the other end himself, that Kitty might pull him over the water, for you see the giant could not go across the Brig o' ae Hair as Kitty had done for he was far too heavy and would have broken it down so he had to try and swim.

Well, Kitty pulled and pulled at the rope till she got to the middle where the purse was, and then she let go the rope and the giant fell into the water and was drowned.

As for Kitty, she ran home with the purse and the beautiful bed cover all covered with jewels and gave them to the king, and he married her as he promised and they lived happy and died happy and never drank out of a dry cappy.

22   *Neil Gillies*

RIOBAIDH AND ROBAIDH AND BRIONNAIDH

THERE WERE ONCE TWO widows and one of them had two sons and the other had one son, and the two were called Riobaidh and Robaidh and the one who was his mother's only son was called Brionnaidh; and they had a croft each and a cow each. And Brionnaidh was so good to the cow – he was such a willing worker – but as for Riobaidh and Robaidh, their cow could do no more than keep alive because they were so lazy about doing anything for it. And then they became envious of Brionnaidh because his cow was so much better than their own and one night they went to the byre and set about Brionnaidh's cow until they had killed it and when they had killed it they left it there and took themselves off home.

When Brionnaidh got up next morning and went out to the byre, the cow was dead. He knew fine who had done it: he was certain that it was they who had done it, but anyway, there was nothing to be done about it. He took the cow out of the byre into the open and began to skin the cow, and when he had skinned it and cleaned the hide he set about folding it up, and he put a half-crown in every corner of the hide as he folded it, and when he had done that, he put it on his back and made for the city.

Now, the others were at home – Riobaidh and Robaidh – watching him: they were watching every move he made, but he made off to the city with the hide and he went to one or two houses there and he asked the people if they would buy a cow's hide which would give out half-crowns every time they shook it. Anyway, no-one there believed him.

At last he came to the inn and the innkeeper came out to the door and he said to the innkeeper that he should buy the hide, and anytime he wanted money, all he had to do was shake the hide and half-crowns would fall out of it.

'Go on now,' said he, the innkeeper, to him, 'shake it now till we see,' said he, 'whether they come out of it.' He [Brionnaidh] gave the hide a shake and out came the half-crowns.

'Oh,' said he, 'I'll certainly buy it,' said he. 'How much will you want for it?'

'Oh,' said he, 'I'll want so much for it,' said he.

Anyway, the innkeeper paid him for the hide and when he had done that he set off for home with a good sum of money for the hide, and when he came in sight of the house, the others were at home watching him.

Riobaidh nudged Robaidh and Robaidh nudged Riobaidh. Off they went to meet Brionnaidh and they greeted Brionnaidh:

'Well, Brionnaidh, here you are.'

'Yes,' said he – Brionnaidh.

'And how did you get on?'

'I got on very well,' said he. 'See how much money I got for the hide.'

'Yes indeed!' said they. 'Hadn't we better kill our own cow now,' said they, 'and take her hide.'

'Well indeed you'd better,' said he – Brionnaidh.

This is what they did. They made for the byre. They set about the cow until they had killed it, and when they had killed the cow they took it out and skinned it, and when they had skinned it and folded up the hide they set out for the city to sell it.

Anyway, when they reached the city they began to shout:

'Who will buy a cow hide?'

And, my goodness, not a soul would have anything to do with them. At last the police threatened them that unless they cleared out of the town they would be put in prison. My goodness, they made for home.

Brionnaidh knew now that they really had their knife in him and that they would stop at nothing if they got a chance at him. So this night what he did was, he said to his mother:

'Mother,' said he, 'tonight you'd better go to my room,' said he, 'and I'll go to your room,' said he.

'Yes,' said she – his mother.

This was what happened. He went to his mother's room and his mother went to his room to sleep.

When Riobaidh and Robaidh thought Brionnaidh was asleep they made for his house and they went in and set about Brionnaidh's mother till they had killed her, and when they had done this they made for the door.

Brionnaidh rose in the morning. He went in to see his mother: his mother was dead.

Oh well, it couldn't be helped. He knew fine who had done it.

Anyway, when he saw this he went and set his mother standing up and dressed her in all the best clothes she had and set off with her on his back to the city.

He reached the city – well, the outskirts of the city anyway – and he came upon a big well there and he put down his mother and set her standing above the well and put a walking-stick to keep her upright; and there was a big house a short way beyond the well and he went over to the big house and knocked at the door and the lady of the house came to the door and asked him what he wanted.

'Well,' said he, 'I would like a drink. I've come a long way,' said he, 'and I'm thirsty.'

'All right,' said she, 'you'll get that,' said she. 'Come in,' said she.

And she made him sit down at the table and spread out all sorts of food on the table.

'Go on then,' said she, 'and take your food there,' said she.

'Well,' said he, 'I left my mother over at the well,' said he, 'and I know that she'd take something too,' said he, 'if she could get it, and I'd better go and fetch her,' said he.

'Not at all,' said she. 'You have your meal and the girl can go,' said she.

'Well, if the girl goes,' said he, 'my mother's rather deaf. If you shout at her and she can't hear you, you'll have to go up and give her a little shake.'

And this is what happened. The girl went and started shouting to the old woman who was standing over the well and the old woman paid no attention whatever. Anyway, she went up and shook the old woman and the old woman went head first into the well.

Och, the girl came back to the house in a mortal panic and told them that the old woman had fallen head first into the well.

'And I believe,' said she, 'that she's been drowned.'

And, my goodness, out rushed the lady of the house and out rushed the man himself and out rushed Brionnaidh. So then:

'You'd better not say a word about it,' said he, the gentleman. He was a gentleman, it seems.

'We shall bury your mother,' said he, 'since things have turned out as they have, and a great wake will be held for her,' said he, 'and you will get a good sum over and above that,' said he, 'if you don't say a word about what has happened,' said he.

'Oh no, I won't,' said he – Brionnaidh.

My goodness, the old woman was taken over to the duke's house and a coffin and shroud provided for her and a great funeral arranged for her, and when this was done, the duke – if he was a duke: he was a gentleman anyway – handed over a great sum to Brionnaidh, and not a word to be said about what had happened.

And Brionnaidh made for home and the others were at their house watching for him till he came and when they saw him and he was getting near the house, then Riobaidh nudged Robaidh and Robaidh nudged Riobaidh and off they went to meet Brionnaidh.

'Well, Brionnaidh, here you are.'

'Yes,' said he – Brionnaidh.

'And how did you get on?'

'Very well,' said he. 'I sold my mother, and I got all that money for her,' said he – showing them the bag.

'Did you indeed?' said they.

'I did,' said he.

'And hadn't *we* better kill our own mother and go off with her?'

'Yes, indeed, you'd better,' said he – Brionnaidh.

And that's how it was: they went off home. They set about their mother till they had killed her, and when they had done that, they set off for the city with her. And when they reached the city they were shouting:

'Who will buy a dead old woman? Who will buy a dead old woman?'

And, my goodness, the police swooped on them – they were to clear out of the city with the old woman or they would be put in prison and never get out as long as they lived.

Riobaidh and Robaidh just had to go back home with their mother, relieved to have got away with it, and Brionnaidh knew now that they would be out to get him again – that they would do anything to him to finish him off. And when Brionnaidh saw them coming he made for the hills and off they went after him – Riobaidh and Robaidh. But Brionnaidh was faster than them and was getting the better of them.

Anyway, when he had gone some distance into the hills, whom should he meet but a shepherd with a number of sheep and a dog. He made straight for the shepherd.

'You'd better take off your clothes,' said he, 'so that I can put them on,' said he, 'and I'll take off my own clothes and you can put them on,' said he, 'and I'm only asking you to do this for a short time,' said he, 'and you'll get that bag of money if you'll do it,' said he – Brionnaidh.

'Yes,' said he – the shepherd. 'I will,' said he.

And he did that: the shepherd took off his clothes and Brionnaidh took off his own clothes and the shepherd put on Brionnaidh's clothes, and he put on the shepherd's clothes.

'Well, now,' said he. 'Carry on now in the direction I was going in,' said he, 'and I'll go the way you were going,' said he, 'with the sheep and with the dog,' said he.

The others appeared, Riobaidh and Robaidh and they followed [the shepherd], thinking it was Brionnaidh. They set upon him with stones and clods till they had driven him into a big loch that was there and when they had done that the man was drowned in the loch and they went home. And Brionnaidh had hidden; there was no sign of Brionnaidh.

Anyway, Brionnaidh went and made for home with the sheep and the dog, and wearing the shepherd's clothes. My goodness, they noticed him coming.

'God bless my soul, is this you, Brionnaidh?'

'It is,' said he, 'I'm home.'

'But I thought,' said he [sic], 'that you had been drowned in the loch.'

'Oh no, I wasn't,' said he. 'When I reached the bottom of the loch,' said he, 'this good man was there before me,' said he, 'and he told me to go back as quickly as ever I could,' said he, 'and that he would give me the dog and the sheep and shepherd's clothes: and that was what I did,' said he. 'The shepherd gave me his own clothes,' said he, 'and I put them on and he gave me the sheep,' said he, 'and the dog.'

'Well then, hadn't you better drive *us* into the loch, and who knows but we may find him too.'

'Well indeed I'd better,' said he – Brionnaidh.

This was what happened. Brionnaidh went after them and set upon them with stones and with clods till he had driven them into the loch.

And when he had done that he went home, and they never troubled Brionnaidh again.

That's how I heard it.

23 *Samuel Thorburn*

THE BUTLER'S SON

A LONG TIME AGO, there was a laird in the Highlands – I cannot tell you where he was – but the butler he had had been with him for a very long time. He was a fine honourable man and his master was very pleased with him. But the butler had a son and when he grew up to the age at which he could be useful for service in the big house, he was brought in there.

He had not been very long there when a lot of gold and silver articles went missing and nobody knew where they were. But it was found out that it was the young boy who had taken them – he'd stolen them. And the laird spoke to his father and said to him that he must send the boy away, otherwise, if he didn't send him away, they'd both have to go together with their whole family, and he would have to get a new man in his place.

The father agreed to send the boy away, and he went with him himself in order to apprentice him to a trade in some place. And he reached the town of Glasgow with him, and on the night he arrived, a man came to speak to both of them in the street, realising that they were strangers that he didn't normally see. They got into conversation and he asked him what business brought him to the town

'I came with this boy,' said he, 'so that I could put him where he could learn a trade.'

'Well then,' said the man, 'I will teach him a trade.'

'What trade will you teach him?' said the father to him.

'Robbing,' said he.

'Well, indeed,' said the father, 'I don't think that will be very difficult for you since it is something like that that has put him here.' And he told the man what he had done.

'That makes him all the better,' said he.

The father handed the boy over to the robber. And he went with him, and the robbers had a queer place where they lived – this one wasn't alone at all, there was a gang of them.

When the boy had had a rest, one of them took him out one night to show him how to work things, and let him get to know the town. He went to a big watchmaker's shop there. And they went in together and the robber said to the man on the other side of the counter that he had come to buy a watch. And he gave a brief description of the kind he wanted – he wanted a gold watch. The man set a box of watches over in front of him, and he looked at them, and 'Have you got another kind?' said he.

'Oh, yes,' said the man.

'Show me some more,' said he.

While the man turned his back, he was looking at the watches and he put one of them down his sleeve. And the man came over with the other box and he looked among them.

'Oh,' said he, 'none of these will do, they're not what I'm looking for.'

'Oh, if they aren't,' said the man, 'it cannot be helped.'

He went away and the young boy stayed. And when the robber had gone off with the watch he said to the man who was over behind the counter:

'Did you see,' said he, 'the thing that that man did?'

'What did he do?' said the man.

'Dash it,' said he, 'he put one of your watches in his sleeve and went off with it.'

The man counted the watches, and wasn't he short of a watch right enough? He ran out to get a policeman – to chase the man, but the man wasn't to be seen. And when the young boy got him out of the way he put the lid on one of the boxes and he put it under his jacket and he himself went and took another road; it was not the road he thought the man who had gone after the robber had taken that he took.

He arrived at the place where the robbers were staying and he went in.

'Dash it,' said the robber to him, 'did you see now how neatly I worked that? Do you think you would be able to do such a thing?'

'Aye, it was very good,' said the young boy, 'but I think I have done every bit as well as you,' and he took the box out from under his oxter and he put it on the table, full of watches.

That was that. It was a night or two later that they left again and went out to the country to rob a house there in which there were riches. And they got in without anyone hearing them. They were going about and there was a cellar in the house and they lowered the young boy down into that cellar on a rope to see if he found valuables there. He wasn't long down when the people of the house heard something and they got up and the robbers fled and got clean away without being caught. The young one didn't know what to do. It didn't seem that there was anyone up there who could haul him up on the rope, nor indeed was there a rope to be seen. But it seems that he had something – he lit a match or something and looked around. In a corner of the cellar he saw the hide of an ox or a cow that had been skinned and the horns and everything on it and the legs. And he couldn't see a better way than to wrap it around himself. And he took one of the legs of the beast in each hand and he began to knock and strike everything around him, and he made a dreadful noise and din. And it seems that somebody came above him and shouted to him, 'Who is that?'

'It is I,' said he.

'Who are you?'

'Oh,' said he, naming the Evil One by name, 'I am he, and if you do not give me the keys of the house so that I can get out of here I will take you and the house along with me on my horns.'

The man looked down. Evidently he had some light and down there he saw the most awful apparition that he had ever seen. There was nothing for it but to throw the keys to him, and he began to open doors until he got outside.

When he got outside, I believe he threw the keys away, but he kept the hide – he took it with him. He arrived at the robbers' hideout and what were they doing – they had sold a lot of the loot they had got, and what were they doing but quarrelling about sharing it. And he put his head with the horns in through some hole, and he banged with the legs on something and he shouted to them very loudly. 'Leave it for me,' said he; 'you have been working for me a long time earning it.' Everybody fled, the one who couldn't grab a bow would grab a sword, and they went in all directions and before he could blink an eye there was not a living soul in the place, and the money was there for him in heaps. He went in and gathered up every last brass farthing of it and took it with him.

He left then and made for his father's house. He got home. 'Oh, you wretched wrecker,' said his father, 'what sent you home here? I will lose my job and we shall all have to go.' But anyway it came to the laird's ears that he had come, or else he himself saw him, I don't know which, and he sent for his father.

'Did I not understand,' said he, 'that your son was sent away to learn a trade?'

'Oh, I did that,' said the other, 'but he wasn't long away when he came home.'

'Well, he couldn't learn a trade,' said he, 'in the time that he was away.'

'Oh well, I think he learnt it very well,' said his father, 'it seems that he did very well while he was away.'

'And what trade was it?'

'Robbing,' said he.

'Oh well, if he learnt his trade as well as that,' said he, 'go home and say to him,' said he, 'that I will put a bullet through his head tomorrow,' said he, 'if he doesn't steal the sheet that will be under myself and my wife as we sleep in the bed tonight.'

'Oh well,' said the father to him, 'you might just as well go and do it now,' said he, 'because he hasn't got the ability to do that.'

'I won't do it just now,' said he, 'until he fails to do that. But if he fails I will do it.'

When his father went home he told this to the boy and the boy was not put out in the least. He went off when night came and there was a body in the churchyard which had been buried a day or two before. And he went and dug it up and he got clothing belonging to himself and dressed the body up with it. He put it on his shoulder and he went to the laird's house during the night when everyone had gone to bed. He got a ladder and placed it against the window of the bedroom of the laird and his wife. And when he put it to the window he had a rope and he tied it to the body down below and went up the ladder dragging the body with him. And he managed to raise the laird's bedroom window and he put its head against the window.

'Here he comes,' said the laird, 'but if he has come he will not go as he came.' He had a gun by his side in the bed, and the one who was outside [was] putting the head of the body in, bit by bit, and when the laird made out the side of its head coming in at the window he fired a shot. And as he did, the man outside threw – gave the body a little push inside and it made a thump on the floor below the window. And the laird jumped out of bed. 'I must go,' said he, 'and put him out of sight somewhere,' said he, 'and we won't let on that he ever came; no matter what people say we won't let on that we ever saw him and there won't be many questions asked about him.'

That is how it was. He got up and went away with the body. And it seems that when the young lad who was outside had got the laird away carrying the body, he went running inside, and he knew which way to go with the previous knowledge he had of the house. And he reached the bedroom of the laird and his wife and, 'Oh,' said he, 'that brute is awfully heavy to carry,' said he. 'I don't know what to get to put him in. Give me,' he said, 'this sheet on the bed,' said he, 'and I will put him in it and go with him.' He got the sheet and he left. The wife thought that it was her husband right enough, but it was not long till her husband came and she was looking for another sheet to put on the bed. She didn't like to waken the household, the servants, and again she didn't want what had happened to be discovered, and she was looking for something to put on the bed. 'Dash it,' said her husband, the laird to her, 'why are you up at this time?'

'Do I not need a sheet for the bed?' said she. 'Did you not take away the sheet yourself,' said she, 'to bury that man you killed as he was coming in at the window?'

The laird realised then that the young boy was too much for him, and that he had better just keep quiet. His father remained in his service and I don't know which way the young boy went after that. I haven't heard any more about him.

THE FARMER WHO WENT
BACK ON HIS AGREEMENT

WELL, THIS FARMER used to fee farm servants, and the contract he made with the servants before he would fee them, he told them the rules, which were that if they went back on their agreement before their time was up, they were to lose a strip of skin from the back of their heads down to their rumps, three fingers wide. And if he went back on the agreement the same thing would happen to him, the servant could do the same thing to him. This was all right, and he would fee someone now and then, and everyone he got he wasn't long, not a moment with him when he went back on his agreement. And he took this strip of skin off them, and they used to be pretty poorly for a long time after, until it healed up.

Anyway he'd had a whole lot of them that this had happened to. But this man, he was a near neighbour of one person this happened to, and he said he would fee with him next, he'd try the job . . . He went to see the farmer and asked him if he needed a farm servant, and he said he did need a servant. 'But,' he said, 'do you know the terms my servants get?'

'No,' he said, 'not really, but I'd like to hear them.'

'Well,' said the man, 'if you go back on our agreement before your time is up, a strip of skin three fingers wide will come off from the back of your head right down your back to your rump. And if I go back on it the same thing will be done to me.'

'Fine, then,' said he. 'We'll try it.'

'If you'll come on these terms we'll manage all right.'

'Yes, I'll come then,' he said.

'Fine.'

Off he went to work with the man.

The morning of the first day he asked the farmer what he had to do today. He said, 'First of all, you've to go and look for the horses.'

'And where will I find them?' said he.

'Try where you think they might be and where you don't.'

'Fine, then,' he said, and off he went. He went over to the byre and got a graip. He came back and climbed up the side of the house. In those days most people had thatched houses: all the farmers did. He set to work tearing down the thatch from a good way up above the door.

The farmer came out and saw him. 'You walking disaster area,' he said, 'what are you doing up there?'

'I'm looking for the horses,' said he.

'You knew fine the horses wouldn't be there.'

'Yes,' he said, 'but you told me to go and look for them where I thought they might be and where I didn't. I knew fine they weren't here, but I did what you told me.'

'Then come down out of that, you disaster area. I'm sorry I ever met you.' However, 'Are you going back on our agreement?' said the farmer.

'No,' he said. 'Are *you* going back on it?'

'Well, no,' said he: 'not yet, anyway.'

Well, this was all right. That day passed and he kept going. Next day he asked him after breakfast what he should do today.

'Make a sheep's footpath [through the bog],' said he.

'Fine, then,' said he. Off he went, taking the dog with him, and gathered every sheep that was to be seen, put them into the fank, and set about cutting their feet off from the knee, and laying them out in a row, one after the other.

Along came the farmer. 'You misbegotten misfortune,' said he, 'what are you doing here?'

'Just what you told me,' said he. 'You told me to make a sheep's foot path, and you've got the feet laid out in a row there as you told me.'

'Are you going back on our agreement?' said he.

'No,' said he, said the servant. 'Are *you* going back on it?'

'Oh, not yet,' said he. He just went and gave him something else to do . . .

Next evening . . . I think it was next evening, there was to be a wedding party in the village, and he told . . . the servant, 'We've got an invitation to the wedding, and you're to come along tonight,' said he, 'and I'll be in charge of supplies, and when anything's running short,' he said, 'give me the eye, cast an eye at me now and then when you need anything.'

He went out to the byre, and got . . . his pockets filled with eyes from the cattle. And he went to the wedding. Every time he got a chance at the farmer he aimed an ox's eye at him as accurately as he could. The farmer began to wonder what he was throwing at him. Then he managed to catch one of the things he was throwing at him, looked at it and realised it was an animal's eye.

He left [at once]. But anyhow, when they got home he went into the byre. Half of all the cattle he had in the byre had not one eye between them. And . . . he went into the house. 'What,' said he, 'you walking disaster area,' said he, 'did you do there last night, taking the eyes out of my cattle?'

'Didn't you ask me,' said he, 'to keep giving you the eye when I was short of anything? Wasn't I doing that at the wedding all night long?'

'Well, that's true,' said he, 'you disaster area. Are you going back on our agreement?' said the farmer.

'No,' said he. 'Are *you* going back on it?'

'Oh, I'm going back on it now,' said he, 'and I didn't do it soon enough.'

'Then I'll take the strip of skin off you,' said he.

He started, and he didn't spare him either, he tore him off a good strip. And the farmer was not fit to do anything much for a good while. He never took a strip of skin off any of his farm servants again after it happened to himself.

WILLIE TAKE-A-SEAT

LONG AGES AGO, there was a cunning old wife staying close to Kylerhea who owned Beinn na Caillich and a good deal of the land around there. Though the old woman was well off, with plenty of goods and chattels, she was very close and mean. Nobody who ever came to her house was invited to come in or sit down. She and the Lochaber men who used to go to the Isle of Skye to raid cattle were in league, for she always helped them on their way as they came and went across the sound . . . The old woman never helped the Lochaber rogues without getting good payment for it, but others never got a sight of her fireside.

However or whatever, there was a shrewd, clever man by the name of William who had come to live at Leac a' Chaoil on the Glenelg side of the sound. And one particular evening, while he and others were talking about the behaviour of the miserable woman, he wagered that he would make her ask him to come in and sit down, for all she could do to stop him. That was all there was to it. William set out for the old woman's house. He knocked at the door and out she came.

(Hag:)   'Where have you come from?'
(William:)   'I have come from Leac a' Chaoil, my dear woman, as night began to fall.'
(Hag:)   'What's your name?'
(William:)   'It's Willie Take-a-Seat.'
(Hag:)   'That's a queer name you have, Willie Take-a-Seat.'
(William:)   'I will indeed, when the goodwife of the house asks me.'
So saying, he went in through the door.

(Hag:)	'If you sit down you'll regret it. You'll get nothing here but the bare floor, potholes and fleas: lean fleas from the floor nibbling your two buttocks without mercy.'
(William:)	'Goodwife, bring me food. Let God come between me and my misery.'
(Hag:)	'You won't get enough food here to cover a winkle's lid.'
(William:)	'I see you have a sheep's head and trotters up there.'
(Hag:)	'Even so you won't get much of it. What you can take away with a rhyme you shall have, but I'm going to start first:

'Two brows, two seers,
   Two ears, two tallows,
Two crooked jawbones,
   Eight fist talons,
The head's high speaker
   And four shanks with marrow.'

The old woman meant to have every bit for herself, and she was quite convinced she had named every part of the head and trotters that was worth eating in the rhyme, and there would be nothing left for the other one. But she didn't know who she was dealing with. Thereupon William answered:

'The man who carves the head has a right
   To the eyes, jowls and brains,
The ear with its roots,
   Jaw's son, cheek and temple.'

It is evident from this that William had the better part, for the things he named in his rhyme are by far the meatiest parts of the head. Then the head was divided and cooked, and William started to eat it.

(Hag:)	'You're a terrible eater.'
(William:)	'I earned it all myself.'

(Hag:)   'Many a one who has earned has given.'

(William:) 'Go to those you have given something and get it back.'

When he had finished eating the meat, William began to sup the broth. That was the way with the old Gaels, to eat the meat first and sup the broth after it. As William was lifting a spoonful of broth to his mouth, the old woman said: 'What a heavy load on that thin shank.'

(William:) 'It hasn't all that far to go.'

(Hag.)   'Short as it is it's uphill.'

(William:) 'No sooner up than it's down.'

(Hag:)   'Oh man, aren't you sharp? I'm sure your father must have been a bard.'

(William:) 'No-one barred him from their house, and you've not barred me!'

---

26   *Gilbert Voy*

THE PARSON'S SHEEP

Away back in the old days in Orkney there were some gey pitiful times. Jimmock O' Tissiebist, wi' a scrythe o' peerie bairns, were warse off than maist: wi' the sheep aa deein', and the tatties a failure, things at Tissiebist wisna lookin' ower bright for Christmas.

Whatever wyes or no, one blashie dark night, Jimmock was away a while, and twa – three days efter, an uncan yowe was seen aboot the hoose. Some of the bairns surely kent the yowe, for one day when ane of them was oot herdin' the kye, he was singin' to himsel' aboot it, something like this:

> Me father's stol'n the parson's sheep
> An' we'll hae mutton an' puddin's tae eat
> An' a mirry Christmas we will keep,
> But we'll say nethin' aboot it.
>
> For if the parson gets to know,
> It's ower the seas we'll have tae go,
> And there we'll suffer grief an' woe
> Because we stole fae the parson.

Well, up jumps the parson fae the other side o' a faelie dyke, and he says tae the boy: 'Boy, look here, if you'll come to the church on the Sabbath and sing that same song, I'll gie thee a suit o' claes and half a croon.'

So, on the Sunday mornin' service, efter the minister had read a psalm and said a prayer, he stood up and he said in an a'ful lood voice: 'I hev the following intimation to make. Stand up, boy, and sing that same song as I heard you singin', herdin' the kye.'

But the peerie boy hed mair wit than that. This is what he sang:

> As I was walkin' oot one day
> I spied the parson very gay:
> He was tossin' Molly in the hay –
> He turned her upside down, sir.
>
> A suit o' claes and half a croon
> Was given tae me be Parson Broon
> Tae tell the neighbours all aroon'
> What he hed done tae Molly!

HOW TO DIDDLE

WELL, THIS IS A horse that . . . I took away to Kelso, to the horse-sale, for to sell, and before I went to Kelso I met Mr Walker fae —, and he says to me, he says, '. . . H' much d' you want for that horse?'

I says, 'I want a hundred pound for't.'

'Well,' he says, 'I'll jist give it ye. Now,' he says, 'I'll tell ye what to do,' he says, 'you take it away along to the Anderson stables at Kelso, and leave it there.'

Ye see,. . . I says, 'Right-oh.' So away I went,. . . and of course . . . Mr Walker . . . paid me, right on the spot. [Comment from Mr Walker – 'By God, you were lucky.'] – I was lucky – so jist before I arrived at, eh, at Anderson's stables, I met Mr Wilson o' —. He says . . . 'Is that horse for sale?'

I says, 'Aye.'

'How much d'you want for't?'

I says, 'I want a hunder pound for't.'

'Well,' he says, he says, 'is it sound?'

I says, 'It's as soond as brass.'

'Well,' he says, 'I'll give ye't.'

'Well,' I says, 'got to be paid the now.'

He says, 'Oh aye,' he says, 'I'll pay ye,' so he gave us a hunder quid. But I gave him the helter shank . . . an a', an I cleared oot, an I forgot, I forgot a' aboot . . . Mr Walker, but . . . I'd an extra hunder pound into ma pocket, what I was wantin', so that's a', 'twas a' 't I was worryin aboot.

So ever, at the finish after I was home, he phoned us up, he says, eh, 'Wha' aboot that horse?'.

. . . I says, 'What aboot it?'

He says, 'The horse that I bought off ye.'

'Oh,' I says, '. . . I gave it tae another man.'

He says, 'Whae was that other man?'

I says, 'Wilson o' —.'

'Oh.' An he says, 'Wha' aboot ma hundred pound?'

'Oh,' I says, . . . I says, 'I've naething to dae wi that now,' I says, . . . I says, 'ye'll have tae . . . fend for yersel aboot that.' So . . . he got on tae the phone . . . tae —, – oh . . . a kind o' argument, and . . . one thing and another . . . and what a' passed atween them I don't know but there were a few days passed and the p'liceman arrived. Ye see? And he got, he got the story off them, ye see, an . . . went away, and 'twisnae long comin back wi' . . . a Summons . . .

So, I went in, and ma mother says to me, she says, 'What was that polisman daein here?'

'Oh,' I says, . . . 'I've got in a . . .' . . . I was t'appear at the court.

So . . . oh, of course, ma mother was in a terrible state, ye see, aboot me havin t'appear at the court . . . so, . . . 'Well,' she says, 'Ye'll have to go and see a lawyer.'

So, I says, 'What lawyer there wis ye gaun tae?'

She says, 'There's, there's a good man at Hawick.'

So . . . away I went to Hawick. I went in and he says, 'Well,' he says, 'What can I do for you today?'

I says, 'I dinna ken what ye can dae for us.' I says, 'I'll ha' to show ye this . . .'

So, showed him . . . and . . . he says, 'Aye,' he says, 'You've got'n yoursel' intae a bit o' a fix.'

I says, I says, 'I ken that a' right.'

He says, ... 'Are ye able to sing?'

I says, 'No.'

He says, he says, he says, 'Are ye able tae . . . deedle?'

'Oh,' I says, 'I could deedle.'

'Well,' he says, 'from now onward,' he says, 'if anybody mentions this to you, jist you say,

Di dee-dle di dee di dee di dee, di dee-dle di dee di dee di dee

'Oh yes, I can dae that.'

So home I goes, an I meets ma mother, she says . . .'How did ye come on, son?' Says I,

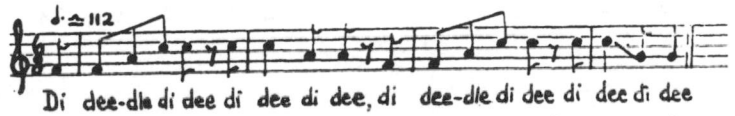

Di dee-dle di dee di dee di dee, di dee-dle di dee di dee di dee

So however, here the court,. . . I was t'appear at the court, an . . . in I goes. And, it wasnae long till . . . 'George Jamieson,'. . . shouted oot, so of course I stood up, an . . . doon at the dock,. . . an the prosecutin fiscal read oot the charge, aboot this a', and the next a', an dear knows a'. [?what he said] – I wisnae listening quite til it a' . . . And eh,. . . th'auld judge looks round tae me, he says, 'D'ye plead Guilty, or Not Guilty?' Says I,

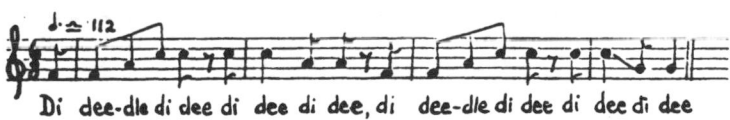

Di dee-dle di dee di dee di dee, di dee-dle di dee di dee di dee

He says, '*Do you plead Guilty or Not Guilty?*' Says I,

Di dee-dle di dee di dee di dee, di dee-dle di dee di dee di dee

So he looked doon at the prosecutin' fiscal, an he says tae . . . I don't know exactly what he was a' saying tae him, but he says, 'Look here,' he says, 'take this man oot o' here.' Ye see? So right enough,. . . an I just walkit oot, and *kept gaun oot*, and just as I was gaun oot I met the s'licitor at the door. He says, eh, 'How did ye come on?'

'Oh,' I says, 'I've gotten off.'

'Oh,' he says, 'I knew ye'd get off,'. . . ye see. 'Well,' he says, 'for tae . . . for tae . . . save time . . .' he says, 'for sending in the account,' he says, 'you owe me . . . three poun.' Says I,

Di dee-dle di dee di dee di dee, di dee-dle di dee di dee di dee

28   *Alasdair Stewart*

THE TAILOR AND HIS WIFE

[THIS WOMAN], her husband was a tailor, and . . . she and the tailor . . . they worked, and they got on well enough, but one way and another they got short of money. Their money ran out, and the tailor said he was going away to practise his trade.

'I must go,' said he, 'as a travelling tailor,' said he, 'and see if I can get a bit more money than I'm getting.'

'Oh well then,' said she, 'off you go then,' said she, 'but I'm not going away at all.'

'All right,' said he, 'you can stay.'

She stayed [at home], and one day, who should come along but the local schoolmaster and . . . the schoolmaster came in and asked – she was just a young woman – the schoolmaster asked if he could go to bed with her, and she said he could if he gave her five pounds.

'Well,' said he, 'you're pretty expensive.' But anyway, 'Well, well,' he said, 'I'll give you that then.'

But anyway, just at that moment what should come but a knock at the door, and when the knock at the door came she didn't know where to put him. She shoved him in the cupboard, and who came in then but the minister himself. In came the minister, and what the minister asked for was just the same thing.

'Oh,' said she, 'all right,' said she, 'if you give me five pounds.'

'You're pretty expensive,' said he, 'but, come, come,' said he, 'we won't quarrel [over it].'

The minister was just getting into bed with her when there came another knock at the door. She shoved him into the cupboard on the bottom shelf. Now the pair of them were in there. Who came in then but the doctor.

The doctor came in, and the doctor asked for the very same thing. And she . . . told the doctor just the same story – that he'd get it if he gave her five pounds.

'Oh, you're pretty expensive,' said he, 'but we won't quarrel [over it].'

The doctor went and got in. There came a 'knock, knock' at the door.

'Oh, here's the tailor coming!' said she. 'He's come home.'

She shoved him on to the top shelf. And in came .. . who was it but the tailor. By now she had fifteen pounds. In came the tailor.

'Have you made anything while you've been away?' said she. 'You've been a long time away.'

'Yes,' said he, 'I've made ten pounds.'

'Huh, well,' said she, 'I've made more than that myself,' said she. 'I've made fifteen pounds,' said she.

'And what were you doing?' said he.

'Taking pictures,' said she.

'And what pictures did you take?'

'I took the teacher,' said she, 'and I took the minister, and I took the doctor. Come over and see them.' She opened the cupboard.

'Ah well, well, well,' said he, 'aren't these good likenesses. I'd take my Bible oath,' said he, 'that that's the teacher . . . and the minister . . . and the doctor, except for one thing you've done to the doctor,' said he, 'you've made that bit of him just slightly . . . a little too long, and I think I'll just snip a bit off it with my scissors.'

When they heard that they made a dash for the door – all three of them.

I don't know what happened to them – they went away then.

THE WREN

WELL, THERE WAS A night of falling and drifting snow and the wren, he didn't know where he could go. He could find no place to go, and such a night of falling and drifting snow that you couldn't see a thing for the drifting. But he came to a sheep there in the field.

'Oh,' said he to the sheep, 'Won't you let me into your wool till morning?'

'Oh no,' said the sheep, 'you can't come here.'

But he came to one little speckled sheep.

'Oh,' said he, 'I wish you would let me into your wool till morning.'

'Oh, come on, you poor thing,' said she. 'You won't do me any harm by being in my wool.'

So he got into the wool and he was sweating, he was so warm. In the morning he got up and when he came out in the morning, the sheep's throat was cut and the sheep was dead.

Oh, he didn't know what he should do. But when he got up in the morning,

'Oh well,' said he, 'I must find the cur who killed my hostess,' said he, 'before I leave here.'

And he rose and went to the farmer – he went to the farmer and said to the farmer – he told him word for word how the sheep had been killed, his hostess, and if he would be good enough to find him the cur who had done that, he would pay for it. And this was refused to him. And he said to the farmer,

'If you do that for me,' said he, 'I'll give you a cask of wine that was washed ashore.'

'Oh, where is it?' said the farmer.

'It's down here on the shore,' said he. 'It was washed in by the sea, but,' said he, 'you can't carry it away. You'll have to take the horse and sledge down to the shore.'

The old fellow came and harnessed the horse to the sledge and he and the wren went down to the shore.

'There now,' said the wren. 'There is the cask of wine for you and I hope,' said he, 'that you'll find the cur who did that to my hostess.'

'Och yes,' said the old fellow.

He looked around when he had got the cask up on to the sledge:

'Get out of here,' he said to the wren, 'or I'll knock your head off with my finger.'

'I believe you would do that,' said he, 'but before you move from there,' said he, 'I'll kill your horse.'

No! I have gone ahead of my story.

'I'll do this to you – I'll spill your cask of wine,' said he.

'What would *you* do that with?' said the farmer.

He started and he was pecking and pecking and pecking away at it:

'Oh my goodness,' said the farmer, 'you'll do just that.'

And what was in the sledge but a big axe. He picked up the axe and the first swipe he took at the wine cask, the wine cask smashed like that! The farmer was left with nothing of it.

'I'll do worse than that to you,' said the wren. 'I'll kill your horse.'

'Ach!' said the farmer, 'what would *you* do that with?'

'Oh, just you let me be,' said he.

He went over to the horse's face and started to peck away under his forelock. The old fellow raised the big axe: the first swipe he took at the horse, he knocked its brains out with the axe. The horse was dead!

'I'll do worse than that to you,' said he, 'I'll break your sledge.'

Oh my goodness, the wren was pecking away at the sledge and everything. The old fellow smashed the sledge to smithereens with the axe. Every time the wren sat down he thought he would get a crack at him but by the time he was through he had smashed the whole sledge.

'Huh!' said the wren. 'I'll do worse than that to you. I'll break your shank.'

Now he was working away at his shank and the old fellow raised the big axe and the first swipe he took at himself in the shank, he broke his leg. The old fellow could not get up from there. But they came down – the boys – and they did not know what the old fellow was up to – why he had not come home. But at long last they came down and took the old fellow up on a bedspread to the house. He came up on the bedspread and they got him into bed: the old fellow was lying in bed now and the bed was beside the window.

The wren came up from the shore. The cows and the bull were there grazing in the field. Oh, he came up to the bull – the wren:

'You haven't got much there, my poor fellow.'

'No,' said the bull, 'I haven't got much here.'

'Oh but hasn't your master got plenty,' said he, 'in the barn?'

'Ach yes,' said the bull, 'but I can't get in to it.'

'Hoch, haven't you got a pair of big horns?' said he. 'Put your two horns in under the door,' said he, 'and you can lift the door off the hinges and you can go in then and eat as much as you like.'

'My goodness,' said the bull, 'I think that's just what I'll do.'

The bull went up to the door of the barn and, as he had told him, he put his horn in under the door and the door came off the hinges, and the door fell down. The bull went in, himself and the cows and there they ate turnips, oats, hay, everything they could find, till they burst and died. There they were, dead.

And after all this he [the wren] came into the barn – or wherever it may have been – and there was a big bitch there with puppies.

'Oh you poor thing,' said he to the bitch, 'you are hungry.'

'Oh yes,' said the bitch, 'I am hungry.'

'Well,' said he, 'if you do one thing for me,' said he, 'I'll give you plenty of food.'

'Will you?' said the bitch.

'Yes, plenty of meat.'

'Well, and what,' said the bitch, 'am I going to do for you?'

'If you will kill the cur,' said he, 'who killed my hostess, I'll give you plenty of meat.'

'Oh I will,' said the bitch.

And it was a fox.

'He is in,' said he, 'in his hole – in his den, and I'll go into the den,' said the wren, 'and I'll send him out by a trick to the door and you'll get a grip on him at the door of the den, and I'll give you plenty of food,' said he.

Well, this is how it was. The wren came in and he said to the fox,

'Och, och,' said he, 'what a state you're in lying there,' said he, 'when there's plenty of food down there,' said he.

'Indeed,' said the fox, 'I dare say there is.'

'I *know*,' said he, 'that there is.'

'Well,' said the fox, 'I'll go out and get some of it.'

The fox came out and, when the fox came out, the bitch caught him and killed him.

'Well, well now,' said the wren. 'You can go down to the shore,' said he to the bitch then, 'and there's a horse there that was killed today,' said he. 'Sit down there,' said he, 'and you'll get as much food as you can eat.'

'Oh, I'm sure I will,' said the bitch.

The bitch went down and she got plenty of food from the horse, plenty of meat.

And now there he was, the wren, and when he was there, there was a night of falling and drifting snow that night, and didn't it happen that the old fellow's window was open. The wind blew the wren in and he landed on the old fellow's bed and the old fellow put out his hand:

'Ah!' said he, 'I think I've got you now. I've got you now,' said he, 'the fellow who did the damage to me. I'll give you what for!'

'Oh, let me go,' said the wren, 'let me go, and I've got a little lump of gold under my wing for you. Well, open your hand,' said he, 'and you'll get it.'

The old fellow opened his hand and the wren made a 'Yoop!' of his droppings on him – in his hand.

'There!' said he. 'I'm not much of a lump of gold, the whole lot of me.'

And he sprang across on to the dresser. But the old fellow got up and he got a stick, a shepherd's crook. He sprang on to the dresser, he sprang on to the shelf, he sprang on to the mantelpiece – the wren. The old fellow was smashing everything, till he had smashed, he had made . . . he had smashed every single thing that was in the house, and he hasn't got the wren yet. I don't know that they aren't still at it.

That's the Story of the Wren for you.

OTHER CLEVERNESS, STUPIDITY AND NONSENSE

THE KING'S THREE QUESTIONS

THERE WAS A PRIEST in Scotland and he did something wrong, and gave great offence to the king – it was one of the Jameses. And he was to be executed. But the king allowed him a chance: if he came to see him in his palace at Scone, and answered three questions the king would put to him, he would go free. And he knew well enough that there were some questions he couldn't answer because of the way someone had framed them – that there are questions that nobody at all can answer if they are put in a certain way – no-one else. Well, this was worrying him a lot, and he was just pacing up and down the house day and night, and his brother, who lived with him and was a simpleton – everybody just called him 'the fool' – he said to him:

'What's bothering you now?'

'Och, what use is it for me to tell a fool like you?'

'Oh, but I might be able to do something, give you advice, or something or other like that.'

Well, he told him how it was, that he was condemned to death, but he had one chance: if he could answer the three questions the king put to him in his own palace, then he would get off.

'Well, there are questions,' said his brother to him, 'that you couldn't . . . that you *can't* answer.'

'And what am I going to do?' said the priest.

'Well, I'll go in your place.'

'Oh no. What's a fool like you going to do?'

'Well, look here. What will happen to me if you are executed? I'm just going to be a fearful idiot wandering through this world, making sport for everyone. Won't you let me go there: if I'm executed, it won't make any difference at all.'

Well, the priest agreed that his brother should go, and he put on the priest's habit, took the priest's staff and set off. He came to the king's palace in Scone; he knocked on the door; a big man came to it beautifully dressed in a fine blue and red uniform and asked him who he was; he told him that he was the priest, and all that, and:

'What do you want?'

'I want to see the king.'

'Come in, he's expecting you.'

He was taken to the king's room, and the king was sitting there on a big throne, with gold chains round his neck and wearing lots of beautiful things.

'Come in.'

He went over to him and took off his hat. The king said to him: 'You know the reason why you are here.'

'Yes,' he said.

'Well, well, then, we might as well just begin now. First question, then – where is the centre of the world?'

'It is right here,' said he; he knocked with his staff on the middle of the floor.

'Oh well, I must let you have that. You know, yes, I believe that the world is round like a ball, and anywhere will do for its centre. Heh, I'll give you that one. Next question, then – what am I worth sitting on the throne here? Just what am I worth in money?'

'Well,' said the man to him, 'you're not worth any more than thirty pieces of silver, anyway.'

'Why do you say that?'

'The best man who was ever born in the world was sold for thirty pieces of silver.'

'You've got it. I must give you that one too. The third one – if you can answer this, you're really damned good,' said he. 'Do you know of anything I'm thinking . . . the king is thinking at the moment, and he's entirely wrong?'

'Yes,' said he.

'What's that, then?'

'You're talking . . . you think you're talking to the priest, and you're talking to the fool, his brother.'

'Well,' said the king, 'anyone who has a brother like that, and that brother a fool, deserves to get off. Away you go!'

30b   *John Stewart*

THE KING AND THE MILLER

A'M TELLIN YE A LITTLE STORY aboot a miller an his daughter: he hed one o the nicest daughters could be seen in the country, an everybody hed a fancy of her. And the keeng – the young king was livin not very far from her an he hed a notion of her, an he didnae know what way for tae gain this girl. An he went doon tae the mill one day, and he said, 'A'm goin to gie ye three questions,' he says, 'miller, an ye know,' he says, 'the keeng's word's never broke. And if ye don't answer me that three questions,' he says, 'your head will go on my gate.'

'Well,' says the miller, 'if A can answer them A'll try ma best.'

He says, 'Ye know,' he says, 'that I can do what I like,' he says, 'I'm keeng o this country, an my word'll stand.'

'Very well,' says the miller, he says, 'what is it?'

'Well,' he says, 'you must tell me,' he says, 'the weight o the moon. That's wan. You must tell me,' he says, 'hoo many stars is in the heavens. That's two. An you must – third one,' he says, 'you must tell me what A'm thinkin on.'

'Oh well,' says the miller, he says, 'A doot my heid'll go on yir gates.'

An he says, 'Gin this time a year an a day,' he says, 'A'll be doon,' he says, 'an ask ye the questions. An if ye're not right,' he says, 'yir head comes off.'

So this poor miller now, he's gaun up an doon, thinkin tae himsel what could he say or what could he do. An there's a young shepherd lad not very far away, an he was helpin him at the hairvest, takin in the hairvest. An . . . the shepherd chap says tae him, 'Gosh bless me, miller,' he says, 'what's ado wi ye? Ye're [? aa] awfae dour be when I cam here first.'

'Yes,' he says, 'laddie, A'm dour. An if you kent,' he says, 'what I ken,' he said, 'you would be dour too.'

He says, 'What is it?'

So he told the shepherd what he wis told be the keeng. An he says, 'You know the keeng's word,' he says, 'goes far.'

'Oh well,' he says, 'A'll tell you one thing,' he says, 'miller,' he says: 'if you promise me tae get your daughter,' he says, 'as a wife,' he says, 'A'll clear ye o that.'

'Well,' he says, 'A can't give her,' he says, 'unless she's willin.' An he goes in tae his daughter an he asks her a question; he says, 'My daughter,' he says, 'ye know,' he says, 'what I've tae suffer.'

She said, 'Yes.'

He says, 'Would you get my life saved,' he says, 'fir tae mairry a man?'

She says, 'A wid mairry,' she says, 'the day, if it wid save yir life.'

'Well,' he says, 'there a man'll save my life if ye marry him.'

'Who is he?' she says.

He says, 'So an so's shepherd.'

'Well,' she says, 'he's as good as what I am. A'll marry him if he'll save yir life, but not, faither, till yir life's saved.'

'A'll bet yez [?] he'll save my life – I think.'

So the shepherd an them agreed that he would save his life. So that day year – it's a Hogmanay night – he was up the side o the dam an who did he meet but this young keeng.

'Good evenin, shepherd' – A'm goin wrong wi ma story now . . . Just a minute . . . A should have said that the shepherd dressed himsel up with a white baerd an put on the miller's suit o clothes on him, and he's away up beside the dam fir tae meet the keeng: this was the night he wis tae meet him an answer his questions. So –

'Good evenin, miller.'

'Good evenin, ma noble keeng,' he said.

'Did you answer my questions?'

'Oh well,' he says, 'so far as I think,' he says, 'A hiv.'

He says, 'What weight is the moon?'

He says, 'The moon'll be a hundredweight. There's four quaarters in the moon,' he says, 'an there four quarters in a hundredweight.'

He says, 'That's very good! Can ye tell me hoo mony stars,' he says, 'as shines in the heavens?'

'Oh, there'll be aboot seven million, five hundred an fifty-five, an if ye dinnae believe me ye can coont them yirsel.'

'A cannae – I cannae coont them,' . . . says the keeng. He says, 'Ye cannae tell me,' he says, 'what . . . A'm thinkin on. This one'll . . . puzzle ye,' he says.

'Yes,' he says, 'A can. You think,' he says, 'ye're speakin tae the auld miller, but ye'll fin' it's his son-in-laa ye're talkin to!'

So the young fella got the auld man saved an married the girl. So that's the end o ma story.

DONALD AND THE SKULL

THIS OLD MAN, he was walking through the wood –
Red-haired Donald he was called. And what did he come across in the
wood but a skull (a man's head, you know – bone, a skull as they called
it.) He kicked it with his shoe like that. 'What,' said he, 'sent you here?'
and the head answered him, 'Speaking sent me here,' it said. The old
man got a fright, but he said to himself, 'I'll tell it to the king, that this
skull spoke to me.' He went to the king. 'Did I not come across this skull
in the wood and it spoke . . .'

'It spoke?' said the king. 'What did it say to you?'

'I asked it, "What sent you here?" "Speaking sent me here." '

'I don't believe you,' said the king, 'but I'll send two of the guards
whom I have at the gate with you, to see if that head will speak to you.
Now if it doesn't speak to you,' said he, 'I'll take your head off, if you're
telling me lies.'

'Oh, it spoke right enough,' said Donald, 'so it did,' and he went off
with those riders. They went to the wood, Donald, and the men that the
king sent with him. They found the head and Donald said, pointing to it
with the toe of his shoe, 'What sent you here?' The skull said nothing.
'What sent you here?' Not a word. 'Well,' said they – they grabbed him
– 'You'll have to go with us. We'll have to chop your head off for telling
lies.' They brought him before the king, you know. The poor man was
trembling, and 'Why were you telling lies?' said the king.

'Oh it wasn't lies . . .'

'It was lies and we'll have to chop your head off for telling lies. But

I'll give you another chance,' said he. 'I'll put three questions to you and if you answer me you'll get off. I'll give you three days,' said he, 'to answer them. You'll come – today's Tuesday and you'll come here on Friday, and I'll give you the questions and if you don't answer me, the noose will go over your head.'

Donald went away trembling and he didn't know what on earth to do. Who should be scything further up the way but Gilleasbuig Aotrom. He went up to him and said, 'For God's sake, Gilleasbuig, won't you help me, in my great need, when I've got to answer these questions for the king on Friday and [if] I don't know, my head is going to . . .'

'Huh!' said Gilleasbuig, 'you let me go there,' said he, 'and give me your cap, your jacket, your trousers and your shoes, and all your clothes.' Friday came, and, 'You will come with me and hide outside there.'

Gilleasbuig went inside, wearing Donald's clothes, and the king – he didn't recognise him – said, 'Well, you've come. Are you ready to answer my questions?'

'Yes.'

'Now, if you don't answer them,' said he, 'it's off with your head. Right, the first question,' said he, 'is, how long will I take to go round the world?'

'The sun takes twenty-four hours,' he said, 'and you couldn't do it that fast.'

'Yes, very good,' said he. 'That's the first one. The second question,' said he, 'what am I worth?' said the king.

'O,' he said, 'they sold our Saviour for thirty [pieces] and I'm mighty sure you're not worth that,' said he.

'Very good,' said he, 'but I'll catch you here,' he said. 'What am I thinking about right now?' said the king.

'You're thinking that this is Red-haired Donald, but you're very far wrong; it's Gilleasbuig Aotrom,' said he.

He got off in this way, and he and the old man, Donald, were going home and the self-same skull was in the wood in front of them, and the old man kicked it. 'What sent you here, getting me into trouble?'

'Speaking sent me here,' said the skull.
That's how I heard it.

---

31   *Colin Morrison*

THE ONE-EYED MILLER
AND THE DUMB
ENGLISHMAN

A SCOTSMAN AND AN Englishman once met in an inn in Edinburgh. They had a drink or two, and very likely three or four.

Said the Englishman, 'I'll lay you a wager that there is a dumb man in our place who can put questions that no-one in your country is able to answer.'

'We'll make it one hundred pounds,' said the Scotsman. 'There is a schoolmaster in our place who can answer every question that a dumb man or anyone belonging to your place can ask.'

'All right. We shall meet here a week today.'

The Scotsman went home and went to see the schoolmaster and he told him all that had been said.

'O,' said the schoolmaster, 'I will not go at all. I will not go at all, at all, at all. If the dumb man,' said he, 'was able to speak, perhaps I would try him, but I will have no idea what he is saying anyway.'

That was that. The Scotsman was going to lose his wager in any case.

But he called in on the miller. The miller was half blind: he had only one eye. He told him what had happened to him.

'Och,' said he, 'I'll go. There's no point in you losing your hundred pounds without having a try at least.'

Off they went then and the dumb man and the miller were put into a room by themselves. They sat there facing each other.

The dumb man put up one finger and the miller looked at him. The miller put up two. The dumb man put up three. The miller closed his fist. The dumb man took an apple out of his pocket. If he did, the miller took a piece of oat bread out of his own pocket. At that the dumb man got up and left.

'How did you get on?' the Englishman asked him.

'O I lost,' said he.

'How did you lose?'

'This is how I lost,' said he. 'I put up one finger to say that there was only one God. He put up two to say that there were Father and Son. I put up three to say that there were Father and Son and the Holy Spirit. He closed his fist to say that these Three were as one. I took an apple out of my pocket,' said he, 'to show him that this was how sin came into the world. If I did, he took a piece of oat bread out of his own pocket to tell me that this was the bread of life. At that,' said he, 'I got up and left.'

When the one-eyed miller came out to where the Scotsman was, the Scotsman asked him how he had got on.

'He got up and left anyway,' said he. 'I think I won.'

'How?' said he.

'He put up one finger,' said he, 'to say that I had only one eye. If he did, I put up two, to say that he had two. He put up three to say that we had three between us. I closed my fist,' said he, 'to give it to him for making a fool of me. He took an apple out of his pocket to tell me,' said he, 'what grew in their country. If he did,' said he, 'I took a piece of oat bread out of my own pocket to show what we lived on. At that,' said he, 'he got up and left and it was as well for him that he did.'

THE POOR MAN'S CLEVER DAUGHTER

THERE WAS ONCE a crofter somewhere in the High-
lands who had a large family. It happened that he was short of meat and
he set off for the hills, determined that his children should have some
meat that night at any rate, and he killed a deer – it was a young deer.
As always happens, there was a black sheep in the fold: there was a man
living at the far end of the village who had a grudge against him, and he
had seen him kill the deer, and he saw him take out the entrails and bury
them in a hole. The poor man took home the deer, and the children had
meat with their meal that night.

But that other man set off and went to the laird's house, and
it so happened that this laird was a magistrate – the only magistrate in the district. He told him precisely what the poor man had done,
how he had killed a deer belonging to him – he'd seen it with his own
eyes, and he could lead him to the place where he'd buried the
entrails. And the laird got into a rage, and sent word immediately to
the poor man to come and see him at his own house: and the poor
man came to see him the next day, as soon as he could. He spoke
very roughly to the man when he got there, and told him that for certain
his house would be pulled down about his ears, and he and his
children would be out on the street. The poor old man was not very
happy to hear that.

He [the laird] told him how he had done him wrong, shooting and
killing one of his animals and taking it home on his back and eating it.
'But I'll give you this chance,' said he. 'If you can answer me three

questions – I'll give you three days to work them out – I'll let you off,' said he, 'so long as you never do it again as long as you live.'

'And what are the questions?' said the man.

He told him that – the questions. 'You must tell me,' said he, 'when the three days are up, what's the only thing,' said he, 'that will never miss what you take out of it – it will never notice the loss. Though you were working at it for years, it would never miss it. Next,' said he, 'what is the most worthless thing on earth – something totally useless? And the next thing,' said he, 'tell me what it is that goes on four feet, on two and on three?'

The man almost went out of his wits – at least, he could hardly find his way home with the turmoil his mind was in. He got home and he would not raise his eyes from the ground. His wife asked him what was wrong, and he wasn't able to answer her. She told him to come to the table for his supper, but he paid no attention to her. Then she went ben to the room and told everything to her young daughter who was there, with her hair cut short above the ears and her face covered with freckles – the state her father was in, that she thought he was half out of his mind.

'You go to him,' said she, 'and see if you can get him to come to the table and have something to eat.'

The girl went through to him. 'Father,' said she, 'what's the matter with you tonight? You didn't use to be like this.'

Oh, he wouldn't answer her.

'Well,' said she, 'I saw you this morning, and I was talking to you. It's a good while,' said she, 'since I've seen you in such good spirits as you were today. What's gone wrong? You're not ill anyway.'

'Oh, I've good reason,' said her father. 'Am I not, my darling,' said he, 'to be turned out of doors and the house set on fire?'

'Why is that?' said his daughter.

'There's a man in the village,' said he, 'who had a grudge against me, and he went and reported,' said he, 'what I did there three days ago, when I killed a deer. He saw that, sure enough,' said he, 'and he told the laird.' . . .

'I see,' said she. 'You had better come through for your meal,' said she, 'and,' said she, 'I'll settle this business for you.'

'Will you, darling?' said he.

'I will,' said she. 'It's easy enough to work out these things.'

'Oh well, darling,' said he, 'it's not easy for me anyway.'

But he went with the girl through to the table, and she sat down facing him, on the other side of the table. And –

'Well, the first question he set for you, father,' said she, 'was what never noticed any decrease. That is the mighty ocean: the ocean never feels a loss. When the tide goes out,' said she, 'it's bound to come in again as it always has. The ocean never misses anything.'

'I wouldn't say you're wrong,' said the old man.

'And the next one,' said she: 'however valuable the thing you put in the fire, even if you put in millions of pounds' worth,' said she, 'set a light to it, and when it goes up in flames you're left with nothing but ashes – it's no use any more.'

'Nor it is!'

'And the next one,' said she, 'that's something you have experienced yourself. I haven't seen you, but you have seen me,' said she, 'going on all fours, when I couldn't walk. But when I once got up,' said she, 'when I got up on my own two feet,' said she, 'it wasn't easy to get me to sit down – I never wanted to sit. But,' said she, 'when you or I get old, when one of our legs is beginning to fail, we try to help it – we get a stick.'

So now there's how the man set off and repeated it word for word to the . . . magistrate the next day.

'Who put all that into your head?' said he.

'Oh,' said he, 'nobody put that into my head,' said he, 'but I thought that that was the right thing to say.'

'Don't you tell me that,' said the magistrate. 'Somebody put that . . . that never came into your head by itself.' He put the fear of death into the old man.

'Well,' said the old man, 'it was my own daughter who told me – who said over those words to me.'

'Your own daughter?' said he.

'That's right,' said he. 'It was my own daughter who told me that.'

'Will you take me to her,' said he, 'so that I can see her?'

'Yes,' said he.

The two of them set off together.

'Is this your father?' said he to the girl.

'That's what my mother said,' said she, 'and she should know best.'

'I expect you're right,' said he. 'Then what induced you to teach your father answers I wanted him to work out for himself, but it was you who answered for him? I never spoke to *you* at all.'

'And what induced an intelligent man like you,' said she, 'with an education . . . ? My father never got any education, but you did, and my father couldn't answer. And unless you got an answer, the house would have been in flames about our ears, and I'd have been out on the street with my father. So I did my best to help my father, just as any daughter or son would have done.'

'Well,' said he at last, 'if you were just a laird's daughter, I'd marry you.'

'But,' said she, 'I'm not a laird's daughter, I'm a poor man's daughter.'

'Since I can't do anything better for you,' said he, 'I'll give you a little present.'

She said nothing.

'I've got a little estate,' said he, 'not as big as this one, and you shall have it.'

'Well,' said she, 'thank you very much, but I won't accept it: I can't make good use of it. But I'd be much obliged to you if you would give what you were offering me – if you gave it to my father.'

'Well, yes,' said he, 'your father can have it, in your name.'

She was delighted with this. 'Can I have that in writing?' said she.

'Oh, you can have that too,' said he, 'and welcome.' He had the gift recorded in writing.

She put it in her bosom: 'Now,' said she, 'I'm a laird's daughter now.'

'Well, yes,' said he, 'you are that.'

'Will you marry me now?'

'By all means,' said he. 'You're a laird's daughter now.'

'Ah, but,' said she, 'even if I marry you, the first thing that comes to your notice, you're so short-tempered that you'll turn me out of doors.'

'Oh, I wouldn't do that,' said he.

'Oh, you would,' said she. 'I wouldn't depend on it – I think you would. You're hasty-tempered and impatient: you might do that to me, and I would end up worse off than I started. But,' said she, 'if it turns out that you throw me out because we've quarrelled, will you grant me my request?'

'What's your request?' said he.

'To take three armfuls out of the castle,' said she.

'You can have that,' said he, 'even if you take away three armfuls in each one.'

They got married, and amongst other things they got the very thing they wanted, an heir – for this magistrate's title went back for maybe five or six generations, and now the last of the line was going to have an heir. There he was anyway: he was born there and he would be the heir. But anyway, he was quite delighted with his heir.

But what should happen but – as might happen anywhere in those days – two of the neighbours there used to club together, and their horses were harnessed together for ploughing. One of them had a mare, and she was in foal. And the other man had a white horse, and they were ploughing together. When the ploughing was over they were turned out on the hill. They weren't needed again till it was time to bring in the corn. But now when the hay and the barley and oats and the rye had been cut, they went to look for the horses. When they found the horses, there wasn't one [sic] of them, but three. There was the white horse, and a foal with him, playing together; but the mother was over there with her head down, grazing, and oh, this old fellow was overjoyed when he caught sight of the foal and saw what had happened.

'That's a fine foal all right,' said the owner of the white horse.

'Oh it is, indeed,' said the old fellow, 'and I badly need it: the mare's just about done anyway; many's the day she's worked for me.'

He put a halter on her, and when he went off with her the other man put a halter on the white horse. But when he led it away the foal followed it. There was no sign of the foal coming to follow its mother.

'Oh,' said the old fellow, 'once he misses her it won't be long before he runs after his mother.' But anyway, the old man got home and the foal never followed him. 'I'll need to go for the foal,' said he to his wife.

'Have you seen it?' said she.

'Yes.'

'Isn't it strange that it didn't follow its mother?'

'No, it didn't,' said he. 'I think it took a fancy to the white horse,' said he: 'it was playing with the white horse.'

'Oh, that's what it was,' said she.

He set off to get the foal. But when he came to get the foal, he found himself no better off. The fellow planted himself on the road in front of him. 'The foal is mine,' said he. 'The foal followed me a good way,' said he. 'It never followed you one step. The foal belongs to the white horse. It preferred the white horse,' said he, 'and now you've seen them with your own eyes.'

'Oh, you poor fool,' said the old man, 'don't you know that the foal is my mare's?'

'No,' said he, 'it's the white horse's.'

But anyway, with all that was going on, out came the man's wife, and when she came out, 'Oh,' said she, 'don't fight, don't fight. You've always been friends,' said she, 'living here as neighbours, as brotherly as could be. I've never seen you the way you are today, and if you're going to be like that,' said she, 'the whole village will know of it. You'd be better to go to the magistrate and he'll settle it for you.'

'Oh, I'll do that,' said the owner of the white horse. But the magistrate heard about it [anyway]. The magistrate summoned them to appear the next day at the – in his field. There were two gates to the field, one to the north and one to the south.

'You go to the north gate,' said he to the owner of the mare, 'and the other to the south gate.'

The old man went with the mare to the north gate. Though he did, the foal didn't follow him. The fellow with the horse went to the south gate, and the foal followed the white horse. And the laird said, 'You,' said he, 'are the owner of the foal: take him home.'

The fellow with the mare wasn't at all happy. He went home miserable. He told the news to his wife. 'What can I do now?' said he. 'I was looking forward to having this young animal: it would have been a great help to me. Now I've been cheated out of it.'

But what should happen but the laird went off next day to the other end of the parish about some business that he had to do there, and this old fellow heard that he'd left home, and he bestirred himself and set off for the laird's house. And he was met by his young wife – the laird's young wife. He greeted her, and she greeted him, and he sat down.

What was his news?

He told her exactly what the laird had done, how he'd given the other man the foal of his mare – that was the judgement he'd delivered about the animals.

'And it was a poor judgement he delivered there,' said she.

'So what are you going to suggest to me?' said the old man.

'Oh, I won't suggest anything to you,' said she. 'If I suggested something to you,' said she, 'you'd tell him about it,' said she, 'in a moment.'

'I won't,' said he.

'Oh yes, you will,' said she.

He was prepared to take his oath that he wouldn't tell. When she heard that, she said to him, 'Tomorrow,' said she, 'the laird is going to fish the upper end of the loch you know well up above your house. You be sure and be by the loch before him, and wait for him there. And take a bag of salt with you on your shoulder, and don't use any of it until you see him coming. And when you see him coming, start sowing the salt. And he will think at once,' said she, 'that this is a lunatic who's moving his arms this way like a man sowing seed.' . . .

[So the old man went to the loch and] the laird went over to him at once and asked him what he was doing there – what he was working at. And the old man told him that he was always short of salt, and he meant to sow salt there, and then he would have enough for the whole year.

The laird said to him, 'Havers,' said he. 'Don't you realise that salt will never grow there, but it will dissolve where you sow it?'

And the old man said to him, 'Isn't it as easy for the salt to grow here as for the foal to grow in the belly of the mother [sic: he means father] horse?'

The laird said to him at once: 'Who taught you that and put it in your mouth?'

'Nobody but myself.'

But he threatened the old fellow with fearful things: if he wouldn't tell who had taught him those words, he wouldn't go home alive. And in those days they could do anything at all, since they alone controlled everything, so that they could do whatever they pleased – might over right. But anyway the old man told him, when he put the fear of death in him, that it was his own wife who had told him.

'That's enough,' said he. No rod was put out on the loch that day, but he made for home. When he got home, he ordered his wife out of the door, never to come back again, and he told her his reason. She realised then that the old fellow had told him what she had said.

'I knew,' said she, 'that it would come to this, and I told you so,' said she, 'that the first time you got angry or upset, you'd turn me out of doors. But now,' said she, 'you'd better fulfil your promise to me.'

'What promise is that?' said the laird.

'Three armfuls out of your house.'

'You can take away three armfuls, and though there were three armfuls in every one you took away you could go – only go, and don't come back.'

'Oh,' said she, 'I'll do that.' And she went in. And the first thing she took out was the heir, the baby in the cradle. When she brought the baby out she set him down outside the door. She came back in promptly and went to the best room, and she took out the charter book, the most valuable single thing in the house, and went out with it and set it beside the cradle, and came back in. She said, 'Are you sitting comfortably there?'

'Yes,' said he, 'I'm comfortable enough.'

'Hold tight,' said she. She put her arms on either side of the chair he was sitting in and lifted him out of the door with a rush, and set him out beyond the cradle.

'Now,' she said, 'you stay there.'

Then she picked up the cradle and put the cradle back indoors. The next thing she put in was the charter book. Then she locked the door on him.

'Now,' said she, 'away you go and don't come in here.'

'Come on,' said he, 'let me in and I'll never cross you as long as I live. You can say anything you like as far as I'm concerned if you'll let me in.' She let him in when he promised that.

---

33   *Jeannie Robertson*

SILLY JACK AND THE FACTOR

Y E SEE, THERE WAS an old wumman, and she had a little wee craftie placie, and she'd one son, and they called him Jack – but he was really right off . . . but she idolized him jist the same, it was the company that she had, an of course he did aa the work aboot the place. But they were very very poor, very very poor; it jist took them to keep theirsels.

But the one day she was gaein awa fae hame, and she said, 'Now, Jack,' she says, 'A'm gaein awa fae hame the day, but A'll maybe be back in time before the factor gings awa – he'll be in by here, maybe, in the efternoon some time. And hae on a big peat fire, so that the factor'll get a good heat while he's sittin waitin upon me, because he'll maybe be here before I come back. And ye'll mind and pit on a good fire.'

An he says, 'Aye, mither, A'll pit on a good peat fire,' he says, 'and A'll hae the fire ready for the factor comin in past.'

'Ah well,' she says, 'laddie, that's whit to dae, an I winnae be awfu lang.' But awa his mither gings onywey.

And . . . of course, she'd been awa an 'oor or twa, when in by comes the factor, lookin for his six-monthly rent, ye see? And the factor says, 'Your mither in, Jack?'

'Na, na,' he says, 'ma mither's awa the day. But she tellt me to tell ye, sit doon and take a rest, and ye'll get a heat, an she maybe winnae be awfu lang. She disnae want ye tae gang awa,' he says, 'until she comes back, and ye'll get yir money.'

'Oh well,' he says, 'Jack, A'll sit doon an A'll tak a rest.' So of course, the factor sut doon upon the chair in front o this big peat fire it wis, as it was a very cauld day, and he made he's sel as comfortable as he possibly could. But wi the heat o this fire, the factor faas asleep.

So poor Jack, he was sittin at the ither side o the fire, tryin to mak *he's* sel as comfortable as he could, till his mither would come in. And of course he's sitting watchin the factor, an the factor fell sound asleep, wi the heat o the fire; an Jack's sittin lookin intil his face.

So suddenly there was a great big flee lichtit on the factor's broo, you see, his baldy broo, and Jack got fascinatit at this flee, traivellin back and forrit ootowre the factor's baldy heid, ye see, an upon his broo. So he watched it for a good while, but bein nae very richt, God help us, he couldnae help hissel, and he says: 'Come aff the laird's bree, man!' But, of course, the flee didnae come aff.

He waits for a wee whilie, he sees this flee still gan roon aboot the tap o he's baldy heid an his baldy broo so he says: 'Come aff the laird's bree, mun!'

But this flee's still sittin on his broo, and he sits for a whilie langer, and he watches it, an he's beginnin to get a wee bittie agitated noo at this flee, so he says:

'Come aff the laird's bree, mun! – Oh God, ye bugger,' he says, 'ye winnae come aff, will ye?' So up gets poor Jack, an he lifts the aix 'at he was the wey o hackin up aa the sticks wi, and he hits the flee, fir tae knock it aff the laird's bree, but of course, he hut the flee richt enough, but he killed the factor! Ye see?

'Course, when his poor mither came hame, she gets the factor lyin wi his heid hammert in two wi the aix. Now she realised what her poor silly son had done, and she knew that this wis one thing 'at he wouldnae get aff wi – that it'd be the means o takin her son awa fae her, and pittin him intae some place. Well, naturally, him bein aa that she had, she was gan tae put up a fight fir to save her son.

So they had a big goat, a big billy goat, and they cried hit 'The Factor'. That was its name.

So now,. . . he wisnae very wise, but he wisnae sae silly as she made him oot to be. So she thocht things ootowre, so as there was only one wey she could save her son, mak him look worse than what he wis, an really mak things look as if . . . he was aa muddlet richt.

So they took the factor, and they buriet him, him and her. See? But she kent that he would tell the police when they comed roon aboot questioning aboot the factor, ye see, she kent 'at he would tell the police. So she killed the billy goat, and she put hit . . . she took the factor oot of the grave that him and her buriet him intil, and she put the billy goat into the same grave – ye see? An she went awa farther, and she . . . made a new grave, an buriet the factor hersel in the new grave – ye see? – withoot Jack's help.

So she went up the lum, and she tellt him to look up the lum, but afore she went up the lum, she made a pot o porritch an milk – ye see? So she tellt him 'look up the lum', and when he lookit up the lum, she teem't doon the pot o cauld porritch and milk. An as hit was comin doon the lum, the poor fool was gobblin it up – ye see? So she tellt him it was rainin porritch and milk; and he thought it, when it was comin doon the lum.

So, whitever, anyway or another, a whilie passes, onywey, and the police was gan roon every one o the hooses, makin enquiries . . . tae everybody, did they see the factor, when they had seen him last, an what time, what 'oor.

So of course they come to Jack an his mither. So they askit her, so she tellt them whit time *she* saa him at. (And of course, remember, she hidit the bag wi the money!)

So whatever, anyway or another, the police question't them upside doon and backside foremost onywey or another, but poor silly Jack says: 'God, aye, man,' he says, 'I killed the factor!' (His mither kent 'at . . . he would say that, ye see, 'at he would tell the truth).

'Oh, you killed the factor,' the police says. 'An whar did ye pit him?'

'Oh God, min,' he says, 'me an ma mither buriet him up here. Come on,' he says, 'and A'll let ye see,' he says, 'whaar I buriet the factor.' So of course the police went up wi him, for tae see whar he had buriet the factor. An his mither come up with him.

'Ma God,' she says, 'would you mind that poor silly laddie,' she says, 'he disnae ken what he's speakin aboot.' She says, 'It's nae richt,' she says, 'you shouldnae be questionin him, an he'll say "aye" tae aathing,' an she says, 'but of course,' she says, 'yeze can dig up,' she says, 'the grave. But,' she says, 'yez'll get a surprise.'

'Noo, haud your tongue, noo, mither,' he says. 'I killed the factor,' he says, 'an me an you buriet him in here.'

'Well, well,' she says, 'it's aa richt. What nicht,' she says, 'wis't – when did you kill the factor?'

'God, mither,' he says, 'A mind fine,' he says, 'it was yon day,' he says, 'it was rainin porritch an milk.'

'O God bliss me,' the policeman says, 'this man,' he says, 'is far,' he says, 'fae bein richt,' he says (when they heard him sayin it was rainin porritch and milk). 'But,' he says, 'nevertheless, we'll hae to dig up this grave,' he says. 'He insists,' he says, 'that he killed the factor, an we'll hae tae dig up the grave.'

So they saw it was a new . . . dug-up grave. So of course they aa started to dig, an they dug up the grave. So they did take oot the thing that wis buriet in the grave. So when they pullt it oot, this was the billy goat, an it had horns, ye see?

So as they were pullin it oot, the poor fool lookit doon on tap o the thing that they were pullin oot of the grave – he was expectin to see the deid man, but when he saw the billy goat comin oot – he still thocht it wis the man, because he said: 'Good God Almighty,' he said, 'mither, he's growt horns an whiskers since we buriet him here last.'

So therefore the police said, 'Oh God bliss me,' he says. He says, 'The poor laddie,' he says, 'ye hannae tae mind him.'

So therefore the case wis droppit, an the factor wis never seen or heard tell o. An the whole thing wis, that the authorities thought that the factor had skedaddlet awa wi aa the money, and . . . wisnae tae be gotten. And therefore it left poor Jack an his mither wi aa the money, an him free o the murder, an aye left tae bide wi his poor aald mither.

---

34   *Willie McPhee*

THE WANDERING PIPER

THIS IS A STORY about a wanderin piper. He jist played here an there an drunk whatever he got. He was a kind o ramblesome old soul, an he done wee jobs forbye – any kin o a wee job he could get to earn a livin wi, he wad dae it; cairried some tools wi him, did odd jobs.

An wan day he was wanderin away along the road and snow began to come down. It was very, very strong and it happened on a Hogmanay night. So he wandered along this road and the storm was gettin worse an worse, an he was gettin blowed here and blowed there. An he wis holdin his old coat roon him an his pipes an his gear an everything in this bag on his back an tryin tae keep hissel warm trodgin along the road. The snow's comin on deeper an it's lyin deeper along the roadside. He had boots so worn they were goin away fae the soles an his toes wis stickin oot o his boots an the snow was going between the sole o his boots an hes fit an he wis fair frostit.

An he's trodgin along an he's trodgin along, till all of a sudden he tumbles owre somethin lyin in the road. He sits doon aside it on his knees an he rakes his hand along the top o this thing, whitever it wis. God! here, it's a man's face! A man wis lyin in the snow an he wis freezin. So he raked the snow right doon off the man, right doon till he come tae his feet. When he lookit at the man's feet, the man had new boots on, split new boots – lovely boots, the best boots that ever this piper ever seen!

He says, 'God,' he says, 'that's a pair o great boots!' he says. He says, 'I think I'll take them off, 'cause he'll never use them again!' he says. 'Puir soul.'

So his fingers were fair freezin. He's slackened the laces an everything an he tried tae pull the boot aff, but no! the boot wouldnae come off, because the boot was freezin tae the sock an the sock was freezin tae the man's fit, he'd been lyin that long. So he tried the ither wan but he couldnae get it aff either. 'Oh, I'll have tae get these boots,' he says, 'I'll have tae get these boots.'

So he pulled the man's trousers up a bit, just up abeen the uppers, an the man's leg was freezin. There were a case o icin roon the man's anklers, the dead man's anklers. He got a chisel and a haimmer oot o his wee bag an he chiselled away the ice, fae the anklers, richt roon aboot the ankler. Pit the chisel back in the bag again and got a wee hacksaw oot an he sawed the fit aff, a wee bit abeen the upper o the boot. He got the two o them aff an tied them thegither an pit them roon his neck an he's away on the road noo.

So he forgot aboot the dead man; he never told nobody. So on he went an he was looking for a place tae sleep. An the snow's still comin doon strong, an he's getting blowed here an blowed there. Anyway he comes roon this corner efter he wis traivellin for aboot hauf an oor, an he sees a light. 'Oh,' he says, 'thank goodness, there a light,' he says. 'I'll maybe get in for a shelter somewhere.'

So he comes along an this was a wee farm, a wee croft at the side o the road, some wee steadins an things. He come along an there was this winda an there was a bright light come through the winda. He keeked through the winda tae see whit he could see. An he sees an old man and wumman sittin an there was a bottle of whisky on the table an there was a great big chicken on the table. It bein Hogmanay night they were holdin their Hogmanay, ye see. An a great big roarin fire was on. 'Oh,' he says, 'this is lovely! I'll get in here for the night!'

So he chapped at the door an the old fairmer ruz fae the chair an come tae the door. He opened the door a wee bit an the wind was blowin an the fairmer said, 'What do you want?'

'Oh,' he says, 'let me in for goodness sake. I'm jist a wanderin piper,' he says, 'an I'm lost and I'm gaun tae be frostit, or got dead, if ye don't let me in! Let me in some place!'

'Away ye go!' says the fairmer. 'We don't want no tramps here. Away ye go! Away ye go!'

An he shut the door on him, ye see. He's stannin there, the piper's stannin there, rubbin his hands. He stood for another wee while an he luckit back the road an he luckit forward the road an he seen there wis naethin else for't, he had tae chap the door again. He chappit at the door again, an chappit hard this time. This old fairmer he ruz again an he come tae the door again. He opened the door an, 'What dae you want?' he says.

'Well,' he says, 'I jist want in. For goodness sake let me in. I'll maybe die.'

'Ye're not gettin in here!' he says. 'There no tramps gettin in here. Away an play your pipes some place else,' he says, 'an ye'll maybe get some place tae sleep.'

He says, 'I'll have tae get in some place.'

'Well,' says the fairmer, 'go round the back an ye'll find a byre or somethin roon there,' he says, 'some place tae sleep. There are some sheds away roon there,' he says, 'sleep doon there.'

So the piper went roon the back, ye see, an he come right roon an there wis this long shed thing an it wis a byre for the cattle. One side o it wis half knockit doon an och! it wisnae very comfortable lookin at aa.

But anyway he opened the door an came right away in an there was two stalls for haudin the kye. An in wan o the stalls there wis this big auld coo lyin, lyin doon, an it wis chowin away, the way it chows its cuid aa the time. It's lyin chewin an when he come close tae the coo, it was a wee bit warmer – the warm breath, ye see. The auld piper looked at the coo an he said, 'I think I could put the boots here,' he says, 'an the breath, the warm breath o that coo wad melt the frost on these boots and I'll get them on.'

So he took the boots off an he left them at the top o the cow, at the coo's feedin place that wis a kind o a crib thing. He pit the boots in there an of course, the coo was chowin away an it was breathin on these boots. So the auld piper went tae the next stall an there wis some straw there an he blusted the bale o straw, he took off his old boots aff him an he got in among this straw an pulled his old coat roon him. In a very very short time he was sound asleep.

So he slept there for a long time. He didnae ken hoo lang he sleppit. He was wakent early in the oors o the mornin, aboot half past six in the mornin, he wakent up. He lucked over an he seen the coo still chowin away. 'I wonder,' he says, 'if my boots is thawed oot yet.'

So he went roon an he got his boots back roond, the dead man's boots. Of coorse the feet came oot dead easy, ye see, oot o the sock, the two o them; he left them doon. 'Oh,' he says, 'that's lovely!' An he tried these boots on an they were lovely and warm wi the coo's breath, ye see. So he laced them ontae his feet. 'Oh,' he says, 'that's lovely. That's beautiful,' he says. 'That's better now. I'll be able to go on the road a bit better noo.' An he sat an he thocht for a wee while. He got his ain two auld boots then, that were all torn, an he pit the dead man's feet intae these boots an laced them up and left the two boots at the cow's head again, ye see. Left them doon there an he lay doon quietly tae see whit wis gonnae happen.

So the auld woman come roon early in the mornin fur tae milk the coo. An she had a lamp in her hand: it wis kinna dark. She had this lamp wi her an she left the lamp doon. She sat doon on her wee stool an wis jist gaun away tae milk the coo an she seen the two boots an she lookit an she seen the stumps o the feet stickin in the boots.

'Oh my God!' she says. 'Oh my God!,' she says. 'That was the piper, the wanderin piper,' she says. 'The coo must have ett him!' she says. 'Oh whit am I gonnae do?' She left the stool an left her pail an she run roon tae the hoose again. She tellt her oul man, 'Come oot tae ye see this!' she says. 'Come oot tae see this!'

He says, 'Whit's wrong. Whit's wrong wi ye, silly oul woman?'

'Come here tae ye see this!' she says. 'The cow's ett the piper,' she says. 'The cow's ett the piper. Come here tae ye see this!'

So of course, the fairmer came an he lookit. 'Oh my God Almighty!' he says. 'It did eat him right enough!' he says. 'That's his boots,' he says, 'ett him all but his boots. Oh,' he says, 'we're gaun tae get transported!' he says. 'We're gonnae get pit away frae the world when everybody fins us oot. We'll have tae bury these boots,' he says, 'an this bits o feet. But the ground's that hard,' he says, 'I don't know where we're gonnae bury them.'

The auld woman says, 'Down in the garden there's a big tree,' she says, 'a big bushy tree there, an the ground'll be softer there,' she says. 'We'll bury him in there.'

'Right,' he says. 'Come on, we'll get the spade, and a pick,' the auld fairmer says, 'an we'll go an bury him there.'

So away they went for the pick an the spade, ye see, an when the auld piper got them away, he jouked oot an went doon tae this big tree an he stood at the back o the big tree an he's watchin the cairry-on.

So they came back wi the pick an the spade, dug a hole an this old fairmer, he's all shakin. He says, 'If anybody fins oot aboot this, we'll get the jail, or we'll be transported. I don't know what'll happen tae us,' he says. 'We'll need tae dae away wi these boots an bury them properly.'

So he dug this hole an he pit the boots in an covered it back up wi earth. Of coorse the piper's standin watchin. They didnae see the piper. An the mist was comin doon early in the mornin. An they buried them up an scattert the snow on the top o them on the ground, so ye'd never hae kent it and away they went.

'Oh,' the fairmer says, 'come on, we better get some hot tea,' he says. 'This is terrible.' So away they wannert, back up tae the fairm again. The oul piper got them jist goin intae the door o the hoose. He blowed up his pipes jist at the back o this tree.

'Listen!' he [the farmer] says. 'What's that?' An the sound come [storyteller imitates drone of pipes, then the tune "The Barren Rocks of Aden"]. The old fairmer, 'That's the ghost o the piper,' he says, 'that's the ghost o the piper!' An they lookit back doon where the boots wis an they seen the shedda o this man standin. Wi the mist they couldnae hardly recognise him an they heard the tone o the pipes comin through. 'Oh as sure as fate,' he says, 'we're gaunnae be hantit. We should have let that old piper in,' he says, 'We're gaunnae be hantit.'

An they're stannin lookin an the piper come oot canny fae the bushes an he come mairchin up canny an he's still playin, comin up tae them. When the ould fairmer seen the ghost o this man, as what he thought, comin up, he says tae his old woman, 'Run for your life!' he says. 'Run for your life, quick!' he says. 'There's the ghost o the piper comin,' he says, 'an it'll have its revengeance on us!' he says. 'Make for your livin life!'

So the ould fairmer an his ould wife run away up the road, ye see. So the ould piper came up an he seen them runnin an he stopped an came up tae the hoose an he stood having a good look efter them. He opened the door an come intae the hoose, an of coorse, the fire was still burnin, ye see. So he rakit up the fire and he got a good heat and there wis a good drop whisky left in the bottle. The ould piper liftit the whisky, drunk the whisky an had a bit o this chicken. 'Well,' he says, 'maybe that's set them,' he says, 'a lesson, for no lettin people in at nicht.'

So I think the piper's still stuck at that fairm yet. An that's the last o my story. The auld fairmer never came back.

---

35   *Alasdair MacArthur*

CAILLEACH NAN CNÙ
AND TÀILLEAR NAN CLÀR

MANY YEARS AGO there was a great, wild old woman living in one of the glens of the Highlands who had the name of being a notorious witch and in full communion with the evil spirits of the world. And among all the old woman's other peculiarities, she was very fond of nuts. She used to have a bag full of nuts hanging on a stake every day of the year, from which she was given the name of Cailleach nan Cnù [the Old Woman of the Nuts]. There was not a horse that fell over a cliff, a cow whose milk ran dry, a girl who lost her sweetheart, but it was Cailleach nan Cnù who had done it. There was not an old man who went fishing, if he got no fish that night and she had met him, but it was Cailleach nan Cnù who had done that.

But at long last, Cailleach nan Cnù was taken very ill, and it looked very much as if she was dying. And she gave strict instructions to her friends, if in fact she died, to be sure to bury the bag of nuts at her head. This was how it turned out: her friends were afraid of her when she was alive, and they were none too sure of her even when she was dead. Anyway, as they had agreed, the bag of nuts was buried at the old woman's head.

There was a smart lad there in the place who didn't believe very much in the old woman's powers and he said to himself one night that it would be a great shame to let such a lot of good nuts go to waste, buried at the old woman's head. Anyway, one night when the family had settled down, our lad took his shovel on his shoulder and went off to the churchyard to dig up the old woman's bag of nuts.

When he was getting near the churchyard who should meet him but a bad character who had the name of being an expert sheep-stealer. And they came upon each other so suddenly in the dark that neither of them had a chance to draw back.

'Hullo!' said the sheep-stealer, 'where in the name of goodness are you going at this time of night with your shovel?'

'Where am I going! I know perfectly well where you're going You're away to steal a wether. Now, since the pair of us have met here, and neither of us on honest business, I'll tell you where I'm going. I'm going to dig up the old woman's bag of nuts. And now, if you give me half of the wether you're going to steal, I'll give you half of the nuts.'

'Done!'

'Well, off you go then, and be sure you get a good wether. And while you're away, I'll sit in the churchyard and I'll pass the time cracking nuts till you get back.'

Now we'll leave the sheep-stealer and the lad with the nuts to their own business and we'll have a look now for a little while at Tàillear nan Clàr [the Tailor of the Boards].

Tàillear nan Clàr was a cripple who had lost the use of his legs. He used to wear a little piece of board on the palm of each hand and under each knee and in this way he could get around on all fours among the houses where there was tailoring for him to do.

He happened to be working, on this particular night that we're talking about, in a house that was just about sixty yards from the churchyard gate, and the house was full of visitors. And as tailors found it useful to be good at telling old stories, there was not a single man in the country round about who was a match for Tàillear nan Clàr at that. And there was Tàillear nan Clàr: reeling off a lot of lies about fairies and witches.

But, anyway, at last one of the party got thirsty, and it so happened that there wasn't a drop of water in the house. There was a smart lad there who offered to go to the well – and the well would be about half a dozen yards from the gate of the churchyard. Off he went with the pail.

As he was getting near the well he heard a nut go crack! He stopped to listen. He heard another nut go crack! He took to his heels and rushed back home, gasping for breath, with his eyes about popping out of his head and swearing by every power high and low that the old woman was sitting up in the churchyard cracking away at the nuts.

'Pah!' said everyone. 'You're nothing but a miserable coward.'

'Give me the pail,' said the Gille Maol Dubh [Crop-headed Black-haired Lad], 'and I'll bring it back full.'

Off went the black-haired lad with the pail in his hand. When he got to the well he heard a nut go crack! He stopped to listen. He heard another nut go crack! Like the other lad, he came back gasping for breath, his eyes about popping out of his head and swearing by every power high and low:

'There's no denying it. The old woman is sitting up in the churchyard cracking away at the nuts!'

'Well, now,' said Tàillear nan Clàr, 'I've wandered many a corner of the world, and I've never come across a houseful of cowards like you,' said he. 'If I had the power of my legs, which I haven't, I'd bring the pail back full from the well, however many old women and men were sitting up cracking nuts.'

'Well,' said the Gille Ruadh [Red-haired Lad], 'I'll carry you there on my back.'

'All right then. Give me a lift!'

The Gille Ruadh took Tàillear nan Clàr on his back, and Tàillear nan

Clàr took a tight grip on the pail in his hand. As he was getting near the well he heard a nut go crack!

'Do you hear that?' [said the Gille Ruadh].

'May I lose my honour, if it's not her right enough!'

He heard another nut . . .

'Did you hear that?'

'It's not canny this, at this time of night,' said Tàillear nan Clàr.

'Will I take you any further?'

'Yes, but be very quiet about it.'

Now the lad with the nuts was getting impatient that his friend, the sheep-stealer, wasn't getting back and he stood up, and when he saw Tàillear nan Clàr on the back of the Gille Ruadh he concluded that it was a wether he was bringing. Anyway, he called out in a loud, ringing voice:

'Is he fat?'

'Fat or thin, you can have him' – and he pitched Tàillear nan Clàr straight into the churchyard.

Anyway, very late that night Tàillear nan Clàr got home, without pail or water, covered with mud and filth and torn by thorns.

And like everyone else who thinks a great deal of himself Tàillear nan Clàr was much less of a hero coming back than when he set out.

THE MINISTER AND THE STRAW

THIS WIS A WIFE 'at they caa't Jannie, an shö bade be hersel in a peerie strae-t'eckit-röf't hoose inside o the hill-daeks, an it wis the kind o a bit o grunnd that 'at shö hed 'at they caa'd a ootset, an it wis jist enoff to keep wan coo. And shö cared this coo like the aipple o her eye: in fact they were a loack o fokk 'at said that shö took more care o the coo as what shö took o hersel. But in spite o all the care 'at shö took o the coo, it . . . [did] no hinder the coo to get a turn o illness. An shö did the best 'at shö could fir the coo, but it cam to the time 'at the coo güd in liftin – that wis, 'at the coo couldna rise hersel. And shö administered all the cures to the coo 'at shö t'owt aboot – shö pluckit her gaw girse, an shö got her tail cut [for 'worm in the tail'] and shö administered the usual pultice o fir tar an söt an saut, and shö even güd to the extent to gie her the cüt krüll: yon was a krüll 'at wis baekit oot o aitmeal, but no fire't, an they turned him i the dog's mooth, an then pat him doon wi the coo to see if it wouldna start her up showin the cüt. But in spite o all her care o intention the coo was nefer like to get baetter.

And then they were ae day that the minister was goin aroond among the fokk: he was veesitin an catechisin. And this was een o the hooses that he veesited. An efter they were feenished wi their drevoasheens, then Jannie be no persuasion would hae the minister to come i the byre an look at her coo. And the baurn oapened aff o the but end an the byre oapened aff o the baurn; an while they were goin through the baurn the minister kind o aibsent-mindetly pickit up a . . . Shetlan ait strae. An he took yon in his haund and he güd in i the byre, and although he kent noathing aboot kye, to please Jannie, he gied the coo a pok here and there, and then he drew the strae back an fore ower her, an he said to Jannie, 'Weel,' he says, 'weel, if shö liffs shö liffs, an if shö dies shö dies, shö's oanly the brute baest onywey!'

But the minister güd on his rodd, an it wis likely as luck would hae it, he wisna been very lang awey when the coo bang't til her feet, an shö appear't to be restored til her noarmal health!

Noo the time güd on a bit, and they were ae day 'at Jannie spak wi een o the sarvant lasses fae the Manse, and they could tell Jannie 'at the minister wis awful ill. And Jannie said awfu little, but shö güd in i the hoose and shö buckled on her best bits o claes, and shö made fir the Manse. And when shö cam to the Manse the mistress said that shö could not see the minister, fir he was lyin in sic a state o illness wi a whinsy boil in his thrott. But Jannie insisted tö the extent that they ot the latest hed to slip her in. And shö güd up the stairs to the bedroom, and although the minister wis awful ill, he kent her an all that: an shö stüd an lookit at him fir a moament an then shö gied a pok here and there ower the bedclaes, and shö fumbled inunder her hap and shö cam oot wi a graet muckle Shetlan ait strae, and shö drew him back an fore ower the baed, an said, 'Weel, bairns, if he liffs he liffs, and if he dies he dies, he's oanly the brute baest onywey!'

And although the minister was lyin in a graet state o illness, he was that much amused at this that he couldna help gaffin, an it wis the means o the boil brakkin in his thrott, an he improved fae that 'oor onwards, an it was no graet lenth till he was restored til his full maesure o health ageen. And Jannie aalways aatributed, ever efter, this to the healin powers o the Shetlan ait strae and the wirds 'at güd wi 'im!

STRUNTY POKES

THERE WAS ONCE A MAN who liked to have everything different from other people and when he was going to hire a man-servant, he made him promise to call everything by queer names which he invented for himself.

'Now, John,' said he, 'when you speak to me what will you call me?'

'Why, sir,' said John, 'I'll call you Master, or Your Honour or anything else you like!'

'No, John, that won't do, you must call me "Master above all Masters." And what will you call my house?'

'I'll call it your house, your mansion, or what you please.'

'You must call it Mount Aupris. And now what will you call my wife?'

'I'll call her my Mistress, or Your Lady, or anything else you please, sir,' said John, who was a most obliging man.

'No,' said his master, 'you must call her Dumbalibus. And what then will you call the fire?'

'Ah, just the fire, I suppose,' said John.

'No,' said the gentleman, 'you must call it "the great flame of light". And now what will you call my trousers?'

'Well, sir, I'll call them your trousers, your breeches, or what you like.'

'You must call them my strunty pokes,' said the master, 'and then what will you call the cat?'

'Oh, just Pussy or Kitty or anything you choose', was the answer.

'No, you must call it the "Great Man of Crayantis". And what will you call the water?'

'Oh, just water,' said John who could not think of any other name for it.

'No,' said the master, 'you must call it Gillipontis.'

Well, the servant did his best to remember these names to please his strange master, and he soon became so used to them that he could say them quite as easily as the old names.

So one night when the man and the cat were sitting at the kitchen fire, a cinder fell out and, as luck would have it, it fell upon the cat's tail and set it on fire. Then what a to-do there was, as it ran squealing up the stairs in a terrible fright, setting fire to everything on its way. The master was by this time in bed, so the servant rushed to his room and beat upon the door crying out: 'Wake up Master above all Masters, waken Dumbalibus, put on your strunty pokes. For the Great Man of Crayantis has gone up to the top of Mount Aupris [with the Great Flame of Light] and if we don't get some help from Gillipontis we shall all be devoured!'

THE FLAYED HORSE

This STORY WAS telled aboot the men here in North Yell 'at hed a . . . a big croft or a small fairm, and they hed a . . . a horse an a geeg. An they were north wan day at Greenbank licensed premises, and they güd into the shop and – most likely gettin aerands – in all probabeelity hed a dram an spent a good bit o time. And they left the horse tied to somthing ootside o the shop, an they were saeveral kigs or baarels o poarter there. And the horse got very impaetient wi waetin, an he wis stampin wi his feet an he brook in the heid o wan o this kigs o poarter; and the horse no doot was likely thristy and hungry boath and he drank this keg o poarter.

And when the men was raedy they cam oot o the shop and they got i the geeg, but they werena gone very far when they saa 'at they were somthing, ir t'owt at they were somthing serious 'at ail't the horse. But they proceeded on their wey fir hom, an gie't the horse his time; but efter a while the horse collapsed completely an entirely. An they unbuck-led him oot o the geeg an they cam to the conclusion 'at the horse wis deid. An to mak the best o a bad job they turn't to an they flay't the horse an güd hom cairryin his skeen.

An efter they were been hom for a while, the – it might til ha' even ha' been the following moarning, they heard some commotion aboot the hoose an they lookit forth what this wis, and then this wis the flay't horse strampin aroont the doors; but he appear't to be very cowld. An very short afore this they were been killin saeveral sheep to saut by fir winter flesh, and they turned oot to the bright idea 'at they would tak this sheep skeens an pit it to the horse in place o his own hide. And they güd an they pat on the skeens ipae the horse and they grew on and . . . the same as if it been his owen skeen. But it wis a more profitable horse then as ever, fir they roo'd him every year and they got the equivalent o five or six fleeshes aff o him. An they were very disappointit when the horse died be owld age!

---

39   *David Work*

KEEP A COOL HEAD!

HE WAS A GRAET LAD for tellin stories, he had a graet lot o stories, and there was a New Year's Day, ice cam on the loch, you see, an all the young fellows cam there skatin. They were aal oot there wan New Year's Day, ice on the loch, an they were skatin an there were wan of this boys 'at geed a bit too far oot, and in the middle o the loch the ice was soft, you ken, an it broake wi him an he geed doon, doon in a hoale, and the other edge o the ice just catched him onder his chin. He slid away under the ice till he came to another hoale, and his head did the same on top o the ice, an when they cam there his heid just stuck on again . . . the frost was that strong, you ken, till it just froze his heid on again!

In the evenin then they were sittin aroond the haerth tellin stories, and this boy was there too, and he was gotten some o the cowld wi his dip in the cowld watter, you know, and he start to sneeze. An he was gan to blow his nose – they just blow their nose wi their fingers then, you ken – an he was gan to blow his nose, an wi the haet, it was kind o thaaed the ice aboot his neck, you ken: he aimed his heid in the fier!

FATE, MORALS AND RELIGION

THE SKIPPER WHO
MAROONED A GIRL

. . . THIS WAS AN OLD woman's house (an old wife's house, as we call it) and the young folk used to get plenty of storytelling and larking about there. This night a boy came in after all the rest, and he asked, 'Why is there a light on in both rooms of the house over there?' This was the crofter's house next door.

'Well,' said the woman, 'if you really want to know,' said she, 'a wife for you is being born in that house tonight.'

The young boy took great offence at this, and everyone started to laugh and make fun of him. And when he was a few years older than that, he went to sea, and he got on so well that he became master . . . at any rate he was an officer on a ship.

After a few years he came home to the place he belonged to to see his friends, and he saw this good-looking young girl there. This was the child who had been born the night he was so offended. He took her with him: he asked her parents if he could take her to send her to a good school and give her a good education. Well, in those days parents were pretty poorly off . . . and her parents agreed that he should take her with him, since he was going to leave her with relatives of his own who would educate her well.

He took her with him, and when the boat was a day or two out from port . . . he made some of the crew lower a boat, and put food and drink in the boat, and go to a skerry close by them and put the girl on the skerry with this food and drink and leave her there. This was done. They had to obey him, and the girl was left on the skerry. It seems that, according to the story, the skerry would be covered [by the tide] and the girl would have been drowned, but they would not have been in sight to see this happening to her. A short while after another ship appeared, following the same course, and they saw someone on the skerry. They stopped and lowered a boat, and a crew went into the boat and they went over to the skerry. They took off the girl.

This man took her with him overseas, and she was well cared for after that overseas. He saw to it himself that she lacked nothing every time he came into port. The girl told him what had happened, that she had been marooned on the skerry and left to die.

When two or three years had passed, the man who had marooned her on the skerry brought his ship into the very port where this girl was being kept. And at a meal they had in the house he took a great fancy to this girl. He started to talk to her and she talked to him and made up to him as much as she could. The girl knew him, but he did not recognise the girl.

The upshot was that he asked her finally, when the ship was ready to sail, if she would be willing to marry him, saying that he was captain of a ship. She said she would, she had no relations in that place, and she would be willing enough.

'All right,' said he, 'when I get back here from the next voyage, we will be married here.'

That was what happened. When they got back from the next voyage preparations were made for the wedding and the wedding took place. When the marriage service was over, the girl turned round to the minister and the people who were by – the congregation. She told them every bit of it, how the prophecy which had been made for this man had been fulfilled.

'And I am the woman,' said she, 'that he took with him as a young girl and landed on a reef in the sea, but another ship saved me. I am finished with him now,' said she. 'I have married him, but I will have nothing more to do with him.'

And with that I parted with the story.

THE HERDIE BOY

THEY USED TO GO in to the kiln and throw a ball of worsted into the kiln, an then start pulling it out; an after a bit . . . if it caught on anything or that it stopped, it wouldn't come any further, the girl used to say, 'An wha hadds in me clew-end?' An then a voice would answer with the name o the future spouse.

Weel the story I've heard is that — it's quite a big farm, there was a poor wee herdie boy at it, of course of very little repute in these days — and the daughter slipped in to the kiln tae find out her fortune: threw the ball in an start pulling out, and it stuck. An she says, 'Wha hadds in me clew-end?' An a voice says, 'Whar but the poor herdieboy sittin at your faither's fireside?' An of coorse she was very angry, she thought the boy had gone out an hidden an playing a trick on her. She'd a big iron key in her hand for the barn; she rushed into the house an there he was sitting, an she walloped him over the head with the key an cut his head!

So he left the house, of course, went somewhere else; and in the course of time — I don't know whether he went to sea or what happened to him, but he made good, anyway, made his way in the world, and he came home an courted an married the girl. And in these days they wore their hair — well, much like now, shoulder-length — and she was combing an brushing his hair one day an she found this mark on his head. And she says, 'My goodness . . . what have ye done tae yir head? Who did that tae ye?'

He says, 'Do you not remember when you did it wi the key o the barn?'

She had even forgotten that he was the boy that was at the father's house.

42   *Tom Moncrieff*

TURNING THE SARK

I REMEMBER MY mother and an old lady who was born in the year 1830 described to me most of the rites which were performed at Hallowe'en time, when the girls tried to find out . . . what their future fortune would be. Well, there was one of these rites – it's described in Burns's poem *Hallowe'en* – where a girl was supposed, if she wanted to see the wraith or apparition of her future husband, to go to a place where three lairds' lands met by a burn, and dip her left sark sleeve in the burn, and then . . . turn it inside out and hang it up before the fire, and then hide away, either in the bed or in a corner, and the apparition of her future husband would appear, and he would turn the sleeve of the sark or chemmy and hang it back.

I remember hearing that a girl nearly brought misfortune, according to the story, . . . on her future husband. She had dipped the sark sleeve in the burn and hung it up, turned it inside out, and then she hid away in the corner, and the apparition came in, a young man in sailor's clothing, and he turned the sleeve around and hung it back. And she was so curious to see him again that she went and turned the sleeve outside in and hung it back, and he came back and he turned it again. And not content even with the second appearance, she invoked a third appearance, and that time he left a sheath knife.

And years later, when she was married to him – she'd hidden the knife in an old chest – he came across it and recognised it. He asked her how on earth she got that knife, and she told him about this ploy that they played at Hallowe'en.

And he said: 'Well, if I'd known that, you should never have been married to me, for I was at sea that night, and I was three times overboard, and,' he said, 'the last time I lost my knife and I nearly lost my life!'

---

43   *Jack Cockburn*

THE STOLEN BLANKETS

MY GREAT-GREAT-GRANDFATHER, Peter Aitchison, farmed Harehead and Greenwood at the same time and was very good to all tramps and vagrants who came, especially in the hill places – he fed them and looked after them and put them on their way.

During one autumn at a time when it was very foggy, a man and his wife knocked on the door very late one night and asked where they were and he told them. They asked for shelter and he said yes, he would put them up for the night as he always did, and he got a stable-lantern and blankets for them, gave them some tea, and then he took them along to the straw-barn and saw that they made up straw for a bed – gave them the blankets and said, 'Now come along at six o'clock in the morning and you will get your breakfast and you will bring the blankets back into the house. Whatever you do, don't run away early in the morning and steal the blankets. You must bring the blankets back, and you'll get your breakfast.'

The man swore, he said, 'You may take God to witness, we'll bring back the blankets whatever else happens.'

When six o'clock came next morning there was no sign of them, and seven o'clock. So, not appearing for their breakfast, my great-great-grandfather went to the barn and found there was no-one there at all and the blankets had gone. He just thought this was too bad, and thought no more about it.

It was a lovely day, but by night-time the mist set down thicker even than the night before, and about the same time of night there was a knock on the door, and when he went, this man asked him could he tell him where he'd got to, for he was completely lost – and this was the same tramp and his wife, and he had the blankets all rolled up. He was completely lost – he had no intention of bringing back the blankets, but the blankets were brought back.

THE SANDAY MAN'S DROWNING

THAT'S THE STORY aboot the owld Sanday man. They were gan to go to the sea the next day, to the fishin, an the wife thowt it was gan to be a storm, an she didna want the man to go. So she blinded aal the windows so as he wouldna ken when it was daylight. And the graith-tub, ye ken, was standin on the floor, to get a run of water in for washin the blankets. And . . . ah, eventually the owld man thowt it was winder that it was never gaan daylight, he thowt he'd get up to see whit wey it wisna, for he was sure, ye ken, that it was piece o the day. So he got up and in the darkness he geed heid stoup into the graith-cog and wis droonded.

THE STRONSAY MAN'S DROWNING

I DON'T KNOW if it wad been a Sanday story, I couldno say, for thu sees, this was a boat gyaan for peats tae Eday, and it was said to be afore the time that they were gettin peats oot o Rowsholm Heid. The wife dreamed the night afore that it cam on coorse and they were aa droonded. And she was that fearful o her man . . . she wouldna let him go, and he had to bide home to watch the bairns, and she geed oot to dö ony oot wark there wis. But when she was been oot, he was been thirsty and he geed to tak a drink oot o this butter- or kirn-milk, and he was geen heid stoup in the kirn and he was droonded.

HAM AND EGGS

THE FARMER? With the cuttin of the crop? . . . He wis
. . . They wis all cuttin, swingin their scyes to the tune of 'Porridge and
brose, three times a day'. An the master wis comin along an he haerd
them, an he went out of sight an listen't, an they wis goin very slow. An
he went home an he told the wife that he would have to change their
diet, ether they wouldn't get their crop cut this summer.

So the wife made fried ham an eggs an just gev them a good tuck-in.
They went back to their wark at one o'clock again, an after they'd gotten
under wey to their wark, the master thoyt he would go an see what they
wis doin. An they wis all swingin the scye: 'Ham an eggs! Take care o
yir legs! Ham an eggs! Take care o yir legs!' and they soon got their crop
cut.

PARING CHEESE

THERE'S A FINE STORY aboot a man that was lookin for a wife wance, and he watched how she ate cheese. So win woman cut a great chunk of this skin and throwed it away: so he thought she was too extravagant, he wouldn't have anything to do with her. And then the second one ate it all: so he thought there was something wrong with her, she was too mean, she ate the skin and all. So the third one gave the skin a bit scrape, you see, and then she ate it: and he married her. Shö was the most successful wife, he thought.

CHRIST AND THE HENS
AND DUCKS

You HAVE HEARD about the old wives' tales and here is one of them for you. The Roman soldiers were in pursuit of Christ at this time and every place they used to come to there was nothing but – 'Did you see the likeness of the Son of God passing here?' There wasn't anyone who would tell them the truth and the greater part used to say that they didn't or, perhaps, that they did a week ago, though He would have been there yesterday.

This day Christ came on men who were winnowing grain and He told them that the Roman soldiers were pursuing him and that they weren't far behind him.

'O, but they certainly won't find You this time,' said they, and they put Him lying face down and they started winnowing grain over Him.

There was a large conical heap of grain on top of Him when the soldiers came, and they asked, 'Did you see the Son of God passing here?'

'Yes,' said they. 'The Son of God passed three Thursdays ago.'

Now the ducks came and they started to eat the grain at the edge of the heap, but then the hens came and they proceeded straight to the top of the heap, and they started to scatter it with their feet. They were scattering more and more, and the men were much afraid that they would uncover Christ before the soldiers' eyes, but at last they left and Christ just escaped and no more.

Apparently the hens were punished for how near they came to delivering Christ into the hands of his greatest enemy that day. That punishment is that every shower that might come down from the sky would drench them to the skin, but to this day the showers will only slip off the ducks' feathers and they won't drench them.

48   *Duncan Williamson*

WHY THE BEETLE IS BLIND

THE TRAVELLERS BELIEVE that Jesus Christ knew that there was goin to be a crucifixion an He took off . . . an He went off on His own where no-one would find Him in His wanderin. An He passed by this field where the people wis cuttin the corn wi the sickles, an He stopped an He spoke tae the men. He says, 'If anybody passes by here an asks fir Jesus of Nazareth,' he says, 'tell them yes, A passed by when ye were cuttin the corn. Tell them the truth.'

An they said, 'Yes, we'll tell them the truth. If anyone comes looking lookin fir You tomorrow we'll tell them the truth, tell them we were cuttin the corn.'

An lo an behold, the next day, when the troops came tae look fir Him, they came tae the men who were in the fields; they were workin in the fields. An they said, 'Did ye see a man called Jesus of Nazareth passin by here?'

'Yes,' he said, 'He passed by here.'

'When did He pass by?'

He said, 'He passed by when we were cuttin the corn.'

So naturally one looked at the other – maybe there wis six or maybe seven, maybe eight o them – looked at the other an says, 'That must be a long, long while ago,' he says, 'when He passed by.' He says, 'Look at the corn. It's all stacked   cut, sheaved an stacked, in stacks, ready fir winter.' He says, 'It must have been a long, long time ago when He passed by here.'

An the black beetle come up oot the earth, an he stopped in front o the troops an he said, he said, 'He passed by here yesterday. Yesterday He passed by.'

An fae that day on for evermore, to the end of Eternity, the beetle remains blind an cannot see; it has no eyes of any description. That wis his punishment fir tellin on Jesus Christ Almighty.

---

49   *Angus MacLeod*

THE MAN WHO STOPPED GOING TO CHURCH

W HEN I WAS A BOY I used to hear a story about a man who lived long ago: and God called him while he was still a young lad. Every day in life he used to attend divine service and go to church. And he continued that way for many years.

But this year he noticed that corn was disappearing from his stack-yard. And he went . . . whether it was a constable or some such man in the village – or it may be it was even the tacksman who had the place – he went to tell him about it. And this man said to him:

'You'll have to . . .' said he, 'if your corn is disappearing through the night, you'll have to sit up and keep watch, and one of these nights you'll see the man. And when he comes, you'll come and tell me who he is.'

Anyway, this night he saw a man coming, and he laid a rope he had with him down on the ground and he began to pull sheaves out of the corn-stack and make up a bundle. And he recognised the man: it was the minister. When he had finished making the bundle he made off with it. And it was the minister of his own church.

Oh, he went back into the house and he never said a word to anyone, and he never went near the man who had told him how to catch the other fellow.

Day after day went by. But Sunday came and all the other folk were going to church and he just stood there at his own door. He saw everybody passing on the way to church but he didn't budge. He had never missed a day in church for the past twenty years – and more than twenty years: yet there had not been a day all that time that he had not been to church. But that day he let everyone go on by him to church. After a while he took a Bible and set off up the glen. It was a fine summer's day and he stretched himself out on the slope of the glen there and began to read the Bible.

But a little while later, he had the feeling that there was someone else with him. He looked up, and a man was standing there beside him looking down at him.

'You're reading,' said the man.

'Yes,' said he.

'You're reading the Bible.'

'Yes.'

'And why,' said he, 'are you not in church?'

The man had never taken it on himself to tell anything of what he had seen – that he had seen a man stealing his corn – till now, but now he told the whole story. He was never going back to church. The minister was just a common thief and a bad man and so forth. He would never go to hear him preach again.

Said the man to him: 'Come on,' said he, 'up the glen with me for a walk.'

He stood up and they went on up. When they were near the burn there, a terrible thirst struck him – the man with the Bible who had not gone to church – he found himself overcome by thirst, and he bent down to the burn and drank his fill from the burn. He stood up then and said: 'Oh,' said he, 'what good water that is.'

'Oh, it's very good,' said the other man. 'Come on a bit further up the glen with me.'

'All right.'

They went on up there, and when they got further up, there was a dead horse lying in the burn with a terrible smell coming from it – a smell of decay.

The other man stopped then and said: 'Don't you think it strange,' said he. 'You told me there how good the water tasted down yonder.'

'Yes, I did,' said he

'Don't you think that strange? Look what it's flowing through. It's flowing through that rotting carcase and . . .'

'Indeed,' said he, 'I never noticed anything wrong with the water. When I drank it the water tasted good,' said he.

'Ah,' said the other man, said he, 'that's the way of it,' said he. 'And that's the way of the Word,' said he, 'too, and the Gospel. It cannot be sullied no matter what mouth it comes out of or from whence it issues. And,' said he, 'don't let what you were telling me keep you from going to church again.'

The man vanished and he was left standing alone on the bank of the burn.

THE KING OF HALIFAX

WELL, I HEARD THAT there was once a man and he was married and he made his living by fishing. And when he got a lot of fish he used to sell it to the people in the village that was in that place. And he had no family.

Well, it seems that the fishing got rather poor – that the fish was getting scarce. And one day he was out fishing and he had covered the banks where he used to get good catches as well as he could and he had not got very much.

And he was just folding away his lines and going home when he heard a splash at the stern of his yawl or whatever kind of boat he had – and he glanced down towards the stern and there was an old man there out of the water from the armpits up.

'You're not having much success with the fishing, man,' said he.

'Oh, no,' said he.

'Well,' said he, 'if you give me what I ask of you, you shall get the fish just as well as you used to,' said he.

'Oh, I don't know,' said the other, 'if I have such a thing to give you.'

'Oh, no,' said he, 'but you shall have it if you take my advice.'

'What was that?' said the fisherman, said he.

'Your first son,' said he.

'Oh,' said the fisherman, said he. 'I'm sure I can do that,' said he, 'if I have one.'

'Well,' said he, 'you promise that you will give him to me when he is fifteen years of age.'

'Oh, I might as well,' said the fisherman, said he. 'I'm sure that nothing of the sort will happen anyway.'

'Well,' said he, 'you cast out your lines, and the first thing you catch, you will set it aside and take it home for yourself, for your wife. You will take it home to your wife and you will keep giving her the fish, itself and the liver – a portion of the fish and a portion of the liver with it – until it is all done.'

Well, the old man disappeared. The fisherman went and cast out the line and he had scarcely let it down when a good-sized fish took it. He pulled it in and when he had taken it off the hook he went and took it and threw it up in a place by itself in the bows of the boat. Anyway he began to fish until at last his boat was almost full up to the gunwales; and night was falling. He went ashore, anyway, and there were people waiting for him as usual for fish and he sold the fish – all except this one. It was the only one he managed to hold on to for himself, and he took it home with him and he asked his wife – he told her how the matter was, and he told his wife to keep that fish aside for herself and to take the liver out of it and to keep cooking a portion of it and a portion of the liver together and to keep taking it herself.

This was how it was, anyway. The old woman took it; and the fish was all used up and the old man started fishing and he was getting as much fish as he could pull in. And what should the old woman do now – his wife, who was well up in years – but become pregnant. And from day to day things took their course until at last she bore him a baby boy.

Well, now the boy was there and time passed and the child was growing until at last, anyway, he came to school age and he went to school. I don't know whether it was far away or near at hand, but he went there, anyway. And when he was getting on for fourteen years of age or thereabouts, there was not a night he came home but his father and mother were crying. And it puzzled him greatly what was making them cry and he would ask them what was going on and, oh, it was nothing, and, anyway, things went on in this way until he was fifteen – more or less – and this night he came home and they were both crying away.

'Well,' said he, 'it looks as if it's because I come home that you are crying every night, but I'm just about finished with school and when I am finished with school I'll be leaving you.'

'Indeed,' said his mother, 'it is hard for me that you have to go,' said she.

And then they told him, the boy, word for word how the matter stood.

'Oh yes,' said he. It seems that I have been given away, whoever it may be who has got me, but when I leave school, I am leaving here and I shall find out what this business is about.'

Well anyway, he finished with school, and this day he got ready to go. He went, too, and he had no idea which way he should turn or where he should go, but, anyway, he set about going and off he went. He came to a town, then, that was there and he was meeting people and they were asking him where he was from and where he had come from and he was telling them. And he told one man there, anyway. This man asked him where he was going. He told him that he had no idea where he was going and he told him how the thing had happened and how this man had come up at the stern of his father's boat and how he had asked him for his first son and how his father had promised – he was so sure, anyway, now that they were getting on in years, that there would be no son – how he had promised him away and everything about it.

'Oh yes,' said this man, 'I'm afraid, my dear lad, that you are in bad hands; that it was the Destroyer himself who came up at the stern of your father's boat and that it is he who has you in his power. But this is what you must do. There are men in this town,' said he, 'men – there are three of them, and they call them hermits and they do nothing but pray all the time, and wherever their food comes from, it comes to them from somewhere, and you go . . . They don't live together. They live some distance apart, where they are, but call on the first one,' said he, 'to see what advice he can give you.'

Well, that was how it was. The lad went off, and he got directions from this man where the place was. He got there, anyway, and he came to the house of this hermit. He knocked at the door and this old man came down and asked him to come in. He went in and:

'Yes,' said the man who was in the house; 'where have you come from?' said he.

He told him and he told him from start to finish how he had come – how his father had met the man and everything. And he [the hermit] took down books and he began to read books – going through them and searching among them and, anyway, then:

'Indeed,' said he, 'I can see nothing here that is of any use for [such] matters, but I know that it is the Destroyer who has you in his power, that it was he, that it was the Adversary himself there. But there is another man, and he is older than me. He is a day's walk from here and it may be you will find the answer there, that this man may have more information than I have.'

But anyway, now, at supper-time, doves came and they brought him supper for both of them.

'Oh well,' said the hermit, said he, 'here is a good omen. Your supper has come here along with mine.'

Well, they had their supper and went to sleep and next day when they got up and got ready, with food and everything, the lad went off.

'Now,' said the hermit to him, said he, 'if you ever come back alive this way, do not pass me by.'

'Oh no,' said the lad. 'If I come this way,' said he, 'I shall call on you.'

'Very well, then,' said he. 'I should like to find out how you get on.'

Well, the lad said goodbye to him and went off and late at nightfall he came to the other man's house. He knocked at the door anyway, and this oldish man came down and asked him to come in. He went in.

Well, he asked where he had come from and the lad told him. He began to tell the story – how he came into this world and everything and about the old man his father had seen at the boat, and what he had done and everything he had asked him to do; and that he had been last night in the house of this hermit and how he had found out nothing – that he had gone through books for a great part of the night and that he had found nothing to tell him what could be done about him, and that he was journeying to see if he could get himself set free somehow. Well, this man started, when they had eaten, this man too started on books, and he worked at the books for a good part of the night and:

'Oh well,' said he, 'there is no information in the books I have here, any more than the other man had, but there is another man, about a day's walk from here and he is far better than I am and it may be that you will find out from him what way you can take or what plan you can devise so that you may be set free.'

But at suppertime, then, his food came to him as it had come last night along with the hermit's food, and:

'Oh yes,' said the hermit. 'Oh well,' said he, 'I think you will be quite successful. Your supper has come here just as mine has and do not despair, for I think you will be quite successful yet.'

And they went to sleep, anyway, and next day, when they got up and had eaten, the lad got ready to go.

'Now,' said the hermit to him, said he, 'if you ever come back this way, do not pass me by.'

'Oh no,' said the lad, 'I shall not pass you by,' said he. 'If I come back alive this way, I shall call on you.'

'Very well, then,' said the hermit, said he. 'I should like to find out how you get on.'

And he went off, anyway, and that evening he came to the other man's house, and when he came to his house, he knocked at the door and this man came down and opened the door and asked him to come in. This man was a good deal older than the others, and he asked him where he had come from and he told him – that he had come from the house of that hermit, that he had spent last night there and the night before that, that he had been in the other one's house and that he had come from home before that and he told them [*sic*] the story from start to finish, how he had come and the thing his father had seen and everything that the thing he had seen had asked of him – the old man he had seen coming up at the stern of his boat.

Well, this man too started – he took down books and started to read them and he worked at them well into the night. But, anyway, at supper-time the doves came bringing their supper to both of them.

'Oh,' said the hermit, said he, 'take courage. Your supper has come here, just like mine, and you are all right so far anyway. We have been given good encouragement. I think you will get on quite well,' said he.

And, anyway, when they had got supper over, he went on with the books until he had gone over them one after the other, and:

'Well,' said he, 'I can see nothing here about anything of that kind at all, but here is what you will do tomorrow. There is a man here, and he is not very far away, who is called the King of Halifax, and he is bedridden now, and,' said he, 'he has a bed in the Evil Place and when he was fit himself, he used to go to see it now and again, but he has a dog now and it is the dog that goes, and if you could get to know that man and you could get to go with the dog and get to the other world, perhaps you could get yourself set free there.'

Well, that was that, anyway. Next day they got up and got everything in order and the lad went and:

'Now,' said the hermit, said he, 'see that you do not pass me by when you come back.'

'Oh no,' said the lad, 'If I come back alive this way, I shall call on you,' said he.

He went off and he got directions to the house of the King of Halifax from the hermit and he came to the house, anyway, and went in, and there was a man there lying in bed and he asked him where he had come from. He told him, that he had been in the houses of these hermits, that it was they who had directed him here, and he told him how the matter was, from start to finish.

'Oh yes,' said the King of Halifax, 'there is a good chance, right enough, that it is the Destroyer who has you in his power. I myself used to go to that place. I had a bed there, and I used to go there as long as I was able, but I have this dog, and it is able to go there now, and you will go with it tomorrow and it will take you there and you will see what can be done for you there.'

Well, that's how it was. He spent that night in the house of the King of Halifax and, anyway, next day he got ready and got it [the dog] and he and the dog set off. The dog took him along. And they came to the other world, and the first person he saw, anyway, it was the Son of God that he saw and he came to Him.

'Well,' said He, 'you have come.'

'Yes,' said the lad.

'Oh,' said He, 'your father did a very foolish thing,' said He.

'Oh well,' said the lad, said he, 'it can't be helped now.'

'But,' said He, 'we shall try to get you set free from him [the Devil]. He has no right to you in a way. You did no wrong at all that he should get you into his power, but it was your father who gave you away, and because of that we shall try to get you set free. We shall go with you to him, to see what he will do about you.'

And the Son of God went and took him with Him and went to see the Devil.

'Well,' said the Son of God, said He, 'here is a lad you got hold of and you have no right to him at all. The lad never did anything that you should get him in your power in any way and it was his father who gave him to you, and the lad is not at all responsible for that, so release this lad.'

'Oh, no,' said he. 'I won't release him at all. This lad was mine, promised to me before he was conceived in his mother's womb.'

'Oh, I know he was,' said the Son of God, 'but you release the lad or I shall put such a number of other chains on you.'

'Though you put on me every chain you could,' said he, 'I will not release the lad.'

'Well, unless you release the lad,' said the Son of God, said He, 'I shall put you in the bed of the King of Halifax.'

'Well,' said he, 'I'll do anything, but don't put me there. I'll do anything you ask as long as you don't put me there.'

'Well,' said He, 'I am asking nothing of you but to release this lad – that you shall have nothing at all to do with him in this way.'

'Oh well,' said he, 'I shall do that. He is free of me,' said he.

And: 'Well, now,' said the Son of God, said He, 'you are all right now. You are free to go now.'

Well, anyway, the dog came, the dog that belonged to the King of

Halifax, and he and the fisherman's son set off. And they came to the house of the King of Halifax and the old man was there lying in bed.

'Well,' said he, 'and how did you get on?'

The lad told him word for word what had passed between the Son of God and the Destroyer and everything, until at last he came to the point where He threatened to put him in the bed of the King of Halifax, and that it was then that he had set him free.

'Alas, alas,' said he, the King of Halifax, 'I shall die tonight.'

And: 'Oh, no,' said the lad.

'Oh yes, I shall,' said he, 'and you must stay here tonight. Don't be afraid at all,' said he, 'and tomorrow, when you are ready, kindle a good fire, a good strong fire, and you must throw me in it, into the fire, and you must wait till I am burnt to ashes and you must keep the fire going till there is nothing left but a heap of ashes so that no bone or any part of me is left. And you must keep a look-out,' said he, 'and three ravens will come from the north and three doves will come from the south, and if it is the ravens that get to me first, before the doves, have nothing to do with me. Leave the ashes where they are. But if the doves get to me first, before the ravens, you are to gather up my ashes and you are to bury them.'

'Oh well,' said the lad, said he, 'I shall do that.'

Well, anyway, that's how it was. Whether he went to sleep or not, the day came, anyway. And the King of Halifax was dead. He went and started to build a fire. And he built a fire outside, a good fire too, and when he had built the fire he managed to drag him outside and put him in the fire – and he was there burning and melting, and wasting away with the fire until at last there was nothing but a little heap of ashes. And the fire had gone out.

Well, now he began – he was looking far and near in the sky to see if it would happen as the man had said.

And, here, suddenly it seemed to him, in the north, that he saw three black things there, coming, and he kept watching them like that, and then he made out that they were birds.

And he kept looking south and there was no sign of anything appearing and it – what was coming in the north – was coming fast. But now he took a look to the south and he saw three other things coming from the south and if the ones coming from the north were moving fast, these were really moving, until at last they came, the three doves there, and they clapped themselves down around the ashes. And the ravens came after them.

'Go on,' said the ravens, said he [sic], 'get out of there. This belongs to us.'

'Oh no it doesn't. There is no doubt,' said the doves, said he, 'that he belonged to you before, but it is not to you he belongs today.'

'Oh, it was for us,' said he, 'that he was working all his life,' said the ravens.

'Oh yes,' said the doves, 'but it was for us that he did his last deed, and so,' said they, 'you get away out of here.'

Well, the ravens went away and the doves went away too, and when they had gone, he got ready and I do not know where he put the ashes but he buried the ashes of the King of Halifax, anyway, and he said goodbye to the dog and went away.

He kept going now and made straight for the house of the hermit with whom he had been last.

'Oh well,' said the hermit, 'you have come.'

'Yes,' said the lad.

'Well, how did you get on?'

The lad told him how it had been from start to finish, and how at last it had been threatened that he [the Devil] would be put in the bed of the King of Halifax and that that was how he had set him free at last.

And: 'Oh yes,' said the hermit. And now they were there talking away and it was getting on for supper-time. And no supper came. And, anyway, it was late at night before the doves arrived.

'Man, man,' said the hermit, said he, 'what went wrong tonight that you are so late in coming to people with their supper?'

'Oh,' said the doves, said they, 'we had great rejoicing in Heaven today.'

'How was that?' said the hermit.

'We had the King of Halifax in Heaven today,' said he, 'and he was greeted with great rejoicing because he got there.'

The hermit fell down dead on the spot.

'Away, away!' said the doves, said he. 'You get away from here. Do not stay. Have your supper and be off. Do not stay here at all.'

Well, the lad had his supper and set off. He came to the house of the other hermit, whatever hour of the night or morning it may have been when he got there. He got there anyway and got in and this one gave him a great welcome, and he asked him how he had got on.

He told him and he told him about the King of Halifax, and how he had come last night to the house of this hermit and when this hermit had heard that the King of Halifax was in Heaven, he had fallen down dead on the spot, and that the doves had told him to go, not to stay there at all.

'Oh yes,' said the hermit, 'they did very well,' said he. 'You did quite right. It is envy,' said he, 'that had put him down, but he will be in the bed of the King of Halifax and the King of Halifax will be in Heaven. He was so envious,' said he, 'that the King of Halifax, poor man, had got into Heaven.'

And he was well cared for there, in the house of that hermit and he went off then next day and came to the other one and spent that night there. He told the story to that one too, how it had all turned out, and he spent that night along with that one.

And he went then and made for home and when he got home his father and mother were blind and deaf. And they recognised him but they could hear nothing. But he began to talk to them and with every word that came out of his mouth, part of their hearing and part of their sight came back to them until at last they were as well as they had ever been; and I came away from there and headed for home, and I left them like that. I don't know what happened afterwards.

ST FILLAN AND THE WHITE SNAKE

W<small>ELL, WE KNOW HE</small> was born in the ninth century and he did a great deal of preaching in Perthshire and there is a place there called after him, just as there is here – St Fillans. Anyway, apparently he came to Kintail and he did a great deal of preaching in Kintail, and Lochalsh too, and he was a famous healer.

But it seems that one time he made a journey to France and, while he was there, he called on a famous French physician and stayed with him there for a while. But the thing that interested the French physician most was the hazel staff he carried – Faolan's hazel stick. This was a stick he had cut beside Loch Long before he set out on his journey and the Frenchman kept on asking about this hazel staff and where he had cut it – and he said that he had cut it in a wood beside Loch Long.

'Well,' said this man to him, 'if you go back to the spot where you cut that hazel staff, you will find a poisonous snake there, and it is white, and if you bring it back to me you will never want for anything, because I shall give you a fortune for it.' And he told him how he could catch the snake.

Faolan came back to Kintail and he went back to exactly the same spot where he had cut the hazel staff. And he took with him a pot full of honey. And when he reached the place where he had cut the hazel staff he built a big fire there and he placed the pot of honey beside the fire. In a short time the snakes began to appear, [attracted] by the heat of the fire and the smell of the honey. The snakes all gathered round it, and a little later what should appear but this white snake, and this was the king of the snakes. And he managed to get it into the pot of honey, and as soon as he had got it into the pot of honey he clapped the lid on it and made off.

He knew very well that the other snakes would be after him as soon as they saw that their king had been captured. He also knew that if he jumped seven running streams that he would be safe enough. And he did this and the River Elchaig, the river down near my house, was the last river he had to leap. He leapt over it and the snakes who were trying to rescue their king stopped.

Anyway, he had the snake in the pot and he took it back to France to this French physician, and he handed it over to him in the pot just as he had caught it, in the honey.

The French physician set the pot on top of a stove and he lit a great fire under it, and when he had done that he said to Faolan: 'You look after that. I've got to go out for a little while, but be careful not to put a hand near it.'

And he went away, and Faolan was feeding the fire with sticks and it the pot began to boil with bubbles coming to the surface, and it so happened that he put his finger – without thinking of what the man had said to him, since he'd told him to be sure not to put his finger near it – he put his finger through one of these bubbles and he burnt his finger, and then he did just what anyone else would do if he burnt his finger, he stuck it in his mouth.

As soon as he put his finger in his mouth he felt a change coming over him, and he knew by the way he felt that something very wonderful had happened to him, and what had happened to him was that he had got this gift for healing that no-one else had, and it seems that this is what the French physician wanted for himself. He had known about it and that was why he had told the other to have nothing to do with the pot. And a little while after the French physician came back and he knew as soon as he got back that he had lost the thing he had been after and I'm sure he was really furious because of that. But anyway, the gift he had been seeking, it was Faolan who had got it as soon as he put his finger in his mouth.

And he went back to Kintail then and he stood on that knoll there in front of my house that we call Tulach nan Deur [The Knoll of Tears], and he was very tired and sick at heart after the journey from France, and he made a verse. And the verse went like this:

> I am sitting here on the Knoll of Tears
> Without skin on toe or sole
> Alas! King of all the airts
> France is far from the head of Loch Long.

And he began to preach here in Kintail and in Lochalsh and a church was built at Kilillan [Cill Fhaolain], opposite us there, and it was called after him, and besides preaching round about here he was a famous healer and because of that and because he was looking after the people in the glens here and they were not afflicted by diseases or anything else, they got to be as strong as anyone you could find anywhere in Scotland and that is the reason why the people of Kintail are particularly strong.

But anyway, he is buried in Kilillan. That is the place that is called after him – but that was not where he died. He died in Iona but before he died he asked that his body should be brought back to Kilillan, the place he loved so much, and a galley came up Loch Long with his body and a sod of turf from Iona to be laid over him. And he was buried in Kilillan there and his grave is still there and I could show it to you if we were over there. But the one unusual thing about his grave, different from any other grave – and there are many people buried there – is that it lies in a different direction. He is the only one lying one way and all the others another way, as you might say. . . . How does his grave lie now? His grave lies north and south and all the other graves lie east and west . . . It is marked by two stones . . . just two flag-stones . . . not big stones either . . . just two natural flags as they were hewn out of the rock, without any writing or anything else on them.

. . . There was more to it than that too. As I have said he was a wonderful healer and there was a spring over in Kilillan and this spring rose through a birch tree that was hollow inside, you know, an old tree, and the spring came up in the middle of it. And the water from this spring, it had the power of healing too, you know. Fillan had blessed it . . .

> All anyone had to do was take a drink from it and whatever was the matter
> with them it was said that it would cure it, and they believed that it had
> this power   If you believe the tales of the old folk it did this . . .

And that spring was there, yes, for hundreds and hundreds of years
till not so very long ago, and it seems that a tinker-woman came along
and she washed her children's clothes in the spring and as soon as she had
done that, the spring dried up. It lost its power of healing as soon as she
did that . . . as soon as she misused it in that way the spring lost all its
powers.

ORIGIN AND
DIDACTIC LEGENDS

THE HUGBOY

THE HUGBOY WAS A GIANT who lived doon in Caithness or somewhere. At any rate he an his wife fell oot aboot something, an he was chasin her in a north direction, an it must have been before the Pentland Firth was made. When he came in sight o her she was goin

up Ireland Brae, so he thought . . . he couldna catch her: he threw a stone at her, but missed, and the stone lies in a field above Ramsquoy. It must have been some soft stane, this, the finger-marks are in it still. She must have rinned a long way, for there's another stone he threw at her in the Lylie Banks at Skaill in Sandwick.

[*Peter Leith jr:*]* He was supposed to be tall enough to wade across the Pentland Firth.

Oh, that's another story.

The Hugboy wanted some faels [turf] to do some buildin wi. So north he came with his caisie [straw basket], scooped up wan handfu – made the Loch o Harray – scooped up another – and made the Loch o Stenness. Gaenin back he stubbed his toe and a divot dropped aff – and that is Graemsay. Then the fettle (that's the rope that hads the caisie) broke, and the whole thing fell oot, and with disgust he left it where it wes – and it remains there as the hills of Hoy.

* Mrs Leith's son.

DUBH A' GHIUBHAIS

THIS IS A STORY I heard from my grandmother before
I ever went to school. If I came to her not very clean she would say,
smiling: 'Here's Dubh a' Ghiubhais' and I had to find out who Dubh a'
Ghiubhais was. As everybody knows the peat bogs in this region are full
of fir. We see the stumps of the trees in the ground, with the roots
running to and fro around them. We can sometimes see the tree lying
in the bog as it fell, and I have sometimes seen these trees look as if part
of them had been burnt. So it must be that this region was covered with
a great forest many hundreds of years ago.

Now the king of Lochlann was very envious of the fine wood with
which Scotland was covered, and he wanted to destroy it. One day he
was so gloomy and worried that his daughter asked him what was
troubling him. He answered that he wished he could find a way to destroy
this Scottish forest.

'I'll do that,' said the princess, 'if you get a witch to put me in the
shape of a bird.' Without further delay the king sent for a famous witch,
and she turned the princess into a beautiful great white bird. She flew
away, and she was not long in reaching the west coast of Scotland. She
came down here and there, and when she struck a tree with a wand she
had under her wing the tree would catch fire. It was not long until the
beautiful white bird had become an ugly black bird with the smoke of
the pinewood, and the people of this country gave her the name of Dubh
a' Ghiubhais [Fir Black].

It was not easy to catch her, and she was doing a lot of damage. But word got out that Dubh a' Ghiubhais had a tender heart, especially for animals. A man at Loch Broom hit on a scheme to get hold of her. The young were taken away from all the farm animals – the calves from the cows, the lambs from the sheep, and the foals from the mares, the kids from the goats, the piglets from the sows, the puppies from the dogs, and even the little chickens from the hens. The mothers were put in one fold and their young in another. When evening came, there was the most dismal bleating, lowing, whinnying, barking and screeching that human ear had ever heard. Dubh a' Ghiubhais was passing on her course of destruction, and her heart was so sore for the poor creatures that she had to come down to earth. No sooner was she on the ground than one of the local people sent an arrow through her heart, and she fell dead.

The king of Lochlann heard what had happened, and he sent a longship with a hardy crew to bring the body home to Lochlann. But when they had sailed out as far as the mouth of Little Loch [Broom] there came a fearful gale which forced them to turn back. They made three attempts to leave with the bier, but at last they saw that Dubh a' Ghiubhais would have to be buried where she had fallen, at Kildonan, at the head of Little Loch Broom. A beautiful green hillock is pointed out there as her resting place.

THE PABBAY MOTHER'S GHOST

THERE WAS A MAN living in Pabbay at one time and his wife was in child-bed. And what they used to give them in these times when they were in child-bed was porridge with butter, and he was making porridge for his wife this night. And when he had the porridge on the fire, a woman came in and sat on the bench. And she never spoke and neither did the man speak to her. But, anyway, when he had the porridge cooked, he asked her if she would take some porridge and she said she would indeed, and he gave her some porridge.

And when she had eaten all he had given her, she got up to scrape the pot. And he asked her if she would take some more and she said she would, and he put the pot back on and filled it again. And she ate all of that too. Well, I can't tell you now how often he put the pot back on but he put it on several times anyway, and, anyway, when she had had as much as she wanted she said:

'There now,' she said, 'that's what I ought to have had when I was in child-bed myself, and it was hunger,' she said, 'that was the cause of my death. But now,' she said, 'as long as a drop of your blood remains, no woman will ever die in child-bed if anyone related to you is attending her.'

And neither there did, and his descendants are still on this island. Yes.

LURAN AND IARAS

ONCE UPON A TIME there lived a man in Stoneybridge who was called Luran, himself and his wife. Luran was always out working during the day, and he did not come home till evening, and his wife stayed at home by herself. But one day what happened was that his wife complained to Luran that a man was always coming around the house while he was away working and that, first of all, he looked in the window and, when he saw that she was alone, he came in and stayed with her all day. And this day she asked Luran to stay at home himself and hide, and when the man came she would let him in and they would catch him.

This is what happened. Luran stayed at home this day and hid in the other end of the house, waiting until the same stranger came – if he did come. It wasn't long till his wife called to him that the man was coming. When he came he went to the window and looked in. When he saw that she was alone he came to the door, and she immediately opened the door. He came in and sat down, but just then Luran appeared from the other end of the house. Out of the door went the visitor with Luran after him. This man set off towards the hill running at full speed with Luran at his heels. Now they were getting close to Loch Iarais out in the hill and, when the man was almost at Tigh Iarais [the house of Iaras] – a huge cairn of stones which is at the edge of the loch – he turned round and said, 'Luran is swift, but for the hardness of his bread, but if Luran's food was porridge, Luran could run down the deer.' Then he vanished and Luran had just to return home.

But he kept thinking of what the man had said to him about the porridge and how swift he would be if porridge were his food. And he began to take porridge instead of bread [oatcakes]. But after being a while on porridge he began to grow heavy and clumsy and he realised that it was to harm him that the man he had been chasing had given him that advice. Luran went back to his usual food and he was as fast and as supple as ever he was and the stranger never again came near the house.

55b   *Calum Johnston*

LURAN

WHEN WE WERE CHILDREN there were plenty of things that were good for us, but didn't seem so good to us. We weren't terribly keen on porridge at all, and sometimes we would be given some encouragement to like it by being told this story.

There was once a man and his wife. He was a crofter. They lived in a remote glen by themselves. They had a good bit of land, and they kept a good stock of cattle on it too. They wanted for nothing: they had milk and butter and cream in plenty and they lived very comfortably.

About Hallowe'en strange things always happen – some of them natural enough, but sometimes supernatural ones: and this crofter, sometimes he would lose some of his stock. One of his stirks would disappear, or one of his calves or something, and he hadn't the faintest idea where it went. Anyway, this time autumn was drawing to a close and Hallowe'en was approaching, and when Hallowe'en came he said to himself that he'd go . . . and keep an eye on the stock that night.

And when night was falling he went out to the fold where his cattle were, to keep an eye on the stock, and he hadn't been there long when he saw two little men dressed in green coming towards him, and he realised at once that these were fairies. Anyway, he watched them: and they came into the fold and seized on the best cow he had and made off with it. He went after them at once, but, oh, the fairies went so fast that he couldn't catch up with them at all: he couldn't hold a candle to them.

In the end he got so exhausted chasing them that he had to sit down on a little hillock for a breather. And the fairies themselves must have been pretty exhausted, and they sat down up the way from him. They began to talk among themselves, and they didn't want him to understand if he heard anything of what they said, so when they spoke about him they called him Luran. One said to the other:

'Didn't Luran run fast?'

'If only his bread were not so hard,' said the other, 'but if Luran were fed on porridge, Luran would outrun the deer.'

And he heard this, and he turned back. And when he got home, his wife asked him how he had fared, and he told her everything that had happened word for word, and how the fairies had carried off his best cow.

'You never got it back?' said she.

'No,' said he, 'but I picked up a hint that will probably help me for all that.'

'What's that?' said she.

'Well, I'll tell you,' said he. 'You'll have to give me porridge and milk every day for the next year.'

'Oh, fine,' said she. 'I'll do that.' And all that year she fed him on porridge and milk, every morning or every evening, whichever he preferred.

And when next Hallowe'en came he said to her: 'I'm going to watch the cattle now.' And he went out as before on Hallowe'en night, and as before the two of them came again and came in among the animals and seized on his best cow. They went off with it, but off he went after them, and they hadn't gone terribly far when he caught them and took the cow from them and brought it home. And the fairies never bothered him or came after him from then on.

So now you know the best advice for any boy who wants to be nimble on his feet: he should stick to porridge and milk.

55c   *Tom Tulloch*

PEERIE MERRAN'S SPÜN

THIS WAS A STORY 'at was telt to the bairns to . . . encourage them to tak their gruel aboot the moarnin. They telt them 'at the fairies güd to cairry the Ness o Houllan – that's a long smaa ness 'at lies oot through the sea here at the north end o Yell – 'at they were goin to cairry him some wey, awey fae the aest'ard o Shetland to help to mak a brig ower Yell Soond. An when they cam yondroo this moarnin they set doon the Ness while they had their brakfast. But when they set them in to their brakfast, then they fand oot that they were een o them 'at wis lost their spün. So een o the leadin fairies said to the rest o them 'at they were bidden to

    'Caa fast an sop shün
    For peerie Merran wänts a spün.'

But they were apparently i thatten a hurry 'at they boltit doon their brakfast, an they never waitit quhile peerie Merran got a laen o wän o their ither spüns. And they liftit the Ness and set aff wi'm ageen. But fir the want o her brakfast peerie Merran couldna tak her equal share o the wight, an when shö got the full wight upon her shö wisna able to cairry it, an shö bruke her back. An fir the want o her cairryin ipö the Ness, the Ness fell, an peerie Merran fell anunder 'm. And peerie Merran is anunder the Ness yet, an the Ness is lyin yondroo broaken in t'ree.

---

56   *Angus MacKenzie*

BLACK JOHN OF THE BLIZZARD

IT WAS IN SPRING and it was a cold day, according to the story that I heard, and a boat came — it was from Harris that the boat came to raid the cattle — she came in to land at a place we call Toilisgir on the Balranald shore with a north-east wind blowing, and she had good shelter coming in there. And that was the first house they came to – the house at Cìrein, and he was ploughing; they went up to him and they must have had information that he was a good seaman. There was nothing else at all for it, but he must go with them to Heisker [a group of islands west of Uist], and the day turned bad with showers of snow.

It was no use refusing: he had to go, and he was in the bow of the boat, and as they were drawing close to the Heisker shore he was being asked: 'What is the name of that reef?' and 'What is the name of this skerry?' And he was making signs to the helmsman, he was making signs to him with his hand to keep close to the shore. And there is a point in Heisker that they call Rubha na Marbh and he – Black John of the Blizzard as they called him – he was in the bow of the boat and he called to Donald MacLeod who was in the stern – it was he who was steering: 'Hold her in,' said he, 'as close to the point as you can get her.'

He held her in close to the point and Black John of the Blizzard stood up and put his hand on the sheet of the fore-sail and made a single leap to the point. The boat came in that close: he escaped and as he went he said, 'Whatever the name of the point was before,' said he, 'it shall be called Rubha na Marbh [the Point of the Dead] tonight.'

The boat was broken up to matchwood there and every man in her was drowned. No-one escaped, according to the story, but John. And because they were so pleased in Heisker, he moved his home from here and went to Heisker.

That is how I heard the story: that that was what caused it to be called Rubha na Marbh.

LEGENDS OF GHOSTS
AND EVIL SPIRITS

MACPHAIL OF UISINNIS

THREE HUNDRED and fifty years ago a man lived in Uisinnis whose name was MacPhail. He and his wife, his son and the son's wife and daughter all lived together. Now the girl had been dumb from birth: she'd be coming on for thirteen and had never spoken a word in her life. Anyway, old MacPhail died and his body was dressed and laid out for burial in an end room of the house. Then the son went off to the township to fetch people and to get whatever was needed for the funeral. He wasn't going to return to Uisinnis until the following morning. The two women and the dumb girl were by themselves in the house, with MacPhail's corpse at the other end of the house.

But as it came near one o'clock in the morning MacPhail's wife to her astonishment heard the girl who had never spoken a word in her life shouting: 'Granny, Granny, my grandfather's getting up! He'll eat you and he won't touch me!'

The woman had a look, and the man who was dead and laid out for the burial had risen to a sitting position. She sprang back and closed the door, but MacPhail was right behind it. Then she began to pile boxes and chests against the door to hold him there. At this, MacPhail began to dig his way out under the frame of the door, and in spite of her efforts to keep him back, his head and shoulders had emerged from beneath the doorway when the cock flew down from the cross-beam on to the floor and crowed three times. Immediately the man who was digging his way out fell dead and there he stayed until the son came back from the township next day.

He was lifted then and buried, but the hole he made underneath the doorway is still to be seen in the old ruins of the house where the thing happened in Uisinnis, and no-one has ever been able to fill it in. The hole is known as 'MacPhail's Pit' to the present day. It's said that people tried more than once to fill it up with stones and earth, but next day it would be the same as before, and not one blade of grass ever grew there — nothing but a foul, dank mire.

58   *Duncan MacDonald*

MÓR PRINCESS OF LOCHLANN

In OLDEN TIMES it was a custom among people to keep a graveyard watch; that meant watching in the graveyard all night, in case anything happened to it. One night this woman was watching in Howmore graveyard and, in order to pass the time for herself through the night, she took a distaff with her, meaning to spin all night. She went to the graveyard and sat down and began to spin. The night was beautiful, calm and warm, and she thought that she would have a good quantity of wool spun before morning came.

But round about midnight, while she was busy spinning, what was she most surprised to see but graves opening on every side, and the people coming out of them and hurrying out of the graveyard. She did not know what all this meant, but she kept on spinning as if nothing unusual was happening.

But after some time, one after another began to return and make for their own graves, and the grave closed over each one, male and female, who went back into it. Thus every man and woman who had gone away had returned except one, and that grave was still open. The time was drawing near to morning and the watcher went and placed the distaff across the mouth of the grave and she sat down to wait until the one who had left it came. At the end of a good while anyway, she saw a woman coming in a great hurry. She came into the graveyard and made for the grave, but the distaff was across the mouth of the grave. She asked the woman who was watching to lift the distaff and let her to her rest because she was tired.

'I shall do that,' said the watcher, 'when you tell me where everyone who was here tonight was, and what left you so long after the others in returning.'

'I'll do that,' said the one who had come. 'Everyone who was here tonight was away at the places where their dwellings were in this world and the way I was so long after the others was that I had longer to go than any of those who left here tonight. I am Mór, daughter of the king of Lochlann and I have been to Lochlann since I left. The boat I was in was lost near land here and I and all who were on board were drowned. My body came ashore and I was buried in the graveyard before there was a graveyard, and people have called the place Tom Móireadh [Mór's Knoll] ever since then. And let me tell you one more little thing. My casket came to land on the shore at the mouth of the ford and nobody found it, and eventually it sank into the strand and it was not to be seen. But to let you know where it is, and the very spot where it can be found, where you see three black stalks of tangle sticking up out of the beach, my casket is just under that. And now lift the distaff off my grave and let me go to my rest for I am tired.'

The watching woman said no more, but she lifted the distaff off the grave and Mor, daughter of the king of Lochlann, went down into it and the grave closed over her. Day had now dawned and she [the watcher] went home. She related what had happened to her and what the daughter of the king of Lochlann had said to her and immediately some people went to the mouth of the ford to dig for the casket, but they never found the three stalks of tangle together. There were tangles in plenty sticking out of the beach but they never chanced on three together, and so Mór, princess of Lochlann's casket is under the strand, still undiscovered, whatever treasure is inside it.

---

59   *Tom Tulloch*

MYZE KEYS

THIS IS THE STOARY relaetin to the owld Kirk o Ness near the Saunds o Breckin. It wis reputed 'at it wis biggit wi a shipwreck't crew – whether that's correct or not I doan't know, but that wis the stoary 'at wis toald. And unfortunately wan o the maen 'at wis . . . at the buildin o the kirk, he wis a man by the name o Myze Keys, and he fell off the scauff'ldin and was so severely hurt 'at it resulted in his daeth. An he was the first män to be böried i the graveyard, an his workmates erected a wuiden heidston til him.

And there wis a croftin house a wee bit farther north, a house be the neem o Taaft, and the crofter 'at wis stoppin i the hoose o Taaft hed occasion to mak himsel a kirn: an he managed to get the whoale o the kirn made till he cam to the bottom an then he couldna fin' a piece o wuid to mak the boddom o the kirn oot ot o. And they were wan day that he wis passin the kirkyaurd, an he geed in, an he pulled up the wuiden tombston and he took him hom wi him an made a boddom til his kirn. An no doot his conscience likely boddered him aboot this act o sacrileege 'at he wis committit, an durin the night sometime he thowt 'at they were an aapareetion that stüd afore his baed, an he thowt that that was Myze Keys. And this aapareetion said til him 'at he wis

> 'Myze Keys
> Come fir his trees
> 'At stüd at his heid.'

But then the man wis cut up the piece o wuid, an he couldna putt it together ageen, and he was in a dilemma to keen whät to do. So he hed a good hunt aroond until he fan' anither piece o wuid that was very seemilar to the piece 'at he wis removed, an he güd an knockit it doon i the kirkyaurd at the män's grave, an he was bother't no more wi the aapareetion.

ALASDAIR MÓR MAC IAIN LAIDIR

WHEN CLANRANALD stayed in Nunton, he had a farm-servant, a big strong man who was called Alasdair Mór mac Iain Làidir [Big Alasdair son of Strong John]. He lived in the Aird Fhada. I know fine where his house was: it's not far from the Well of Clach an [?Déidhir], a little to the north-west of it.

And he often used to go fishing, on the craigs or at the loch. And the Gaels in the old days had a taboo about this business of fishing: they used to say 'late to loch and early to river'. But what happened was that Alasdair went this night late to the river – going against this custom – never thinking that this had any meaning or that he would come to any harm by it. And he went to Abhainn Muileann Iain Duibh [the River of Black John's Mill]. That's out above Nunton, out beyond the drainage channel that's there today. Evidently there was once a mill on that river and there was plenty of water there, though there is very little now.

Anyway, he went out at nightfall. There was no-one with him. He began to fish with a frame-net. He had not been fishing for long – he was getting a few all right but not very many – when a man came up behind him and this man said to him: 'Could you do with some help?'

'I could use it,' said Alasdair.

Anyway they started . . .

'Which would you rather – beat the water or start with the net?' [said the man].

'Oh, I'll work the net myself,' said Alasdair. 'You can beat the water.'

And they started fishing that way, anyway, and they were catching plenty of fish, and Alasdair was just throwing it behind him – in a cleft behind him as he pulled it in.

This man who had appeared kept saying – though Alasdair didn't recognise him and he had no idea who on earth he was – he kept saying to him every now and again: 'It's time to share the catch, Alasdair.'

But, glancing behind him, Alasdair saw that it wasn't shoes or proper feet that the man had but cloven hooves.

They kept on like that, however, all night, and the man who had appeared would say to Alasdair: 'It's time to share, Alasdair.'

'Oh no, not yet,' said Alasdair. He would answer him promptly and say: 'Oh, not yet. There are still fish in the river.'

They kept on like that, anyway, until it began to get light and when it was getting light they heard a cock crowing.

Alasdair said to him – knowing he was not at all canny: 'You can go now.'

The darkness was lifting and the dawn coming up.

'Oh, I'm not going to go at all.'

'You can go,' said Alasdair. 'The cock has crowed.'

'Aha,' said the man who had appeared to Alasdair, 'it's just a poor autumn cackler.'

'Ho, it's nothing of the sort,' said Alasdair – the cock had just crowed again – 'That's the black cock of the March month of spring.'

The man vanished: he saw the flames of fire shooting up into the sky. When he looked behind him there was nothing left but . . . a heap of something like horse dung.

But before the man disappeared he had said to him: 'This will be visited on the son or the daughter or the grandchild or the great-grandchild.'

And towards the end of that same autumn when they had come home to Alasdair's house one evening . . . one or two of the family had come home and they were getting ready for supper: his daughter went out with a pot of potatoes to drain the water off it just outside the door. That was also taboo – to go outside with the potato water after sunset.

She never came in. Someone went out and there was no trace of her. A dreadful thought struck them: she might be dead. They found the pot in fragments outside the door and the potatoes scattered around. They began to search for her body. There was not a corner of the Aird Fhada that they did not search, back and forth, and then at sunrise they came across her body, with every bone in it broken, at Clachan na Mollachd [the Stones of the Curse]. That's the place where the Nunton sheep-fank is today. There are two stones there and the faces of them are still red, blood-coloured – grey stones, but they have this red mark to show that she was killed at that spot.

That's how I heard it and I heard it from two old men when I was young and they were already old at that time . . .

60b   *Mary MacLean*

THE NIGHT FISHERMEN

It was from my grandfather I heard this story, when I was very young.

Apparently there were two old men over at Cladach Kirkibost, and in those days they used to go fishing on the lochs, and usually it was best to do it by night. They arranged this time, these two old men, to go to

such and such a loch in the morning . . . very early on Monday morning.
Well, they set out, and it seems that Monday morning had not begun; it
was late on Sunday night that they left the house. They got to the loch
and began to fish.

They didn't have much success at all at first, but a stranger – a tall,
handsome man – came by them and asked if he could join in fishing with
them. They agreed, and he began fishing with them and they hadn't been
at it long at all before they had landed a good catch of fish. When they
were going to share out the fish the old men asked the stranger how he
wanted to share the fish. And it was a peculiar answer he gave them, but
this is the answer exactly word for word as I heard it:

'A *cealasag* here and a *cealasag* there, and if there's a *cealasag* left over
that's for me.'

Well, just at that moment, as they were going to begin sharing out
the fish, a grouse-cock crew and the stranger disappeared. And when the
men looked there wasn't a trace of the fish left, but it had turned into
mud, or something of the sort.

MACPHEE'S BLACK DOG

T HERE WAS A MAN living here in Benbecula once upon a time, and it was in Balivanich he lived, and he was a shepherd. He was shepherd to the whole village. And it was the laird in those days who . . . his word was law for every township in the place. And, anyway, he had one shepherd and his name was MacPhee.

He had two dogs – a bitch and a dog. And he had never been able to work the dog, although there was no question that the mother was very good.

At shearing time they used to gather men together for the shearing and they used to . . . They had a sheiling out at Staingeabhal in Benbecula: twelve men this night in that sheiling with MacPhee in charge of them and they were waiting for daybreak . . . to get on with the shearing.

And during the night . . . It was beds of heather they had. And during the night, anyway, every man of them said: 'I wish I had my sweetheart here with me.'

MacPhee was in another room and he had a fire there and he was wearing a plaid and had a shepherd's crook. And women began to come in. It is said that they had beaks of bone. And every one of them went through into the other room. And MacPhee was sitting by the fire and a woman came and sat down beside him. She didn't say a word.

He had the two dogs there – the dog and the bitch. And he thought it was very strange, this woman coming in and sitting beside him. And a good while later he noticed blood seeping through under the door from the other room and he said to himself: 'Something's not right here. I must try to get away.'

He stood up, anyway, and took his crook. The woman beside him held on to him. 'You're not going at all,' said she.

'Oh,' said he, 'I'm just going out. You keep hold of the end of my plaid and I'll be back in in a moment.'

When MacPhee got outside he stuck his crook in the turfs in the wall of the sheiling and tied the end of his plaid to it. And he made off.

Well, now, his home was in Balivanich and it was a long way off, so he made off as fast as he could. He heard a great noise behind him: oh, a great noise coming after him. And he didn't know what this could be.

And, anyway, he said: 'I'll slip the dogs,' said he. 'Bios-eara, Bios-eara, MacPhee's Black Dog!' said he. 'If you won't go tonight you never will.'

Off went the dog and off went the bitch. MacPhee kept going to try and get home to Balivanich. He reached home. His wife was in bed. They had plenty of milk and he said to his wife: 'Lay out,' said he, 'every basin of milk you have,' said he, 'in front of the house. If the dogs come,' said he . . . 'I'm quite sure they'll be very thirsty,' said he, 'and unless there are basins of milk laid outside and water,' said he, 'we'll be . . . they'll devour us.'

They laid out every basin of milk they had and plenty of water and MacPhee closed the door and barricaded it from inside . . . And in the morning when they rose MacPhee's Black Dog and the bitch were lying there swollen up like balloons outside the house without a single hair left on their bodies. And it must have been something very strange there when the dogs were stripped of hair.

And that's the end of my story . . . I've heard that story a score of times, but I know Àirigh na h-Aon Oidhche [One Night Sheiling] myself, and if you came with me . . . if I went along with you – I can't walk it for sure – I'd show you Àirigh na h-Aon Oidhche.

ÀIRIGH AN T-SLUIC

T HERE'S A PLACE on the north side of Loch Skiport called Airigh an t-Sluic [the Shiel of the Slough], and here's the story that was told of how the place got its name.

There was an old woman who lived by herself at a place called the Bay of Alasdair's Children on the north side of Loch Skiport. This night the old woman was very ill and to all appearances dying. That same night that the old woman was on her death-bed, a ship came into the bay and anchored there. The skipper came ashore and came up to the old woman's house. When he saw how far through she was he went back to the ship and came to the old woman's house once more and put a Bible at her head and a Bible at her feet. Then he left her and returned to the ship.

A little while after he had gone aboard he and the crew saw a ball of fire coming and going round the old woman's house. Then a little later they heard a voice calling her to come out, and they heard the old woman answering. She said, 'How can I go out when there's a Bible at my head and a Bible at my feet and the little cock, the son of the hen, on the roost above me?' The ball of fire came a second time and a third time, and they heard the voice calling the old woman out, and each time she answered, 'How can I go out when there's a Bible at my head and a Bible at my feet and the little cock, the son of the hen, on the roost above me?' After the third time the ball of fire came no more.

Next day people gathered and a coffin was made for the old woman and they set off to bury her. But when they were a little distance from the house the coffin began to get heavy, and got heavier and heavier, until at last they had to put it down at the place that's now called the Shiel of the Slough. They just buried her there and the hole in which she was buried is still to be seen. It never dried up but remained a black pool with a nasty grey-green scum on the water. And that's how Airigh an t-Sluic got its name.

62b   *Tom Robertson*

THE COCK AND THE SKIPPER

THEY WERE A CROFT hoose on the side o a hill, an wän day they were a smack 'at cam into the voe, and the crew cam ashoer an cam op to the hoose, and they hed tae. And efter they were hed tae, then the skipper o the boat says to the old man in the hoose, he says: 'Could you sell wis a haen, fir wir Sonday denner?'

An the owld man i the hoose says, 'No.' He says, 'There a cock, a old cock here,' he says, '. . . he's startit craain i the middle o the night, an we cannae get ony rest for him. So,' he says, 'we'll gie you him.'

But they were wän thing that the old man didnae kaen. Twa nights afore dis . . . dey were awaa, aboot wän o'clock i the moarning they were a light 'at cam in ower the hill, an cam doon the hill an cam doon to the hill daiks, and then the cock crew, and the light disappear't. An the night afore dis the sam thing wis happen't: the light cam in ower the hill an cam doon to the hill daiks, and the cock crew, and the light disappear't. But the owld man didnae kaen dat, of course: he said to the skipper o the boat, he says, 'You can tak that old cock,' he says.'He's only keepin us oot of sleep.'

So they took the cock and they göd back aboard the smack and sailed oot the voe . . . And that night they were a light 'at cam in ower the hill an cam down, an cam down to the hill daiks an they were no cock to craa. So . . . the light cam in ower the hill daiks an cam doon to the hoose, an next moarning the hoose was burnt to cinders.

---

63   *Donald MacDougall*

TARBH NA LEÒID

THERE IS AN ISLAND a few miles west of Uist that they call Heisker and it's a low-lying island with little water. In summer, when the water was scarce, the women used to go out to do their washing in a loch some distance from the village. They went out two at a time, for it was said that a water-horse lived in this loch. It was also said by an old man in the place that it could happen that the water-horse would come to the village and that it might do fearful harm, and he advised the people to rear a bull and never to let it out of doors in case it might be needed some day.

But this year, anyway, whatever the reason, there was one woman who went out alone to do her washing. She finished her washing and she was tired and it was a fine warm evening and there was a sunny little knoll there and she lay down on the side of the knoll. When she had been there for a little while she saw a fine-looking, handsome man approaching. He came right over to the place where the woman was and he said what a fine evening it was. She said it was indeed.

'You're pretty tired,' said he, 'after all your washing.'

'Oh yes,' said she.

'Ah, I'm pretty tired myself,' said he. 'Would you have any objection,' said he, 'if I sat beside you and took a rest?'

'Oh, I don't mind at all,' said the woman.

He sat down beside her and when he had been sitting beside her for a while he said to her: 'I'm getting sleepy,' said he. 'Would you have any objection,' said he, 'if I laid my head in your lap?'

'Oh, I don't mind,' said the woman.

The man laid his head in the woman's lap and when she had been looking at him for a while, she noticed that there was gravel from the loch among his hair, and water weeds. She looked at him more closely then and she suddenly noticed that he had hooves for feet and it was then she realised who she had there – it was the water-horse.

He was fast asleep and snoring now and she didn't know what on earth she should do. But she had a pair of scissors in her pocket and she took them out and cut a circle out of her coat where the water-horse's head was resting, and she managed to slip away cautiously, but when she got a little way off she took to her heels.

She was getting near the village but it wasn't long till she heard a neighing behind her and looked back, and there was the water-horse coming, and coming pretty fast at that.

Apparently the man who was in charge of this bull that they were keeping in case the water-horse came, his name was MacLeod and the bull was called Tarbh na Leòid. When she was getting close to the village she began to shout:

'Turn loose Tarbh na Leòid!' she cried. 'Turn loose Tarbh na Leòid!'

Some people in the village heard the shouting and the bull was let loose and some others went out to meet the woman. The bull and the water-horse met and hurled themselves upon each other. Sometimes the water-horse seemed to be winning, and sometimes the bull seemed to be winning, but at last the bull started to drive the water-horse back and he drove him out into the sea at last and they both disappeared.

The woman went home and took to her bed and it is said that she never rose again.

But a long time after that a horn – one of the bull's horns was washed ashore, and it is said that it was used for a great many years as a bar across a gateway in Heisker, and it's not so very long since some people saw it – a little over . . . just about forty years ago, it's said it was still to be seen in Heisker.

LEGENDS OF FAIRIES
AND SEA-FOLK

DANCING IN THE FAIRY HILL

I WANT TO TELL you now . . . I don't believe a single one of you will believe me. It's about the fairies, the fairies.

At this time there were two farmers across by Loch Etive side, and this year it was getting on towards Christmas and they were needing drink for Christmas, and they put their heads together and decided they would come over to Kingshouse since that was their nearest inn. And they came over a day or two before Christmas and arrived at Kingshouse, and I'm sure they had a dram, and had a cup of tea, and they ordered a three gallon jar of whisky – for you couldn't get it in bottles in those days, but you could get any quantity in a jar – a half-gallon or a gallon or two gallons or three gallons, whatever you wanted.

But they asked the innkeeper to wrap the jar up in straw in case it got broken on the way and when they were ready to go they said: 'We'll take turns at carrying the jar.'

And it was put on the back of one of the farmers and tied really tightly with straw ropes all round till it was so firm that it wouldn't shift and: 'We'll be off then,' said they.

They set out and they had to go across the moors, as you know, over to Etive, and when they had got about half way, night fell, and they sat down to have a smoke.

And one of them said: 'Look! Look! Look at that light up on the hillside there. Nobody lives up there,' said he.

'No,' said the other, 'and I wonder what light it can be.'

'We're not in a hurry anyway,' said he, 'so we can go up and see what's going on.'

And they set off up the brae. They hadn't gone very far up the hillside when they heard the sound of the pipes. And the man who had the jar on his back, he was a well-known piper himself and he said to the other farmer: 'Do you hear that? There's something going on here. Hurry! Hurry!'

And it was the man with the jar who was leading and when he got there he was a good bit ahead of the other farmer. There was a fine, bright light there, an open door and a piper inside the door with as fine Highland dress on him as they had ever seen on anyone, playing away there. And he took a look inside – the man who was carrying the jar. There they were, dancing – women in silk dresses. Oh, he was so taken with this that he went right in. He was no sooner inside than the door closed.

The other farmer came up. He wasn't very far behind and he came up and there was no trace of his companion. He couldn't make out what had happened. He searched up and down there and he couldn't make out what had happened. There was nothing for it at last but to head for home.

He got to his own house, then called on the wife of the man who had been carrying the jar . . . – the other farmer – and told her what had happened.

Oh, there was no-one there who would believe him. They didn't know what the man was on about at all. But at last he came under suspicion and policemen came up from Inveraray and took him away and he was brought to a great public trial there. He told them every detail from start to finish just as it had happened. There was no-one there who would believe him either and he was sent to prison.

He spent some time in prison and then he had to face another public trial, but the farmer had nothing to tell but the same story. He told everything . . . just the same story. At last they got so sick of questioning him that they let him go home.

And the better part of a year after that, on Hallowe'en of all nights . . . They say the fairies are out in force at Hallowe'en. And the fish are spawning at that time of year too – salmon and trout in the burns about Hallowe'en time.

And this farmer – he said to the lads round about: 'Come on out to burn the water, and we'll get some fish.'

They went out at night and I'm sure they got a fair catch of fish, and what had the farmer brought to catch the fish but a hay-fork. And they worked their way through the burns and I'm sure they got a good haul of fish.

They were coming home by the very track they had taken the night he lost his companion – the piper who had been carrying the jar – and they sat down. The farmer said to the lads: 'Do you see that light up yonder?'

'Yes.'

'That's where I lost my companion last year. Come on up!'

The lads wouldn't go . . . They weren't keen to go there. They had heard so much about this business. But at last they went – one of them went with him. And he set off up the brae carrying his fork and when they got there, there was the fine bright light and a piper inside the door playing away, as I told you before . . . women in silk dresses, and who should he see right in the middle but the farmer – with the jar on his back just the same as ever, dancing away, dancing away!

'Well,' said the farmer to himself, 'I'm not going in.'

But he stood in the doorway with one foot outside and the other in, and he stuck the fork – the hay-fork – he stuck it in the lintel of the doorway, because he knew that if there was steel in the doorway the door couldn't shut.

There he was. They were dancing away and when they had finished that dance they swung into the Reel of Tulloch, and one of these times the man with the jar – the farmer with the jar on his back – came swinging round close to the door.

The farmer in the doorway grabbed him by the shoulder: 'Out of here! Out of here!'

The farmer with the jar on his back stopped. He stopped: 'Take it easy, boy,' said he. 'We've only just got started.'

'Started or finished or not,' said he, 'come on out of here!' He got him outside the door.

The instant he got him outside the door he pulled the fork out of the doorway. The door closed just as it had done the first time. He said to his companion, 'Where have you been all this time? What were you . . . ?'

'Och, I was dancing all the time.'

'Get on home now!'

He didn't . . . The other farmer . . . didn't bother offering to take a turn at carrying the jar because he . . . the other man was so used to having it on his back anyway. But they got home and he went into his own house and the wife of the man with the jar stared at him and: 'Man, man,' said she, 'where have you been all this time?'

Oh, he gave her no answer at first; he just sat down.

'Man, where have you been all this time? It's the better part of a year now since you went missing.'

'Och, I've been dancing all the time,' said he.

'Oh in that case,' said the other, 'you ought to be a pretty good dancer by now!'

But then his wife said: 'Man, what's that you've got on your back there?'

They had a look and . . . they got going on it, cutting the ropes that were round it. There were so many knots and it had been . . . so long on his back anyway. They cut them through and lifted the jar off his back and set it down in the middle of the floor. And they drew the cork and they just made a Christmas Eve of it there and then.

THE FIDDLER O GORD

THIS IS A STORY fae the district o Sandness, which is near Papa Stour. The croft was occupied by a man 'at güd away one night, away to the craigs to fish – fir fish. So he was comin hom one night, wi his büddie o sillocks an waand, and as he passed a certain knowe, he wis awaar 'at they were a light sheenin oot an he güd up tö examine this, an he saa 'at . . . the trows wis dancin inside. So he güd in, bein a fiddler, an the knowe closed up behint him, until they were noathing left to shaa any doorway.

An his fokk that night waetit fir him to come hom wi the fish, an he niver like to com, and all night they waeted an i the moarnin they were a search party güd oot an they lookit, huntit the coast an they fand no sign o him. An time güd by and it was pitten doon 'at he wis geen ower the craig and the sea was teen him and the tide was taen his boady.

So time güd by an eventually his faimly grew up an moved awey, and his name wis forgoaten. And the time cam when they were a whoale century wis passed fae that thing happened: they were a new faimly livin i that croft. So one night i the haert o the winter the owld granfaither was settin at the fire, the son an his wife was settin i the shairs an their bairns wis playin them aroond the flöir, when the door oapened an they appeared a oald man i the door, cled in rags wi a long quite baerd, cairryin in his haand a fiddle. And of coorse the bairns dey laached at this, they t'oucht this wis a man 'at wis silly. He cam in ower the flöir an he says, 'What are you doin here? This' my house!' And dey t'oucht it a graet joke and they laached at him, and they made a fül o him –

everyboady but the old granfaither settin at the fire, smoakin his pipe. He listened.

And he says, 'What are you doin here? Dis' my house: you've got to get oot o hit. Quhaar's wir fokk?'

And every time he would say his [piece] then the young eens laached at him; till at last the owld grandfaither spaekin fae the fireside says, 'Well, quat is your name?' An he telled him his name.

'Well, they wir,' he says, 'dey were a man o that name 'at used to bide here long, long afore my day, but,' he says, 'he . . . he disappeared one night, an never cam home.'

And be noo da laachin fell silent, an everyboady was awaar 'at they were something queer goin on here. So this figure i the door says, 'Well, quere is my fokk den?'

And the old grandfather fae the fireside says, 'Your fokk is aal däid.'

'Well then,' he says, 'if that's the case, then,' he says, 'A'll go an join them.' An he turned him an güd oot. Now they were one growin lad among the faimly 'at wisna laached at him, and he rase an güd furth efter this aald man, an he güd oot an he followed efter him, an he creepit up t'row the yaird among the keel to watch him. An this old fellow wi the fiddle goes [?owre] up aroond to the back o the yaird daek, quhar they were a wal, an he lifts the fiddle til his neck, an he looks up ower the knowe to quar the Merry Dancers was sheenin i the northern sky, he lifts the fiddle til his neck and he plays a tune aince or twice ower. And the boy inside the yaird daek watchin aal of a sudden saa him collapse.

An the boy oot ower the yaird daek an he ran, and he cam to the spok whar the man wis faan at the side o the wal, and there he fand the remains of a man that was been däid fir a hunder year, an a peerie fiddle. And he aalways minded that tune; and when that boy grew up he could play that tune, and that tune's been handed doon to this day.

65   *Bella Higgins*

THE HUMPH AT THE FIT O THE GLEN AND THE HUMPH AT THE HEAD O THE GLEN

WELL, THIS IS THE STORY o the Humph at the fit o the glen, an the Humph at the head o the glen, this wis two men, an they were very good friends. But the wan at the fit o the glen, he wis very humphy, he wis near doublet in two wi the humph that was on his back. The other one at the top o the glen, he wisnae jist quite so big in the humph, but he wis pretty bad too.

Well, Sunday about they cam to visit one another, wan would travel up aboot three mile up tae the top o the glen, tae spend the day wi his friend, the Humph at the heid o the glen. An then the Humph at the head o the glen next Sunday would come down to the Humph at the fit o the glen an spend the day.

So anyway, it wis the wan at the fit o the glen, he had tae go tae see the Humph at the head o the glen, it wis he's Sunday tae walk up tae the heid o the glen tae see his friend. Well, he had a wee bit ae a plantin to pass, an when he wis comin past this plantin, he hears a lot o singin goin on. He says: 'Wheesht!' – an a' the song they hed wis:

'Saturday, Sunday,
Saturday, Sunday,
Saturday, Sunday.'

an that's the length they could get.

'Gosh!' he says, 'I could pit a bit tae that song.' An he goes:

'Saturday, Sunday,
Monday, Tyoooosday!'

O, an he heard the lauchs an the clappin o the hands.

'Goad bliss me,' he says, 'what can that be?'

But this wis three kind of fairies that was in the wood. And the wan says to the other: 'Brither, what dae ye wish that man,' he says, 'for that nice part he put tae wir song?'

'Well,' he says, 'I wish him that the humph 'll drop an melt off his back,' he says, ' 'at he'll be as straight as a rush. An what dae you wish him?'

'Well,' he says, 'I wish him tae have the best of health,' he says, 'an happiness. An what dae you wish him, brither?'

'Well,' he says, 'I wish him,' he says, 'full an plenty, 'at he'll always have plenty, tae he goes tae his grave.'

'Very good!'

Och, this man wis walkin up the glen, an he feels hissel gettin lighter and lighter, an he straightened hissel up, an he's wonderin what's come ower him. He didnae think it was hissilf at all, 'at he could jist march up, like a soldier, up this glen.

So he raps at the door when he came tae his friend, the Humph at the head o the glen, and when they cam out, they ask't him whit he want', they didnae know him.

'Oh,' he says, 'I want tae see So-an-So, ma friend.'

'But who are you?'

'Och,' he says, 'ye know,' he says, 'the humphy man 'at's lived at the fit o the glen,' he says. 'A'm his friend, ye know me.' An he . . . told his name.

'Oh my!' he says, 'whit . . . whit . . . whit happen't tae ye? Whit come owre tae ye?'

'Oh wheesht,' he says, 'if you come down,' he says, 'wi me, or when ye're comin down next Sunday,' he says, 'listen,' he says, 'at the wee plantin as ye're gan doon the road, an,' he says, 'you'll hear singin.' An he says . . . he told him 'at they only had 'Saturday, Sunday, Saturday, Sunday,' but he says, 'I pit a bit tae their song,' he says. 'I says "Saturday, Sunday, Monday, Tyoooosday", an,' he says, 'I felt masel,' he says – 'everything disappearin from me.' An he says, 'If you come down,' he says, 'you'll be made as straight as whit I am.'

Anyway, this man's aye wishin it wis next Sunday, an he's comin – when Sunday cam – he's comin marchin down the road, an jist at the wee plantin he hears them aa singin, the song, the bit 'at the ither humph pit oot tae it, ye know. They're goin:

> 'Saturday, Sunday,
> Monday, Tyoooosday!'

'Wheesht,' he says, 'I'll pit a bit tae that.' He goes:

'Saturday, Sunday,
Monday, Tuesday,
Wednesday, Thursday,
Friday, Saturday'

mair 'n what he put. Aand, he got no clap.

He says, 'Whit dae ye wish him, brither?' he says, 'that man, for destroyin our lovely song?'

He says, 'I wish him,' he says, 'if his humph wis big, that it'll be a thousand times bigger: an whit dae you wish him?'

He says, 'I wish him,' he says, 'to be the ugliest man,' he says, 'that ever wis on the face of the earth, 'at nobody can look at him: an whit do you wish him?'

He says, 'I wish him to be in torture,' he says, 'an punishment tae he goes tae his grave.'

Well, he grew an he grew, tae he wis the size o Bennachie – a mountain. An he could hardly walk up. Well, when he come tae his house, he couldnae get in no way or yet another. Well, he had tae lie outside, an it'd took . . . ta'en aboot seventeen pair of blankets tae cover him, tae cover him up. An he's lyin out winter an summer till he died an it ta'en twenty-four coffins to hold him. So he's buriet at the top o the glen.

THE THIRSTY
PLOUGHMAN

Y ES, WELL, IT WAS two men from Brusda, that this was about. They were down ploughing in Siabaidh on a hot, hot day in their bare feet. And as they went up the knoll they heard a woman working away at a churn. And the one called Ewen said to the one called Donald: 'Oh, Donald,' says he, 'if the milkmaid had my thirst, what a drink of buttermilk she would drink.'

Donald said to him: 'Oh, I wouldn't care for it.'

They turned down [the field] and when they came up ploughing the next furrow a bonny woman in a white apron was standing there with a jug of buttermilk. And she offered it to the one who had asked for it and he refused to take it: he was afraid. And the one who wouldn't care for it, he went and drank the buttermilk, saying that it was the best he had ever tasted.

'Oh,' says she, 'you who asked for the drink,' says she, 'and did not accept it, a short life and poor living to you. And the one who did not ask for the drink and took it, a long life and good living to you.'

Apparently when poor Ewen went home he took to his bed and never got up again, with the anxiety that the witch from the knoll had caused him – or the fairy or whatever it was.

And it was in Berneray itself that that happened.

THE HUNGRY PLOUGHMAN

THERE WERE ONCE two men who were working near a fairy knoll. The day was hot and they sat down in the shade beside the fairy knoll for a breather, and they began to eat the bite of food they had. I'm sure they hadn't much kitchen [to flavour their bread] anyway, but one of the two said, 'I wish, myself,' said he, 'that we each had a good bit of meat out of the fairy knoll along with the poor bite we have here.'

The words were hardly out of his mouth when a young, beautiful woman, dressed in light blue clothes, approached them, with two plates, and a piece of meat on each plate. She offered them a plate each. One of the men took it from her, but the one who had made the wish would not accept it; he was kind of afraid. When the woman saw that he was refusing the meat, she grabbed the meat off the plate and she struck the man with it on the temple. And ever after this there was a running sore on the man's temple; fluid kept dripping from his temple where the fairy woman's meat had hit it.

THE TALE OF THE CAULDRON

THERE IS A LITTLE island south of Barra which we call Sandray. Nobody lives there now: there's nothing there but sheep. But I can remember when there were families living there. And evidently at that time there were a lot of fairies there too, and some of the people got to know them quite well.

One of the fairy women was in the habit of coming to one of the houses every day to ask for a loan of a cauldron, and the housewife had a rhyme which she always used to say when she gave her the cauldron, to make sure she got the cauldron back. Anyway, one day the woman of the house, she had to cross over to Castlebay to get some shopping she needed, and she told her husband: 'Now,' said she, 'when the fairy woman comes for the cauldron, you must say to her what I always say –

"A smith must have coal
To heat cold iron:
A cauldron must have bones
And be put home unharmed".'

'Oo yes,' said he, 'I'll say that to her sure enough.'

'That's fine, then. I'll go to Castlebay, and I hope you'll manage everything all right.'

'Oh, it'll be all right,' said he.

And his wife left and took the ferry over to Castlebay. And the husband was at work in the fields close to the house for part of the morning, and then he saw the fairy woman coming. And, oh, she had the fairy way of moving. You couldn't see her feet touching the ground at all, but she was coming just as if she was treading on the tips of the grass. And he got scared: he ran home and barred the door and huddled himself into a corner somewhere.

The fairy woman came on all the same and tried the door, and she couldn't get in. Then she jumped up on to the wall-head, and from there to the top of the roof. And in those houses it was generally a fire in the middle of the floor that they had, and a lum above it to let the smoke out. Whatever words the fairy woman spoke to the cauldron, it leapt off the pot-chain and shot off out through the lum, and she caught hold of it as it came out and went off with it. As for him, poor man, he stayed there, knowing just what he would get from his wife when she came if the cauldron hadn't come back, and he just sat there brooding all the rest of the day.

Anyway, when evening came and darkness began to fall, his wife got home from Castlebay, but the cauldron had never come home. And she asked him about it, and, oh, he told her how he'd got scared when he saw the fairy woman coming and run into the house, and he told her every detail – how she'd got up on the top of the roof, and how the cauldron had leapt off the pot-chain and shot out through the roof, and how she had gone off with it and he had been too scared to say a word of the rhyme she had taught him, and he hadn't seen the cauldron since.

'Oh, you useless fellow,' said she, 'now we'll be without a cauldron, and what are we going to do?' And she started nagging and complaining.

However, she got ready and put on her outdoor clothes and set off to go to the fairy hill. Well, she knew where it was, and she got to the fairy hill, and the entrance was open. And she looked inside, and there was no-one in but two old grey-haired men, one on either side of the fire, dozing after their meal, and she could see the pot on the fire. And she went cautiously over and seized the pot off the chain and out she went. But as she was going out the pot struck against the doorpost, and flashes of fire came out of it, and this woke the old men. And one of them cried after her:

'[?Tuneful] woman, dumb woman,
Who has come to us from the Land of the Dead,
Since you have not blessed the *brugh* –
Unleash Black and let go Fierce.'

And he began to unleash the dogs to send them after her.

She was keeping going as fast as she could, and when the dogs got too close to her she would throw them a bone out of the pot to delay them, and that would delay them for a little, but after a short while they would catch her up again and she would throw them another bone, until at last the pot was almost empty. And when they came up and were making for her, and she just threw them the last bone she had and as Providence would have it, she was getting near home by then, and the dogs at the house heard the howling of the fairy dogs and came out to meet them and put them to flight.

She got home with the pot and . . . you may be sure her husband was glad to see the pot coming back. There was great rejoicing, and they even did a little dance in the middle of the room, they were so delighted to get the pot back.

And the fairy woman never bothered them or came after them or their cauldron from that day on.

BAKING IN CREAG HÀSTAIN

WELL, AS I HEARD it, there was once a girl, and late in the evening she went out to look for the cows. The cows were further away than she thought and at last the mist came down on her. She kept going and lost her way, but she still went on until night fell. And she went on till at last she saw a faint light far away, and she decided to make straight for the light.

When she got there she went inside and she realised that . . . that it was a [fairy] knoll she had got into. It was full of fairies in there, women and men, young people and old people. But the knoll closed behind her, and the girl could not get out.

They were searching for her all over the place for a long time, but there was no trace of the girl, and in the end they stopped looking for her. They had given up hope of her being alive.

But the girl was in the knoll and when the fairies went out every day they used to leave her there, herself and another little old man who was getting too old to go out, and the task they set her was baking. And they told her, 'When this girnel of meal is all finished,' said they, 'we'll let you out of the knoll.'

She was baking every day but the meal in the girnel was not going down at all. She kept on and on at it, but finally she realised that no matter how long she kept on baking, if she was to be there till the girnel was empty she would be in the knoll for ever.

But then, one of those days, she said to the old man who was inside with her, 'I'm afraid,' said she, 'that I never will get out of this knoll.

The girnel is showing no signs of going down at all.'

'Oh well,' said the old man, 'if you do as I tell you, the girnel will go down right enough and it won't be all that long till it's empty. Every time,' said he, 'that you're baking, the meal that's left over on the board, you must put it back in the girnel, and you must do that every day.'

Next day she started baking as usual. The meal that was left over, she put it back in the girnel. She kept on like that from day to day and it wasn't long till she noticed that the meal in the girnel was going down and down, till at long last there came a day of days when the girnel was empty.

She went to the fairies and said to them, 'Now,' said she, 'I'm going to get out of this knoll. The bargain we made was that when the girnel was all finished you would let me go.'

'And,' said this fairy, 'is the meal finished?'

'Yes,' said she.

He looked into the girnel and the girnel was empty and: 'Well, then,' said he, 'we'll let you go, and we don't have anything to give you for all the time you've been working for us here, but I'll grant you,' said he, 'your first wish. Go ahead and ask.'

'Well,' said she, 'the first wish that I ask is that I should be a good worker.'

'Oh, very well then,' said he. 'Your wish has been granted. Farewell,' said he. 'My blessings on yourself,' said he, 'but my curses on the mouth that taught you.'

The girl went away, and as she was going out at the door she heard the screams of the old man. I suppose they were . . . that they finished him off there and then.

But the girl went on homewards and got to the house. She was years older by now and her mother could not recognise her. But she was wearing a plaid her mother had made for her . . . before she had left home and got lost, and it was in tatters now. And her mother knew her by this plaid – that this was the plaid she had been wearing when she went away years and years ago.

It is said that this gift was passed on to her descendants right down to the present day – that they were splendid workers and that they could get through far more in a short time than anyone else could..

. . . They called them Sìol Sìdheadh Chlann Anndra [the Fairy Race of Andrew] that was the name they went by . . . There were stories about several of them. One of them emigrated at the time when people first started going out there and he took . . . he was hired by a farmer. The day after he was hired he and the farmer and the farmer's son went out. Well, it was all scythes in those days. The machines they have now hadn't come into fashion, and the farmer and his son started cutting with scythes, but he [The man who had been hired] sat down at the end of the field. But after a little while the farmer came over to him and said to him, 'Have you any intention of starting work today, now I've hired you?'

'Oh, you carry on,' said he. 'It's a long time yet till evening. I'll catch you up by the evening.'

The farmer took this so badly that he stopped speaking to him. They came home at dinner-time . . . after he had sat at the end of the field all morning. They had their dinner and came out again. But when they came out this time, he set to work binding sheaves. And before dusk fell, all that the farmer and his son had cut with the scythes in the morning, and all they cut after dinner, he had . . . there wasn't a sheaf unbound when they went home . . . It was said that that happened in Canada.

[Donald A. MacDonald:] 'Now, it is said that those people are still in Uist – do people know which families belong to them?'

Oh yes, they do.

JOHNNIE IN THE CRADLE

IT WAS A MAN in a farm . . . a man and his wife, they werenae long married, ye see, and . . . they'd a wee kiddie, and . . . they christened its name Johnnie, see? But it was a very crabbit wee baby this, it was always goin, in the cradle, it was . . . day after day, it would . . . it was never satisfied, it was always goin 'nyaaa, nyaaa, nyaaa', jist that way a' the time, ye see. So here, there was another neighbourin man, the tailor, used to come up and visit this farmer, ye see, he'd a small craft. And when they come up tae the farm, they used to always have a wee drink of whisky between them, ye see, an a bit talk and a game o cards, an somethin like that, ye see. So anyway it was the day o the market (I think in them days . . . if I can mind, it's every six month or every year, there was a market day); they went away with their . . . loadit up their van wi pigs or anything, or cattle, they went away tae the market with them. So, it was a very warm day, an jist as usual, Johnnie wasnae growin, it was aye aboot the same size, no gettin [? oot o the bit] and it was aye goin 'nyaaa, nyaaa' greetin away.

So here, they were in the . . . down in the byre. The man was cleanin oot the byre, ye see, an the man says, the tailor says to the farmer, he says, 'You're awfy worried-lookin,' he says. 'What's wrong wi ye?'

'Och,' he says, 'it's market day the morn,' he says, 'my wife,' he says, 'me an the wife hed a bit o a row,' he says, and . . . 'she wanted to come wi me to the market. She's been . . . stayed closed in the hoose,' he says, 'watchin the wean,' he says, 'an that,' he says, 'gettin kin' o fed-up. She wants to go to the market, she wants to buy some things. And she's naebody to watch the wean.'

'Oh, but,' says the tailor, he says, 'if she . . . I'll no see naebody . . . wee Johnnie wantin a nurse. I'll nurse the wean.' See? So . . . 'if she wants to go.'

So the man says: 'No, no,' he says, 'I dinnae think she would let ye dae that, but we'll go doon an see anyway.'

So he went roon wi the tailor, and he asked his wife if she would let the tailor watch Johnnie, 'till ye would get a day at the market'. So the woman was pleased, ye see, and the next morning come – to make a long story short – the next morning come, and they packed up their van, yoked up the horses – I think it was two horses they had in them days – and away they went to the market. So the man was in, and he was doin something, the tailor, sewin at a pair o trousers or makin a suit, or something at the side o the fire, finishin off a job, and he hears a voice sayin: 'Is ma mother and faither awa?' See?

So the tailor looks roond, and he didnae think but for one minute it was the baby that was talkin. See? So he looks roond, he goes over tae the windae, he looks oot the windae an that, but he could see nothing. He goes back and sits in the chair again. He thought the baby was sleepin: it stopped cryin.

So he says . . . he hears the voice sayin again: 'Is ma mother an ma faither awa tae the market? Are they away?' So he looks roond, and this was the baby haudin its wee hands at each side o the pram; it was sittin up. An it says . . . Of coorse, the tailor was a wee bit . . . he got kin' o feared like, an he looks at the baby an he kin' o kep' hissel, an he says: 'Yes,' he says, 'they're away tae the market, Johnnie,' he says. 'What is it?'

He says, 'If you look in the boddom press,' he says, 'there's a bottle o whisky,' the baby says, 'take it oot an gie me a wee taste.' See?

So he takes the bottle o whisky oot . . . he went an sure enough, the fairmer [sic – he means tailor] opened up the boddom o the press, and here was the bottle of whisky! And he took the bottle o whisky, and took a taste o whisky, and teemed oot some for the wee baby – the wee baby took the whisky an drunk it. See? So it says, 'Are there ony pipes . . . hae ye got a set o pipes in the hoose?'

'No me,' says the tailor, he says. 'I cannae play the pipes,' he says, 'but,' he says, 'I like to hear the pipes.'

'Well,' he says, 'go oot to the byre and bring me in a strae, an I'll play you a tune.'

So of coorse the tylor got up, an oot he went . . . brings in a strae. (It wasnae a bashed strae, it was a roon strae, it had to be roon, so that the fairy could blow through it, ye see?) Takes the straw in, and hands it tae Johnnie, an the tailor's watchin everything, see? He was worried, the tailor, noo; he was thinkin aboot the mother an the faither, and this wee Johnnie bein the fairy, see? Didn't know what to say aboot it . . . He sut doon an he's watchin. He says, ah, 'Can ye play a strae?' the tailor said.

So the fairy says, 'Aye,' he says, 'I'll play ye a tune on the pipes.' Sut doon, and it played the loveliest tune on the pipes that ever ye heard – through a strae! The greatest music, pipe music – he [the tailor] says he heard lots o pipers in them days, the MacCreemons an a' them, pipin, ye see?, but he says he never heard the like o it in his life, this wee baby in the pram. He knew it was a fairy then, ye see, it was playin the pipes!

So . . . they had a good talk together, this fairy an the tylor, ye see, so it says, 'Is it time for ma father and mother to come hame yet?'

So he says, 'Aye,' he says, 'they'll be hame in aboot half an 'oor.'

So he says, 'Well,' he says, 'ye better take a look an see if they're comin.'

So the fairmer [sic – he means tailor] went oot, and looked oot the windae, and he says, 'Aye, here they're comin up the lane.' Ye see?

So of coorse, the wee fairy, he says, 'I'll have tae get back into ma pram again.' And it lay doon on its back an it's goin . . . when the mother come to the door the wee bairn started goin again, 'nyaaa, nyaaa', greetin away, ye see?

So here noo the tylor was worriet. But he broke the news aff to the fairmer, see, and tellt the fairmer.

'Oh,' he says, 'I don't know,' he says, 'what I'll dae.'

But in them days, what they done wi a fairy, they got a girdle, ye know a girdle for bakin scones. They pit it on the fire, and they took – in them days, to pit away a fairy – they took horse's manure off the road, or anywhere at all, ye see, an they put it in a pan an burned it in a pan, and the fairies seen that, an they took fear an they disappeared. Ye see? Put it on the tap o the pan. This was ma mother used to tell us this.

So here – the fairmer asked him what was wrong. So he tells the fairmer.

'Well,' he says, 'I'll have to break it to ma wife,' he says. 'But,' he says, 'I don't know how I'm goin tae do it, it'll break her hairt,' he says. 'I can hardly believe this.'

'Well,' says the tailor, he says, 'I'll tell ye what I'll dae. You an your wife,' he says, 'go . . . wait for a while, and go tae another market. Let on there's another market, that the stuff wasnae half sellt, there's two days' market. And go through . . .' (in them days, there was a hole fae the byre right to the kitchen, ye could look through a hole in the wall, through to the byre. Ye see? Ye could see the cattle, an everything) 'go into the byre, and lift the curtain back, and listen tae everything that's goin on. Ye can see what I'm tellin ye,' says the tylor, ' 's true. It's a fairy ye've got for a wean.' See?

So, anyway, the next mornin come, and they packed up their things as usual, lettin on that they were goin tae another market. And they went through tae the byre. And here, they're sittin. An it heard . . . the mother an the farmer heard the wee fairy sayin tae the tailor, 'Is ma mother and father away? Is ma mother and father away tae the market?'

So the tylor spoke kin' o loud, ye see, to let them hear them. 'Oh yes,' he says, 'they're away to the market,' he says, 'Johnnie,' he says, 'you'll be wantin a drink.'

'Aye, get the whisky oot,' he says, 'and gie me a drink.'

Well, the woman nearly fainted when she heard the fairy speakin . . . her ain baby speakin to the tailor, ye see? So efter this went on, the next mornin, they never said nothing when they found oot it was a fairy.

The farmer come in . . . the baby's father come in . . . got the girdle

. . . And the fairy looked wi its eyes wild, watched the mother . . . the father pittin the girdle on the fire, seein nae floor or nothin on the table . . . wi'oot any bread gettin baked, ye see?

Next thing come in, was wi a bit o a half o a bag full o the horse manure, an a big peat fire. An he put some o the horse manure on tap o the griddle, like that. And the fairy begun to get feared noo, its eyes got kin o raiset up, and it was gettin feared when it seen the girdle. And just as the farmer was comin forward to reach for wee Johnnie in the cradle, he just made a dive like that, and made a jump up the lum – went up the lum itsel, and it cries doon the chimley: 'I wish I had 'a kent my mother – if I'd 'a been longer with my mother,' he says, 'I would ha liked to ken her better.'

That was . . . Ye can take that meaning out o that, what the fairy said, back doon the chimley . . . disappeared.

That was a story ma mother told me, years ago. Heard it often. It was supposed to be true, that story . . . My mother was a Campbell . . . Argyllshire Campbells.

A FAIRY CHANGELING

[THIS IS THE STORY of a woman] that lost her own baby
. . . She was feeding it and she couldn't give him enough. And she went
to an old man in the village. There was always a wise man in every village,
you know, that advised them what to do. And she said, 'I don't think it's
my own child I've got. It doesn't matter how much porridge,' she says,
'I give him. He's not satisfied. Whereas my own child,' she said, 'couldn't
take all the porridge. He never finished the porridge I gave him.'

'Oh well,' the old man said, 'I'll tell you what. It can't be your own
child, but I'll tell you what to do. Just you pretend you're going away
from your home, and that you're going for some distance. And keep
hiding around the place. And when he thinks that you're gone just peep
at the window and see what happens.'

So . . . this happened and she went to peep at the window. And the
one that was supposed to be the baby was an old fairy bodach . . . on his
elbow in the cradle playing the chanter. So she went back to the old man
in the village again; she told him what happened. 'Now,' she says, 'how
am I to get rid of him?'

'Well, I'll tell you what,' he says. 'Just you take him with you the
next time you're going to cut seaweed.' They used to cut the seaweed
for fertiliser. 'And put him on the top of . . . a rock, the very top of a
rock. And pretend you don't see the tide coming in, but keep away from
the tide yourself, a good bit. And keep cutting the seaweed round the
rock on which the . . . baby is. Keep an eye on him all the time. But keep
away from the rock until the tide surrounds the rock.'

So this is what she did. And when the old man . . . saw that the tide was right round the rock and that he couldn't get . . . off without swimming, he stood, . . . a real fairy man, and started with his fists and swearing at her, that he would do this to her and that to her. And some of the other fairies came to his rescue. And she said, 'He'll be there,' she said. 'I'm going to leave him there,' she said, 'till you bring my own baby back! And not until then will he be rescued . . . from that rock.'

And they brought her own baby back, and brought the old bodach with them.

70a　　*Angus MacLellan*

A WOMAN SAVED FROM THE FAIRIES

I'VE HEARD THIS story about a man called Somhairle MacDonald. He lived on the mainland. He was a rich man; he had all the money he needed. And he used to go out shooting. This day he had been shooting in the hills and he was coming home towards nightfall, and he sat down on the side of a knoll for a rest. And there wasn't a breath of wind. What should he see but a wreath of mist coming over the top of the mountain facing him across the glen.

He had never seen mist move as fast as that, and this really astonished him when it was so calm. He thought it must be something unnatural. He had heard that shot would never harm an evil thing, so he went and put a sixpence in his gun. And the mist was coming within range, and he could see a black shadow in the middle of the wreath of mist. And he fired at it and the shot went off, and the mist vanished.

But then he heard a pitiful moaning further down the hill, and he got up and went down there, and there was a woman wearing nothing but her nightdress, and both her thighs bleeding where the sixpence had grazed them. He spoke to her, but he could get nothing out of her but a shake of her head or a movement of her hand. He started to bandage her legs and stopped the bleeding. She couldn't speak a word. He didn't know what to do with her: he couldn't bring himself to leave her there. He went and lifted her on his back and took her home with him, and they put her to bed, and he looked after her himself.

Her legs healed up then and she got up, and she used to work about the house, and there was nothing a woman's two hands could do that she wouldn't do but she couldn't speak a word. His people carried on at him for ever having anything to do with her, saying she couldn't be a right woman, and he should take her and leave her where he had found her. Well, he couldn't bring himself to do such a thing.

Then he went to see an old man in the village and find out what advice he could give him. He told him how he had found her and how his people were on at him to take her and leave her where he had found her. 'And I can't bring myself to do such a thing,' said he. 'There's nothing a woman's two hands can do that she can't do,' said he. 'There's no sort of ironing or washing or cooking,' said he, 'that she's not able for.'

'Oh well,' said the old man, 'don't send her away just now,' said he, 'but when a year is up,' said he, 'go out,' said he, 'and sit in the same place where you were sitting when you saw the wreath of mist,' said he, 'and stay there a while,' said he. You just might hear or discover something about her,' said he, 'before you get rid of her.'

Well, when the year was up MacDonald went and took everything he needed and set out for the hills, and took his seat on the very spot where he had been sitting when he saw the wreath of mist. Night came on and he saw nothing and heard nothing, and he was getting cold then and he got ready to leave. When he got to his feet and looked up the hill, a knoll above him was open and a light was showing. He started off up the hill.

There were people inside there, and one man standing handing round drink to them all in a cup, and he stood outside watching them. The man who was handing round the drink said: 'Well,' said he, 'it was a year ago tonight,' said he, 'that I meant to have my wedding here,' said he, 'but things went wrong,' said he. 'But I left her one thing to remember me by,' said he. 'She won't be able to utter a word until she gets a drink out of my cup,' said he.

When he heard that, he rushed in. They all shouted to get him out, get him out.

'I won't go out,' said he, 'until I get a drink like the others have had.'

'You can have that,' said he [the man with the cup], 'if you undertake to be just like ourselves.'

'I will,' said he.

He went and put some of whatever this stuff was that he had into the cup, and handed it to him. He just emptied what was in the cup on the ground, stuffed the cup into his pocket and made off. The whole band went after him: he had nothing but fall after fall until he got home. But he got home: he went to his bed and stayed there all day.

When he got up in the evening, he went and got the cup and he washed the cup clean, dried it and filled it with milk. And he went down to the kitchen, and she was working in the kitchen, and he held it out to her. 'Here,' said he, 'drink that,' said he to her.

She waved him away – she wasn't going to take it at all.

'Take it,' said he, 'and drink that!' said he.

Oh, she shook her head – she wasn't going to take it at all. He drew his sword. 'Take that and drink it,' said he, 'or I'll run you through on the spot with this sword!' said he.

She looked at him and trembled, and she took the cup and drank it off. When she had drunk what was in the cup, 'Ah, God be thanked,' said she, 'what a lot of good that drink has done me!' said she.

'You seem to have found your tongue with it, anyway,' said he.

'Yes,' said she.

'What sort of woman are you?' said he to her.

'Oh,' said she, 'just a woman like any other.'

'Then what brought you,' said he, 'to where I found you?' said he.

'Well, that's something I don't know anything about,' said she. 'I had married,' said she, 'the proprietor of a hotel,' said she, 'in Edinburgh,' said she. 'And the wedding night,' said she, 'when we went to sleep,' said she, 'that's the last thing I can remember,' said she. 'The next thing I knew was you bending over me,' said she, 'bandaging my legs, which had been wounded,' said she.

'Aye, aye!' said he. 'Then are you wanting to go home now?' said he.

'Ah, yes,' said she, 'if you think it is all right for me.'

'Oh well then,' said he, 'get ready,' said he, 'and I'll go with you myself.'

The upshot was that he and she set off for Edinburgh, and when they got to Edinburgh she knew her way around well enough, though he had never been there. At last she got to the hotel where . . .

'Well now,' said she, 'here's where I lived.'

'Well then,' said he, 'we can go into the kitchen,' said he, 'and you mustn't let on that you belong there at all,' said he, 'and we'll see what we can find out,' said he. (And he had come armed.)

'Oh,' said she, 'I'll do whatever you ask me.'

They went into the kitchen and the servants were bustling hither and thither, one this way and one that, and there was one girl, and every time she passed, she would stop a moment to stare at the woman. The woman was keeping her face hidden. And he asked if they could get something to eat there.

'Well, you can,' said the cook, 'but almost any other day we'd have been better able to serve meals than we are today,' said she. 'But you can have something to eat,' said she, 'if you'll wait a minute.'

'What's the matter here?' said he to her.

'Well, I can see you're a stranger here,' said she, 'if you have to ask what's the matter.'

'Oh yes,' said he, 'I've never been in the town until today.'

'Well, it's a sad tale we have to tell today,' said she. 'The lady of the house has been confined to her bed for a year past,' said she, 'and I believe she is not expected to live another day,' said she.

'Aye, aye!' said he. 'Has a doctor ever seen her?'

'Oh, he's spent all he has on doctors,' said she. 'For all that they've never done her the slightest good,' said she.

'Oh well, that's extraordinary,' said he. 'Mind you, I'm a doctor myself,' said he, 'and I'd be very willing to look at her,' said he. 'You never know, I might be able to keep her alive a little bit longer,' said he.

'Oh, in that case,' said she, 'I'll tell him that,' said she. She went through to her master and said: 'There are a couple there,' said she, 'who have come into the kitchen,' said she, 'a gentleman,' said she, 'and a lady too along with him,' said she, 'and he says,' said she, 'that he is a doctor. I told him,' said she, 'that the lady of the house has been confined to bed for a year past,' said she, 'and he has offered to come and look at her,' said she, 'in the hope that he can keep her alive a bit longer.'

'Oh well,' said he, 'it's too late for doctors now,' said he, 'but since he's offered to come through himself,' said he, 'tell him to come.'

She came back and asked him to go through. He went through. . . .

. . . 'They tell me,' said he, 'that you have had her in bed for a year past.'

'Oh yes,' said he.

'Ah, well,' said he, 'I don't believe she's so far gone yet,' said he, 'that we can't maybe do something for her,' said he.

She was lying facing the other way, and oh, she didn't look as if she had long to live.

'Turn over,' said he, 'and let's see your face,' said he.

Oh, she couldn't: she wasn't able to stir.

'Oh, you aren't so far gone yet,' said he, 'that you can't manage to turn over. Turn over,' said he, 'when I tell you.'

Oh, she couldn't.

'Oh,' said her husband, 'don't bully her,' said he. 'She hasn't long left to live,' said he.

He turned to him – 'Are you,' said he, 'going to teach me my own business?' said he, drawing his sword. The other man backed out of the door. He went over and bolted the door.

'Turn over when I tell you,' said he to her.

She began to wail, but in the middle of all the commotion she turned to face him.

'Can't you . . . couldn't you turn over, now?' said he. 'Now sit up,' said he.

'Oh, I can't, I can't!' said she.

'Oh, you can do it,' said he. 'Sit up!' said he.

She burst out crying and screaming, but in the end here she sat up.

'Can't you manage to sit up, now?' said he. 'Now get out of bed,' said he.

'Oh, anything, anything but that!' said she.

'Out of that bed,' said he, 'or I'll put this through you!' said he, drawing his sword.

She flew off in a ball of flame and vanished.

He turned round and went and opened the door. 'Come in now, my dear fellow,' said he, 'and have a look at your bed,' said he.

He came in. 'Ah, God preserve us,' said he, 'where is she?' said he.

'She's in Hell,' said he, 'where she belongs,' said he. 'Come through now,' said he, 'with me.'

He went through to the kitchen, and the woman was sitting in the kitchen.

'Is that your wife?' said he, turning to him.

'Oh, Lord, yes. This is my wife!' said he. She got up and came to him.

'Well, she's the more likely of the two, anyway!' said MacDonald to him. 'The fairies carried her off and the Devil took her place.'

They wanted to keep MacDonald there with them for good. They didn't want to let him go home again at all; they wanted him to stay with them.

That's what happened to the woman he found in the hills.

A DEAD WIFE AMONG
THE FAIRIES

[THIS MAN'S WIFE] died, a young wife . . . young man
. . . and he took great thowt aboot it, the man did. It was afore this now
lighthoose was built, oh, I don't know how long before. Well, they were
a small wardro there where the lighthouse is built, which . . . you ken a
wardro . . . a small buildin o stones, a small cairn buildin.

Well, they were an owld wife here 'at was a kind of . . . kind o
witchie-wife; I don't know whether she was, but she was supposed to
be well up in the Bläck Airts onywey, an he went an got advice fae her.
An he wondered if there could be nothing dön aboot it yet?

She said, yes, they could be something dön aboot it indeed: but he hed
to get a . . . hev a very thick oaken stäff, an a Bible, an a bläck cät. An he hed
to go to the wardro at the brae o Versabreck wi the full moon, and there
was supposed to be a sort of heathery cave under this wardro. And he hed to
go there an cry on his wife be neem. An he hed to hev the Bible open at a
psälm, I think, and he was supposed tae recite a verse or two o this and
throw in the bläck cät, an the wife would come [? just rising up] just like
that. But the fairy foak would try to stop her. But . . . she said, when he heard
his wife spakin he hed to jump in and use the stäff and use it withoot mercy
until he got a howld o his wife, an she would come oot just like that.

An he dös it. And . . . of coorse she hed to go bäck afore daylight,
though, but he spoke tae her all night, every full moon. Thät is the story.
That's what this man [? hed to do]. I heard me fäther sayin it.

A MAN LIFTED BY THE
SLUAGH

THE HOUSES IN THE old days [were] thatched houses
that had no chimneys or anything else in them but a fire in the middle of
the floor. Well, when they were lighting the fire, do you see, the house
would be full of smoke. There would be a window on the west side of
the house and it would have a shutter on it. They would open that shutter
and the window would be wide open. And it was said that the *sluagh* was
going around and if they found the window open, with nothing blocking
it, they would shoot anything, they'd kill anything that was in the house
if there wasn't an iron bar across it, but if the bar was across it they
couldn't do anything.

There was one man in the township we belonged to and his house
was above the shore and it was said that the *sluagh* used to lift him. But
this night anyway he had gone out of the house and he didn't come in.
His wife was worried about him and so were his children. The children
went to bed but the wife stayed up at the fireside. On . . . well after
midnight he came home.

'But Heavens,' said she, 'where have you been?'

'Well, it was no small distance from here,' said he. 'I've been in
Heisker,' said he, 'and I've visited all the islands.'

'How did you do that?' said she.

'When I went outside,' said he, 'the *sluagh* was just waiting for me,'
said he, 'and I simply went off with them.'

'You'll be dead,' said she, 'for lack of food.'

'Well, indeed, I'm not that,' said he. 'I got my fill of warm milk in Heisker,' said he. 'And I was told,' said he, 'to shoot one of the girls – the girl that was milking the cows,' said he. 'And I hadn't the heart to shoot the honest lass,' said he. 'There were hens on the roost,' said he. 'I shot a hen, and the girl stayed alive.'

And that's the way I heard it.

72   *Nan MacKinnon*

A MAN WITH A FAIRY LOVER

I HEARD ABOUT A MAN who had a fairy lover and, anyway, he was saying to himself that the affair was going too far and that it was time for him to leave her. He used to go to the hunting-hill, as they called it, to hunt, you know, and he had been going with this fairy woman for some time – she would meet him and he was going with her, and the time came when he said to himself that it was time for him to break with her, that he had gone a bit too far. So he broke with her and then he stopped going hunting to the hill: he was afraid to go to the hill in case he met her, since he had given her up.

Anyway, this day he thought he would go to an island to hunt, and he took two dogs with him and set off in his boat. Anyway, when he was coming in to the landing-place – he was right at the landing-place – the fairy woman appeared coming down.

When he saw her he began to row out as hard as he could, and she came down to the landing-place and she pulled a *cnèibeag* out of the hem of her mantle. (You know what a *cnèibeag* is? . . . a little scrap of yarn . . .) She pulled a *cnèibeag* out of the hem of her mantle and threw it so that it hit the boat, and she began to pull the boat in, and the boat was on the point of touching the shore and . . . He remembered a knife she had given him, and anything it touched it would cut, you know, and he took the knife out of his pocket and put it to the thread, and the boat moved out from the rock and she called after him then: 'MacPhee of the Black Dogs,' said she, 'you have left me on the point.'

That was that, time passed and he married another woman – a woman from his own township and he never went near her [the fairy woman] now, but, just wait, his wife was expecting a baby now, and then her time came and there was no sign of the baby coming. But, anyway, he said to himself that he would go to the hill to try and see her, just to see what she would say to him – the fairy woman.

He went to the hill and she met him: 'What's your news today, MacPhee?' said she.

'Indeed, I do have news,' said he. 'There's a goat down yonder,' said he, 'in prolonged labour.'

She paused for a moment: 'That seems very strange to me,' said she, 'with the pearlwort under her foot. But,' said she, 'it's not the goat at all,' said she, 'but your wife.'

And she took a black belt out of her pocket: 'You put that belt on her,' said she, 'when you get home,' said she, 'and she'll be quite all right.'

And he took the belt and put it in his pocket. When the fairy woman parted from him, he wound this belt round a stone. The stone split in two.

And he went straight to the goat-pen and plucked the pearlwort. (You know the pearlwort? You've heard of the pearlwort: that little flower they call the pearlwort? . . . Oh, it grows here in summer, lots

of it – a slender little white flower it is, with just the one flower . . .)
He went straight to the goat-pen and plucked the pearlwort and put it
in the bed – his wife's bed – when he got home, and the child was born
and she was quite all right.

That's how they found out that the pearlwort has healing powers.

73a   *Kate Dix*

THE FAIRY SUITOR FOILED

THERE WAS A HOUSE at Bornish in South Uist, and it
was just a little thatched house, but many a one called there. Every house
at that time had a partition in it. And they killed their cow when it grew
old. And they used to dry the hide to make garments and boots and all
sorts of things out of it, even laces: they made laces for their shoes. And
the cow's hide was hung over the partition.

And there was one girl in the house with her father and mother. And
the girl was very beautiful, and she used to go to the hill with the cattle
every day and come back in, and go out again in the evening and bring
them home. And there was a man who used to meet her in the hill, a
bonny lad – she had never seen anyone so handsome as him. And he
would walk with her till she was nearly home, and he left, and came

back, and it went on like that for six months. She used to wonder — for she was deeply in love with the lad — why he never said a word to her, and how nobody had ever seen him before. She asked everyone, but they had never seen or heard of such a man at all.

She went to a kind old tinker woman who lived down there, and she told her the whole story.

'Oh, my dear,' said she, 'when you go home, take a strand from the tail of the cowhide hanging on the partition, and wash and clean it and make it up into a bonny plait, and lay it aside. And before long that lad will ask for a lock of your hair. And when he asks for a lock of your hair you must go and give him the plait you got from the cow's tail.'

As the poor old woman said, that's how it happened. It wasn't long before the lad asked her for a lock of her hair, and she said, 'I'll bring it for you tonight when I go for the cattle.' And she did that.

And when they were holding family worship at midnight, the hide over the partition began to hop. It began to hop, and jump, and hop like mad. They leapt to open the door, and out went the skin. They went after it, everyone who was around, with dogs and men and horses. They couldn't catch it or keep up with it until it reached the knoll they called Cnoc an t-Sìdhein [the Fairy Knoll]. It stopped there and it went and vanished from sight, and they never found the hide again.

And they said that if the girl had given him her own hair, she would have gone and she would never have come back again. That's what I heard.

KEEPING OUT THE SEA MAN

WELL, THIS HAPPENED in a hoose – it was supposed to be somewhere in the Sooth Parish o Sooth Ronaldsay. It was a man, a widower man and his daughter, they lived together on a wee croft. And there was one night, the man – he was awey, he was in bed before the girl. An the next mornin she tell'd him she'd haen an aafu experience. She'd barred the door an was sittin at the fire when the door opened an a man came in. An he sat aal night beside her. An she said there was somethin funny aboot him, she said, an she didna like to ask him who he wis or what he was doin – there was somethin queer aboot him.

Saa he says: 'Ye're no barred the door right,' he said. 'I'll bar the door mesel the night.' So when that night cam he barred the door an made sure it was fixed an geed awey tae his bed. In the mornin she said the sam thing happened – the door just opened an the man came in.

'Ah weel,' he says, 'I think he must be a sea man.' So he says: 'But I'll sit op the night an wait tae he comes in.' So they barred the door as usual, an sittin one at each side o the fire, an the door just opened and the man waaked in. Oh, the old fellow said, 'Oh, com in, com in,' an made him very welcome. 'Sit doon!' an start to taak awey aboot different things tae him, an he says: 'Mön,' he says, 'I'm hevin an aaful bit o bother.'

'Oh,' he says. 'What's wrong?'

'Weel,' he says, 'there a sea bull teen to comin an haantin a quey [heifer] I hev in the byre, an no matter hoo I fasten the door, or hoo I tie her, he gets in an he's in there all night, an he's just ruinin my quey. I donno what I'm gaan to do wi her.'

'Ah,' he says, 'that's aesy pitten right, mön. Aal ye need to do is cut some hair aff o her tail, an pare her hoofs, an pit the hair an the parins abov the byre door, an he'll no be able to com in.'

'Oh,' he says, 'thanks very much' – he was terribly grand, he would try that. So he geed awey to bed an left them: sam thing, he sat to mornin an awey he gaed.

So that day they clippit a lock of the girl's hair an pared her nails an pat it all together an stuck it up abov the door, barred the door as usual an sat waitin. Aboot the usual time he cam: they heard the sneck o the door liftin, an the door tried but shö wouldno open. An they hears him sayin: 'Eh my,' he says, 'there mony a man done themsels ill wi their tongue, and I'm don the sam.' An that's the last they're hard o him.

I heard my mother tellin that one. It was her mother that had told it – she belonged to the Sooth Parish . . . She would have known where the hoose was an probably who the folk was, or was supposed to be.

MACCODRUM'S SEAL WIFE

Yes, I HEARD A STORY long ago from the old people about that. They were known as the MacCodrums of the seals and I heard the story of how it came about too.

In those days people used to go beach-combing much more than they do now. They used to go looking to see if seaweed had been washed ashore for manure . . . And bits of timber would get washed ashore, and there would be iron bolts attached to them and things of that kind, you know. And things were not so easily come by then as they are today – they were hard to get. And they always went beach-combing looking for such things.

It was said that this man, one of the MacCodrums, was beach-combing one day. And, anyway, he was taking a rest beside a certain bay and he sat down in the shelter of a rock. And he looked out and what should he see but this group of seals making for the beach in the bay.

He kept an eye on them and they came ashore and walked up above . . . No, they didn't walk, but they made their way up beyond the tide-wrack and they dragged themselves up the bank. And then – they took off their skins and the moment they took off their skins, they changed into beautiful women.

They turned back and out to sea they went. They were playing and swimming there. But anyway he noticed that one particular woman among them – that she was much more beautiful than the rest though they were all beautiful enough – that one of them was especially beautiful compared to the others. And the skin she had been wearing was especially beautiful too compared to the skins of the others.

He said to himself: 'Well, I'm just going to try and get that skin for myself and I'll make one dive for it to see if I can get hold of it before they can get ashore.' And at that he got up and made for this lovely skin. But they noticed him and up they rushed on to the land and every one of them made for her own skin but he made for this skin and he managed to get to it before the woman did. He seized the skin and thrust it under his arm. The others seized the other skins and out to sea they went – in the shape of seals as they had been before.

The woman was weeping and begging him to give her the skin so that she could go with her companions but there was no moving him. 'No,' he said. He was going to keep the skin. At last he made for home with the skin under his arm and the woman following behind him weeping and begging for the skin – but he just kept going and paid no heed to her. He got home and when he got a chance he hid the skin behind the rafters in the barn . . .

Anyway, as things turned out, he and this woman got married and apparently they lived happily together. But it seems it was the end of harvest-time when this happened and he was getting the corn in. And when he got the chance a day or two later when he was building a stack, he managed to get the skin from behind the rafters in the barn and he hid it in the corn-stack without being noticed. He kept on doing this every year – and that was always the last stack he put into the barn in the spring – and when he was getting the stack in he hid the skin behind the rafters till he made the next stack next year, and he always left that stack out last after the others.

Year after year went by and things were going very well for them, and she was an excellent wife and a good mother to the children – they had children by this time. Anyway, one particular year, in spring he was getting the last stack in as usual, and by this year the children were growing up and some of them were helping him to get the stack in. They got the stack in and he went and got the skin as usual and hid it behind the rafters in the barn.

But this night the mother was getting the children to bed and one of the children – one of the girls – said to her mother: 'Oh mother,' said she, 'what a beautiful thing father had in the stack today,' said she, 'in the corn-stack.'

'What was it, darling?' said she.

'A fur coat,' said she, 'as beautiful as ever you saw.'

'Could you tell me, darling,' said she, 'where he put it?'

'Certainly,' said she, 'he put it behind the rafters in the barn.'

'Oh well,' said she, 'I'm going away and leaving you, and I'll be away for a while, but I'll come back again,' said she. 'And you won't be short of fish. You keep a look-out for me.' And she kissed the children and went away.

Anyway, the woman was never seen again – and there was no sign of the skin. And they reckoned she had got hold of the skin and that she had got back to the sea just as she had been before.

Anyway, at a certain time of the evening, sometimes, there was a big reef down there facing the house and a seal used to land on the reef, and it would be crying, with a fish in its mouth. And they reckoned that this was her coming back to look for the children and waiting there for them on the reef with the fish.

That's how I heard the story.

RESCUED BY A SEAL

THIS IS A STORY 'at was told by my father, and it was a handed-down story to him. And hit was about a crew . . . of men that went to some skerries . . . to shoot seals. And when they were shootin the seals, the wind and the sea got that rough 'at the men got back to the boat – except one, he was so busy clubbin the seals that . . . by the time that he was ready they couldn't get him off the rock, and they had to leave him. And so, he was sittin waetin, just didna know what to do, when a seal popped up an spoke to him, an said: 'I'll put you to your shore if you'll do wan thing for me.'

And he says, 'What's that?'

'To bring my son's skin back 'at that men took.'

And . . . 'Oh yes,' he said, he would do that.

'Well,' he [*sic*] says, 'come on my back, then. Maek a slit on each side where you can taek a grip, so 'at you don't tumble off, and I'll land you.'

So she [*sic*] did this, an the seal landed him at the shore. Then he went along to the store where they had the seal-skins, and the seal was followin him at the sea. And . . . he came out with a skin and he said, 'Is that it?' and she said, 'Yes.'

And he gave her the skin and the seal disappeared and the man came home. And they aal thought that he was dead, an when he came in, they were bakin the scones for Christmas, and he oapent the door an waaked in on them, and they got the shock o their life when they saa him. So he told them this story . . .

I think it was either Sule Skerry or Ve Skerries, I don't remember.

THE LIMPET PICK

Noo HAVE YE HEARD THE STORY about the man 'at wis down i the ebb gettin lempits? Well, ye know, what they caal't the lempit pick, he wis like a piece of . . . a bit of a broken knife, you see, an a wooden handle on it. An when he was down i the ebb gettin this lempits, he saa a big seal lyin . . . not very far away. Now he craaled along, an he had noathin but juist the pick, you see, wi this olt broken portion of a knife on the end, 'at he was pickin off the lempits with. Well, he got cloase enoff 'at he thocht he would maybe get this sael, so he lifted this pick an he cam down on him: he cut the skin, but the sael made a bassel an away he went. He didnae get him. But he [the seal] took his lempit pick with him!

Now years after that he went – him an some more went tae get a boät. And they cam into this house and then they were a poor, they said, a poor old body sittin up in a coarner. And they tälked fir a time, and then this old body took a good look at this man, an then out o the holl i the wall shö pulled out something, an she held it up, an she said, 'Do you know that *skjön*?' (Now *skjön* was the name . . . fir their knife, in fac' . . . i the haaf days . . . the *skjön* wis the name fir the knife 'at they cuttit their bait an all that with, it hed to be the *skjön*.) An then this wis the saem old lempit pick 'at he wis stucken i the sael, and this was supposed to be the olt lady, you see, this was supposed to be the saem seal 'at he stack the knife in . . .

(I heard aa this olt stories, ye know, when A wis a boy, an I sät listenin . . . what you learned then, you see, you'll never forget. An yet somethin, you know, fae not very many years ago, you will forget it –

may come to your mind some time. But fir my age, you see, you live in the past . . . Everyone comin to my age an before that, you see, they're livin in the past. Aal . . . that happen't an aal that they heard . . . i their youth, you see, he's there.)

77   *James Henderson*

THE MAGIC ISLAND

I DON'T KNOW EXACTLY where, but it was supposed to be aff o some o the North Isles or the West o the Mainland, but there was a faimily, father an mother an two sons an a daughter. Well one mornin the daughter went away to take lempit for bait at the shore, an she didna come back when she should ha' come. So they gaed aff to look for her, but there was no trace o her ever fund: they thought, weel, the only thing was she had slippit ower the face o a rock and wis drooned.

Oh, some while efter that, maybe years efter that, the faither and the two sons gaed aff to the sea, fishin, wan day. Came a very thick fog, and they thought – they'd no compass in the boat, an there was very little wind, but they got oot the oars an tried to pull as near as they could for whar they thoyt the shore wis. Efter a whilie they did mak oot some land, an they cam in on a beach, but it was a strange place to them, they'd never seen it afore, but there wis a boat landin place there, so they brang the boat up an hed a bit o look aroond. They saa a path, so they folla'd the path, an it led up tae a good big hoose. They thoyt the best they could do wis knock at the door añ see if they could get some informaetion as to whar they wis. So they knockit on the door, a man cam to the door an they tell'd him what had happened them.

'Oh,' he said, 'com in, com in,' jist com in an wait tae the fog cleared an they would soon see whar they wis then. So they cam in: a grand weel-furnished hoose, an wha wis the mistress o it but the lass that was supposed tae have been drooned years ago. So when they saa that they thought there wis somethin kind o queer aboot it, an they didna like to ask ony questions.

But . . . she asked hoo they wis, an oh, they wis aal fine, an she said, oh, they would hev somthin tae aet, set doon a grand diet to them tae aet. An they wis taakin awey aboot different things, an the man said, did they hev ony baests that they would sell?

'Oh yes,' the old fella says, 'we hev a coo, a grand coo 'at A wis thinkin on sellin indeed.'

'Weel,' he says, 'A'll buy her. What dae ye want for her?'

Oh, he named a good price for her, he would want that onywey –

'Oh,' he says, 'A'll give ye that,' an he paid him in gold sovereigns.

So he thought, 'Noo . . . A'll fin oot whar this place is,' so he says, 'Weel, ye'll hev to tell me noo what wey to com here, or A'll no be able to tak the coo tee ye.'

'Och,' he says, 'don't you worry aboot that. A'll com for the coo masel.'

So . . . wan o them said, 'I think 'at the fog's offerin to lift a little.'

So the . . . lass says tae them, 'Weel, afore ye go, are they onything here in the . . . in the hoose 'at ye would fancy to tak wi ye?'

An the man said, 'Oh, ye're welcome to onything 'at's here, jist pick onything ye would like an tak it wi ye!'

So the lass, she gied them a kind o look, I suppose thinkin 'at they would say, 'Well A'll take – A'll tak you wi us!' Hooever, they lookit aroond an they saa a grand big gold dish, an they said, oh, they would like tae hev that. So she handed it to them: 'Well,' she says, 'tak it an go!'

So they gaed doon to the boat, and the man gied them a hand to laanch, an he said, 'Jist pull ower that way a bit.' So they pulled oot an the island disappeared in the fog, an the fog lifted an they were no distance aff o their own land. So they pulled for home, an soon as they cam in, the wife was meetin them at the shore very agitated. She says, 'An aafu thing's happened.' She says, 'Wir best coo's lyin in the byre deid!'

'Ach,' the man says, 'let her be gaan, she's ower weel paid for!'

So that wis the end o that.

---

78   *Tom Tulloch*

THE LAST TROW IN YELL

THIS WIS WAN O THE HIDMAST, if not *the* hidmast trowie hadd 'at wis in Yell: it wis in a knowe at Burnside in Collyifa. An aboot yon time they were a fiddler o graet repute in Collyifa be the neem o Rabbie Anderson, and the trows would aye meet him efery year an invite him to play tö them ipö owld Yül E'ën; an he wis graetly delighted wi this, fir although he would naither aet or drink in asaed them, everything 'at he laid his haund til through the coorse o the year prospered til him, and he thowt 'at this wis a very good bargeen, an he aye lookit forward to goin. But he never telled anybody whaur he wis been the Christmas Eve, an the fokk all kind o winder't whar Rabbie wis been, but he . . . never telt them at all. An they envyed him of coorse upon his graet prosperity durin the coorse o the year, but he held his tongue, he telt no body.

And then they were wän winter 'at he never saw anything tö the trows, and they never met him or ever invited him. And Rabbie wis gettin a bit alairmed aboot this, fir he was wonderin whit wey 'at it wis . . . [would] eyffect his prosperity fir the comin year. So they were ac night comin brawly weel on fir Yül 'at he made upon him an summed up his courage, and he güd in to the trowie hadd. An when he came in there, they werena a sowl in sight aless wän owld wife, an shö wis sittin on a doil-hoit at the fier, and he axed her whät on aerth wis come o all the rest o the fokk 'at was here the last time he wis? And shö said that he might ax; shö said they were a minister come to Collyifö, an he had thatten a volabeelity o preachin an prayin 'at the trows could not suffer it at all – they got no paece, and they were all hed to clear oot to Faera. The last wan o them wis gone, but shö t'owt 'at shö wis ower owld tö . . . start life in a new place ipö the face o the aerth, an shö t'owt 'at shö would just end her days whar shö wis. And that was the hidmast o the trows that ever was telled aboot in . . . North Yell!

. . . That was supposed to be James Ingram: he was minister o the parish o North Yell an Fetlar fae yghteen-t'ree to eighteen-twenty-wan . . .

. . . As it was telled i my boyhood days aboot faeries 'at they were supposed to be a more kind o a gentle, gossamer bein as what the trows wis: . . . the faeries wis more or less a hairmless race, and . . . they were more up fir gai'ty and all that kind o – The trows wis . . . same as if it wis more cloasely assoaciated til a aert'ly bein, 'at they could aither be good or bäd, accoardin to whit wey you dealt wi them . . . Yondroo at the Burn o Skoildigil on your wey to Gloup . . . that wis supposed to be a graet trowie hadd, an they were different fokk 'at said that when they were aroont that burn 'at they could hear the trows wäshin their leem!

LEGENDS OF
WITCHCRAFT

THE BROONIE

Dae ye ken what a Broonie is? No? Well, in Scotland we have a Broonie, a spirit creature – not only fairies an witches an waarlocks an aa that kind o things but we also have the Broonie. But the Broonie wis a very helpful spirit, an it couldn't take on a very nice form. It used tae look terrible, an everybody was frightened o it, and it kept away oot o the sight o people if it could. It was mostly covered in brown hair like a coconut; it had iron teeth, and its eyes were the same as they'd been half plucked out and tried to be . . . pushed back in again! An its feet were at least a yard in length – so that everybody was terrified o the Broonie. But they'd nae reason to be, it never – a Broonie wis never haerd tae dae any harm tae anybody.

But, all they done, was they attached themsel tae a family, and they would work for this family. Mostly, they liked to work in a mill, an they nearly always went fir mills, but nut always, they would work at other things as well, but mostly inside things. Now, near this place there lived a young miller, an he lived wi's mother. An his mother dabbled aboot in the Black Art an witchcraft an charms an aa that kind o thing, an this young fella, he was her only son. An there wis a fairmer's daughter, an she would have gave anything for him, she really cared aboot him. But he wis courtin a servant lassie on another fairm. Now his mother wisnae very pleased at that, she thought he should ha' took this fairmer's daughter, an she said, 'Look,' she says, 'a big fairm an everything, an it would be yours, because her father's gettin on a bit now.'

He says, 'I cannae help it, mother,' he said. He says, 'I love Katie,' he said, 'an A'm gaunnae marry Katie.'

She says, 'Ye're naw gaunnae marry Katie,' she says, 'because Katie's gaunnae dee, an you're gaunnae marry the fairmer's daughter!'

He says, 'Never, mother!' He said, 'A'm gaunnae marry Katie, the servant lassie.'

So his mother wisnae very pleased at aa. But in spite o his mother, he did marry Katie, and he went an lived at the mill: there wis a wee empty hoose there. An his mother wis aboot a mile away from them. So they were very happy an worked away, an of course the ineviteable happened, Katie wis wi child. And they were pleased an happy aboot it. The mother she never came near them, ye see, she jist stayed in her ain wee place.

But one mornin the young man came in an he said, 'Katie, I dinnae want tae alarm ye,' he said, 'but I think there's a Broonie on the place.'

And she paled and said, 'What?'

He says, 'Now, dinnae get alarmed,' he says, 'but A'm near sure there's a Broonie on the place. Aa last week,' he said, 'an aa this week, every mornin when A went doon tae the mill,' he said, 'the bags are [?stashed] up right at the side o the waa,' he says, 'all milled. So naeb'dy else would dae it but a Broonie.'

'Oh dear,' she says, 'we'll hae to clear oot o the place.'

'No, no,' he says, 'dinnae get alarmed.' So one day he caught a glimpse o the Broonie, and he said tae Katie, 'If ye come doon caanie wi me,' he said, 'ye'll see him. Now A'm waarnin ye, he's no a bonnie sight, but,' he said, 'he'll dae ye no harm.'

So he took her and they would sit and watch, you see, and she did get a glimpse o the Broonie. And she recoiled a bit, ye ken, but och, she wis a fine lassie, and she said, 'Well, folk cannae help what they look like,' she said, 'I don't suppose. If you tell me that he'll no hairm us that's the main thing.' So gradually she went doon and she made a bed intae a wee bothy place for the Broonie, and he gradually let . . . her see him. And she got that she didnae mind his appearance, an she got quite used to seein him now and then. So he went there and he worked, and she brought him maybe a – milk or something like that an left it fir him anyway, an oatmeal an that, but she lost all her fear o him.

Now she wis gettin near her time. And she wis wonderin, an her man wis wonderin what they were gaunnae dae. He says, 'A dinnae ken whether tae ask ma mother or no.'

She says, 'No, dinnae ask yir mother.' But she didnae huv tae ask the mother, because the mother came up, when she knew the lassie wes near her time, and oh, she couldnae have been friendlier! She started tryin tae help her the every way: she says, 'Look, A've brought ye a bonnie wee black cat kitten,' she says, 'a wee black cat, look, tae keep ye in comp'ny when ye're confined,' she said. 'And it could be any day now, so A'll do up your hair' – you know how women always wear long, long hair at that time – 'A'll do up your hair,' she says, 'an you'll no have to comb it while you're in bed,' she said. 'And A'm gaunna make ye two lovely soft feather pillows.' So she went away and she filled two pillas wi ravens' feathers; she turn't the foot o the lassie's bed towards the door, and she tied up her hair, an every here an there she was puttin witches' knots in it. 'Course the lassie didnae ken this. And this wee cat wis always comin up an sittin beside the lassie.

So, sure enough, the lassie went into labour, and the young man says, 'A'll get somebody.' He says, 'A'll go fir the howdie woman.' (This was a sort o midwife that jist – no trained or anything, but they were good at that, it wis a gift – and everybody in that district went for this woman.)

And she says, 'I don't know if she'll come' – because everybody in the district had haerd that there was a Broonie on the place, an a lot o folk wouldnae even pass there at night in the dark, fir fear o the Broonie. And she says, 'Dinnae leave me here,' she said, 'dinnae leave me' – because this was her secont day in labour. She said, 'I do need somebody, but I dinnae want ye to leave me.'

He says, 'Well, A'll get the Broonie to go!' So when it got dark, he got a big lang coat and a hat wi a big wide brim, an he said, 'Look, A want ye to go an get the midwife fir Katie.'

He says, 'All right.' So he pulled up the collar o this coat . . . hat doon – it was dark anyway – and took a horse, and away he went along this bridle path to where the midwife stayed. And he came to the door, and he said, 'It's Katie that's no weel,' he said, 'and I'm sent fir ye.'

She says, 'Oh well, A'll jist come alang wi ye.' So her man helped her up on the horse's back beside the Broonie, and they're away·on the road. But it bein dark, and just a bridle path, they couldnae go very fast. And she says, ye ken, 'I hope I dinnae see that Broonie!' She says, 'I'm terrified o the Broonie.'

And the Broonie says, 'Na, dinnae worry.' He says, 'I can assure ye, fir certain, that ye'll no see anything worse than whit ye're cuddled intae the noo' – because she had her airms roond aboot the Broonie, ye see?

So they got tae the hoose, and the young man cam oot and lifted her aff the horse, and she came in to where Katie was. And the Broonie went back to the wee bothy.

But another couple o days went past and there was still nothing doin. Six, seven, eight days went past. No, nothing happenin. An the young lassie was in absolute torture, agony all the time. She wis absolutely done. An this young man says, 'I know, A'll bet ye a shillin,' he says, 'this is the work o my mother.'

So doon he went tae his mother's hoose, and he says, 'Mother,' he says, 'will ye tak that spell aff o Katie?' He says, 'I ken ye've did something.'

She says, 'I will not.' She said, 'I told ye that she was gaunnae die, an you were gaunna mairry the fairmer's dochter!'

He said, 'No. No, mother, fir God's sake!' He says, 'Ye've nae idea o the torture that lassie's gaun through.'

'Nae mair than she deserves,' she said.

So the young man, he knew that this would happen, his wife would die in agony, and he ran away wi his heid in his hands. An he had naebody to go tae: he ran tae the Broonie, and he told the Broonie: he was greetin on the Broonie's shoother. He says, 'O dear, dear, what am I gaunnae dae? – an it's aa the fault o my mother!'

'Well,' the Broonie said, 'A'll tell ye whit ye can dae.' He said, 'Take me doon tae yir mother.'

'Oh no, no,' he said, 'that wouldnae help at aa,' he says. 'Supposin I took God himsel doon tae my mother,' he says, 'I ken her too well.'

'Ah, but,' he said, 'you jist take me doon, becuz,' he said, 'I can become invisible. But before ye go doon,' he said, 'A'll tell ye what tae say. Just try an put a smile on yir face, an run in an say, "Oh, mother, mother, you've got a beautiful young grandson!" and see whit happens,' he says, 'an A'll be invisible.'

So the laddie wis a bit perplexed wi this . . . but anyhow he done it. He went down wi the Broonie, an he ran in an he says, 'Mother, ye've got a beautiful young grandson.'

And she says, 'What?'

He says, 'Oh yes, mother, a beautiful boy. It's lovely!' An he says, 'A cannae wait, A've got to go back to Katie.' So he's out the door, but the Broonie was still standin there, invisible, ye see.

An when he went oot the door, this auld woman started stampin her feet an cursin, 'Who told him aboot the witch's knots in her hair? Who told him aboot that black cat? An who told them aboot the raven's feathers? And who told them that I'd turned her feet tae the door?' she says. 'I wonder who could have told them that.'

And then the Broonie of course, he's whipped away after the young man, caught up wi him an he says, 'I ken whit's wrong now.'

And when they went intae the hoose, they heard the lassie screamin, an this young fella says, 'No, no, I cannae go near her! I cannae look at her like that.'

'Well,' the Broonie said, 'I must dae it.' An the Broonie ran up, opened the door – and when the midwife saw him she's out the door, and the sparks were fleein fae her heels as she ran away up through the fields and things! And the Broonie went, an the lassie was in such a state she couldnae care who it was. He says, 'I've came,' he says, 'tae try an help ye.' And, 'Come on, Katie,' he said, 'let me loosen oot yir hair, ye're sweatin there,' an he loosed oot her hair an took oot aa the witch's knots. And he turned her bed wi her feet tae the south, and he said, 'Gie me that pillas.' He took the pillas, and he shouted tae her man, he said, 'Are ye doon there?'

He says, 'Aye.'

He says, 'Well, here' – and first of all it wis the cat that landed on his chest: he throwed the cat doon, an he says, 'Take that an strangle it some place.' And he said, 'An that pillas, take an burn them.'

'Oh,' the man says, 'A cannae touch ma wife's wee cat,' he says: 'Katie'll kill me fir her kitten.'

He says, 'Dae it!' But he couldnae, so the Broonie took it an he jist twisted the head aff it, an he says, 'Ye can dae it now,' he says. 'Go an bury it, or burn it! Best thing is tae burn them.' So the fella's away wi this pillas an this cat's body to burn them. An the Broonie went ower tae – he says, 'Katie, ye're gaunnae sleep now,' he said, 'and when ye wake up ye'll feel fine.' And she did, an when she woke up, she did have a beautiful wee baby boy in her airms.

And that Broonie stayed on that place until the fella's mother died, till the auld woman died. And then it jist disappeared, the same way as it had come, never wis seen again. But the young couple lived happily there ever efter that – an they were pretty well aff, wi aa the stuff that the Broonie had milled fir them. An that's the end of ma story!

LONDON AGAIN!

THIS WAS A FISHERMAN. He lived down Wester Ross way, in Kintail. He and his sons used to go out fishing every day and one day when they were out, the weather turned bad on them. And he had to clear a headland – like the point of Aird Mhaoile down here – and he could see that he had no chance of clearing the headland. The only way of escape was to let her run aground. He let the boat run in to the shore and some people spotted him and they came together. And they got out of the boat safe and drew her up, but her keel was broken.

They went home and when they had had a meal, [he thought] it would be just as necessary for them to go out the next day as it had been today. He decided to go to the wood to see if he could find a tree that would make a keel for the boat. He took an axe with him. He searched all through the wood but he couldn't find a tree that suited him – when he found a straight one it was too thick and it would take [? too long] to trim it down to size and it would never be ready. And he still couldn't find one . . . When he found one that wouldn't need too much trimming, it had a twist in it and it was no use.

At last night fell and caught him in the wood. He kept trying to find his way out and when he did get out of the wood he had no earthly idea which way he should turn. Then he saw a light in the distance and he made straight for it, and when he reached it there was a neat little house there, and he went in.

When he went in there was no-one there but three old women and one of them was very old indeed. She was sitting by the fire. Another of them was quite active, moving about the house. And he asked if he could stay there till morning. They looked at each other and one of them said grudgingly that he could. They invited him to sit in by the fire.

Then the one who was sitting by the fire got up and went over to join the other two. They began to talk among themselves but he paid no attention: he thought they were talking about him. But then one of them turned and said to him that he had better go through to the other room – that there was a bed there and he could sleep there till morning and he would be better there.

'Oh,' said he, 'I'll be fine here beside the fire till morning.'

'Oh, you'd better go and lie down in bed. We won't . . . no-one will bother you, and you can take the lamp and keep it lit if you like.'

He went through to the room and when he got into the room there was nothing there but the bed itself and a table and a big chest over beneath the window. He undressed and went to bed and he just turned the lamp down. He didn't put it out. He was lying there in bed but he couldn't get to sleep. He was thinking of the folk at home – they would be looking for him and no trace of him to be found.

But then he heard one of the old women coming to the door, but she just peeped round it with one eye. He pretended to be asleep and snoring. At last she came right into the room.

She went straight over to the chest, and took a cap out of the chest and tied it on her head – and she turned round:

'London Again!' said she.

Away went the old woman. He was left without a trace of her.

Then he heard another of them coming to the door and this one did not hang around the door for so long. She came in and she too took a cap from the chest and put it on her head. It was just 'London!' and away after the first one.

Then he heard the old one coming, tripping over her own feet for fear that she was late. She just made straight for the chest and took out a cap and on to her head with it, and it was just 'London!' and away after the others.

Here he was, left all alone. By God, he thought he wouldn't stay any longer there. He got up and got dressed and when he was ready to go he thought he would take a look in the chest to see what was there, since he had such a good chance. And he opened the chest and there was nothing in the chest but two or three of the same kind of caps he had seen the old women putting on. He examined them, and here he tried one of them on and it was a perfect fit for him.

'London Again!' said the old man. Away went the old man and in the twinkling of an eye he was standing in a whisky cellar in London – and the three old women were lying there dead drunk. The taps were left running where they hadn't managed to turn them off, they were so drunk.

He didn't disturb the old women. He turned off the taps and went around trying a sip of every kind of drink that was there: he certainly needed it. And then he thought he would sit down and he sat down, and the place was very stuffy, and he took off the cap and put it in his pocket. And what should he do but fall asleep.

The waking he got was the cellarman showering him with kicks. There was no sign of the old women.

'You bloody rogue, you've been coming here long enough till you've ruined me and finished me – but it's caught you out at last!'

He shouted for the police. The poor old man was seized and dragged off and thrown into prison. And then he was taken to court. The old man kept telling them what had happened to him and how he had come to be there.

Hoots! Who was going to believe that! It was no use trotting out all his lies here. Who on earth would believe that! The man had been missing stuff for ages and every policeman in London and every detective had failed to catch the thief till he caught him himself. And it wasn't so much what was being drunk as what was being spilt!

The result was that he was sentenced to be hanged. And on the day he was to be hanged a great crowd of people gathered to watch the execution: they used to hang them in the open air in these days, in full view of everyone.

The old man was led out and the hangman led him up to the scaffold, and he told him that he had ten minutes now to say anything he wanted to say before he was hanged.

Oh, he said he had nothing to say that he had not said already but that they were hanging an innocent man.

'Hah! You're anything but innocent!'

He put his hand in his pocket: what should he find but the cap. 'Can I wear this on my head,' said he, 'while you're hanging me?'

'Oh, you can wear anything you like on your head,' said the hangman.

He took the cap and tied it on his head:

'Kintail Again!' said the old man.

Away went the old man and the gallows and the hangman into the sky and on the way home he threw the hangman off the gallows and he was drowned.

He and the gallows got back to Kintail and he had a fine smooth piece of timber to make a keel for the boat.

And that was what happened to him.

THE TAILOR AND THE FISHING WIVES

W E ALWAYS USED to hear it said that tailors, they were extraordinarily 'tathainte' – that's the word we have anyway, whether they use it in many other places or not. They were witty and they were eloquent, they were quick to pick up anything and good at telling things. And I don't think what was said about them was right:

> 'A tailor is no man, nor yet a man two
> A raven could push over a cliff two score and two.'

I don't believe those words at all, that they were appropriate for tailors.

But anyway, this particular tailor was like the rest of his kind: he had sharp eyes and open ears for everything that might be going on in the houses where he was working. And the custom in those days was that the tailor went from household to household, as we put it, and from township to township, and he made all the clothes for the family he went to before he left for the next house or the next township, wherever he was needed.

This one was most particularly fond, according to the story, of fresh herring. And when he came to this parish, a long way from his own home, what should be the first breakfast he got but fresh herring. He praised the herring and said that that was his favourite dish.

His hostess said to him, 'In that case,' said she, 'you can have it, tailor, every morning as long as you stay here.'

When he'd finished the clothes for that household he went to the next house where he was wanted, and began to work on the clothes of that household too. And he got the same thing; whether word had gone ahead of him or not he didn't know, but it was fresh herring he got for his breakfast. He enjoyed this, and he praised it to his hostess, and she said, 'Oh, you can get that all right here. We have it every day,' said she. 'You can have it every morning, tailor, if you like.'

To shorten the tale now a good part of the night has passed, we need only say that: when he left the second house and went to the third in the same parish, what was his astonishment to get fresh herring in the morning in the third house too. This puzzled him: he couldn't see anyone going fishing and he didn't hear of anyone coming round to sell herring, and where the herring came from he didn't know, but he enjoyed it all the same.

He made up his mind, as men of his trade were inclined to do – they had to get to the bottom of anything that intrigued them, and find the meaning of it – and the tailor decided, once the end of his work in this household was in sight, that he wouldn't go to bed this night at all. They always used to say to him, 'It's time you went to bed, tailor. You're tired,' his hostess would say, when everyone in the house but her was in bed already. He told her this time, 'I won't go to bed at all tonight, mistress. I'll have finished my work by the small hours of the morning, and I'm heading for the hills tomorrow, as there isn't another family in this parish needing me.'

'Tut, tut,' said she. 'That will never do, tailor, staying up all night with a long day in front of you tomorrow.'

'Oh, it'll never do otherwise,' said he. 'Then I'd be crossing the hills after dark,' said he, 'and I'm not so good at walking the hills in the dark as I used to be. But anything you have to do, mistress, you go ahead and don't bother hiding it from me. I'll keep right on sewing.'

'Well,' said she, 'since you've decided to stay up, I'll tell you what's happening, and you mustn't breathe a word about it.'

'I won't, I won't,' said the tailor. 'I'm not accustomed,' said he, 'to carry tales from house to house. I keep my ears open for what I can hear and my eyes take note of what I see,' said he, 'but I don't bear tales from house to house,' said he. 'I keep them to myself.'

'Very well,' said she, 'I won't keep anything from you, tailor. I have two women friends,' said she, 'round here. We go out,' said she, 'two or three nights a week to fish for herring, and that's the fresh herring you get in the mornings.'

And: 'Oh gracious,' said he, 'couldn't I go with you?'

'If you like,' said the woman, . . . said his hostess, 'when the other two come,' said she, 'I'll put it to them. And I'm quite sure they'll agree, since you know so much already.'

Her friends came, but they weren't at all pleased when they saw that the tailor was at the fireside.

'Don't keep anything from me, ladies,' said the tailor. 'Whatever you have to do, do it. I know well enough how to hold my tongue travelling about.'

So they just had to set about their business, and the tailor was taught a spell. They had to go down to the seashore where there was a rocky stretch, and each of them had a sieve hidden there, and one or two spare in case someone else joined the company that was going for a night's fishing. The tailor could have one of these. Each of the three had a coil of heather rope, the three women, and these were tied – the ends of them tied to the tailor's sieve and the tailor's sieve moored by a heather rope to a big rock on the shore. The women would put out [in the sieves] after repeating the spell – the whole lot of them – and the tailor with them nearest the shore; and when the heather ropes had been paid out to the end the fishing would be over: there would be a herring on every heather tip that stuck out of the rope. And then they would . . . the tailor was to start and haul in the ropes towards the shore.

And that was what happened. Everything went well with them and the tailor had memorised the spell without any mistakes. They boarded their sieves, each of them, and the tailor sailed out a bit beyond the seaweed of the shore in his own sieve, with the end of the three ropes made fast to it. He paid them out . . . and when they were fully paid out the tailor shouted, 'The ropes are fully paid out. With the Lord's blessing fish well.'

Down went the tailor's sieve, down went the women's sieves, and the screaming started and the swimming started. But the tailor didn't look to see what was happening to the fishers – he just grabbed for the heather rope to pull himself to land, and as soon as his sieve touched the shore he leapt out of it and headed for the hills. He thought they were all drowned. He didn't stop to think of the scissors or needles he had left behind, just of covering the miles ahead. Wet as he was, he got to his own house as dawn was breaking in the morning.

And he was most surprised when he heard the news, a few days later, that the women were alive and well as ever. Because their sieves had been made fast to the tailor's sieve, they had managed to pull themselves to the shore.

And I wouldn't much have cared to eat that sort of herring, but all the same the tailor enjoyed it. That's a little story for you tonight.

---

82   *Nan MacKinnon*

DUART'S DAUGHTER

ONCE UPON A TIME MacLean of Duart sent his daughter to be educated, and oh, she was away for a good while. I don't know how long she was away: anyway she was a good while away, and she came home then. And just on the Sunday after she came home, she and her father went for a walk in the hills. And her father said to her, 'How much have you learned now?' said he.

Now there was a ship out at sea. She said, 'I have learned enough,' said she, 'to bring that ship in,' said she, 'to the shore.'

'Right, then,' said he, 'why don't you bring it in?'

The ship began to come and it kept coming in and kept coming in until at last it was on the point of going on the rocks. And it went on the rocks. And her father said to her, 'Will you not save them now?' said he.

'Oh,' said she, 'I don't know how to do that!'

'Well, if that,' said he, 'is the sort of education you have had, I would rather your room,' said he, 'than your company, and I will never have your sort in the same place as myself.' And when he got home, it was said that he built a great fire, and he put her in a basket and cast her on top of it, and burned her. It was the Black Art that she had been learning.

83a   *Donald MacLellan*

THE THREE KNOTS

IT happened once upon a time when the autumn work was over and the people had got the harvest gathered in safely in the island of Heisker in Uist, they thought they would go to Lewis to visit their friends there. They took a big strong boat with a capable crew and set off.

They had fine weather and they got to Lewis. They knew a lot of people in Lewis – they had relatives there. A certain man among them went to a house and greeted the woman of the house and she was very glad to see him. He had not been in the house for long when a tall black-haired girl came in, and he was on such familiar terms with the woman of the house, that he said to her when the girl had gone, 'To whom,' said he, 'does that black ugly girl belong?'

'Is that what you say?' said the woman of the house. 'I don't know but that you may fall deep enough in love with her before you leave Lewis.'

'Indeed,' said he, 'I won't fall in love with her: whoever else may fall in love with her, I won't.'

But this is how it turned out: they went home from their visit that night, and there he was, longing for the night to come again, so that he could get back again to visit that house. And the girl came to the house as usual and he hated her more than the Devil, yet he was longing just as much for the next night to come so that he could go there.

So it went on but when it came to the end of the week, one said to another: 'We've had a good long visit now and it's time for us to be making for Heisker.'

And they agreed that it was.

'Well, I think we'll be off tomorrow.'

And they got everything ready for going. They got up next morning and, oh, it was blowing a gale: they could not possibly get away. There was nothing for it but [to go] back to where they had been before. Next day again they got up. They went down to the boat and got her ready and just as they were starting to get the masts up, it blew up a gale. There was nothing for it but to give up. They could not get away.

They were walking up from the harbour, going back to the houses where they had been staying, and they met a little creature of an old woman and: 'Well, my good lads,' said she, 'I'm sure you're wearying at the delay in this place.'

'Oh indeed,' said they, 'we are.'

'Oh,' said she, 'it is no wonder, seeing what sort of place you kept going to. What will you give me if you get fine weather to go tomorrow?'

'Oh indeed, anything at all you want we'll give it to you.'

'Well,' said she, 'all I want is a pound of snuff.' And: 'Which of you is skipper of the boat?'

The man told her who was skipper of the boat.

'Well,' said she, 'send one of your lads to my house tonight and I'll give you something which will help you on your way.'

That's how it was. One of the lads went to her house and she gave him a thread with three knots on it.

'Here you are now,' said she, 'and you give that to the master of the boat and you'll have a good day tomorrow, and you'll get away. And if you . . . if the skipper does not have enough wind, he can untie one knot. And if that is not enough for him and he would like more wind, he can untie the second. But whatever you do, don't untie the third one.'

They went off, and what the old woman had said turned out to be true. It was a fine day and they went and hoisted the sails and set off with a nice little breeze of wind, and, oh, they could be doing with more wind if the old woman really had such powers – to get more wind, for they were in a hurry to get back home since they had been away so long – and they untied a knot. The wind came up a good deal better, but, ah, they would like more, they would like more! And then they untied the second knot. Then it was . . . it was just as much as the boat could take. She was at full stretch.

Now they were getting close to Heisker and they had had a fine voyage, and one of them said to the other: 'We ought to try the third knot to see what powers the old woman had.'

And: 'Well, we're close in to land: we're safe now anyway, no matter what happens.'

They untied the third knot and the man at the helm turned and looked behind him and he just had time to say: 'Oh!, oh!' he said. And three huge seas came and swept the boat up and left her high and dry on land. And all they had to do was jump out on dry land at a place they call Port Eilein na Culaigh (Port of the Island of the Boat) in Heisker.

83b   *Andrew Hunter*

THE THREE KNOTS

NOW YE KNOW AAL THE boats 'at came to Shetland in wän time – 'course that's a long time ago – they took them across from Norroway, and they wir aal put together with wooden pins, the boats. An when they got them across to Shetland, they re-fästen't them wi galvanise naels. An some men went across to Norroway to bring acroass a boat fir theirselfs. An they säid they wir aaful weel treat'. An before they left, the old lady o the house gev them a bit o string (or a bit o rop maybe; I couldna say whit it wis) wi three knots on it.

'Now,' she säid, 'if you wänt a fair wind an a fine passage, take off the first knot. An if you think that ye're not maekin a quick enough passage, take off the second one. But,' she said, 'fir God's sake doan't take off the third one!'

So when they wir gettin hom, pretty near their destination, the one säid to the other, 'Well, the two knots is off, an I non think that thir any

harm o takin off the third one.' So they took off the third one, an afore
they got the boat landit he wis a proper gale! He wis a flyin gale . . . But
they got the boat; they landit the boat, but I suppose they had a bad time
gettin her landit. Yes!

84   *William Matheson*

DARK LACHLAN AND THE WITCHES

W HEN I WAS IN SOUTH UIST I used to ask about the
MacMhuirichs [hereditary bards to Clanranald], and in South Uist they
were best remembered as having the Black Art, and here's a story I heard
in this connection:

Alasdair, laird of Boisdale, wanted to marry MacLeod of Dunvegan's
daughter, and he left Loch Boisdale with a ship's crew to ask MacLeod for
her. He took Dark-Haired Lachlan son of Donald MacMhuirich with him.
MacLeod's daughter had two maids-in-waiting and they were afraid that if
the laird of Boisdale got their mistress they would not be needed any
longer. One of them was a witch, and what did they do but set off, the
pair of them, to meet the Uist ship in the form of two ravens. When they
reached it, the witch settled on the masthead and the other one flew round
her crying to her: 'Drown Alasdair of the Cows! Drown Alasdair of the Cows!'

But her reply was always: 'How can I drown Alasdair of the Cows with Dark Lachlan son of Donald MacMhuirich hunched over the tiller?'

In the end Lachlan reached for his gun and loaded it with a silver coin. He shot at one of the ravens and knocked out a shower of her feathers. They fled at that.

The laird of Boisdale kept on his course, and when they got to Dunvegan the whole household was in confusion because one of MacLeod's daughter's maids was ill. 'I'll cure her,' said MacMhuirich. He went into her room:

'You imp of Hell!' said he, 'if you had stayed in your own place this wouldn't have happened to you!'

He rubbed the muzzle of the gun three times round the wound and it healed. However, the story doesn't tell whether the laird of Boisdale got the hand of MacLeod's daughter or not.

85   *Donald Sinclair*

JOHN MACLACHLAN AND THE GIRL

DOTAIR RATHUAITH – I think it was John was his name, John MacLachlan, as far as I can remember. The sweet singer of Rahoy . . .

Yes, the Rahoy Doctor knew Tiree pretty well, because he was always there, especially around Balephetrish . . . But it was about Mull, that's where he spent most of his time. And there were no cars then, nor bicycles either, just horses.

Anyway, he got word this night to go to some place in Mull where there was a woman ill. And he set off with his servant – each of them had a horse – and they were going past a house there. And what were they doing in the barn of this house but there were girls there working at *luadh*, that's in English waulking cloth. And it was quite a sight to see, and the doctor and his servant stopped to listen to the songs they were singing, for they used to sing a variety of songs for waulking . . .

And the servant said, he said admiringly: 'Hasn't that girl a good voice?' said he.

'It's very good,' said the doctor, 'over a black toad.'

And he explained to the servant that there was a toad – she had swallowed a toad drinking water – there was a toad inside her. 'It won't be long,' said he, 'until they send for me.'

And it was not long until the doctor was sent for. He examined the girl closely and carefully, and he told them to put on a good peat fire. They did. And he said to the girl, 'Sit by the fire.' He asked them had they any meat in the house.

'Yes,' said they. Wires were got and a lump of meat was put on the wires to roast in front of the fire. Then he asked them to bring in a basin of water. The basin of water was set down on the hearth-stone, and he himself was sitting beside the girl.

The meat began to roast, anyway, and there was a fine smell through the house. But what should happen to the girl but she began to feel sick, and she told the doctor, 'I'm sorry,' said she, 'but I think I'm going to be sick.'

'Ach,' said he, 'that's quite all right.'

And the girl began to vomit, and she vomited up the toad, and the toad fell into the basin of water, and the doctor caught it just like that!

'How do you feel now?' said he.

'I'm fine,' said she.

'Yes,' said he, 'that's the thing that was making you ill. Any time you are in Mull to cut peat, mind and watch how you drink the water. There are no toads in Tiree at all,' said he, 'but there are plenty of them in Mull.'

And that girl was fine after that. But the Rahoy Doctor had the Black Art too. He had the Black Art too. That's something nobody has today . . .

86   *William MacDonald*

THE DANCING REAPERS

THERE WAS A FARMER or maybe a landowner in Brae Lochaber once, and his name was MacGregor, and he was supposed to have the Black Art – to know magic. But anyway he was away this time – he had left home on some particular business, and when he had settled everything he had to do he was on his way home, and he was passing the house of a farmer thereabouts, and it was about midday and he was pretty weak with hunger, and he said to himself that he would go in and ask . . . see if he could get a bite of food to eat, to help him on his way home.

He went in, and there wasn't a living soul in the house but the farmer's wife, and she . . . had her sleeves rolled up and she was so busy . . . as busy as could be, working to get the bread baked. He told her he was hungry, cold and weak and that a bite to eat . . . he needed a bite to eat.

'Oh, I can't give you food just now,' said she to him, 'I'm so busy,' said she, 'with the reapers out in the fields,' said she, 'busy cutting oats there,' said she, 'with it being such a fine day, and they'll be home in a minute for their dinner,' said she, 'and if there isn't . . . I must have the bread ready before they come and I can't give you a thing.'

'Right enough,' said he. He turned on his heel and out he went, and as soon as he was out of the door the farmer's wife sprang into the middle of the room and began to dance and this was the song she was singing:

'A 'fear mór liath a thàinig bho'n iar
　　Dh'iarr e biadh 's cha d'fhuair e mìr.'

'The big grizzled man who came from the West
Asked for food and got not a bit.'

But anyway at dinner-time, when . . . dinner-time had come, they realised the people who were reaping in the field, that they had . . . had no word to come in for their dinner, and the farmer told the maid – she was working at the oats with them – to go home and see what was holding up dinner, why they hadn't got it. She went home, and the farmer's wife was dancing in the middle of the room there and singing, and she went in and sprang alongside the farmer's wife [dancing] and singing the same tune:

'The big grizzled man who came from the West
Asked for food and got not a bit.'

They were . . . They realised that the girl who had gone home, the messenger who had gone home had not come back, and another girl was sent home. She went inside and she too sprang into the middle of the room singing:

'The big grizzled man who came from the West
Asked for food and got not a bit.'

They went in one by one, and at last the farmer was left by himself reaping out in the field. He went home, and he was still wondering what could be wrong, so he didn't go inside at all, but he peeped through the window, so. Everyone . . . his wife and . . . the maids and the young men and everyone was out there on the floor dancing to:

> 'The big grizzled man who came from the West
> Asked for food and got not a bit.'

They were turning and reeling there, and seemingly you never in your life saw such a dance. 'Heavens,' he said to himself, 'there's something wrong here today,' said he. 'I won't go inside at all,' said he.

He set off then and went over to a house not far away, and he asked the housewife there if she had seen anybody that day, or if anyone had passed on the road that day or anything . . . ?

'Such and such a man passed by,' said the lady to him, 'and I saw him pass.'

'Oh well, if you did,' said he, 'he caused me this trouble,' said he, 'and I'll have to go after him.' He went into the stable and brought his best horse and leapt on its back and saddled it [sic!] and off he set in pursuit of the . . . of MacGregor. Oh, he caught up with MacGregor then, and said . . . he begged him to release the people who were dancing in the house.

'Well,' said MacGregor to him, 'when you go back,' said he, 'you must look,' said he, 'on the lintel above the door, so,' said he, 'and you'll find an oaken pin,' said he, 'stuck in there – what they call a magic wand,' said he, 'and you must pull it out, so,' said he, 'and maybe that will release them.'

He went back and stabled his horse and went in, and . . . he found the magic wand in the lintel above the door right enough, and he gave it a tug, and when he did every last one of the people who had . . . been dancing collapsed on the floor, they fell on the floor there in a dead faint. They spent three days and three nights lying there before they could move a muscle.

THE BORROWED PEATS

THERE WERE ONE occasion a woman had started to churn the milk . . . Usually when they started to churn they were not only lookin for the butter, but for the kirn milk, or Scotch cheese, which was the curds, and to produce that, when the butter was removed they had to pour in hot water into the buttermilk, to produce the curds; so they always hung a kettle over the open fire to heat water, to have it ready.

Now it happened, when this woman had started to churn her milk, a neighbour woman whom she suspected of havin sinister intentions came in and asked if she could get some kindling, because her fire had gone out. And she insisted that she should give her some coals from under the kettle. So she gave her the coals, but she 'plunged and plunged the kirn in vain' after that, and nothing – no butter came.

Now it happened that a packman came in, a pedlar – and they usually knew all the country gossip and all the leegends about witches and so forth – he asked for a drink. And nobody in those days would ha' given a man water if they had buttermilk – buttermilk, or blaand, which was the whey produced after the kirn milk had been made, was the favourite drink, and a very good drink it was too, especially the blaand. However, she had none at the time, so she dipped the cup into the churn, took out some o the milk she'd been tryin to churn and handed it to him. The packman took a mouthful or two, and then he said, 'Well, gödwife,' he says, 'ye're no gettin the göd o yer milk!'

She says, 'No, I know it.'

'Well,' he says, 'do you suspect anybody?'

She said, 'Weel, the neighbour wife has just been in an gotten colls oot o anunder the kirnin waater.'

He says, 'Did you gie them to her?'

She says, 'Yes, she insisted that I should gie them.'

He says, 'Weel, ye're gien awaa yer luck.' He says, 'If she comes again, tell her to tak them tae hersel, and then.' he says, 'hadd the kirn staff as hard ipo the bottom o the kirn as ye can, an,' he said, 'döna let her awaa till she gies you back what she's taen.'

A few days later she was tryin tae kirn again, as usual gettin nothing. In came the neighbour wife and she said, 'Lass, my fire is gaen oot again,' she says. 'Could thu gie me twa colls?'

She said, 'Yea, tak them to theesel.'

'Na, na,' she says, 'thu gie me . . .'

'No,' she says, 'A'm t'reshin at this kirn an I haena time, so thu'll just hae to tak them to theesel the day.'

Well, reluctantly she reached into the fire wi the tongs, and then the wife put the kirn staff on the bottom o the kirn, and the witch roared oot – she says, 'Oh my Loard, thu's burnin me. I'm roastin.'

'Oh,' she says, 'thu can roast till thu gies me back what thu's taen.'

So she started an muttered her – some sort of a rhyme, an she says, 'Oh, it's aa right noo.' An . . . 'course the wife let her go, an the kirn fill't wi butter.

THE BORROWED PEATS

Yes, I HEARD ABOUT a tailor who was working in a house one day as they used to do in those days: when someone had clothes to make they fetched the tailor to the house. And the tailor came to stay in this house and he was working away at the clothes. And the housewife, she was churning.

Well, what happened was that one of the women from next door came to ask her for a burning peat from the fire, and she said: 'My fire,' said she, 'has gone out,' said she. 'Could you let me have a peat?'

And she picked up the tongs and took out a peat, and when she had gone out with the peat the tailor got up and took another little peat out of the fire and put it in a tub of water.

Well, now, it wasn't long till the very same woman was back again asking for another peat and: 'That one went out on me,' said she. 'Could you let me have another one?'

And the housewife gave . . . She let her take another peat, thinking nothing of it, and the tailor went again and took another peat out of the fire and put it in the tub of water.

And she came back again a second [*sic*] time and said it had gone out on her — she'd have to get another one. Anyway, the tailor did the same again when she had gone: he put another peat in — he put it in the tub. And she didn't come back again.

And the housewife said to him: 'Why,' said she, 'did you put the peat in the water?'

'Didn't you suspect anything yourself,' said he, 'or did nothing strike you [as odd]?'

'No, indeed, it didn't,' said she. 'I had no idea what she was up to.'

'Well, I know,' said he, 'what she was up to. There's not a single scrap of the butter you had in the churn there,' said he, 'that she wouldn't have taken away,' said he, 'if she had got away with a peat. And if she ever comes back again and does the same thing,' said he, 'you do,' said he, 'what I've been doing,' said he, 'and she can't do you any harm.'

There you are now.

88 *Nan MacKinnon*

MILK IN A TANGLE

A FAIR LOT OF PEOPLE came across from Barra to Vatersay one time, and there were women among them too and a good lot of young lads. And the milk cows were on the beach. And the young lads noticed when they were on the beach that there was one woman there who had a black tangle [seaweed stem] behind her back, and she was holding it at both ends. And she stood on the beach with it, and they noticed when they crossed back that she still had it and she was holding it by both ends just as she had been when she was over in Vatersay.

And one of the young lads said to another, 'What now,' said he, 'has she got there?'

'It can't be anything good anyway.'

'I wouldn't mind,' said he, 'cutting that tangle in half.'

He sneaked up behind her anyhow, and he took a knife to the tangle and cut it in half. And the shore was flooded with milk across on that side [of the ferry]. She had got the cows' milk in the middle of the tangle and held on to it by both ends, but she lost every drop of it.

ROBBERS, ARCHERS
AND CLAN FEUDS

THE GIRL WHO KILLED
THE RAIDERS

IN THE DAYS OF cattle-raiding, long, long ago, there was a family up at Cladach a' Chaolais – a man, his wife and two doughty daughters. This spring day the sky was threatening, it looked like snow, and the father said to his daughters that they had better drive in all the cattle before night came, for it was looking really bad. There had been flurries of snow the day before this. The girls set off and when they got out to where the cattle were, the first thing they noticed was that a bonny red heifer of theirs was missing. They began looking for it, and they found tracks in the snow that had fallen the day before, and they saw a place where a cow had been driven into a bog and they realised at once that this was the work of raiders. The elder girl said to the younger, 'You go home with the cattle, and I won't come home till I find the red heifer, wherever it is, if it's not been killed.'

She set off, and she knew well enough where raiders used to ship the cattle they stole from that part of the country, out there by Eaval, and she made straight for the spot. There were no highroads in those days, but off she went as fast as she could over the moor till she got to Eaval. Just as she had thought, she saw a tent there, and she went into it, and there was a pot on a fire inside, and the fire had died down. She looked in the pot, and what was in it but black puddings fully cooked. She was hungry, and she cut off one of them and ate her fill of it.

She considered what to do for a while, and on looking around she saw a sword on the floor, and she seized it, ready to do battle with anyone for the heifer. Just as she was thinking everything out she heard a cow bellowing, and she peered out cautiously, and the raiders had come into view with a great herd of cattle. She stayed there, inside the opening of the tent, and she heard one of them say, 'We had better tie up the red heifer before we go in to eat.'

'Never you mind about the heifer,' said another. 'You go in and get food ready for us, and then we must be getting away once we've had a bite to eat, with the state of the tide.'

This man made for the tent, and as soon as he was right inside the tent he got the sword right on the back of his neck, and he fell dead on the spot without a peep. She dragged him over behind her. The people who were keeping an eye on the cattle began to wonder why the man who had gone in had not come out again, and they asked another man to go in. The same thing happened to him, and to one of them after another until there was only one left outside. He came over cautiously, for he had a strong suspicion that there was something wrong in the tent. He spotted her, and ran off down towards the coble, but the girl managed to hit him with the sword and cut off his ear. He pushed off the coble and got away with his life, and he went on board a great galley that was at anchor out in the bay.

After that she untied the red heifer and let loose every one of the cattle there. She got home late that night, with the sword still in her hand, and told her father what had happened.

'You must seek the sanctuary of the church,' said he, 'as fast as you can, and if you manage to reach it before they come in pursuit of you, they won't be able to touch you.'

She got to the place, and came home, and no pursuers or anyone appeared.

One wild night over a year after that, her father heard a knocking at the door. He answered it, and there was a man there asking shelter for the night, if only sitting by the fire, the night was getting so bad.

'Come in anyway, and we'll see what we can do for you.'

Men wore their hair long in those days, and his had grown down to his shoulders. He got a bed, and he had such a good night that he said he would be glad if he could stay with them for a few days, until he got the horse he was looking for.

So he stayed. He went to look for a horse every day, and came back every evening to this house, where he had started to court the elder daughter. After a short while they agreed to get married, and the stranger bought the horse he wanted the next day, and got ready to leave a day or two after that. The girl was to go along with him, and in those days they had no means of transport but a cart or a horse, but they agreed that she should ride behind him on the horse. So she did, and they set off at daybreak, and kept to a track along by the Claddachs all the way. The wind was rising all the time, and when they were out by Bagh Mór, near Cnoc Cuithein yonder, didn't a gust of wind lift up his hair on the windward side, and the girl was horrified to see that he had lost an ear.

'Goodness,' said she, 'how on earth did you come to lose your ear?'

'Oh, I assure you you won't go too far, and you won't be a lot older than you are now,' said he, 'before you know how I lost my ear.'

The horse was bridled with a bent rope, and he took her down from the horse and tied her hands and feet [with it]. He left her there and ran off to get his companions, who would have been waiting for him with a boat, whatever they were going to do with her. The horse was grazing near her, and she rolled herself over close to it to see if she could manage to put the knot on the bent rope tying her hands behind her back to the horse's mouth, in the hope that he might cut through it. Then she got close to the horse's mouth and raised her hands behind her back, and when the horse saw the knot of bent there he started to chew at it. At last he cut through the knot and freed her hands, and it didn't take her long to get her feet free herself. Then she jumped on the horse's back, and he found his way back to where he had come from, and she was home early in the evening. And she never heard nor saw more of the man with the one ear.

SPÒG BHUIDHE

THERE WAS A TIME there long ago, before reapers and binders and harvesting implements of that kind came, people used to go from here, and from all the islands, down to . . . to Lowdie they called it – that means the Lothians – to work at harvesting, and they used to earn what was a good wage in those days. And they'd come back home, anyway – walking most of the way of course – and plenty of them got robbed on the way home as well.

And it seems there was a place down near Perth, a certain bridge, and a lot of people were always getting robbed there on their way home from this harvest work. Some man met them on the bridge and robbed them of their money, and it was Spòg Bhuidhe [Yellow Paw] . . . Why they called him that I don't know, but Spòg Bhuidhe was what they called the man who met them there.

But, anyway, there was a man from here who used to go every year, anyway, and this year he was on his way home and he called at an inn not far from the bridge and had a dram, and he also had a meal there. And it was night and . . . Anyway, what should he be given to eat but black puddings along with various other things. And, well, he was rather afraid of going to the bridge at night after hearing so many stories about people being robbed there so often, and as he looked at the plate he saw one black pudding there and it was shaped like a pistol or, as we say, a revolver, and he said to himself, 'Well, I'll just put this in my pocket and if anyone bothers me I'll take it out and they won't know, as it's night anyway, that it isn't a pistol I've got, and I'll give them a fright if nothing else.'

And, with that, he slipped one of the black puddings into his pocket.

Oh, he ate his meal anyway, and had a rest, and then he left and off he went on his way. Oh, he was getting nearer and nearer to the bridge, and he was a bit afraid too, but, ah, just as he got near to the end of the bridge he noticed this big man standing there in a cloak. Ah, there was no going back now anyway – he kept on – but when he came up to him the man said, 'Hand over your money or you're dead.'

'No,' he said, 'I won't part with my money that easily. Many a day I sweated to earn it. I worked hard for every penny of it.'

'If you don't,' said he, 'I'll have your head off.'

'No,' said he, 'but I'll have your head off and every spark of this will be . . . ,' and he took the black pudding out of his pocket and stuck it against the man's chest. The man just gave one leap and ran off into the night. The man went on his way and he got safely over the bridge. No-one troubled him after that – he got home safe anyway.

But he went the following year, anyway, he went away for harvest work as usual. When the work was done he was on his way home and he called at the same inn, just as he had called the year before that, and he was given black puddings again just as he had got the year before too. Oh, the inn-keeper was . . . He came over to him and said, 'How did you get on the night you were here last year?' said he. 'You were here one night just like this – you called here on your way home from your work. You didn't have any trouble at the bridge, did you?'

'Oh, well, as a matter of fact I did. There was a man waiting for me at the bridge,' said he, 'but, my goodness, he got quite a fright! Just like tonight I was given black puddings along with other things for my meal, like this, and I thought I'd put one of them in my pocket – it looked so like a pistol. And I put it in my pocket and when the man stopped me at the bridge I just took it out and stuck it against his chest and told him that he'd get every spark of this if he didn't clear off. He got such a fright,' said he, 'and didn't he run for it!'

'Oh, well,' said he, 'wasn't that good! That was some fright he got!'

'Yes,' said he, 'he got a fright all right! Anyway, I got home safe.'

But anyway after having a rest he set off as he had done the year before, and, ah, he was frightened enough coming to the bridge this time as well, but he carried on. But, oh, sure enough, as he came up to the bridge the big man with the cloak was right there before him, just as he had been the year before. He kept going anyway but when he had almost come up to the man the man said, 'Hand over your money or you're dead.'

'No,' said he, 'I'm not handing it over like that – it wasn't so easy to come by. I've had to work many a hard day for it.'

'If you don't,' said he, 'you're a dead man this minute. Your black pudding won't save you tonight like it did last year.'

'If not,' said he, 'this will.'

And he had bought a revolver this year, and he took the revolver out of his pocket and he fired it at him and killed him there and then.

He went straight back to the hotel. He told them that a man had stopped him at the bridge and tried to rob him and that he had killed him – that they'd better go with him to see who it was. Oh, they couldn't find the hotel-keeper anywhere, and off they went, and when they got there who should it be but the hotel-keeper.

It was the hotel-keeper who had been robbing everyone who called at the hotel. When they had left he would go by a short-cut and be at the bridge before them, and he robbed everybody – that's how he did it. He thought it was a black pudding this man had, just as he had the year before, and that he was safe enough, but he was badly mistaken this time.

DARK FINLAY OF THE DEER

THERE WAS A STRONG, wild man of the old people long ago who lived in a little glen between two estates we call the Kintail Estate and the Kilillan Estate, and this place was called Coille Rìgh. The man had a few cattle, from which he made his living and his wife's living.

But when Finlay went out this particular evening there were some of the cattle missing, and Finlay knew every corner of the hills like the back of his hand, and he knew very well what had become of them, seeing that in these old days there were people they called reivers, who made raids on poor folk and carried off their cattle nobody knew where. but these old folk – they had lost them.

And Finlay said to himself that there was no use beating about the bush, he must go after them. Off he went, and on he went, but in the end, long as the way was he wasn't long finding it, till he reached the country of Lochaber, where they said there were a lot of these reivers in the old days. And the reivers were asleep when old Finlay got there. And Finlay fell upon them as Samson fell upon the Philistines – they didn't get away to tell the tale: Finlay killed them on the spot.

Finlay went home without another thought – himself and the few cattle that were left, very pleased with himself and hoping never to be raided again as long as he lived, and he brought the cattle home.

Weeks passed and weeks passed and things were going very well, but one of these mornings Finlay set out to herd the cattle again to the *aonach*, as we call it – the hill pastures. And when he grew tired of driving the cattle this way and that, then he sat down for a rest. When he looked about him at a hilltop we call Màm an Tuirc, on the boundary between Killillan and Kintail, there he saw three men coming down the hill, and Finlay knew very well that they were strangers. Not only did he know them for strangers but he thought they were avengers coming in search of someone, and he said to himself then that he might as well sit where he was and there he sat.

They came down the hill until they came up to Finlay and one of them said to him: 'You're a stranger in these parts?'

'Oh, no, I'm often . . . I know this district well.'

'Then do you know anyone round here they call Dark Finlay of the Deer?'

'I know him well: I'm his herdsman.'

That was all the reivers wanted.

'Well, you'll have to excuse me,' said Finlay, 'I'm such a cripple,' said he, 'that I won't be able to keep pace with you.'

'We'll help you ourselves.'

Well, well, they helped Finlay along step by step until they came to Finlay's cottage. When they came to Finlay's cottage: 'See, there's my [*sic*] cottage.'

And his wife was standing in the doorway. And when they got to the door Finlay said to his wife: 'See, here are some strangers I've met: take them in and I'm sure they could do with a bite to eat.'

'Come in, gentlemen,' said she, 'till you get some food.'

'Oh, we're not hungry. What we're looking for is the man of the house – is he at home?'

'The man of the house is at home, right enough, but the man of the house isn't keeping well. He hasn't got up yet.'

That was the best news they could ask for, but the woman asked them in, and she was preparing food as best she could and at the same time edging towards where old Finlay's bow was.

She put the bow and arrows out through a hole there was at the back of the cottage. There was no glass in the windows in those days at all, except that they might have clods or divots in them [?until] the daylight came.

When Finlay got his bow and arrows he came round to the door of the cottage and he looked in and he said to them: 'Here you are just as it was when Noah built the Ark, when he said: "Noah shall be inside and you shall be outside and the foxes shall be drowned." But I'm outside and you're inside and it's you who shall be drowned.' And he killed the three of them.

That's a fine end to the story of Dark Finlay of the Deer. John Finlayson from Drumbuie recounting it.

---

92 *Duncan MacDonald*

GILLE-PÀDRUIG DUBH

Rubha an tigh mhàil [the Point of the Rent House] is the name of the place in Loch Eynort where Clanranald's rent house was, where the tenantry paid the rent annually in grain. And this year, when rent day arrived, they were gathering there from every airt with sacks of grain. And Clanranald had a man in the rent-house measuring the grain with a peck measure. Who should arrive but Gille-Pàdruig Dubh, with two sacks of grain. The measurer began to measure, and the last peck of grain he was measuring was short.

'Oh,' said the measurer to Gille-Pàdruig Dubh, 'this peck of yours is short; you haven't enough grain to fill it, and it should have been full for the rent you have to pay.'

'You wait a minute,' said Gille-Pàdruig to the measurer, 'and it will be full presently,' at the same time catching him by the back of the neck and pulling the sgian-dubh from his own side; and he slit his throat with it, and held him above the peck measure until it was full of his blood. 'There now,' said Gille-Pàdruig, 'it's full now.' And he got himself ready and returned home.

Now, when Clanranald in Ormiclate heard of the deed done by Gille-Pàdruig Dubh to the man who was receiving his grain, it was difficult for him to decide how to get his revenge on him. He was reluctant to fall out with him because Gille-Pàdruig was a noted archer, and his like was too useful to Clanranald any time he was threatened by enemies. But the method he chose was this: he sent for Gille-Pàdruig Dubh to come to him at Ormiclate and to bring Iain Dubh, his son, with him, saying that there was a stranger in his house just now from the mainland, and that he had laid him a wager that he had an archer on the estate who could break an egg on his son's head with an arrow at such and such a distance without harming the man. And he named the day on which Gille-Pàdruig had to be in Ormiclate with his son.

Now, when the day came, Gille-Pàdruig set out, himself and his son, and he left the Geàrrachan, for that is where his dwelling was, and they both reached Ormiclate. You may be sure they were received with open arms there! They were welcomed with food and drink. Then they discussed the feat that they had to perform and they went outside. Gille-Pàdruig made his son stand in a particular place in front of him, and Clanranald and his lady and the stranger who was with them were standing on the graddaning hearth in order to see how the matter went. Gille-Pàdruig took an arrow from his quiver and he stuck it through the garter on his right leg, and he took another arrow and stuck it through the garter on his left leg. The egg was then placed on the top of his son's head. 'Go on, son,' said Gille-Pàdruig, 'turn your back to me.'

'I need not, Father,' said his son, 'because if you do me any harm it won't be your fault.'

Then Gille-Pàdruig took the third arrow from his quiver and put it in his bow, and he took good aim and released the arrow, and he shot the egg sky high.

'Very good,' said Clanranald, 'I am pleased that you performed the feat in the presence of the stranger who is here from the mainland, when I know that he has no-one on his lands who could do as much. But will you tell me now, what was your reason for sticking an arrow through each garter at the beginning?'

'Yes,' said Gille-Pàdruig, 'if I had done my son any harm, one would have landed in you and the other in the lady.'

'Away, away!' said Clanranald. 'It's no good trying to do anything with you.'

Gille-Pàdruig and Clanranald parted on friendly terms then, and he and his son went home to the Geàrrachan, and no further revenge was taken on him for the man he killed in the rent house at Loch Eynort.

GAUN TAIT AND THE BEAR

THIS HAAPENED i the days when this islants wis still anunder the Norse domination. And there a place in Fetlar 'at they caa Öri [written Urie]. They're been considerable bueeldins there. An this wis wan o the maen places in Fetlar, an this is whar the Norse tax-gatherer älways cam to gather his taxes fae the Fetlar fokk. And this parteeclar day he wis collectin taxes, an among the Fetlar maen they were a Gaun Taet. An he – pairt o his taxes wis bein peyed in butter, an when the Norse tax-gatherer weyed it upon his bismar then he hed it lighter as what Gaun Taet's bismar was hed it, and they got intil a row. And this Gaun aevidently wis a graet big powerful män, an he saezed the bismar fae the tax-gatherer an he struck the tax-gatherer i the heid wi him an he felled him ston deid. Noo, no doot the tax-gaitherer hed heenchmen along wi him, and they reportit this crime back hom i Norrawa an Gaun Taet wis summonsed afore the keeng o Norrawa, tö . . . the keeng tö pronounce punishment upon 'm.

An when he appeared afore the keeng, he hed his baer feet – he apparently wis aalways hed his baer feet, an his taes wis very big an muscular, an the keeng wis impressed wi the pheesical appearance o the man, an he remarkit about the graet big knobs 'at wis on his taes, an this would ha' been knobs o muscles. An Gaun said if they in any wey offended the keeng, he would shün get clear o them. And they were a shaurp aix lyin some wey aboot, and he pickit up the aix and he knockit off wan or two o the humps aff o his taes. And this impressed the keeng graetly, 'at a män could be so brafe an t'ink so little o paen, an he t'owt

ROBBERS, ARCHERS AND CLAN FEUDS

'at it wis a peety fir such a fine spaeshimen o a man to be condemned to daeth. An he considered fir a moament an then he said to Gaun 'at they were a bear graetly troublin the paalace grunds, an if he geed oot an captir'd this bear an browt it back to the palace alive, he would pardon him.

An Gaun liffed in Fetlar all his life: he was never seen a bear or kent what lek a bear wis. He kent 'at it was a very faerce aanimal, and he left the palace in a very despairin mood and he wandered aboot, an finally he cam upon a owld wife livin in a peerie hut be hersel oot i the edge o the foarest. An he geed in til her an he telt the wife his dilemma. And the wife said til'm 'at it wis butter 'at wis browt him to this, an the oanly thing 'at shö kent o, wid it be 'at butter would bring him oot ot o it: and shö telled him to go oot an buy a tub o butter, an set it oot fir some wey 'at the bear could get aat it, and this might mak him listless an droosy. So Gaun he geed oot an he bowt the tub o butter an he güd where he t'owt 'at the bear would be likely to come, and he waeted paetiently fir twa 'r three nights and the bear did put in a appearance. And the bear lickit oot the whoale tub o butter, and then it seem't to be saitisfied as faur as hunger wis consairned, an it made it droosy an sleepy, an Gaun trailed him all the wey an the bear curled up an güd to sleep. And Gaun pounced ipö the bear an he wis thatten a big strong män 'at he oaverpower't the bear, an he hed his rops wi him and he tie't the bear's fower feet an tied his jaas, an he took him upon his shooder, and he laundit the bear at the keeng's feet i the paalace!

An the keeng was graetly impressed wi this, fir he t'owt that the bear would kill Gaun and that would rid him o the trouble o haein to sentence him to daeth. But when Gaun arrifed afore 'm wi the bear, he was as good as his wird, and he telled him to tak the bear an disappear fae Norraway back til his owen countree, and that 'at he was to get into no more trouble, and he was not to pit in a appearance here ageen or he widna be dealt wi so leniently! So Gaun took the bear, but it's no recoardit what way he came back to Shetlan, but he couldna harbour the bear in Fetlar among the fokk, an he got a piece o chaen fae some wey, an he took the bear an he band i the sooth end o Lingey, that's the peerie

421

isle 'at lies aff here i Gütcher. And the bear traivel't roond aboot in a circle an tör up the aert' and ultimately he die't wi starvaesheen. An A'm been at . . . the circle whar the bear tör up – braa twa'r three year fae syne noo – an it's a circle maybe aboot fifty to sixty yaird, maybe fully bigger as that in diameter, an it's described as almost a perfect circle, and the grund hes the appearance as if it is been toarn up wi some wild aanimal. But the circle is still there fir anyboady to see if they in any wise misdoot the stoary!

94   *John MacDonald*

THE EARL OF MAR A FUGITIVE

THIS . . . SON OF MacDonald of the Isles, he was known as Domhnall Dubh Ballach and he had a powerful host of Highlanders as fine as a man could meet in a month's travel. And who should decide to come . . . to come and attack him and bring him to battle but the Earl of Mar, and he came over from the Braes of Mar, between there and Perth. And where did they meet but at Inverlochy, where the factory has been built today . . . This was in 1431. And Domhnall Dubh Ballach won the battle, and he put the Earl of Mar to flight.

The Earl of Mar fled, and he went up by Lianachan and up that way until he reached Glen Roy. And when he was nearly at a place they call Corriechoillie he went into an old woman's house and asked her for food.

'I haven't any food ready, but if you'll wait a moment,' said she, 'I'll get you something.'

'I haven't time for that,' said he, 'they're on my heels. But give me a little pinch of meal and I'll make myself a meal somewhere.'

She did what he asked. He got the meal, and at the first burn he got to, once he thought he was safe, he put the meal into the heel of his shoe with a splash of water and ate it with a twig. And he said:

'Hunger is a good cook:
Foul fall the man who scorns his food.
Cold barley gruel from the heel of my shoe –
The finest meal I have ever had.'

And he went . . . Since night was falling then – between then and the morning he travelled up Glen Roy, and when dawn began to break, in case he should be seen he managed to get into a house belonging to a man they call O'Brien. And there wasn't much food in the house and the stranger was hungry –

'But I'll tell you what I'll do for you,' said he. 'I'll kill our only cow and you can have it, to eat.' And that was what was done.

He stayed three days there, sleeping on a bed of heather, and the blanket or, as they said, the coverlet that was over him was the cow's hide. And when he had rested and recovered, he left at nightfall, heading for home, his own place. And he told him: 'If you think you are being blamed or anyone bears a grudge against you for saving my life, come to my place and I will make you welcome.'

That was what happened. He [O'Brien] felt as he saw it that they were down on him for saving the man, and he went to his place . . . the Earl of Mar's. And as he came up to the place there was a porter out there at a great gate, and nobody was to be let into that place unless he was given a sign from the house or a word from the doorway. This wretched little man came along, and he was most astonished to see the

Earl inviting him to come on up to the house, and surprised at the shaking of hands there was up there and how welcome he was made.

The Earl said to him: 'Come into my house, and you shall have the best room in it and the best food I can give you, just as I got from you; and if you're not wanting to go back to Glen Roy, you shall have lands on my estate, and you can stay there as long as you live.'

That was what happened. The old man decided that he was as well to stay there and never to go back to Glen Roy, and they never heard of him again there: he lived on the Earl of Mar's lands.

95a   *Angus MacLellan*

PAUL OF THE THONG

. . . IT WAS SAID THAT it was in Scolpaig Castle that Dòmhnall Hearach was murdered . . . He was of the Clan Donald. And this is how they killed him: they had a thong hanging from the rafters to see who could [leap up and] put his head through the noose that was on it. And he got his head through the noose and the man who was [holding it] below pulled on the rope and they strangled him like that. [And afterwards that man was known as Paul of the Thong.]

And when his wife began to get uneasy about him not coming home, she went down – she knew where he was – she went down to look for him, and he was dead and they had burnt his eyes out with red-hot irons. And she said: 'If you cooked him,' said she, 'why did you not eat him?'

One of them gave her a kick in the backside and she went out and she said: 'Who knows,' said she, 'but that there may be under my girdle what will avenge him yet.'

And she was pregnant . . . and she fled then and went to Skye and she was delivered there and bore a baby boy.

And the boy was always asking her what had become of his father and she would not tell him; but when he was about sixteen or seventeen years old she did tell him, and then he began to make arrows, a bow and arrows.

Then he set out from Skye with some others, and he said he was going to avenge his father. And they came ashore at Eubhal and they came to the house of an old woman there, and they knocked at the window and she said: 'Is this Aonghas Fionn,' said she, 'the son of Dòmhnall Hearach?'

'It is,' said he.

'Go out then,' said she, 'and get the wether that is out at the back of the house,' said she, 'and kill it, so that you can eat it,' said she, 'before you go.'

And he did that and they cooked the meat and had a meal and went on their way.

And he left the road at Bayhead – they all left the road at Bayhead – and cut across . . . the Druim Ard.

And he [Paul] was on the top of a corn-stack in Paiblesgarry and he noticed them and he said: 'Aonghas Fionn,' said he, 'is coming. It's time for me to go,' said he.

He jumped down from the stack and made off and he cut across [the sands at] Tràigh a' Locha . . . Aonghas Fionn went and cut across by Cachaileith a' Ghàrraidh Bhig [Gap in the Little Dyke], as they called it, across by Balranald.

And in these times, if anyone could get his finger in the keyhole of the church, nothing could be done to him. And he made for Rathad Mór a' Rìgh (the King's Highway) and Aonghas Fionn kept after him, and he was catching up with him fast. And when he was across the ford Aonghas just took an arrow and fired it at him, and the arrow pierced the sole of his foot – Paul's foot.

And there was a man in Goular whom they called Goll and Paul had put his eyes out. And when Aonghas Fionn brought Paul down at the church, his [Goll's] daughter saw them and said: 'There are men,' said she, 'over by the church.'

'Oh,' said he, 'Black Paul,' said he. 'Take me over there by the hand,' said he.

And she led him over and he shouted to them to leave him [Paul] alive till he got at him. And they left him alive till he got there, and this was the death he gave him – he chewed his testicles. That was how they put him to death. [The place is still called Leathad Phòil, Paul's Slope.]

95b   *Donald Morrison*

MURCHADH GEÀRR'S BIRTH

SOME SAY, ACCORDING to tradition, that it happened like this: his father, he was laird of Lochbuie, and he was getting on in years, and Duart captured him. And he put him in an island out there at the back of Staffa, which they call Cairnburg. And . . . he imprisoned him there and he left the ugliest woman in Mull with him, to prepare his food, and I suppose they had all the facilities they had in those days. That was going on fine, but events took another turn; the woman who was in Cairnburg with him grew – she wasn't very well, and she was sent – taken away from there, and taken to Torloisk – down here, MacLeans again. And the Ollamh Muileach [the Mull Doctor], he was over by Loch Scridain there, Pennyghael, and he was MacLean of Duart's doctor. And this man, he was asked to come and see to the woman when it was needed, and he said he would. And Duart said to him, 'If it's a son, strangle him, but if it's a daughter, let her live.' And it was a son, and apparently the Ollamh Muileach went back, and he said that it was a daughter. And he [the baby, Murchadh Geàrr] was kept in hiding until he grew up; he was up in a place up here they call Glencannel, with some of the MacGillivrays in hiding there, until he grew up to be a man, and then he came to the fore. And, yes, you know . . . if there hadn't been anyone to succeed the man who was in prison, no family – in Cairnburg you see, Duart would have had Lochbuie along with the rest! . . . That's the story I heard handed down.

MURCHADH GEÀRR'S RETURN

BUT THEY GOT STRONG, Lochbuie, you see, and they ousted out the MacFadyens. And then it came to the point when Lochbuie and Duart were fighting one another and . . . the head of Lochbuie was Murchadh Geàrr or 'Dumpy Murdoch' they called him. And he lost the castle and he hooked it off to the Earl of Antrim for assistance.

And the mother of the first Earl of Antrim was a daughter of MacDonald of the Isles, that's Islay. And his mother was over there with him and she was always asking him to put Highlanders over there. And at last he gave her that but not in one year. The story says, the traditional story says that he filled the seven glens in Antrim with Highlanders from the Butt of Lewis to the island of Arran. And that went on for a long time.

But at this time he [Murchadh Geàrr] lost his castle – Duart got a hold of Lochbuie and he fled to the Earl of Antrim for assistance. And he asked for assistance and Antrim said to him that he would give them thirteen big swordsmen and a boat, a *currach*, and they had to row. Now a *currach* is a boat made of skins, with a wooden frame. They were common in these old days. And they rowed her from Derry up to Craignure there, to Java, and they came ashore there. It was getting near to the night. And they dodged along by Craignure. And there was one of them that loitered behind. And some of the Mull men were dubious about them and they asked this man, 'What's your name?'

He said, 'Today I was a Morrison but now I am a Son of the Night'.— He didn't know where he was going.

But it passed like that and they went on to Lochbuie to the castle and Dumpy Murdoch got in touch with the dairymaid, she knew him. And her opinion was that – The cows were in one park on this side of the castle and the calves were in the other . . . They had shielings in these days, you know. And she told them, 'Let the cows and the calves among one another and chase them, two or three of you, and make them roar till they make a big noise, and then the people in the castle will come out to see what's wrong, and when they come out, you rush in.' And it worked and they got a hold of the castle and they had it ever since until it was sold by – well, by the last chief of Lochbuie that I remember. And now it belongs to a Lewisman, it's sold. Aye, that's the way. And the castle's there yet, the ruins of it. I was never in Lochbuie.

96 *Gilbert Clark*

THE BATTLE OF TRÀIGH GHRUINNEART

MACLEAN OF DUART – Lachainn Mór of Duart – was married [sic] to the mother of MacDonald of Islay. MacDonald was just a child – a young lad, not a child but a young lad – when his father died, and at that time MacLean of Duart thought it would be a good chance to get Islay in his own name and under his own control. And they came to

Islay – a place they call Mulindry where the MacDonalds had their great houses, their long house. And, as it turned out, they failed to come to terms because MacDonald's advisers were stirring him up against his mother's brother and the result was that they made the Mull men prisoners. But they got free: they came to terms and they got free.

But after that the dispute got even worse. Lachainn Mór gathered the host and the ships of Mull to take Islay by force. The MacDonalds in Islay did as best they could. Word went out to Arran, to Kintyre and to all their kinsfolk round about to come and help them.

And there was a witch – they called her the Doideag Mhuileach – the Doideag Mhuileach, whom MacLean of Duart kept as an adviser, and she told him there were three things he must not do, before he sailed against the Islay men. He must not . . . or rather he must go three times sunwise round a green knoll that was in front of Duart Castle, but instead of that, MacLean went clean against the old woman and went three times round this mound widdershins. The second thing: she told him if he got to Islay that he was not to put in to land at a place they called Nòstaig, a sandy bay on the north-west of Islay. And the third thing, not to take a drink of water from the Well of Niall Neònach.

When he got to Islay he put into Nòstaig. He marched across to the side of Tràigh Ghruinneart: it was a hot day in autumn and they just came to the well and had a drink of water . . . well water. They didn't know that this was the Well of Niall Neònach. But all three things were done contrary to the old woman's advice. And there was a fourth. I don't know if it was the old woman who told him this or who it was: not to raise his standard on Cnoc nan Àighean, and he did that too.

Anyway, the MacDonalds on the other side were gathering every man they could. They had MacAoidh of the Rhinns, a man famous for his skill at arms; and the Ollamh Ìleach was a famous physician to the MacDon-alds. And there was a man they called Mac a' Phrìor: he was well-known as a soothsayer, like Coinneach Odhar [the 'Brahan Seer'] and men of that sort. And he said to MacDonald – he told him he could tell him how the day would go for him, but that he would have to promise him a piece of land that they called Seann Fheòirlinn – Sunderland we call it today –

and Coul, as a reward. MacDonald promised faithfully that if the day went well for him they [sic] could have that.

Well, the battle was joined and it seemed as if the Islay men would have the worst of the day, because the Mull men were above them on the high ground. But as the battle went on more men arrived to help the Islay men.

And there was a little man there – a wretched little man who had come across from Jura, and he offered his services to Lachainn Mór. And Lachainn Mór turned round and said that he could not bear to look at such a miserable creature among his men. This enraged this wretched little man so much that he went over to the MacDonalds and said to MacDonald, 'Will you take me into your army?'

'I certainly will, even if there were a thousand like you.'

'Well,' Dubh-Sìdh said . . . that was what they called this little man, Dubh-Sìdh – . . . a Shaw from Jura, and Dubh-Sìdh said to MacDonald: 'If you take care of all the rest of the Mull men, I'll look after Lachainn Mór myself.'

And I'll tell you later how this happened.

The battle began. As I've said . . . the Mull men were up on the high ground and the Islay men were down below. Anyway the Arran men arrived to help them, and this is what they did because they were late: they came to land at Portnahaven . . . and they marched up by the side of the loch and up by a place they called Boirechill, this side of Traigh Ghruinneart: and what should they come upon but a party of the Mull men down below them, away from the battlefield. I don't know what the Mull men were doing there, about two miles away from the battlefield. But the Arran men came upon them unawares and killed every single one of them. And to this day they call that place Torr na Muileach [the Mull Men's Mound], at the back of Lyrabus.

Well, when Lachainn Mór and his men saw this band approaching, they thought there was a great host there and their courage began to fail them and they moved down to a place they call Sliabh a' Chath [the Battle Brae] and the Islay men got a better chance to get a footing up on firm ground.

And there were trees, patches of woodland there at the time, and this Dubh-Sìdh climbed up into one of the trees – and the day was hot. MacLean of Duart took off the steel armour that was protecting . . . his breast, and he bent down over the well to have a drink of water. And as he tood up Dubh-Sìdh planted an arrow in his breast and killed him.

And the army, his army, panicked now and they fled, and they came to a church with the Islay men in pursuit – they came to the old church of Kilnave, a few miles down beyond Sliabh a' Chath. They went in there thinking they would be in sanctuary but the Islay men had gone berserk so that they set fire to the church, and every man who was in there was burnt to death except for one who managed to escape. And the Islay men were after him, but he must have been pretty fast: he managed to keep ahead of them. He swam out to sea near Nave Island – and there's an islet there – with an arrow in his thigh. He swam out till he reached this islet they call Badaig and he stayed there, at the back of the islet, till the Islay men had gone away. And he came ashore then and he stayed on in Islay ever after, and we still have people whom they call to this day Clann Mhuirich na Badaig . . . the Curries of Badaig.

But I've got ahead of my story. I should have told you about . . . how the Arran men got on.

When Lachainn Mór fell and the battle was over, one of the Arran men came along, Angus MacDonald, a near kinsman to MacDonald of Islay. He saw a fine ring on Lachainn Mór's finger. He bent down to pull this ring off but the ring was so tight that he couldn't get it off. He cut off the finger. And one of the Mull men was lying near him. This man was still alive and this infuriated him so much that it gave him a burst of strength, the Mull man, and he reared up and planted an arrow in Angus MacDonald and killed him. They carried off the body of Angus MacDonald . . .

Well, in those days it was the custom among the Gaels – the Highland clans – that their closest female relatives were by them on the battlefield. And so it was with Lachainn Mór: he had his foster-mother and her son with him when he came . . . The day after the battle, when things had settled down, his foster-mother and her son Duncan brought a slype and a horse to take Lachainn to Kilchoman and bury him in the High Church of Kilchoman. Now the man was so big and massive that his feet were sticking out at the front of the slype and his head was jolting from side to side at the other end. Duncan began to make sport of it – laughing. His mother asked him what he was on about.

He said: 'What a come-down for Lachainn Mór – lying there on his back nodding to and fro like that!'

This made his mother so furious that she drew a knife and killed her own son. That's the place they call Carn Dhonnchaidh [Duncan's Cairn] to this day, a little settlement where there were a lot of crofters after that time.

Anyway his foster-mother went on with the few men she had with her and Lachainn Mór was buried at the west end of the High Church of Kilchoman. But tradition says that at that time the church was different and that it was inside the church that Lachainn was buried, though today, the building being different, he lies outside the church. And to this day they speak of the tombstone of Lachainn Mór of the Two Hearts. There's a great stone slab there. I'm sure that it's an hour-glass that's on it, though the people believed that it was two hearts that were carved on this slab.

And when everything had settled down the Ollamh Ìleach was given a great reward and MacAoidh of the Rhinns was rewarded for his services, and this Mac a' Phrior, he got the estate of . . . Coul and Sunderland and these two pieces of land were held separately from the rest . . . of this part of the island till a few years ago. That piece of land had a separate proprietor.

And, as I've said before, the Arran men, instead of going back to Portnahaven and taking the boats they had left there back to Arran, they crossed the moors and got boats on the other side of the island to take them across to the mainland, and from there they could get over to Arran.

And as everyone [in Islay] knows, a few years after that, fighting broke out among all the clans so that the poor MacDonalds had to flee to Ireland at the end of the day, though Colla Ciotach fought many a battle trying to win back the land of his ancestors.

They built a fine big castle out in Antrim, by the shore, right opposite Islay, and ever since that time, for this part of the island and especially the Rhinns, there has been a warm feeling and a great deal of trade between the two countries . . . up to the time of just before the First World War, when the fishing declined as in many parts of the Highlands, and the young lads went off to the war. Since then the link between the two islands has fallen off, till now there's not much trade or understanding of each other between the two countries, though there was a great warmth for many centuries since that time, three hundred years ago: this place had a warm feeling for Ireland.

SELECT BIBLIOGRAPHY

This select bibliography includes the principal sources cited in the Notes which follow. As abbreviated titles have been used in the Notes, for ease of reference here sources have been listed alphabetically in order of these abbreviations.

AFH Hannah Aitken, ed.: *A Forgotten Heritage*, Edinburgh 1973

Arv Scandinavian Yearbook of Folklore, Uppsala 1945–

AST Peter Buchan: *Ancient Scottish Tales*, Peterhead 1908 (reprinted from the *Transactions of the Buchan Field Club*)

AT Aarne-Thompson type number in Antti Aarne and Stith Thompson: *The Types of the Folktale*, Helsinki 1964 (FF Communications No. 184)

Béaloideas The Journal of the Folklore of Ireland Society, Dublin 1928–

CSD Mairi Robinson, ed.: *The Concise Scots Dictionary*, Aberdeen 1985

F Types from the University of Edinburgh School of Scottish Studies provisional catalogue of fairy and other supernatural legends

FL, FLJ, FLR *Folk-Lore/Folklore*, London 1890– (successor to *The Folk-Lore Journal*, 1883–9, and *The Folk-Lore Record*, 1878–82)

FLI Sean O'Sullivan: *The Folklore of Ireland*, London 1974

FOC Alexander MacGregor: *The Feuds of the Clans*, Stirling 1907

FOS Ernest Marwick: *The Folklore of Orkney and Shetland*, London 1975

FTFL James MacDougall: *Folk Tales and Fairy Lore* (ed. George Calder), Edinburgh 1910 (partially reprinted as *Highland Fairy Legends*, ed. Alan Bruford, Ipswich 1978)

FTI Sean O'Sullivan: *Folktales of Ireland*, London 1966

FTTC Duncan Williamson: *Fireside Tales of the Traveller Children*, Edinburgh 1983

GAB J. G. McKay, ed.: *Gille A'Bhuidseir/The Wizard's Gillie*, London n.d.

GFMR Alan Bruford: *Gaelic Folk-Tales and Mediaeval Romances*, Dublin 1969 (also as *Béaloideas* 34)

GMK Alan Bruford, ed.: *The Green Man of Knowledge and other Scots Traditional Tales*, Aberdeen 1982

The Highlands by Calum I. Maclean: three differing editions, London 1959, Inverness 1975 and Edinburgh 1994; cited by chapters only

KBA Sheila Douglas, ed.: *The King o the Black Art and other Folk Tales*, Aberdeen 1987

LEM Lady Evelyn Stewart-Murray's MSS. (see note to tale No. 11)

ML Types from Reidar Th. Christiansen: *The Migratory Legends*, Helsinki 1958 (FF Communications No. 175)

MWHT J.G. Mckay, ed.: *More West Highland Tales*, 2 vols, Edinburgh 1940 and 1960.

OLM The Viking Society, *Old - Love Miscellany* of Orkney, Shetland

PRS Robert Chambers: *The Popular Rhymes of Scotland*. Cited from the 'New Edition', reissued at various dates later in the last century: the first edition was published in 1826, but the tales, or most of them, do not seem to have appeared until the third ('much enlarged') edition of 1841.

PSFA W. Grant Stewart: *The Popular Superstitions and Festive Amusements of the Highlanders of Scotland*, Edinburgh 1823 (facsimile reprint London 1970)

PTWH John Francis Campbell: *Popular Tales of the West Highlands* (4 vols); cited from 2nd edition, Paisley 1890–93, or by tale number where possible: see Introduction note 25 for publication history.)

SA Sound Archive of the School of Scottish Studies, University of Edinburgh .

SD K. C. Craig, ed.: *Sgialachdan Dhunnchaidh*, Glasgow n.d. (after 1944)

SND W. Grant and D. D. Murison edd.: *The Scottish National Dictionary*, Oxford 1931–76.

SOCB Séamus Ó Duilearga: *Seán Ó Conaill's Book* (translated by Máire MacNeill), Dublin 1981

SS *Scottish Studies*: The Journal of the School of Scottish Studies, University of Edinburgh, Edinburgh 1957–

SSH John Gregorson Campbell: *Superstitions of the Highlands and Islands of Scotland / Scottish Highlands*, Glasgow 1900

SSU Angus MacLellan: *Stories from South Uist* (translated by J. L. Campbell), London 1961

STT D. A. MacDonald and Alan Bruford, eds.: *Scottish Traditional Tales*, privately printed, Edinburgh 1974

T *Tocher*: Tales, songs and traditions from the archives of the School of Scottish Studies, University of Edinburgh, Edinburgh 1971–; cited by numbers, not volumes

TGP Peter Narváez, ed.: *The Good People. New Fairylore Essays*, New York 1991

TGSI *Transactions of the Gaelic Society of Inverness*, Inverness 1871–

BIBLIOGRAPHY

TIF Types from Seán Ó Súilleabháin and Reidar Th. Christiansen: *The Types of the Irish Folktale*, Helsinki 1963 (FF Communications No. 188)

TMI Types from Ernest W. Baughman: *Types and Motif Index of the Folktales of England and North America*, The Hague 1966 (Indiana University Folklore Series 20)

TUD Joe Neil MacNeil: *Sgeul gu Latha / Tales Until Dawn* (translated and ed. by John Shaw), Edinburgh 1987

UAB Pàdruig Moireasdan: *Ugam agus Bhuam* (ed. D. A. MacDonald), Steòrnabhagh (Club Leabhar), 1977

W Types from the School of Scottish Studies' provisional catalogue of witch legends (see *SS* 11: 1–47)

W&S Lord Archibald Campbell (general ed.): *Waifs and Strays of Celtic Tradition*, Argyllshire Series (5 vols.), London 1889–95

WSS John Gregorson Campbell: *Witchcraft and Second Sight in the Highlands and Islands of Scotland / Scottish Highlands*, Glasgow 1902

Seven of these tales can be heard as
they were told on the cassette

Scottish Tradition 17

SCOTS STORY TELLING

GREENTRAX RECORDINGS
C9017 Edinburgh 1995

The tales included from this book are:
The Three Feathers (Andrew Stewart, Blairgowrie)
**The Humph at the Fit o the Glen and the Humph at the
Head o the Glen** (Bella Higgins, Blairgowrie)
Silly Jack and the Factor (Jeannie Robertson, Aberdeen)
The Boy and the Brüni (Tom Tulloch, Yell)
Keeping Out the Sea Man (James Henderson, S. Ronaldsay)
The Fiddler o Gord (George Peterson, Papa Stour)
The Greenbank Pony (Tom Tulloch, Yell)

With three other stories:
One-Eye Two-Eyes and Three-Eyes (Betsy Whyte,
Montrose)
Daughter Doris (Davie Stewart, Kintyre)
The Angel of Death (Stanley Robertson, Aberdeen)

*All recordings are from
The School of Scottish Studies'
Sound Archives*

NOTES

Abbreviations have been used for frequently cited sources: for full details of these publications see the Select Bibliography.
Other abbreviations: AJB Alan (James) Bruford, DAM Donald Archie MacDonald

Where the name of the transcriber and/or translator is not given, these functions were carried out by the editors. Tale titles in brackets were supplied by the editors or collectors rather than the storyteller.

Introduction

1　See Edwin C. Kirkland, 'The American Redaction of Tale Type 922', *Fabula* 4:248–59, and Alan Bruford, ' "The King's Questions" (AT 922) in Scotland', *SS* 17:147–54.
2　See Neil Philip, *The Cinderella Story*, Penguin Folklore Library, Harmondsworth 1989:17–20 and *passim*.
3　*The Scots Magazine*, May 1976, p. 208.
4　*FL* 47:190–202.
5　*The Scots Magazine*, July 1976, p. 342; August, pp. 446 and 448. In fact until very recently I had forgotten one other previously published Scots text, the only one told at full length, in a little book of rhymes and games from Forfar collected by Jean C.Rodger, *Lang Strang*, Forfar n.d. (1948):45-6, 'Bedtime Story', where the trousers are 'stuntifiers' and the cat is 'Old Killiecraffus'.
6　Walter Gregor, *Notes on the Folk-Lore of the North-East of Scotland*, Folk-Lore Society, London, 1881, Chapter X, 'Evenings at the Fireside' (adapted from 'Evenings in the Farm Kitchen' in his earlier *An Echo of the Olden Time from the North of Scotland*, Edinburgh 1874, which gives a fuller description of the stories). Quotation from p. 55 of the later book.
7　*Ibid.* p. 57.
8　*T* 31:64–5, from Mrs Kate MacDonald.

9 T 31:62–3.
10 A. T. Cluness, *Told Round the Peat Fire*, London 1955:134 ff., 'The Wreck of the *Harvest Rose*'. The Laaf fishing (the *a* is actually short, but the double *a* is established by convention) affected life throughout Shetland for most of the 18th and 19th centuries, since it took most of the men away from home for the summer months, and its stories of heroism and hardship have permeated the islands' tradition.
11 Gregor, *op. cit.*:55–6.
12 *Ibid.*:57–8.
13 *PTWH* 1:V–VI.
14 *Ibid.*:VI–VII.
15 Tom and Liza Tulloch, SA 1978/68.
16 T26:81.
17 Betsy Whyte's *The Yellow on the Broom* (Edinburgh 1979) and the Introduction to Duncan Williamson's *Fireside Tales of the Traveller Children* (*FTTC*, 1983) and several of his later books fill in parts of this picture.
18 See David Buchan. 'Folkloristic Methodology and a Modern Legend', in Reimund Krideland (ed.) Folklore Processed (Studia Fennica Folkloristica I, Helsinki 1992): 89–103. The quotation from Pendennis, episode 19, which first appeared in 1850, is on p. 90–91.
19 See *GFMR* part 1, and for theories on the Fenians, J. F. Nagy, *The Wisdom of the Outlaw*, Berkeley 1985 and Kim McCone, *Pagan Past and Christian Present*, Maynooth 1990, chapter 9.
20 Some folklorists use 'variant' where we use 'version', and literary terms such as 'redaction' where we use 'variant'.
21 Duncan Williamson's *Fireside Tales of the Traveller Children* (*FTTC*, 1983) is the first of half a dozen published by Canongate, of which perhaps the most interesting is *Don't Look Back, Jack!* (1991); *A Thorn in the King's Foot* (Penguin Folklore Library, Harmondsworth 1987) is the best of those published outside Scotland. Stanley Robertson's *Exodus to Alford* (Balnain Books, Nairn, 1988) is the only one of several books from these publishers to consist mainly of traditional tales. See review in SS 30:107–16, and biographical features, with tales and ballads, in T33 (Duncan) and T40 (Stanley).
22 Actually printed as 'the volfe, of the varldis end', but an emendation ('volle' or 'velle'?) has been suggested since Chambers *PRS* if not before. See *The Complaynt of Scotland*, ed. A. M. Stewart, Scottish Text Society, 4th Series, vol. 11, Edinburgh 1979:50.
23 *AST*: 4; 'The Red Etin' begins on p. 13.
24 P. C. Asbjørnsen and J. I. Moe, *Popular Tales from the Norse*, translated by Sir George W. Dasent, Edinburgh (Edmonston and Douglas) 1859. Campbell's title as well as his choice of publisher followed Dasent's.
25 See *PTWH*, and *MWHT* 4.
26 See *W&S*; the volume editors were the Revd Duncan MacInnes, the Revd James

MacDougall (see also *FTFL*) and the Revd John Gregorson Campbell (see also *SSH* and *WSS*.)

27 Carmichael is best known for his collection of Gaelic prayers and charms *Carmina Gadelica*, but he published a number of stories including *Deirdire* (Edinburgh, London and Dublin 1905), which is considerably edited from its oral original (see *Scottish Gaelic Studies* 14.1–24). Father Allan MacDonald's work is described in Amy Murray's *Father Allan's Island*, J. L. Campbell and Trevor Hall's *Strange Things* and elsewhere, but as far as I know none of the stories from his collections have been published in full. For Lady Evelyn Stewart-Murray see notes to tale No. 11, 'Lasair Gheug', below.

28 Campbell's *Sia Sgialachdan* (Edinburgh 1939) and Craig's *Sgialachdan Dhunnchaidh* (*SD*, Glasgow, after 1944), both privately printed for the editors, publish only Gaelic texts, though Campbell provides English summaries. Craig's other publications of stories are similar, but come from J. F. Campbell's MSS. Campbell's *Tales of Barra Told by the Coddy* (privately published, Edinburgh 1960) and *Stories from South Uist* (*SSU*, 1961) on the other hand, give only the English translations. For a fine independent collection recently published from Cape Breton Island, Canada, in Gaelic and English, see *TUD*.

29 See *T*39 for an appreciation of Calum Maclean's work.

30 John Mackay Wilson, a Berwick printer, published a series of these tales retold by various authors in up to ten volumes, reissued many times in the late nineteenth century, but easier to pick up cheaply than to read.

31 Volumes 1 and 5 of *W&S* are largely clan legends.

32 These were collected by John Dewar, one of J. F. Campbell's former helpers, and translated by another, Hector MacLean, for the Duke of Argyll; one volume of the translations has been published (*The Dewar Manuscripts*, vol. 1, ed. John MacKechnie, Glasgow 1964) but DAM has begun to work on a more scholarly edition including the Gaelic text.

33 V. Y. Propp, *Morphology of the Folktale*, Bloomington (Indiana) 1958. Revised edition, Austin (Texas) 1968.

34 See notes to tale No. 30, below.

35 See *SS* 22: 1–44, *Arv* 37:117–24 and 103–9, and *T*31:35–66.

Children's Tales

1a *The Old Man with the Ear of Corn* SA 1969/5 A8. Recorded from Mrs Dolly Ann MacDougall, Urugaig, Isle of Colonsay by the editors, with Ian Fraser. *T*3:98–9 (with Gaelic text); *STT* No. 2. A family tradition which Mrs MacDougall, a farmer's wife with an interest in her island's lore, passed on to her children and grandchildren. AT 1655, 'The Profitable Exchange', classified among tales of lucky accidents, is in some ways closer to chain tales like 'The Old Woman and her Pig' (AT 2030, compare the Gaelic *Biorachan Beag agus Biorachan Mór* or *Murchag is Mionachag*, *PTWH*

No. IX): there the elements in the chain are connected by a logic which has no relation to the real world – a mouse asks for a cat to hunt it – and the same is true of the exchanges here. The girl in the sack exchanged for a load of stones comes into many ogre tales, but here she has no reason to expect she will be thrown into the loch: the story ends as inconsequentially as it began.

1b *The Old Man with the Grain of Barley* SA 1968/183 A4. Recorded from Mrs Kate Dix, Berneray, Harris, transcribed and translated by Ian Paterson. *T*20:124–7 (with Gaelic text), part of a feature on this remarkable Gaelic storyteller and poet, who had held on to her native language and traditions through over thirty-five years in Oban and Sunderland with a husband who never learned Gaelic, though he made sure his children did. Here the sequence of lucky accidents has a happy ending and indeed seems to be intended from the beginning: it seems more usual for them to happen in different houses. Compare the Barra version in *Béaloideas* 4:105.

2 *The Grey Goat* SA 1964/6 A1. Recorded from Hugh MacKinnon, Cleadale, Isle of Eigg by DAM in February 1964. *SS* 9:108–13 (with Gaelic text); *STT* No. 3. Hugh MacKinnon, an outstanding source of local historical traditions and a meticulous stylist (see feature filling all of *T*10), needed some persuasion to tell this story normally told by mothers to children, which he learned from his own mother probably before 1900. AT 123, 'The Wolf and the Kids', in Gaelic includes stylised formulae which would not be out of place in a hero tale: in fact Alexander Carmichael interpolated the impressive oath the birds swear in the published text of the Deirdre story he recorded in Barra (see *Scottish Gaelic Studies* 14:18). We have tried to render the style of this language in the translation.

3a *The Fox and the Wolf and the Butter* SA 1965/10 B4. Recorded from Calum Johnston, Eoligarry, Barra by DAM in March 1965. *STT* No. 25. For this notable Gaelic piper, singer and storyteller (another who had spent all his working life away from his native island) and his sister Annie, see the feature in *T*13, with an appreciation by Dr John Lorne Campbell. AT 15, a trickster fable often told in Europe of the clever fox and the stupid bear, as usual in Gaelic replaces the bear by the wolf (*madadh-allaidh*, 'wild dog', opposed to *madadh-ruadh*, 'red dog', the fox) which has not been extinct in Scotland so long. The clever names for the babies to be christened are the main point of the story, but Gaelic versions add the oath in which, as J. G. Campbell says (*W&S* 5:117), 'the Gaelic C corresponds to the English Wh', giving the nonsense asseveration a very questionable sound. The cask of butter washed up on the beach adds a touch of Hebridean local colour. See *SS*8:218–27 for a version from Hugh MacKinnon, with a sequel.

3b *The Cats and the Christening* SA 1977/14. Recorded from Tom Tulloch, Gutcher, Yell, Shetland by Peter Cooke. *T*30:359–60, part of an extended feature on this devoted bearer of all aspects of the traditions of North Yell. The emphasis on the possibilities for improvisation in such children's stories, and on the moral, is typical of Tom's careful recreation of the tales he heard from his mother and her sister. Here for once the trickster does not get away with it. In the Grimms' version of AT 15, 'The Cat and the Mouse in Partnership', the cat simply eats her partner when she is found out. (There are no unusual dialect words: 'paul(ly)' is simply the North Yell pronunciation of 'pal(ly)'.)

4   *The Boy and the Brüni* SA 1975/179 A4. Recorded from Tom Tulloch, Gutcher, Yell, Shetland by AJB. An earlier and rather less detailed recording is in T11:96–7, *STT* No. 20. The core of the story corresponds to that of AT 327, 'The Children and the Ogre' (best known as 'Hänsel and Gretel'), but it is a very individual Yell form. A summary of it noted in the last century is in Laurence G. Johnson, *Laurence Williamson of Mid Yell*, Lerwick 1971:119–20. Tom felt that the story must have been known in other parts of Shetland, associated with other landmarks than the Erne's Knowe (Eagle's Knoll – the K is pronounced), but we have heard of no other versions. Tom not only noted this opportunity for improvisation but suggested a moral, a warning against playing with your food, though as the final result is wealth for the boy's whole family it hardly seems a clear warning! The giant's rhyme preserves the Scottish equivalent of 'I smell the blood of an Englishman' as Peter Buchan and Robert Chambers noted it early in the last century (PRS:92): compare the form in No. 7 below.

The dialect of North Yell pronounces 'ken' as 'keen' and has disconcerting double prepositions like 'in atil' and 'oot ot o'. The following list may help with words which are less obvious variants of English. *Aless*: unless, except; *atil*: until, to; *'at*: that; *brüni*: a bannock, large round oatcake; *byre*: cowshed; *caudereen*: cauldron; *croople*: crouch, squat; *fand*: found; *güd*: went; *ipae, ipo*: on; *keen*: ken, know; *kye*: cows, cattle; *oagit*: crawled; *peerie*: little; *row* (rhymes with 'cow'): roll; *shoakit*: choked; *skrauflin*: scrabbling, clambering; *stoop o the mill*: upright of the frame supporting the corn-grinding quern; *til*: to; *t'owt*: thought; *t'rot*: throat; *tyoch*: tough; *wän*: one; *yondroo*: there.

5   *(The Wee Bird)* SA 1956/112/1. Recorded from Jimmy McPhee, a fourteen-year-old traveller boy, by Hamish Henderson in an encampment at the berryfields of Blairgowrie, Perthshire. Original transcription by Robert Garioch. T4:124–5; *STT* No. 31. AT 720, 'My Mother Slew Me; My Father Ate Me', the Grimms' 'The Juniper Tree'. This boy's version preserves some of the starkness of the older Scots story as told by Chambers ('The Milk-White Doo', *PRS*:49–50): the murderer is the child's own mother, not stepmother, and the father recognises what he is eating. But as in all cairds' versions the girl is killed for breaking a jug, fractionally more understandable than in Chambers hare she was to put in the pie but 'tasted it a' away', and (as in some versions designed for children) the victim comes back to life, and here explains that her mother was possessed by the Devil. Most other cairds' versions (e.g. *KBA* 152–4) make her a stepmother, call the two stepsisters 'Applie and Orangie', and include the rhyme, central to most versions, which the bird sings to various shopkeepers and is rewarded by the presents it drops to the father and sister and the axe or millstone for the stepmother. The Christmas setting, because the presents come down the chimney, is now usual; in Chambers the dove just 'threw sma' stanes down the lum' to get the others outside. *Peeping* here probably means cheeping, rather than looking. Here is the rhyme as recorded with a rather fragmentary remembering of the story by Hamish Henderson from Andrew Stewart and Donald Higgins, Blairgowrie (SA 1955/191 A8; *T4*:126).

Ma mammie kilt me,
Ma deddie ett me,
Ma sister Jeannie pickit ma banes
An put me atweene twa marable stanes
An A grow'd intae a bonnie wee doo, doo.

6　*Liver and Lights* From a typescript of 'A Scottish Nurse's Stories' given to the School of Scottish Studies through Hamish Henderson in 1968 by Miss K. M. T. Bannerman, an Edinburgh lady then in her seventies. *T8*:239. The stories had been read to Miss Bannerman when she was fourteen or fifteen from the manuscript from which she later typed them, by her Aunt Jemima, Mrs Campbell Lorimer, née Bannerman, daughter of a New College Professor, who had written them down from memory: she was told the stories by *her* Aunt Ceil, Mrs Cecilia Cunningham, née Douglas, who had heard them in Fife, when visiting friends of the family at Rossie, from their old nurse, whose name was Jeannie Durie. This chain seems to carry the substance of the stories and a few remembered words of Scots dialogue back to about the middle of the last century.

This story is a variant of AT 366, 'The Man from the Gallows'. Baughman (*TMI*:9–10) lists two English-language variants: someone finds a bone (etc.) and quite innocently uses it in soup, or as in Mark Twain's *How to Tell a Story*, a corpse buried complete with a golden artificial limb is dug up and robbed of it. This Scottish variant seems closer to the summary in AT, where a man feeds the entrails of a corpse to his wife, though here it is not on the gallows and the motivation is the wife's *greening* – a craving, often of a pregnant woman. In a still more sinister variant in *Shetland Folk Book* 8, the craving is specifically to taste the liver of a dead man. Like a fragmentary recording made from Mrs Annabella Clouston in Orkney in her hundredth year, it includes the wife's repeated line 'Lang lies Lowrie at the mill the night': he is not a professional miller as in the Fife story, but has to grind his own corn in one of the little local watermills of the islands, often used at night, to leave the day for work outdoors.

The questions at the end and the terrible shriek also link our story with Chambers' 'Aye She Wished for Company' (*PRS*:64–6; cf. AT 336), where a skeleton comes in bit by bit to a woman and a series of quiet questions and answers about its different parts ends with a sudden shriek of 'FOR YOU!' designed to terrify 'the juvenile audience'. Other Scots words: *e'en*: eyes; *how*: hollow; *howk*: dig; *thraw*: twist; *traivel*: walk; *wyte*: blame – 'Its' last words may be a misunderstanding of something like 'Ye aucht [are due] the wyte o't'.

Fortune Tales

7   *Silly Jack and the Lord's Daughter* SA 1954/90 A5. Recorded from Jeannie Robertson, Aberdeen, telling it to her young nephew Isaac, by Hamish Henderson. Transcription by Robert Garioch. *STT* No. 14. Jeannie Robertson (Mrs Regina Christina Higgins, to give her her official married name) is remembered more for her singing than her stories, but she was the first caird Hamish Henderson recorded telling stories (see *T*6:169–71), though her repertoire of traditional tales (as against lively anecdotal reminiscence) was not large. The hallmark of her style is involvement with her characters and the stress given to the bond between parents and children: less all-forgiving than her sister-in-law, Stanley Robertson's mother (cf. *T*40:175), she lets the elder brothers be killed as due punishment for their greed and disregarding the mother's blessing, but praises Jack for his kind heart.

This very simple pattern of story can be assigned to the tale-type AT 577, 'The King's Tasks', and it all springs from the 'bannock and blessing' opening, found in both Scots and Gaelic (e.g. *PRS*:90–92; *PTWH* No. XVI). In the latter example the sons ask their mother to 'cook them a bannock *(bonnach)* and roast them a cock *(coileach)*'. The Gaelic word reflects the sound rather than the meaning of Scots 'collop', a slice of meat, and this part of the formula at least seems to have come from Scots to Gaelic. The significant choice, however, found also in Ireland and elsewhere, is between the big bannock (or bigger half) with the mother's curse or malison and the small one with her blessing. The wee mannie is one of Propp's 'donors' (see Introduction p. 27), who sets a simple test for generosity or greed, and the magic object he gives the successful candidate takes charge of the rest of the story. It not only fights the giant, dragon and snake by itself, as you might expect of a sword, but provides Jack with food and a horse.

Notice that John is perceived as a different name from Jack. The giant's words, unlike those in 'The Boy and the Brüni' (tale No. 4 above), are clearly influenced by 'I smell the blood of an Englishman', which must have reached Scotland in chapbook versions of 'Jack the Giant-killer' or the like. 'Feel the smell', however, is pure Scots. Other Scots words: *cray* seems to be Jeannie's regular word for a grey (or white?) horse; *puddocks' spewins*: frogs' vomit; *wal* (rhymes with 'pal'): a well.

8   *The Tale of the Brown Calf* SM 1961/10. Recorded from Annie Johnston, Glen, Barra by Fred Macaulay. *STT* No. 13. For Annie, Calum Johnston's schoolteacher sister, see also *T*13:162 ff. In this case she is collector rather than storyteller: the recording, whether the story is read or learned by heart, follows almost verbatim a Gaelic text she published in *Béaloideas* 6:293–7, taken down in 1930 from her neighbour

Elizabeth MacKinnon (Ealasaid Eachainn 'Illeasbuig), who was born in Vatersay before 1860 and spent much of her childhood in Sandray. Both her parents were storytellers, and Annie had already published a story from her in *Béaloideas* 4.

AT 510B, 'The Dress of Gold, of Silver, and of Stars', is much more usual than 510A, 'Cinderella' proper (with the stepmother and ugly sisters) in the older tradition of Britain and Ireland. See Neil Philip, *The Cinderella Story*, Penguin Folklore Library, Harmondsworth 1989, for a recent study and selection of versions of both and some kindred stories from all over the world. Here the helpful brown calf (the Gaelic word is actually masculine), replacing the artificial 'fairy godmother' who first appears in the seventeenth-century French version of Perrault, explains what is usually left to be deduced, that it incarnates the heroine's dead mother. The hen-wife (*cailleach nan cearc*), whose daughter replaces the ugly sister at the end, is a stock character in both Gaelic and Scots who plays the same role in Chambers' Fife version (*PRS*:66–8): she is usually a villain, linked with the stepmother, but there is also a helpful hen-wife at the beginning of Chambers' story. The bird's rhyme, with chirping high vowels and a typical Gaelic repeat of the first couplet after the second, has been translated partly following Chambers'

> 'Nippit fit and clippit fit
> Ahint the king's son rides;
> But bonny fit and pretty fit
> Ahint the cauldron hides'.

'Scullery' translates Gaelic *cidsin dubh*, 'black kitchen', where the dirtiest work was done. Campbell's Islay version (*PTWH* No. XIV) has a quite different rhyme, but shares with Chambers the typical Scottish Protestant feature that the prince sees the heroine in church, not at a dance.

9   *The Three Feathers* SA 1956/128 B2. Recorded from Andrew Stewart, Perthshire traveller then living in Glasgow, by Hamish Henderson in 1956. Transcription by Robert Garioch. *T*14:225–234. Andrew, who soon after emigrated to Canada, was the youngest of the large family sometimes rather misleadingly all called 'the Stewarts of Blair', because of the prominence of his brother Alec and his wife Belle and their daughters, who lived in Blairgowrie, in the folk music revival (see Maurice Fleming's article in *T*21:165–9 and the introduction to Sheila Douglas' *The King o the Black Art* (*KBA*, 1987) for appreciations of the whole family). At least three of the brothers, Alec, John and Andrew, and their much older sister Mrs Bella Higgins, have all been recorded telling stories learned mainly from their parents. Andrew had perhaps the most uninhibited, racy, impromptu style of the four: it is clear in some stories that he has forgotten what came next, but he is never at a loss for words.

Though this tale-type (AT 402, 'The Mouse (Cat, Frog, etc.) as Bride') is widely known throughout Europe, the opening with the feathers and other major details correspond so closely to the Grimm version that it seems almost certain that one of the popular published translations is the original source. But caird storytelling has added masses of vivid detail: this version, like ones told by Andrew's brothers and his cousin Willie McPhee, is several times as long as the Grimm text and far more enjoyable to hear and even to read. The only Scots words that might need explanation are *guttery*: muddy and *meat*: food of any sort. *Brae steeds* seems to be just an odd pronunciation of 'brave' or 'braw'.

10   *The Green Man of Knowledge* SA 1954/101 B26. Recorded from Geordie Stewart, Aberdeenshire traveller, by Hamish Henderson in Jeannie Robertson's house in Aberdeen. Geordie, then a young man of twenty-four, had learned the story from his grandfather, and it is possible that like some other longer wonder-tales it was considered as the speciality, almost the property of this particular Stewart family. Certainly he seems to have learned no other comparable story. After nearly thirty years during which they lost contact, Hamish Henderson found Geordie Stewart again in Banff and after a discussion of the story recorded a complete text with some interesting differences (SA 1983/157–8). It naturally lacks some of the spontaneity of the original recording, which combines a young man's rather tongue-in-cheek attitude to the conventions of the 'Land of Enchantment' and the simpleton hero (whom he depicts largely as a devil-may-care Buchan farm servant, cheeky rather than backward) with a pride in recalling the whole of his family's ancient story. The colloquial narration, interspersed with well-characterised dialogue in broad Doric for Jack and what to Geordie were English forms ('shall' for 'will', 'well' for 'wal', 'ladder' for 'lether' and so on) for the Green Man and his daughter, rattles on at such a pace that I have made dozens of small revisions of the original transcription by Hamish Henderson and Tom Scott first for the original version of this book (*STT* No. 12), then for the collection where it was the title story (*GMK*:11–27), and again every time I have played parts of it to a class, and I am still not sure exactly what Geordie said in many places.

The text was first published in *SS2*:47–85 with a typically wide-ranging essay by Hamish Henderson on its tale-type, AT 313, 'The Girl as Helper in the Hero's Flight', and its possible parallels with the Middle English 'Sir Gawain and the Green Knight' as well as Sanskrit and Welsh Romany versions. The type is notable for a variety of quite different beginnings to get the hero into the power of the villain (here the Green Man) and different tasks he is then set, even within Scotland: the Gaelic variants published and summarised by J. F. Campbell (*PTWH* No. II) are enough to prove this. The only other published versions I know from Lowland Scots sources are Peter Buchan's 'Green Sleeves' (*AST* 40–47); 'Nicht, Nought, Nothing', written down by Miss Margaret Craig, near Elgin, for Andrew Lang and first published by him in *Revue Celtique* 3:374–6; and Willie McPhee's very individual variant, 'The Nine-Stall Stable' (*KBA*: 132–7) which begins more like 'Silly Jack and the Lord's Daughter' and had a different ending each time in the book and two versions I have heard him tell since. Geordie Stewart's version is longer than any of these, particularly with the journey and guidance by donors at the beginning, and has three distinctive features: Jack *wins* at cards – having practised against the dog who in most versions of the story is not mentioned until he 'kisses' the hero near the end – and yet still goes on to find the Green Man's castle (more usually a task set to the loser

SCOTTISH TRADITIONAL TALES

of the game), apparently from sheer cussedness; his third, rather quickly passed over task is to clear ants out of a wood (at an earlier stage perhaps the ants helped Jack to find pearls from a broken necklace, as in Willie McPhee's story, or sorted different types of grain for him, but this seems to be how Geordie heard the story and still told it in 1983); and the 'Magic Flight' episode ends with the Green Man and his elder daughters being burned by the 'spark of fire'.

North-east Scots words, forms (see also above) and phrases: *aa*: all; *aafae*: awful(ly); *aathing*: everything; *abeen*: above; *chap* (at door): knock; *claes*: clothes; *dee*: do; die: *deem*: girl (dame); *den*: valley; *fa*: who; *fae*: from; *far*: where; *fin*: when; *feel*: fool; *fit*: what; *gae, gaun*: go, goin; *geeny*: guinea; *gey*: very; *gie*: give; *ging*: go; *mair*: more; *meer*: mare; *'oor*: hour; *peer loon*: poor boy; *pinkie*: little finger; *quyne*: girl; *thackit cot*: thatched cottage; *weisht I*: wish I had; *yin tee*: that (yon) too.

11 *Lasair Gheug, the King of Ireland's Daughter* Lady Evelyn Stewart-Murray's MSS, No. 197. Recorded from Mrs MacMillan, Bridge Cottage, Strathtay on 3rd June 1891 by Lady Evelyn, a daughter of the seventh Duke of Atholl, whose collection of Gaelic folklore was stopped by her parents within a year as an unsuitable occupation for a lady. Lady Evelyn was immediately exiled to the Continent at the age of twenty-three to prevent her fraternising further with peasants (though Queen Victoria had praised the Atholl family's interest in Gaelic!) and never returned, but her brother Lord James, later the ninth Duke of Atholl, brought home her manuscripts and began to edit them with a view to publication, and after his death they were presented to the University of Edinburgh's School of Scottish Studies by the present Duke in 1958. The 240 stories and songs in the collection cover most of West Perthshire, where Gaelic was still many people's first language in 1891, and are an invaluable record of the traditions and dialect of the area. We hope for a complete publication of the collection, now being translated and edited by Mrs Sylvia Robertson, before long.

This story was published by AJB in *SS* 9:153–74 as 'A Scottish Gaelic version of "Snow-White" ', with the Gaelic text and notes referring to the only comparable Scottish versions, published by Kenneth MacLeod in *The Celtic Magazine* 13 (1888):212–18, and Irish parallels. In fact it is a conflation of elements from 'Snow-White' (AT 709) with a framework from'The Maiden without Hands' (AT 706). It is not strictly a Perthshire story either: Lady Evelyn noted of Mrs MacMillan, one of the few people from which she recorded *Märchen*, that she was 'a Badenoch woman, her father was a MacDonald, Badenoch, & her mother a Fraser from Lochaber', and all her stories came from her mother or her mother's mother, 'so these are Lochaber tales'. The heroine's name Lasair Gheug, 'Flame of Branches' or 'Limbs', may be a version of Lasair (Fhion-)Dhearg, '(Wine)-Red Flame', a favourite name for heroines in Irish tales. The false accusations and eventual revelation by getting round the 'baptismal oaths' (*briathran baistidh*) – apparently meaning a vow not to tell a Christian soul – belong to AT 706. The *eachrais (eachlach) urlair*, 'floor groom', apparently a sweeper, is a female character who replaces the hen-wife as the stepmother's evil genius in many Gaelic tales, and her seemingly small demands are typical. The hands usually cut off as a punishment (and miraculously restored) in this type are softened to finger-joints (which can be three to correspond to the three offences), but their bleeding serves to introduce the 'Snow-White' elements, apart from the queen's demand for her step-daughter's heart and liver, normally motivated by jealousy of her beauty. The prince in cat form, replacing the dwarfs or robbers, is in Irish versions of AT 709 and other Gaelic tales, and is as usual disenchanted by sleeping with the heroine. The most typically Gaelic feature, also shared by the Scottish versions and those Irish texts which do not clearly derive from Grimm, is the replacement of the (obviously modern) mirror on the wall with a speaking trout in a well. The salmon in a spring as a metaphor for truth or poetic inspiration is a basic image of early Irish mythology, and its smaller relative the trout was often kept in drinking-wells in Scotland and Ireland up to recent times to purify the water. It seems quite possible that the Gaelic version represents the earliest form of this tale-type. The prince's second wife who removes the poison grains (reading *siolain neimh'* for Lady Evelyn's *siolain 'n eigh*, 'grains of ice') is also regularly found in Gaelic versions, though the neat solution of marrying her off to the heroine's father, once more widowed, is not universal.

Riding the wild boar in and out of the church is a motif found in versions of AT 875 (see No. 32) and the story of Diarmaid and Gràinne (*PTWH* No. LX), where the heroine has to be neither on foot nor on horseback and neither indoors nor out, though the latter condition is confused here. The end of the story, in keeping with the formal and repetitive language of the rest, is an elaborate version of a typical 'end-run', a formula apparently designed to show that the story must be true, because its teller was at the wedding, which then destroys the illusion when all the gifts to prove it are lost, and brings the audience back to the real world.

12 *Sùil-a-Dia and Sùil-a-Sporain* SA 1969/120 A1. Recorded from Donald Alasdair Johnson, Ardmore, Iochdar, South Uist, transcribed and translated by Angus John MacDonald. *T*7:222–9 (with Gaelic text). Donald Alasdair Johnson (1890–1978) was first discovered in 1969 by Angus John MacDonald, then an Honours student of Celtic at Aberdeen University, doing part-time collecting work for the School of Scottish Studies in the Uists, simply knocking on doors to ask if anyone there knew old songs or stories (see *T*2:36–7, *SS* 14:133). Mr Johnson had kept telling the stories he learned from his father to himself as he worked, for lack of an audience when ceilidhing and appreciation of the longer stories faded out, and at the age of seventy-nine had still a remarkable repertoire of them and a stylish manner of telling, adding formulaic descriptions to the scenes he pictured as if of his whitewashed kitchen wall in front of him (*SS* 22:14 ff). He had served in the Merchant Navy, worked in Glasgow as a docker and fought in Flanders in the First World War, before coming back to Uist to work as crofter, postman, stonemason and joiner; he also composed and sang Gaelic songs, had played the pipes and still played the melodeon, but his stories were his great gift and a volume of them is in preparation. They were a family inheritance: one derived from a sixteenth-century Irish literary satire, *An Ceatharnach Caol Riabhach* (published from Donald Alasdair in *SS* 14:133–54), was taken down from his father's father in Eriskay by Alexander Carmichael in 1865,

and DAM has published a comparison in Gaelic of the two versions in *Gaelic and Scotland* (ed. W. Gillies, Edinburgh 1989):185–221.

This story, which Donald Alasdair was also filmed telling, is an international moral type, AT 613, 'The Two Travellers (Truth and Falsehood)'. The gathering of cats, rather than demons or a variety of animals, is a peculiarly Gaelic feature, and the name of their leader, apart from the echo of 'Old Calgravatus' (see Introduction), is only known in South Uist stories. The names of Sùil-a-Dia, literally 'Eye-to-God' can be understood as 'Trust-in-God', and Sùil-a-Sporain as 'Trust-in-Purse': the latter is called 'Mac Mharais' at the end, perhaps implying that he is condemned to execution (*marbhadh*).

13 (*Ceann Suic*) SA 1972/175 A5. Recorded from Mrs Christine M. Fleming (née MacLeod), Berneray, Harris, transcribed and translated by Ian Paterson. *T*9:30–33 (with Gaelic text). Mrs Fleming's source Ceit Tharmoid (Kate daughter of Norman) was Mrs Catherine MacDonald, née Paterson (1857–1941), Berneray. Mrs Fleming, 'Curstaidh Mèri Ruairidh Chaluim', was working as a nurse in the Southern General Hospital in Glasgow when Ian Paterson (himself a Berneray man) first recorded her in 1967.

AT 500, 'The Name of the Helper', the Grimms' Rumpelstilzchen, or the Suffolk Tom Tit Tot, is a popular type world-wide, usually about an impossible task with textiles, though more often it is only spinning: the inclusion of weaving here is appropriate to a story from the home of Harris tweed. The Lowland 'Whuppity Stoorie' (*PRS*:72–5) is exceptional in being about a female fairy who cures a sick sow. Usually the person who overhears the name is either the heroine herself or another mortal: the introduction of good and evil groups of fairies here, not to mention their killing and eating each other at the end – fairies are quite often killed in Gaelic tradition – is an unusual twist.

14 *The Captain of the Black Ship* SA 1968/42A. Recorded from Angus John MacPhail, Locheport, North Uist, and transcribed by Angus John MacDonald. *STT* No. 11. Angus John MacPhail (Aonghas Iain Dhòmhnaill 'ic Phàil) was a crofter and stone-mason who inherited his storytelling ability from his father. His family came to Locheport from the Sollas area on the other side of the island when they were evicted in a notorious mid-nineteenth century clearance.

The tale type is AT 506A, 'The Princess Rescued from Slavery', one of several international types where the hero's helper or donor is a 'Grateful Dead Man'. This one was well known in Scots-speaking areas through the long ballad 'The Turkey Factor'. It incorporates one or other variant of the Dick Whittington's cat motif (AT 1651 on its own), replacing the first cat in a mouse-infested country with the first coal (as in *PTWH* No. XXXII) or as here the first (salt) herring, typical British exports worth their weight in gold, usually in Turkey as the nearest rich non-Christian culture: The way it is reached in this version through a 'magic mist' suggests that it really stands for the other world, but the story comes back to earth immediately after with the ingenious way of giving the dead man a Christian burial with things that would be found on a herring boat.

15   *The Three Good Advices* SA 1955/150 B5. Recorded from Andrew Stewart, Perthshire
      traveller, by Hamish Henderson. Transcription by Robert Garioch. *STT* No. 10. A
      non-magic 'novella' of good fortune, AT 910B, 'The Servant's Good Counsels',
      which has been popular in Gaelic since a version was incorporated in the 'Middle
      Irish Odyssey', the thirteenth-century *Merugud Uilix meic Leirtis* ('Wandering of
      Ulysses son of Laertes'). In modern versions the wise master who gives the advice
      becomes a baker simply because of the device of the money hidden in a loaf; the third
      piece of advice about breaking the 'half-loaf' (the term normally used at least until
      the 1950s for a single Scottish 'plain' loaf, baked in pairs which were broken up for
      sale) replaces the counsel to think twice before acting — this stops the hero killing
      the man he finds in bed with his wife, before he realises it is his own grown-up son.
      This scene is probably inconceivable to a caird, and this traveller version cuts it out
      along with the second scene, where the hero is advised not to lodge with the young
      wife of an old man, who murders her rich husband and accuses the hero's companion
      who lodges there. It is replaced by a typical caird 'Burker tale', where the hero
      escapes being murdered for his body in the manner of Burke and Hare, something
      which all cairds were taught might happen to them (giving them a healthy distrust
      of strangers), so that even forty years ago a settled traveller like Stanley Robertson
      grew up with a dread of doctors, hospitals and universities. The red hair of the
      warning is regularly linked with evil in popular belief. In the first episode too,
      Burkers replace the usual bandits on the short-cut. Scots words: *bud*: bided, abode,
      stayed; *parritch*: porridge; *reed* (see *CSD* under *ree*): an animal pen, pig-sty, stone-
      walled yard etc.; *the morn*: tomorrow.

Hero Tales

16   *The Story of the Cook* SA 1955/131 B4. Recorded from 'Alexander Stewart, travelling
      tinsmith', by Calum Maclean at Muir of Ord, Easter Ross, in July 1955. *STT* No.
      18. Calum Maclean gives a detailed and entertaining account of his visit to this caird,
      a very stylish narrator of Gaelic tales in a devil-may-care caird manner, and his
      mother Grace in their camp near Muir of Ord, in the second half of Chapter VI of
      The Highlands. He is one of three fine storytellers from this traveller clan, all named
      Alexander or Alasdair, in this book, but we have not yet succeeded in establishing
      his relationship to the others, and apart from Calum's account he remains a mystery.
          The story is a combination of AT 303, 'The Twins' and AT 300, 'The Dragon-
      Slayer', which in Scottish Gaelic versions often, as here, has a series of many-headed
      giants in place of the dragon or sea-monster. 'The Twins' in Gaelic as throughout
      Europe usually frames the other tale, but most cairds tell it without the inset, so this
      is an unusual version. It includes traces of the aristocratic Gaelic literary tradition,
      such as the detection of the queen's own son by his innately modest behaviour (in
      many versions they are not the king's sons, but born from the eating of magic fish).
      Some elements are very old folk motifs: the animals born on the same night (from

their mothers eating the same fish, though this storyteller only remembers about them when they are called for late in the story); the gate that shows whether the hero is alive or dead; and the small mutilations required to wake him, reminiscent of tribal initiation marks, which eventually also help to identify him. Others are typically Scottish or Gaelic clichés – the description of the giant, so exaggerated it can hardly be pictured, with twenty-six dead old women tied to his shoelaces, apparently as a lunch-pack (we have translated for sound as much as sense, as with the list of magic healing objects at the end); the hen-wife as trouble-maker; and later the appearance of the witch, asking to be let into her own house, in the form of a hen, though she is addressed as 'Old Woman' and apparently grows into one. There is a bit of British history – 'River George' is probably a corruption of 'Royal George', a man-of-war from Nelson's navy. Finally, there are the touches of humour in description and dialogue, especially the cowardly Cook and the landlady's excessive respect for him, which are all Alasdair Stewart's own. *Caman*: a shinty stick.

17 *Conall Gulbann* SA 1959/41 B4–42 B1. Recorded from Angus MacLellan, Frobost, South Uist, by Calum Maclean. The indented passages and the alternative ending are added from another recording of the story from Angus MacLellan, SA 1963/14 A1, made by DAM. *STT* No. 15. Angus MacLellan, 'Aonghus Beag mac Aonghuis 'ic Eachainn', was the only Scottish Gaelic storyteller recognised in his lifetime by the award of an MBE, thanks to the efforts of Dr John Lorne Campbell, who recorded, edited and translated his *Stories from South Uist* (*SSU*, 1961) and his autobiography *The Furrow Behind Me*, published when Angus was already over ninety.

This is perhaps the most popular of all Gaelic literary hero-tales in oral tradition. The original romance was almost certainly written in the early sixteenth century, when 'the Turk' was actually invading Christian Europe, for the ruler of the Irish region of Tyrconnel (most of modern Co. Donegal), possibly the famous Manus O'Donnell, whose realm was named from his fifth-century ancestor Conall Gulban. For a full discussion of the variants of the story and its motifs, see *GFMR*:72–9, or *Béaloideas* 31:1–50. Scottish versions use a motif from far earlier Gaelic literature, the begetting of a half-supernatural son in an otherworld dwelling or *brugh* (though in Uist recently this word could mean something more like 'hovel'), simply to ensure that the hero has a fairy grandfather who can help him in time of need. The result is that Conall loses much of his heroic quality when, like Jack in 'Silly Jack and the Lord's Daughter' (tale No. 7 above), he wins a battle with a sword that fights by itself. In fact the description of this sword and the battle was such a long run that it used to be recited alone as a set piece: so much of its archaic language, meant to impress, has become incomprehensible in oral transmission that we have concentrated on conveying the alliteration and rhythm of the Gaelic rather than attempting to translate every word. A Gaelic text of this story from Angus MacLellan was published by J.L. Campbell in *TGSI* 44: 11–24.

The 'waking motif' is a folk borrowing from the previous tale-type, but the sword in the bed is a mediaeval chivalrous motif it shares with the original romance. The alternative ends show that Angus MacLellan learned the story from at least two sources. One was Donald MacDonald, the father of Duncan who told the next story: Duncan's version (*SD*:45–58) has a long series of abductors each of whom had once had Conall's bride but lost her to the next in the series. It ends with a race which Conall wins, and Macan Mór is not killed, as in the original romance and the main text here. However, Angus had also heard the story from Alasdair MacIntyre, another famous South Uist storyteller, and he may be the source of the ending where (as in many folk versions) Macan Mór, originally just a very large hero, is killed like a typical folktale giant.

The *Tanhuisg* were originally *amhuis*, 'mercenaries', satirised by the author of the written tale by being depicted as ogres. The Tuathanach O'Drao was originally Duanach ('Poetie') the Druid; Conall Ceithir Cleannach ('Four-Headed') seems to be a version of the early Irish hero Conall Cearnach ('Victorious'). A *buckie* (Campbell of Islay's Scots rendering) is a small sea-shell, a winkle.

18 *The Man in the Cassock* SA 1953/34 A4–35 A1. Recorded from Duncan MacDonald, Peninerine, South Uist, by Calum Maclean. *STT* No. 16. Duncan MacDonald, 'Dunnchadh Clachair', had perhaps the largest and most varied repertoire of stories and songs recorded from a single Scottish Gael, though not much of it can be played on tape: most of it was taken down by Calum Maclean when working for the Irish Folklore Commission, by Duncan's son the poet Donald John MacDonald for the University of Edinburgh's School of Scottish Studies, and others like K. C. Craig, either straight on to paper or using recordings which were erased after transcription. A feature in *T*25:1–32 includes appreciations from William Matheson and Peggy McClements and reminiscences from Duncan himself as well as a sample of his repertoire.

The five long hero-tales which Craig published as *Sgialachdan Dhunnchaidh* (*SD*, after 1944) seem to have had a particular meaning for Duncan, and a study of five versions of this one taken down from him and one from his brother Neil (see *SS* 22:27–44) makes it fairly certain that both brothers learned the story virtually word for word by heart from their father, whereas they told other stories in a more usual way, choosing different words each time to describe the same events. Duncan was almost certainly descended in a direct male line from the MacRury seannachies, hereditary historians and storytellers to the MacDonalds of Sleat, and a comparison of the introductory episode of this tale with its solitary incomplete seventeenth-century manuscript written by Hugh MacLean in Kintyre in 1690 (National Library of Scotland MS 72.1.36, published with translation in *Éigse* 12:301–26) shows such close verbal correspondences that it seems quite possible that the story was learned by heart from a manuscript before 1700 and passed down substantially unchanged for two and a half centuries. Duncan himself knew it as 'The Man in the Cassock' (literally 'of the Habit', in the sense of a clerical uniform, but the literal translation could be misleading) but he was told by an old man that his father had also called it 'The History of the Hermit' (*Eachdraidh an Dìthreich*) a more conventional form of the title in the 1690 MS.

The mysterious, yet rather comical, hermit must really be a supernatural character, perhaps the Irish pagan deity Manannán who often plays such roles in mediaeval tales: the way that no time has passed at the end of this version, or that in others Murchadh goes to bed in the hermit's mansion and wakes up next morning on a bare hillside with the stag and hound beside him, shows that this was a visit to the otherworld. However, the burlesque in-tale, almost entirely lost in the only MS, but the longer part of the story in a dozen oral versions, depicts him as a powerful secular warrior, apart from his curious weapons, with no stronger magic powers than his opponents in some episodes and unable to escape his in-laws' plot to prevent him taking home his bride. His epithet *Feamanach*, sometimes claimed to mean a sort of giant, actually seems to be a corruption of an obscure word *fimineach*, translated by an eighteenth-century Irish dictionary as 'hypocrite', no doubt because he is not all he seems. The word *gruagach* (literally 'hairy') is also confusing. In Irish romances like the original of this it means a warrior with some magical powers, a sort of elf-knight, while in Scottish Gaelic poetry it means a maiden, so in this version the Gruagach of the Stag and the Hound is female and her pursuer and her brother are male gruagachs (the name of her estate, Tiobart, means 'Well', because usually it is reached by diving down one, not travelling over the sea with 'water helmets'). Murchadh is a straightforward historical hero, son of the great Brian Bóramha ('Boru'), king of all Ireland, and killed like him in the Battle of Clontarf in 1014: there is an early reference to his otherworld adventures, which survive in this and at least one similar tale (cf. *GFMR:136–43*). We have tried in the translation to give an idea of the rather tongue-in-cheek formality of this story's language, a superb piece of blarney, meant to be spoken not read but otherwise rather reminiscent of the mixture of archaisms and slang Standish H. O'Grady used to translate early Irish tales in his *Silva Gadelica*. *Geasa* are spells which must be obeyed. The hermit's epithet 'Feamanach Fabhsach' seems to mean 'false hypocrite', because he is not all he seems. The 'Cailleach Eana-to-Ghlas' is just an old woman in grey clothing.

19 *The Story of Ossian* Linguistic Survey of Scotland Gaelic tape 965. Recorded from Alasdair 'Brian' Stewart, Culrain, Easter Ross, by David Clement. *T*29:292–301 (with Gaelic text), the last item in a feature on this youngest of the three traveller Alasdair Stewarts, one of only two living storytellers known to us who still tell the longer Gaelic heroic tales. He learned this story from his grandmother, Mrs Susie Stewart (née MacArthur) born in Argyll, who died in 1938 aged ninety-one, whom he used to visit regularly during the winters when the clan were housed in Lairg, Sutherland, asking for stories and getting them only when she was in the mood.

Ossian (James Macpherson's version of Scottish Gaelic Oisean, Irish Oisín, meaning 'little deer') is the most usual narrator and so supposed author of the mediaeval ballads of the Fenian (or Ossianic) Cycle. He is supposed to have told them to St Patrick, who wrote them or had them written down. This story is not based on any surviving ballad or romance, but is known in the oral tradition of both Scotland and Ireland: part of it is supposed to explain why the accounts we now have of the Fenians have gaps in them, and also to prove that 'there were giants in those days' among men, beasts and birds. See *PTWH* No. XXXI for other versions, and

Béaloideas 54–5:48–56 for a comparison of Scottish and Irish versions. There are various explanations of how Ossian lived longer than the other Fenians: in Ireland he goes to the otherworld or Tír na nÓg, the Land of Youth, where time passes faster, as in tale No. 64. Here he has a magic ring from his fairy wife who came to him as a hoodie crow (*feannag*): the taboo on mentioning what form he first saw her in is paralleled in *PTWH* No. LXXXVI and a story of literary origin, *Léigheas Coise Céin*, 'The Healing of Cian's Leg' (cf. *W&S* 2:206–77 and *GFMR*:134–6).

20   *The Princess and the Pups* SA 1976/109 B3. Recorded from Mrs Betsy Whyte, Montrose, by Linda Headlee (now Williamson) on 7th August 1976. *123:258–61*, the first story in a feature on this remarkable traveller woman, well-known for her autobiographical books *The Yellow on the Broom* (Chambers, Edinburgh 1979) and *Red Rowans and Wild Honey* (Canongate, Edinburgh 1990). A third volume now in preparation will include versions of most of her stories, so we have used fewer than we might have chosen otherwise: but this one is so unusual that we cannot leave it out. Like the previous story it comes from the Gaelic cairds of Argyll, through Betsy's mother, the source of most of her stories, who was a Johnston born in Argyll and sang Gaelic songs, though her generation did not speak Gaelic. Betsy remembered about it and told it unexpectedly to AJB in July 1976, to his astonishment, and made the recording next month at his request. Five or six years later, when Betsy was asked to tell it to students in the University of Edinburgh's School of Scottish Studies, she could remember nothing about it.

This story is part of the Fenian Cycle and accounts for the origin of Fionn's hounds Bran and Sceolang, born to his aunt who had been turned into a bitch by her husband's fairy lover, and snatched as puppies along with the king of Dublin's new born baby by a giant from the sea: Fionn himself goes in pursuit, with the help of a set of wonderful helpers evidently borrowed from a version of the international *Märchen* AT 513, 'The Extraordinary Companions'. It forms part of the late-mediaeval written frame-tale *Feis Tighe Chonáin* ('The Feast at Conan's House'), and is translated by James Carney, *Studies in Irish Literature and History* (Dublin 1955), Appendix A. It became popular in oral tradition, and though none of the names have survived in Betsy's Scots, her story is much like the Argyll Gaelic version in *W&S* 3:1–16. *Chore gaanies* is caird cant. *Canny*: slowly; *hijcht or hair*, more often *hilt or hair*, is a variant on the phrase 'hide or hair'; *wyde, widd*: wade, waded.

Trickster Tales

21   *The History of Kitty Ill-Pretts* 'A Scottish Nurse's Stories' (Jeannie Durie, Fife, mid-nineteenth century: see above, note to tale No. 6). *T*18:67–71. A lively version of AT 328, 'The Boy Steals the Giant's Treasure', the English 'Jack and the Beanstalk'. Scottish versions, however, consistently have a girl as hero. Compare Walter Gregor's 'Mally Whuppie' (*AFH*:114–7) and J. F. Campbell's 'Maol a Chliobain' (with summaries of three other Argyll Gaelic variants, *PTWH* No. XVII).

Gregor and Campbell's best variant also share the bridge made of one or two hairs. At the end (1:274) Campbell mentions a similar story called 'Kate ill Pratts' from Perthshire, referred to by a reviewer of Chambers' *Popular Rhymes (PRS)*, which is evidently this tale and title. 'Ill pratts' or 'pretts' is Scots for 'naughty tricks'. *Cappy*: wooden cup; *money*: mony, many.

22 *Riobaidh and Robaidh and Brionnaidh* SA 1965/15 B2. Recorded from Neil Gillies, Glen, Barra, by DAM on 30th March 1965. *SS* 10: 92–104 (with Gaelic text); *STT* No. 21. Neil Gillies, 'Niall Mhìcheil Nill', was a fine storyteller with a vigorous dramatic style: his sisters were known as singers, and the daughter of one, Flora MacNeil, has a national reputation. AT 1535, 'The Rich and the Poor Peasant', Hans Andersen's 'Big Claus and Little Claus', often has two persecutors of the trickster hero in Gaelic: see *PTWH* No. XXXIX. The tale-type is beautifully constructed, with one episode leading logically to the next, but it is typical of trickster tales in two ways: the villains are incredibly gullible, persuaded by greed to do things like killing their mother for sale, but the 'hero', though he starts as their victim, is also totally amoral, asking his mother to change beds with him so that she is killed in his place. In the final episode the 'hero' is usually to be thrown into the loch (or river or sea) in a sack or barrel and persuades the shepherd to take his place with promises of wealth or salvation.

23 *The Butler's Son* SA 1953/158/1. Recorded from Samuel Thorburn, Glendale, Skye, by James Ross in July 1953, and transcribed and translated by him in *SS* 7:18–27. *STT* No. 22. Sammy (Somhairle) Thorburn, Waterstein, learned his stories before 1914 from his father, 'Somhairle Beag', well-known as a storyteller in Glendale. The Thorburns were one of the Border families who came to the Highlands as shepherds after the Clearances, but learned Gaelic and adapted completely to the local culture. AT 1525, 'The Master Thief' can involve many episodes, but Gaelic versions usually end with the test, after which the hero may give up crime and settle down: cf. *PTWH* No. XL, and contrast No. XVIId in which he is hanged in the end, as prophesied, despite all his success.

24 *The Farmer Who Went Back on His Agreement* SA 1969/91 A2. Recorded from Angus John MacPhail, North Uist, by Angus John MacDonald. Transcribed by Mrs Peggy MacClements. AT 1000, 'Bargain Not to Become Angry' is the first of what Aarne listed as 'Tales of the Stupid Ogre'. These are actually just short motifs, nearly always strung together in groups, and this one, which holds together a group, is always told of a mean farmer rather than a giant or devil in Scottish and Appalachian versions, where the penalty with a strip of skin is also normal. This is probably why the trickster is often called Mac a' Rùsgaich (Mac Rùsgail, Mac Rùslaig), 'Son of the Stripper', as in 'Campbell of Islay's' *PTWH* No. XLV, though he also features in stories of seduction. The theme must have helped to relieve the feelings of ill-treated farm labourers much as both ballads did. Some of the words are hard to translate, as Campbell found: the agreement is not to repent (*gabhail aithreachais*) or 'take the rue', as Campbell says; the names the farmer calls the trickster mean literally 'son of misfortune' or 'son of bad luck', a pattern well-established in Gaelic but sounding

rather oriental in English, so we have translated freely. The second episode (AT 1005, 'Building a Bridge or Road with the Carcasses of Slain Cattle') in Gaelic versions apparently involves building a causeway across a bog, *stadhar chasa-caorach*, 'sheep's feet stepping-stones (?)' a phrase Campbell had never heard, which may only survive through this story. The third (AT 1006, 'Casting Eyes') involves another old idiom, *damh shùil*, 'an ox eye', a fixed stare which might be described now as 'bug-eyed' – but that would not fit the story!

25   *Willie Take-a-Seat* SA 1956/55 B1. Recorded from the Revd. Norman MacDonald, native of Staffin, Skye, by Calum Maclean. Transcribed by Morag MacLeod. Norman MacDonald served as minister in several parts of the Highlands and Islands (he was in Islay when this was recorded) and collected traditions in all of them. He was a modern example of the folklorist ministers of the late nineteenth century, and published articles on Gaelic legends and beliefs in the Swedish folklore journal *Arv* (vols. 14 and 17), with the encouragement of Calum Maclean. This story, from which a long historical introduction about the old woman and the cattle-raiders has been cut out, accordingly has a rather studied literary style, and may largely derive (like tale No. 35, see below) from a published text of the late nineteenth century. Again the words of the dialogue are difficult to translate, and we have simply given an approximation which aims to convey something of the flavour and sound as well as the meaning of the words. The final pun in the Gaelic on the word *bàrd* is fairly pointless: 'he was neither tall nor short (*cha b'àrd is cha b' iseal e*) but of a middling height', so we have substituted an English pun with rather more relevance. The basic type, the native variant of AT 1544, 'The Man Who Got a Night's Lodging', is extremely popular in Gaelic, but the hero's name must surely have been influenced by a Scots version which has not survived: in '*Uilleam Bi'd Shuidhe*' the name in Gaelic has no particular significance, and is not the most common name (like Seán in Irish versions), but 'Willie Set Ye Doon' or the like in Scots sounds like an invitation, 'will ye . . .' The later part of the story, which does not always appear, resembles AT 1533, 'The Wise Carving of the Fowl', a popular theme in early Ireland, but the wording of the rhymes is very obscure.

26   *The Parson's Sheep* SA 1969/154 A2. Recorded from Gilbert Voy, Orkney/Glasgow, by AJB on 20th December 1969. *STT* No. 23; *GMK*:39–40. First published in *SS* 14:93, with comparisons of other Orkney versions of this type, AT 1735A, 'The Bribed Boy Sings the Wrong Song' and one from Jeannie Robertson. Gib Voy was an Orcadian from Inganess in the East Mainland who had lived fifty years in the Glasgow area without losing his native accent, more notable perhaps for his knowledge of songs, some of them used by his son Erlend in the group The Clutha, than for stories. He heard this song-story from his father, who used to sing it at weddings before 1900 'much to the disgust of my mother', and it may have been Gilbert himself who added an invented Orkney name and extra dialect when he was asked to contribute to an Orkney record, 'A Night at the Bu', in the 1930s. The tale-type has translated its rhyme into several languages – it is first recorded in sixteenth-century Spain – and the same story told all in verse as a ballad (in quite different words)

has also been recorded in Orkney and Aberdeenshire (*T4*:118–21). Orkney words: *blashie*: rainy; *faelie dyke*: turf wall; *peerie*: little; *scrythe*: a swarm; *uncan yowe*: strange ewe.

27 *How to Diddle* SA 1974/190 B1. Recorded from George Jamieson, Selkirk, and transcribed by Ailie Munro. *T*15:247–9. AT 1585 'The Lawyer's Mad Client (Patelin says "Baa!")', a mediaeval joke against lawyers which has spread throughout Europe and beyond. Whistling or animal noises or anything that suggests the accused is 'not all there' may replace diddling, but the pun between the words for cheating and singing without words adds an extra point. The tune here seems to be from Johann Strauss's 'Blue Danube': for a longer and more Scottish diddle compare a Gaelic version of AT 1351, 'The Silence Wager' (*SS* 10:182–7), with the same title as the next story.

28 *The Tailor and his Wife* SA 1955/132 A8. Recorded from Alasdair Stewart, Easter Ross traveller (see above, note to tale No. 16) by Calum Maclean. *STT* No. 24. AT 1730, 'The Entrapped Suitors', another mediaeval joke, here satirising three other professions. Tailors are often portrayed as weaklings, but the use of the scissors proposed here also comes into an eighteenth-century cartoon. 'Taking pictures' translates the Gaelic *A' tarruing dealbh*, which could mean drawing portraits before it suggested photography.

29 *The Wren* SA 1957/40 A8–B1. Recorded from Alasdair Stewart ('Aili Dall'), Sutherland traveller, by Hamish Henderson. *STT* No. 26. This third Alasdair Stewart (actually the oldest and the first recorded) was the uncle of 'Brian' (see above, note to tale No. 19) and wintered with his family in Lairg: Hamish Henderson travelled with them for several weeks on their summer routes in 1955, 1957 and 1958, and recorded a great range of tales from Aili Dall ('Blind Sandy' in Scots – blind only since middle age). This animal fable is rather different from his many hero and wonder tales, but has the same vivid, colloquial, throwaway style. It is a version of AT 248, 'The Dog and the Sparrow', but the trickster hero is an even more insignificant bird than the Grimm story's sparrow, though at the same time the wren, 'King of the Birds', has a mythological aura that makes him more believable as a nemesis on the farmer who despises him. The plot is less logical than in Grimm, where the sparrow is avenging the dog she has befriended on the carter who ran him over. The carter's load of wine, normal in the Rhineland but not in Sutherland, is ingeniously explained, but the killing of the wren's sheep 'hostess' (the Gaelic word means literally 'godmother') by a fox – how does he find out? – is no reason for his inexorable persecution of the farmer: we have to forget logic and just enjoy the tale.

Other Cleverness, Stupidity and Nonsense

30a *(The King's Three Questions)* SA 1967/1 A3. Recorded from Angus Henderson, Tobermory, Isle of Mull by AJB on 26th January 1967. *T*5:156–9 (with Gaelic text); *STT* No. 28. Angie Henderson, a retired blacksmith and crofter from Tobermory, was an old friend of the University of Edinburgh's School of Scottish Studies who passed on all sorts of information to our fieldworkers, including some quite old stories learned like this one from his father, also a blacksmith. This is a typical Gaelic version of AT 922, 'The Shepherd Substituting for the Priest Answers the King's Questions', perhaps best known in English as the ballad Child 45, 'King John and the Bishop'. The pattern corresponds best to the 'Old French Redaction' in Walter Anderson's classic study of the type: see SS 17:147–54 for a study of Scottish variants, including the type which opened our introduction. The final question is usually simple: "What am I thinking?"

30b *The King and the Miller* SA 1955/37/1. Recorded from John Stewart, Perthshire traveller, by Maurice Fleming. T21:169–71; GMK:28–30. This John Stewart, the father of the 'Stewarts of Blair' (see above, note to tale No. 9), was noted as a piper as well as a storyteller, and unusually for a caird, kept a farm at Tullymet for some years. Maurice Fleming, a journalist from Blairgowrie who for many years edited *The Scots Magazine*, was the first to record old John and several of his family in 1955, not long before he died. His Scots traveller variant of AT 922, learned from his parents, corresponds to Anderson's 'German Servant Redaction' and seems to have arrived across the North Sea, whereas the Gaelic redaction probably followed the Highland chiefs' wine route from France by the West Coast of Ireland. *Dour*: gloomy; gia: by (the time).

30c *(Donald and the Skull)* SA 1972/32/6. Recorded from Donald John MacKinnon, Horve, Barra by Peter Cooke and Morag MacLeod; transcribed and translated by Morag MacLeod. T5:152–5; SS 17:50–53 (both with Gaelic text). Donald John MacKinnon (or 'Rabbie Burns') was probably the best-known bard composing Gaelic songs in Barra in the 1970s. His tale is an unusual combination of the questions from 30a above with a frame borrowed from a moral tale well-known in Africa and among black people in North America: see Richard Dorson, *American Negro Folktales* (New York 1967):146–8. The African tale simply ends with the beheading of the character corresponding to Red-Haired Donald (Domhall Ruadh) on the spot when the skull fails to speak. The most likely source for the Barra version is perhaps a tea clipper or other large merchant ship in the days of sail, where both Hebridean and black sailors were often in the crews. Gilleasbuig Aotrom, on the other hand, is a historical eccentric from Skye (see T45:163–8), who became known to Gaelic speakers elsewhere mainly through the writings of the Revd. Norman MacLeod.

31 *The One-Eyed Miller and the Dumb Englishman* SA 1957/10 A1. Recorded from Colin Morrison, Barvas, Lewis by James Ross on 5th April 1957. T1:24–27 (with Gaelic text). The Scottish variant of AT 924, 'Discussion by Sign Language' has been catalogued under 924A, where the debate is understood by at least one participant to be about theology, but its heading 'Discussion between Priest and Jew' is hardly applicable here. The defeated party is normally English in Gaelic and in Scots, and Walter Gregor mentions it being 'greatly in favour' at the farm fireside (*Notes on the Folk-Lore of the North-East of Scotland* (London 1881):56–7). In this version, do not ask how the dumb man explained how he lost!

32 *(The Poor Man's Clever Daughter)* SA 1966/50 A1. Recorded from Peter Stewart, Barvas, Lewis by John MacInnes. *STT* No. 29. Peter Stewart, 'Pàdraig Sheonaidh', was originally a traveller tinsmith from the Ross-shire mainland, who in middle life was given a site beyond the cultivated ground of Barvas, where he built himself a house and settled down: his skill as a storyteller was appreciated by the more open-minded of his neighbours. AT 875, 'The Clever Peasant Girl', uses various sets of riddles in different versions, but always ends with the heroine's complete victory: the ending here emphasises her independence much better than that in the catalogue, where the king is 'moved to forgive her' when she takes him as her dearest possession.

33 *Silly Jack and the Factor* SA 1954/90 B15. Recorded from Jeannie Robertson, Aberdeen, by Hamish Henderson, and transcribed by him for the booklet of the University of Edinburgh's School of Scottish Studies' privately published disc A002 (1962). *T*6:172–5; *STT* No. 27. AT 1600, 'The Fool as Murderer', is well-known as a trickster tale, but Jeannie's obvious sympathy for the mother of a handicapped child puts it into a different class. She learned this story from her mother, William Stewart's daughter. AT 1381B, 'The Sausage Rain', can appear as a separate tale, but here reinforces the message of the goat in the grave: both types, and AT 1381E, 'Old Man Sent to School' (see *T*38:40–41) are also well-known in Gaelic. *Bree* and *broo* both mean brow, forehead; *craftie placie:* croft; *flee:* fly; *hannae:* haven't; *lichtit:* alighted; *lum:* chimney, smoke-hole; *'oor:* hour; *teem't:* emptied, poured.

34 *The Wandering Piper* SA 1991/7 A1. Recorded from Willie McPhee, Perthshire traveller, by Alan Bruford on 1st March 1991. Transcribed by Sheila Douglas as part of a short feature on Willie McPhee, *T*44:77–90, in which she introduces this last survivor (born 1910) of the older and more traditional generation of traveller storytellers, a piper too like his cousins the 'Stewarts of Blair' (see above, note to tale No. 9), and a welcome visitor to classes in Scottish Ethnology like the one where this recording was made. AT 1281A, 'Getting Rid of the Man-Eating Calf', is known from Finland to Mexico, and many Gaelic versions also tell it about a piper, but this version is unusual in the way the piper exploits the misunderstanding. Duncan Williamson's father (*FTTC*:127–35) told it quite differently as a tale of his own escape from the Burkers (cf. tale No. 15 above). *Blusted:* broke up; *canny:* cautiously; *chapped, chappit:* knocked; *forbye:* also; *jouked:* dodged; *luckit:* looked; *shedda:* shadow.

35 *Cailleach nan Cnù and Tàillear nan Clàr* SA 1969/13 B3. Recorded from Alasdair MacArthur, Port Ellen, Islay, by the editors and Ian Fraser. *STT* No. 9. 'Alasdair Logan', a distillery worker from Lagavulin, was taught this story by his mother, born Kate Logan, daughter of a shepherd on the small island of Texa, for a competition at the 1929 Islay Mòd, which he won. His mother had been fostered by a minister who taught her to read and write Gaelic, and she had apparently found this story in a book; indeed the naming of the characters and the rather formal language of the story, which Alasdair still knew more or less by heart, suggest that this was a re-telling of the traditional story polished up for a Gaelic book or magazine around the end of the last century. Compare tale No. 25 above; like that story, this *Schwank*, AT 1791, 'The Sexton Carries the Parson', is extremely popular in Ireland and in

Gaelic Scotland, where the 'gouty parson' of Continental versions is always replaced b, a crippled tailor. It is told in Scots too, and our servitor mentioned in the Introduction told me a version of this too that he had heard in a club.

36 *The Minister and the Straw* SA 1978/68 B2. Recorded from Tom Tulloch, North Yell, by AJB. *T*30:358–9. A variant of AT 1845 (where the catalogue description does not suggest that the remedy, a placard with similar words hung round a calf's neck, is successful) known also in mainland Scotland. The boil in the throat burst by laughter appears in a different story told of the Beaton doctors of Mull (cf. tales 85 and 95b above) and Maclaine of Lochbuie. There are many Shetland words, forms and usages: *bang* is used of any sudden movement; *be no persuasion* is shorthand for 'she couldn't be persuaded not to'; *cut*: cud; *drevoasheens*: devotions; *gaff*: guffaw, laugh loudly; *gaw girse*: 'gall grass', stonewort, used to cure cattle of liver and gall-bladder diseases; *hap*: shawl; *hill-daeks*: boundary of the common grazing; *krüll*: a thick oatcake, hastily or not at all cooked; *a loack o fokk*: a lot of people; *ootset*: a piece of land reclaimed from the moorland common pasture; *Shetlan ait strae*: a straw of the native 'black' oats; *slip*: let go; *söt an saut*: soot and salt; *strae-t'eckit-röf't*: roofed with straw thatch; *whinsy*: quinsy, inflammation of the throat.

37 *Strunty Pokes* 'Tales of a Scottish Nurse' (Jeannie Durie, Fife, mid nineteenth century: see above, note to tale No. 6). *T*3:82–3. See also the beginning of the introduction for this tale-type (AT 1562A). *Strunt* in Scots can be a form of 'strut', or mean 'go into a huff', and *poke* is a bag. The other words sound vaguely Latin, but it is difficult to see what they came from: 'Gillipontis' perhaps suggests the Hellespont, 'Crayantis' Creation (?) and 'Dumbalibus' may originally have been 'Dame . . .' rather than dumb.

38 (*The Flayed Horse*) SA 1975/179 A2. Recorded from Tom Tulloch by AJB. Probably an Irish tall story originally, with many parallels there: the detail that the barrel contains porter supports this. Versions have been collected throughout Scotland, including a variant where not alcohol but the Evil Eye makes the horse seem dead, but the story seems very popular in Shetland and is often told as having happened in Yell, though I have recorded a version set in Quarff in the South Mainland. Tom Tulloch believed that this version was given its precise setting – the family concerned would have been named to local audiences – by one of his own elder brothers. In Shetland *aerands* rather than Scots 'messages' is the word for shopping; *geeg*: gig, small open carriage; *ipae*: on; *roo'd*: plucked (wool from a Shetland sheep – the normal practice instead of shearing); *strampin*: stamping, trampling.

39 (*Keep a Cool Head!*) SA 1971/263 A7a. Recorded from David Work, Shapinsay, Orkney by AJB. *T*11:86; *GMK*:78. David Work, JP, of Ness Farm was a prosperous farmer and cattle-breeder, who could also spare time to welcome a visiting fieldworker and remember songs and anecdotes from the old days. He heard this tall tale from an old neighbour who had moved to Shapinsay from the island of Sanday: it is certainly a migratory type and has been recorded in North America (*TMI*:579, motif X1722*(b)) and is known in Northern Ireland. *Aimed*: threw.

Fate, Morals and Religion

40 *(The Skipper Who Marooned a Girl)* SA 1965/80 A3. Recorded from Peter Morrison (Pàdruig 'Illeasbui' Phàdruig), Grimsay, North Uist by DAM, whose appreciation of this fisherman, crofter, weaver, bard, storyteller and expert 'on the whole spectrum of the traditional life of his community' is in T16:303–5. A more detailed appreciation in Gaelic is in Pàdruig Moireasdan, *Ugam agus Bhuam* (*UAB*, 1977), where the Gaelic of this story is on pp. 37–8. *STT* No. 30. The type number AT 930A, 'The Predestined Wife', can be used to cover a range of stories with an infinite variety of details, but all illustrating the inevitability of fate.

41 *(The Herdie Boy)* SA 1977/80B. Recorded from James Henderson, South Ronaldsay/Burray, Orkney by AJB. T26:88, part of a feature on this outstanding tradition-bearer – an expert on the whole spectrum of traditional life in his native South Ronaldsay, despite forty years away working in Edinburgh, mainly 'on the buses'. This is a brief example of the corresponding type about a predestined *husband*, AT 930, 'The Prophecy', told as a local legend: the farm could have been named though it was not. Most Orkney farmhouses had a corn-drying kiln on the end of the barn where the divination with the 'clew' of wool, one of many popular ways of foretelling who you would marry practised at Hallowe'en, could be carried out, and tricks certainly were sometimes played on girls who tried it. Boys (and girls) had to be employed as herds, often from the age of eight or nine up and for next to no pay, to keep the sheep and cattle off cultivated ground, up to 1914 as field walls and fences were still almost unknown in Orkney. An Orkney Mainland version of this story is briefly told by John Firth in *Reminiscences of an Orkney Parish* (1920), Chapter XXIII, and I have heard (but unfortunately never seem to have recorded) a version about a 'scaw'd' (scabby-headed) boy in Unst from Tom Tulloch. *Hadds*: holds; *whar* in Orkney is often used as a form of *wha*, 'who', as well as 'where' (*whar piece?*)

42 *(Turning the Sark)* SA 1970/231 B1. Recorded from Tom Moncrieff, North Roe/Virkie, Shetland by AJB on 12th September 1970. T7:220. Tom was yet another person happy to pass on his knowledge of all sorts of tradition, most of it from the northern tip of the Shetland Mainland where he was brought up, but some from the old lady mentioned, who came from Lunnasting in the east, and some from the southern tip, where he came to work on Sumburgh aerodrome during the Second World War, married and settled down. This story of a type of Hallowe'en divination using a nightdress (sark, chemmy, slug) is told with variations – e.g. the man reappears because the girl is just too frightened to put away the sark, rather than because she turns it again deliberately – throughout Shetland, and was known in Orkney and possibly elsewhere. The point here is not so much that the vision comes true, but that it is dangerous to its subject. The international type is AT 737, 'Who Will be her Future Husband?' Baughman (*TMI*) lists five English versions from the Borders to Cornwall and two from North America, involving other customs such as

sowing hemp-seed and laying a 'dumb supper', and two Irish ones are listed in *TIF*.

43 *(The Stolen Blankets.)* SA 1966/19 B7. Recorded from John W. Cockburn, Cock-burnspath, Berwickshire by AJB in February 1966. *T1*:29. Jack Cockburn, a gentle-man farmer whom I have known from the age of eight, is another all-round contributor. This story, which could quite well be true, could also be an un-recognised international tale-type or perhaps rather a 'modern legend' of fate or divine justice. I had already read a very similar story in Gaelic about a Kintyre farmer and a caird, collected by Lady Evelyn Stewart-Murray in 1891 (LEM No. 29) before I recorded this.

44a *(The Sanday Man's Drowning)* SA 1967/114 B1. Recorded from Willie Ritch, Rothiesholm, Stronsay, Orkney by AJB on 8th October 1967. *T3*:88; *STT* No. 33a. Willie Ritch at Newbigging received me kindly when I cycled out to the far end of Stronsay on my first visit, and took me to see his old neighbour Tom Stevenson (aged eighty-nine) in the nearby Longbigging: in this case the younger man's version, which came from his mother, a native of Sanday, was recorded first. It is a variant of AT 934A, 'Predestined Death'; compare ML 4050, 'The hour has come but not the man', where a traveller is forcibly prevented from crossing a river in spate by people who have heard this cry from the river spirit or water-kelpie, but drowns, in some versions, in a tub of water in the dark shed where he is shut up. This version is rather nastier, because the *graith-cog* was a tub of stale human urine, 'kept for scouring blankets' in Orkney, to supply ammonia, just as it was used for waulking tweed in the Hebrides. *Heid stoup*: head first, head over heels.

44b *(The Stronsay Man's Drowning)* Same tape and publications (*STT* No. 33b) as tale No. 44a above, recorded from Tom Stevenson, a retired seaman from Stronsay with a fund of short legends and anecdotes. By the last century peat was scarce in Stronsay and non-existent in Sanday, so it had to be brought by boat from the neighbouring island of Eday, though it could be carted from the far end of the peninsula of Rothiesholm (pronounced 'Rowsome') at the south of Stronsay itself. Whole milk was churned in the old deep 'plout kirn' in the Northern Isles, and when the butter was taken out, the churn of buttermilk would be left for drinking, while another was filled with fresh milk.

45 *(Ham and Eggs)* SA 1969/46 B7. Recorded from Roderick MacKenzie (aged eighty-eight), The Olad, South Ronaldsay, Orkney by AJB on 11th June 1969. This anecdote came up in the course of an informative interview on many aspects of local life at the end of the last century with one of the oldest men in the island, but still a very lively one. It really should be heard to be fully appreciated – obviously there is a tempo change from the mowers' first chant to the second. Porridge (oatmeal boiled in water) and still more brose (oatmeal with boiling water poured over it) were the usual basis for the diet of farm servants throughout the North of Scotland, and there were many complaints about the rarity of meat or anything else but kail (cabbage) to vary it. The type (AT 1567G, 'Good Food Changes Song') was well-known in Gaelic as well as Scots and English: both chants might be in Gaelic, but DAM remembers his grandmother telling it in Gaelic with the 'Ham and Eggs' chant in

English. *Ether*: or else; *scye*: scythe; *thoyt*: thought (a typical South Ronaldsay pronunciation).

46 *(Paring Cheese)* SA 1969/53 B6. Recorded from Mrs Ethel Findlater, Dounby, Orkney by AJB on 25th June 1969. *T*1:31; *GMK* 54. Here again the story came up in the course of a long interview about Orkney life and food: 'Ethel o Breckan', well known for her repertoire of old songs and ballads since Dr Otto Andersson from Finland recorded her in 1938, and as a 'character' in her own West Mainland community, stayed in Edinburgh for a few days on the way back from an SWRI trip to London and recorded some excellent oral history as well as songs. This miniature moral tale, AT 1452, was in the Grimms' collection and is known throughout Europe and North America to many who would consider themselves storytellers.

47 *(Christ and the Hens and Ducks)* Recorded from Roderick MacDonald, Carnoch, North Uist, and transcribed by Angus John MacDonald at Christmas 1967 (fieldworker's own recording erased after transcription). *T*1: 14–15. 'Ruairidh na Càrnaich', then over eighty, a highly respected member of the crofting community, enjoyed the all-round knowledge of tradition (much of it learned from his grandmother), appreciation of music and soundly rooted world-view more typical of an earlier generation of Gaels. The cycle of stories about Christ and his pursuers does not seem to have been noticed in the Aarne-Thompson (AT) canon, but includes origin legends told in various parts of Scotland, by Protestants as well as Catholics. The miracle of the quickly completed harvest, as in the next story, was originally associated with the Flight into Egypt of the new-born Jesus and his family, but these stories of an apocryphal pursuit of an adult Jesus apparently before his trial and crucifixion have either developed from it in folk tradition, or may possibly reflect myths once told about a pagan divine hero.

48 *Why the Beetle is Blind* SA 1978/94 B3. Recorded from Duncan Williamson, Argyll-born traveller living in Fife, by David Clement and Linda Williamson. Printed in *T*33:155–6, as part of the feature in which this outstanding traveller storyteller and all-round tradition-bearer was first introduced to the public by Barbara McDermitt, with a note by AJB and a selection from his vast and varied repertoire. See note 21 to the Introduction for some of his later publications. This 'holy story' represents a minor but important area of his storytelling: all traveller stories have morals, and a surprising number (considering that few cairds went to church – for anything but funerals – even a hundred years ago, when almost everyone else did) have an explicit if not an orthodox Christian message. Many caird families, including Duncan's own, are of Irish descent, and such tales are plentiful there outside church (which Irish travellers too avoid). Sometimes the crop sown one day is being harvested the next, and in Gaelic versions of this story the dung-beetle *(ceard-dubhan)* protects Christ but another sort of beetle *(daol,* perhaps the cockroach) betrays him.

49 *(The Man Who Stopped Going to Church)* SA 1964/32 B10. Recorded from Angus MacLeod, Bragar, Lewis, by John MacInnes. *STT* No. 34. Angus MacLeod (Aonghus Phàdraig) had a deep knowledge of local history from both oral and written sources and knew the value of each, as well as of songs and less localised traditions such as

this story. This is a recognised international *exemplum* (a parable which may be used to illustrate a sermon), AT 759A, 'The Sinful Priest', very well-known in Ireland. The normal theme is the efficacy of the sacrament of the Catholic Mass, the miracle of transubstantiation, even if performed by a sinner (hence the medically doubtful analogy of pure water passing through a rotting carcase) but the message can still be understood in a more general sense when the story is told as here by a Calvinist Protestant. A tacksman was a small landowner who usually held his land from the clan chief.

50 *The King of Halifax* SA 1971/54A–B1. Recorded from Donald Alasdair Johnson, Ardmore, South Uist by DAM in March 1971. *SS* 16:1–22 (with Gaelic text and note on the type); *STT* No. 35. (In translating, we have not attempted to reproduce all the instances of 'said he' which are so much a feature of the Gaelic text.) AT 756B, 'The Devil's Contract', is usually associated in Scotland with the mediaeval scholar Michael Scot, who studied in Muslim Spain before becoming astronomer to the Emperor Frederick II in Sicily, and so got the reputation of being a magician in the legends of both Italy and his native Scotland. In Ireland (e.g. *FTI*:144–9) as in a Ross-shire caird's version (*T*33:188–95) the repentant sinner is usually a fictional cleric or scholar who has made a pact with the Devil, but in Eastern Europe he is usually a robber, and this may be how the King of Halifax should be seen. Halifax may be an English euphemism for Hell, with which it is associated in the saying 'Hell, Hull or Halifax', based partly on the sound and partly on a reputation for harsh sentences in their courts; however, its bad name in Gaelic may rather derive from the use of Halifax, Virginia, as a prison for Loyalists, including many Highland settlers, during the American War of Independence (*SS* 16:20).

The opening of this version is identical with the opening of many wonder-tales, the birth of a child after the mother has eaten magic fish; sometimes this also involves the promise of the first son as in 'The Sea-Maiden' (*PTWH* No. IV, and variants, AT 300, 302 and 303), where the mermaid is also a sea-monster and hardly less sinister than the Devil. Donald Alasdair Johnson also told a story of this type. The three hermits are like donor figures in wonder-tales, helping the hero on his way, but the third one has another function at the end, where he is punished for questioning God's mercy to the sinner. The King of Halifax neither performs a spectacular penance (as characters such as Michael Scot in other versions do when they hear for the first time of the bed waiting for them in Hell – but he already knows about that!) nor does he do much to help the boy (the Son of God is the one who argues with the Devil), but what he has done is evidently enough to ensure his salvation. The doves and ravens at the funeral pyre regularly appear in Scottish versions of this story (and other stories like that of the burning of Coinneach Odhar, the 'Brahan Seer') and in Breton ones, but seem rare if not unknown elsewhere. The revival of a character on hearing the story they want appears at the end of other Gaelic tales like *An Tuairisgeal Mór*, also in Donald Alasdair's repertoire.

51 *(St Fillan and the White Snake)* SA 1972/13 B3. Recorded from Duncan Matheson, Camus Luinie, Kintail, Wester Ross by DAM and Ian Fraser. *STT* No. 36. Duncan

Matheson, a genial, bearded crofter, known as 'Stalker' from one of his past employments as a deerstalker, is skilled in many country crafts: he was invited to Australia to build a cairn of stones from every parish of Scotland for their bicentennial, and has been filmed thatching houses with heather and rushes. He is also an authority on Kintail legends and Gaelic songs who has contributed to the *Transactions of the Gaelic Society of Inverness* as well as the archives of Edinburgh University's School of Scottish Studies. St Fillan (Faolan, early Irish Faelán, 'Wolfling') is a Dark Age missionary associated with Kilillan in Kintail, but better known from Strath Fillan in Perthshire where his relics are kept and he may in fact be buried – though there may have been more than one saint with this fairly common name. The basis of the legend is actually an international *Märchen* type, AT 673, 'The White Serpent's Flesh', though the result of tasting the snake is not understanding animals' speech as in the type catalogue but the power of healing, as in *PTWH* No. XLVII. The incident may be set in France because mediaeval Gaelic doctors went there, to Montpelier, to study medicine; and the way in which Faolan tastes the snake's juice seems to be modelled on the way Fionn mac Cumhaill got his 'thumb of knowledge' by using it to flatten a bubble on the skin of the magic salmon he was roasting, and then putting it in his mouth to cool. The verse about the Knoll of Tears is a version of one attributed to St Columba, mourning the distance from Iona to Derry. The indented paragraph about the healing well (which seems to be the reason why St Fillan is depicted as a medical missionary) is inserted from the conversation after the story was told, and the following paragraph about how the spring lost its powers is a migratory motif attached to several holy wells in the Highlands.

Origin and Didactic Legends

52 *The Hugboy* SA 1966/43 B9 (b + a). Recorded from Mrs J. J. Leith, Harray/Stenness, Orkney, by AJB on 29th August 1966. *STT* No. 37. Mrs Leith, an important source for women's work, songs and many aspects of Orkney life, is described in a brief feature in *T*47. She became a good friend whom I always visited on fieldwork in Orkney, but on my first visit in 1966 she was rather shy of the tape-recorder and read this and other stories from notes left by her late husband Peter Leith (senior), which may be direct from oral tradition but could owe something to a version in the Viking Club's *Old-Lore Miscellany*. The two legends are both typical origin legends on different improbable scales. In fact 'hugboy' is the name originally not of a giant, but of the guardian ghost of the first settler in a farm, the dweller in the howe or burial mound, Norse *haug-búi* – not usually as sinister as Tolkien's 'barrow-wights', more like a Brownie (see tale No. 79), sometimes helpful, sometimes mischievous (*FOS*: 39–42).

53 *Dubh a' Ghiubhais* SA 1955/164 B7. Recorded from Ann Munro, Laide, Wester Ross, by Calum Maclean on 13th September 1955. *STT* No. 38; *T*39:114–7 (with Gaelic text). Miss Munro was the teacher at Laide Primary School when Calum called

in that afternoon, and she vividly describes how he enthralled the children in T39:97–8; his own account of how she had revived Gaelic in the school is in Chapter 7 of *The Highlands*. Neither of them mentions her own traditions which he recorded, including this excellent version of a local legend. This story seems to be a deliberate invention to account for the blackened pine stumps in peat bogs (once split into 'fir candles', see introduction p. 5): princesses and witches from Lochlann (Norway) often appear in Fenian ballads, and may have spread from these, perhaps in the wake of the Ossianic controversy, into local legends, where they are often said to be buried in cairns which may in fact be Neolithic chamber tombs or even natural hillocks. Seven versions are summarised in a catalogue of witch legends (*SS* 11:25–6) where this is numbered (W)10.

54 *(The Pabbay Mother's Ghost)* SA 1958/161/1. Recorded from Nan MacKinnon, Vatersay, Barra by James Ross. T38:46–7 (with Gaelic text) – this is the last item in a feature which opens with a description of Nan by Barbara McDermitt, who visited her the year before her death in 1962. This small friendly woman, who never married but raised the four young children of her sister who died suddenly during the Second World War and kept house for their father from the time he was discharged from the Navy until he died, was famous for her vast repertoire of songs, but recorded great quantities of proverbs and stories (mostly local legends) too. This is the shorter and more coherent of two stories accounting for the success of local families (male as well as female members) as midwives.

55a *(Luran and Iaras)* Donald John MacDonald MSS, pp. 77–9, taken down from his father Duncan MacDonald, Peninerine, South Uist (see above, note to tale No. 18). Translated by Peggy McClements. T28: 218–9 (with Gaelic text). This South Uist variant of the Luran story (F128) is the only one that involves a fairy lover; in others the fairies may steal Luran's cattle, Luran may steal a fairy cup (cf. tale No. 70a) or cauldron (cf. tale No. 67), or Luran may be the name not of the herdsman but of his dog (*SSH*:52–7) – the one common element is the comment about the hard oatcakes, usually followed by advice to eat porridge (*lite*) or something softer, and normally this is misleading advice, which the fairies hope will slow him down. The only origin element in this variant is that other versions explicitly say that the fairy suitor was called Iaras and the loch and cairn were called after him.

55b *Luran* SA 1965/10 B3. Recorded from Calum Johnston, Barra, by DAM. T13:172–5 (with Gaelic text); *STT* No. 39a. Here the story has been turned upside down to encourage children to eat their porridge (*brochan*), by claiming that it not only makes you big and strong, but makes you light and nimble, which the usual version of the story makes it clear is just a fairy confidence trick. (*Brochan* can certainly mean gruel, a thinner mixture than *lite* (porridge), but it probably means ordinary thick porridge here.)

55c *Peerie Merran's Spün* SA 1973/59 A7. Recorded from Tom Tulloch, North Yell (who heard it from his mother as a child) by AJB in April 1973. *STT* No. 39b; T28:205; *GMK*:92. This is both an origin legend and a didactic legend, with the same message as the last one (though this one actually says 'gruel'; according to John Graham's

Shetland Dictionary 'gruel' in Shetland means porridge!). At least in this case porridge gives strength, though it sounds as if the weakening of just one small female (Merran is the Shetland form of Marion) among the hundreds of fairies who would be needed to carry a whole headland was enough to bring it down, in the manner of the kingdom that was lost all for the want of a horseshoe nail. More usually it is sandbars and reefs that are said to be the ruins of a broken fairy bridge; the Ness of Houlland, a promontory continued by a line of two islets, looks very like a broken bridge, but it points north-west into the open Atlantic, so it cannot be interpreted as a bridge to anywhere believable and must be on its way to Yell Sound at the other end of the island. Some of the usages as much as the words may need explanation: *caa*: shift (food, in this case); *laen*: loan; *quhile*: until; *shün*: soon; *smaa*: narrow; *thatten*: such; *wänts*: lacks; *yondroo*: there.

56 *Black John of the Blizzard* SA 1962/51 B2. Recorded from Angus MacKenzie, Hougharry, North Uist, by DAM in October 1962. *STT* No. 40. Angus MacKenzie ('Aonghas (mac Alasdair) 'ic Anndra') was a crofter, carpenter and wheelwright who for some time taught woodwork in North Uist schools, as well as being a fine raconteur and a composer of local humorous songs. There is some factual basis for this story: (1) historical records confirm the tradition that cattle-raiding was carried on by boat in the Western Isles (cf. tale No. 89), and the feud between the MacLeods of Harris and Dunvegan and the MacDonalds of Sleat, who were overlords of North Uist, in the early 1600s certainly included such raids by the MacLeods, one of which led to the Battle of Carinish in 1601. (2) The nickname 'Black John of the Blizzard' (Iain Dubh a' Chafaidh, more exactly 'Black-haired John of the Drifting Snow') apparently belongs to a real person who seems to have been claimed as ancestor by people in the small island group of Heisker, and there may well have been a genuine tradition that he moved there from the furthest west part of the main island of North Uist. (3) There is a headland called Rubha na Marbh, 'The Point of the Dead', in Heisker. Almost certainly, like similar names in other small islands, it means the place where the local dead were embarked for burial in a churchyard on the main island. On this basis, we may suspect, this dramatic and improbable story was simply invented to explain how the point and the pilot each got their names.

NOTES

Legends of Ghosts and Evil Spirits

57 *MacPhail of Uisinnis* Donald John MacDonald MS 3:236. Recorded from his father Duncan MacDonald, South Uist, on 7th July 1953 (see above, note to tale No. 18). Translated by John MacInnes. *T*8:240–1 (with Gaelic text and detailed notes). Uisinnis is a hilly peninsula protruding from the area to the east of the highest hills in South Uist, now totally uninhabited, and a suitable setting for this nearest approach to a vampire story from Scotland. Other versions set the story less far back and make the sinister grandfather an incomer, a shepherd perhaps from the Lowlands (he is called Crawford in one version, but usually MacPhail) rather than a native Uist man. He will eat his wife and daughter-in-law, but not his granddaughter who is of his own blood. The internal door would have been hung in a wooden frame, including a wooden doorstep (*maide-buinn*) on top of the packed earth floor, and the dead man was digging though the earth under this doorstep. This is almost an origin legend, accounting for the pit (an unusually large hole of the sort that may appear in the middle of any earth-floored ruin whose roof has fallen in and let in the rain), but it is actually a migratory type: versions are localised in 'the hills of Ross-shire' (*WSS*:52) and Berneray, Harris.

58 *Mór Princess of Lochlann* Donald John MacDonald MS 1:68–72. Recorded from his father Duncan MacDonald, South Uist, on 2nd May 1953 (see above, note to tale No. 18). Translated by Mrs Peggy McClements. *T*25:12–15 (with Gaelic text). This is a variant on a story well known in Uig, Lewis, where the woman is the mother of the prophet Coinneach Odhar, known on the mainland as 'the Brahan Seer' but claimed in Lewis as a native, who foresaw the future by looking through a stone with a hole in it given to his mother by the Norse princess. It is not clear why Hebridean graveyards, far from anatomists and resurrectionists, should have needed to be watched, and some versions of the Lewis story say that the woman did it as a dare. 'The mouth of the ford' seems to mean the seaward end of the ford across the sands between South Uist and Benbecula. A tangle (*stamh*) is a stalk of coarse seaweed (cf. tale No. 88).

59 *(Myze Keys)* SA 1970/244 A1. Recorded from Tom Tulloch, North Yell, by AJB (the first story he ever told me). *T*30:352–3. Tom was gravedigger at the kirkyard of Ness or Breckin from 1937 to 1976, in succession to his father. Similar stories about gravestones or standing stones taken, for instance, to replace the threshold of a house are common enough, but this is the only one I know with a wooden grave-marker. Like several other old Shetland churches, this one was apparently said to be an 'aamos kirk', built by the survivors of the shipwreck to fulfil a vow (*aamos*) made when their lives might have been lost in the storm. Possibly they were supposed to be Dutch: the name 'Myze Keys' sounds like a combination of the Dutch names 'Mies' and 'Kees'. 'Tree(s)' in Shetland could mean anything made of wood in these almost treeless islands, from a 'gruel-tree' (a spurtle to stir porridge) to a 'rigging-tree' (the ridge-pole of a house). *Biggit*: built; *fan'*: found; *keen*: ken, know; *kirn*: (butter-)churn; *krockit*: knocked; *scauff'ldin*: scaffolding.

60a *Alasdair Mór mac Iain Làidir* SA 1963/51 A1. Recorded from Donald Alec MacEachen, Aird Bheag, Benbecula, by DAM on 21st October 1963. *STT* No. 45a; F114. Donald Alec MacEachen was a first-rate local antiquary with a deep knowledge of his native island whose untimely death was a sad loss to Gaelic tradition. It is difficult for us now to understand why breaking this seemingly arbitrary taboo should bring what seems to be the Devil to threaten the man with death. In *FTFL*:302–7 a mainland Alasdair Mór is threatened by an Uruisg (a water-spirit shaped like a satyr or the god Pan, with the hind-quarters of a goat) who simply turns up without mention of any taboo, presumably because he haunts this river: he certainly intends to eat Alasdair. The taboo against emptying potato water (or any dirty water) after sunset, however, has a long history in Ireland (see Séamus Ò Duilearga's paper in *Féilsgríbhinn Eóin Mhic Néill* (ed. E. Ua Riain, Dublin 1940):522–34) though again the penalty is being taken by the Devil or the fairies rather than violent death. A cock hatched in March was believed in Scotland and Ireland to have special powers against evil.

60b *(The Night Fishermen)* SA 1968/217 A1. Recorded from Mary MacLean, Grimsay, North Uist by Angus John MacDonald. *STT* No. 45b. In this version of the story there is a clear Protestant Christian message: the punishment is for breaking the Sabbath, though unwittingly. As in the mainland Argyll version cited above (tale No. 60a), the stranger makes it quite clear that the other fishers are to be part of his share of the catch – *sgiolam* there like *cealasag* here seems to be a word made up for the occasion.

61 *MacPhee's Black Dog* SA 1968/227 A9–B1. Recorded from Peter MacCormick, Hacleit, Benbecula, by Angus John MacDonald. *STT* No. 43, F112. Peter (Pàdraig) MacCormick was one of a group of fine storytellers in Benbecula recorded by Calum Maclean in the 1940s and 50s, though he tended to be overshadowed by his wife Kate, a quite remarkable traditional singer. Versions of this legend are attached to lonely places called Àirigh na h-Aon Oidhche all over the Highlands: the Benbecula one, marked on the Ordnance Survey map as an ancient monument, may not have been a sheiling at all. Sheilings in their main traditional use as sleeping quarters and dairies for the girls and unmarried women looking after the cattle at the summer pastures were natural places for young men to come courting, and the wish of the unmarried men to have their sweethearts follows naturally, but a wish for something impossible brings nemesis. The women may be called fairies, witches, Green Women (as in the variant which inspired Water Scott's *Glenfinlas* in Part III of *Minstrelsy of the Scottish Border*) or *baobhan*, a name originally given to the Old Irish war-goddess Badb, the hoodie-crow, and used in modern Ireland for the Banshee. They may have bone beaks or cloven hooves, but the young men evidently do not notice them in time. The Black Dog, useless until 'his day comes', belongs to a more elaborate form of the legend about MacPhie of Colonsay and a party of hunters in a cave on the Isle of Jura (*SSH*:109–22). Dogs which fight supernatural opponents regularly lose their hair in Gaelic tales, and the 'battle fury' cooled by milk and water is like that attributed to Cú Chulainn in Old Irish tales. The cry to the dog, '*bios-eara*' (the hyphen simply shows the stress is on the second syllable and the *s* is not a *sh* sound) is meaningless in Gaelic but appears in several South Uist and Benbecula

versions of this story (sometimes with a T, 'bisterra' in English spelling). It might simply be a corruption of a command used by Lowland shepherds to their dogs.

62a *Àirigh an t-Sluic* Donald John MacDonald MS 3:239. Recorded from his father Duncan MacDonald, South Uist, on 7th July 1953 (see above, note to tale No. 18). Translated by John MacInnes. *T*11:92–3 (with Gaelic text). Like the previous tale, this story concerns a lonely sheiling, its name could be translated as 'the Sheil of the Pit', and Peter MacCormick followed the previous tale by telling a version of No. 57 above (*STT* No. 42) set not at Uisinnis but at this place a few miles further north on the east side of South Uist, where he had been himself and seen the pit dug by the dead man. He said the old man's body was too heavy to move when his son used the conventional funeral blessing in the name of the Lord, but could be moved when he said 'Let's set out in the name of the Evil One'. In the present story the old woman is apparently a witch who cannot be taken by the Devil because of the captain's Bibles and her own cock. The quite different emphasis in the story that follows is more usual.

62b *(The Cock and the Skipper)* SA 1974/196 A1. Recorded from Tom Robertson, Collafirth, Delting, Shetland by AJB on 18th September 1974. I met Tom Robertson, son of a fine storyteller in this isolated community and unlike many younger Shetlanders very interested in his own traditions, by chance at his now abandoned croft-house of Quam at the head of the valley, and this was the first of his father's stories he recorded for me. In this more typical version there is no suggestion that the targets of the supernatural attack are themselves evil, only unlucky in failing to realise that the cock has protected them: in effect this is a tale of fate. Compare a very similar Gaelic version from Nan MacKinnon published by Anne Ross in *SS* 7:219–20, and an Irish one, *SOCB* No. 109; the same point is made by an Irish inland variant with different details, *FTI* No. 35. *Tae*: tea; *voe*: inlet.

63 *Tarbh na Leòid* SA 1956/159/3. Recorded from Donald MacDougall, Sruthan Ruadh, Malacleit, North Uist by DAM. *STT* No. 46. Donald MacDougall, retired blacksmith and crofter, is a cousin of DAM, and descended from a long line of MacRuries, armourers, blacksmiths and bards. He has recorded many interesting songs and stories: an important source of his stories was his great-aunt Christina MacRury. The Scottish Gaelic water-horse (*each uisge*) may tempt men or children to ride it and then plunge into a loch, but it also appears as a young man who seduces girls and if successful devours them (*SSH*:203–15; F58). There might be some relationship between this story and a Norwegian legend, 'The Sea-Horse and the Sea-Serpent' (ML 4085), but the sea-horse there acts as a protector and the *each uisge* is a creature of freshwater lochs, not the sea – which makes it unusual that here it is driven into the sea. Sacred bulls appear in early Irish tales such as the *Táin*, and it is not surprising to find a Gaelic bull bred as a protector. On the other hand the story seems to have Norse roots: the Norwegian equivalent of the water-horse (which can take both horse and human form) is called *nökk*, Old Norse *nykr*, and DAM has pointed out that the loch in Heisker that must be meant in the story, 'some distance from the village', is called Loch Snigreabhad (Sniogravat on the Ordnance Survey

map), which almost certainly goes back to Old Norse *nykravatn*, 'loch of the *nykr*'. The name *Tarbh na Leòid* also does not mean 'MacLeod's Bull', but it might come from the Norse name of the ancestor of the clan, Ljótr – or from an obscure Gaelic word *leòd*, 'mangling'.

Legends of Fairies and Sea-Folk

64a *(Dancing in the Fairy Hill)* SA 1971/303 A8. Recorded from Archie MacKellaig, Glenfinnan, Lochaber by Alasdair MacDougall, a Morar man living in Corpach, who told us the story as he had learned it from Mr MacKellaig when we visited him in 1972, and then found us his own recording, made about Christmas a year or two earlier at a ceilidh in the storyteller's house. *STT* No. 47a. By 1972 Mr MacKellaig, a notable tradition-bearer, was eighty-eight years old and thought too frail to be recorded by us. This is clearly a practised version, not perhaps as formal in language as one learned straight from a book, but careful to include all the details of the plot and provide credible dialogue. The type, F22, is rare outside the Highlands and Islands of Scotland: we know of no Irish versions, but there is a similar tale from Denmark and several versions of one from Wales where the main difference is that the fairies are dancing outside in a ring and simply disappear with one man. The story is very often associated with a named 'fairy hill' in many parishes of the Central Highlands. The man who goes into the fairy hill is either one of two, rescued as here by his companion after a year, or in a variant, one or occasionally more men go in and emerge after a hundred years or so, as in the next story. See *SS* 24:44–5 for a brief discussion of the type by AJB: a full treatment by AJB is due to be published in *Béaloideas* vol. 61 or 62.

64b *The Fiddler of Gord* SA 1974/204 B1. Recorded from George P. S. Peterson, Brae, Shetland by AJB. Tune recorded from him by Peter Cooke, SA 1977/114, and transcribed by AJB. *T*26:104–5. George Peterson was born and brought up on the island of Papa Stour, though his working life as a schoolmaster until he retired a few years ago was spent on the Shetland Mainland, and his much admired poetry, storytelling and fiddle-playing (he also played the tune transcribed with the story) all centre on his native island and the adjacent West Side of the Mainland. He has practised storytelling both to his family and in public, and has twice been a guest performer at the Netherbow storytelling festival in Edinburgh, as well as contributing two stories to Ernest Marwick's *Folklore of Orkney and Shetland* (*FOS*, 1975). He told this story in impressive hushed tones. In fact he did not learn the plot of the legend directly from oral tradition, though his father came from the district of Sandness opposite Papa Stour, where it is set, but found both story and tune in *The Shetland News* of 8th January 1963, where 'Sigurd o' Gord' was contributed by 'JPSJ', according to George Peterson a Shetlander who had emigrated to New Zealand. This tale combines the other variant of F22, related to another Shetland tale of long absence in the otherworld, 'The Bridegroom and the Skull' (*GMK*:68–71, cf. AT 470A), with two other themes known in Shetland, the fiddler asked to play for the fairies or trows (often at a fairy wedding) and the tune overheard from the fairies. Dialect words, forms and phrases include: *büddie o sillocks an waand*: basket of young coalfish and rod; *faan*: fallen; *fae*: from, since; *fand*: found; *flöir·* floor; *güd furth*: went out; *keel*: kale, cabbage; *knowe*: knoll, hillock; *laach*: laugh; *Merry Dancers*: Aurora Borealis; *peerie* little; *qu(hu)ar, quère*: where; *quite*: white; *shaa*: show; *shair*: chair, bench; *spok*: spot; *taen, teen*: taken; *t'oucht*: thought; *trows*: trolls, fairies; *wal*: well; *yaird daek*: kailyard dyke, cabbage-patch wall. *Hissel* (strees on last syllable) : himself; *humph* : a hump or a hunchback; *plantiu* . plantation, wood.

65 *The Humph at the Fit o the Glen and the Humph at the Heid o the Glen* SA 1955/153 A4. Recorded from Mrs Bella Higgins, Blairgowrie, Perthshire, and transcribed by Hamish Henderson. SS 10:89–92; STT No. 48. Mrs Higgins, born Isabella Stewart, was an older sister of Andrew, John and Alec Stewart and daughter of old John (see above, notes to tales Nos. 9 and 30b) and a fine storyteller herself, as well as hostess of many ceilidhs recorded by Hamish Henderson and Maurice Fleming in the 1950s. This expertly told story is one she learned from her mother, born Agnes MacPhee, though her children often claimed she was a Campbell (see the end of tale No. 69a above). The legend is often more precisely localised than here, but it is so widely known (from Japan, where a boil on the cheek replaces the hunch back, to South America) and is so like a 'fairy-tale' with its helpful fairies that it is catalogued with *Märchen* as AT 503. Many Gaelic versions have been recorded in Scotland and Ireland, nearly all based on the completion or spoiling of a song naming days of the week (in other countries all that the first hunchback may have to do is join in the dance). Gaelic versions normally begin with Monday, Tuesday (*Diluain, Dimàirt*), and Wednesday completes the song; the mistake is to go on to Friday, unlucky to fairies as well as Christians – but cf. *T*26:106–9, from Flora Boyd, Barra, where the mistake is to mention Sunday to non-Christian fairies. Scots travellers seem just to have chosen days for their sound (cf. *KBA*:53–4, from Mrs Higgins' brother John Stewart), but they sing out the words to a clear tune, where nearly all the Gaelic recordings I know have a vague chant – though Flora Boyd, a fine singer, has more indication of a tune. *Hissel* (stress on last syllable): himself; *humph*: a hump or a hunchback; *plantin*: plantation, wood.

66a *(The Thirsty Ploughman)* SA 1968/183 A5. Recorded from Mrs Kate Dix, Berneray, Harris and transcribed by Ian Paterson. STT No. 49; *T*20:132–5 (with Gaelic text); F111. Though it is normally said to be dangerous to taste fairy food or drink, it is worse to wish for something (cf. tale No. 61 above) and then refuse it when it is hospitably offered. Buttermilk (the liquid left after butter was churned) was always said to be good for quenching a thirst.

66b *(The Hungry Ploughman)* Donald John MacDonald MS 1:11–12. Recorded from his father Duncan MacDonald on 1st May 1953 (see above, note to tale No. 18) *T*25:14–15 (with Gaelic text). Translation by Mrs Peggy McClements. Gaelic *annlan*, Scots 'kitchen' means anything like cheese, butter, eggs or meat eaten with a staple like bread or potatoes. This story is generally told about buttermilk in Gaelic, but probably the first version ever published is a variant from the south-west of Scotland, contributed by the poet Allan Cunningham to Cromek's *Remains of Nithsdale and Galloway Song* (London 1810:301) where the fairies spread a 'green table' with cheese, bread and wine as a reward for ploughing in a circle well clear of a fairy thorn-tree.

67 *The Tale of the Cauldron* SA 1966/16 A1. Recorded from Calum Johnston, Barra, by DAM. *STT* 50; *T*13:196–201 (with Gaelic text). This adds some details, like the 'fairy way of moving' (*siubhal sìdhe*), to the version also set in 'Sanntraigh', *PTWH* No. XXVI; the legend (F98) is also localised in Lewis and Raasay. Again there is a contradiction: fairies generally fear iron, but they can use this cauldron (the word is perhaps too grand for the ordinary 'three-taed pot' or 'kettle' which hung on a pot-chain over every croft fire in the last century), though the mention of cold iron in the rhyme may have helped to get it back safe and full of bones to make soup (again, fairy food which was harmless). The second rhyme is particularly interesting: 'tuneful' may refer to the ringing of the pot against the doorpost, 'dumb' to the fact that the woman said nothing, but does 'Land of the Dead' (not in other versions) merely mean mortals? Had she used the name of God and blessed the *brugh* (cf. note to tale No. 17 above for this word) it might have disappeared, but the dogs could not have harmed her.

68 *(Baking in Creag Hàstain)* SA 1957/84/2. Recorded from Donald MacDougall, North Uist by DAM. *STT* No. 52. This story (F54) is definitely a local legend. Like tale No. 64 above it is localised in numerous reputed fairy dwellings; in Uist Creag Hàstain, a remarkable rock rising from the machair at Paible, though not named here, is the site usually mentioned, and the descendants of the woman involved are still known as incredibly fast workers. The secret of her escape involves *not* doing the normal thing, which was to make a little oatcake (*bonnach fallaid*) out of any meal left over from making full-sized oatcakes. 'No thrifty wife would think of dusting the baking-board into the meal girnel', according to Dwelly's Dictionary (*s.v. fallaid*) – but this was just what she had to do, though other versions (e.g. a Harris version in *SSH*:67) may suggest otherwise. The fairy who gave her good advice is out of place in legend as against wonder-tale, and pays for it.

69a *Johnnie in the Cradle* SA 1955/151 B11. Recorded from Andrew Stewart, Perthshire traveller, by Hamish Henderson and transcribed by him for the University of Edinburgh's School of Scottish Studies' first set of discs. *STT* No. 53. A typically racy telling of one of the commonest changeling tale-types in Gaelic and Scots, F62. Andrew Stewart evidently had not heard of the itinerant tailors who stayed in houses, so he explains this character as an obliging neighbour. In Gaelic versions the changeling, once it has betrayed that it is a fairy replacing the human baby, is generally simply thrown into the fire, or a river: some Lowland accounts say the changeling was roasted on a girdle over the fire, and only cairds as far as I know mention adding dung on the girdle – it sounds here as if just heating the dung was enough, but Betsy Whyte's more circumstantial account (*T*27:174) makes it clear that this is a toned-down version. The end should be the reappearance of the real child in the cradle.

The message of the story should be that before treating a child that cries a lot and does not grow in this way, you should wait for it to betray itself by something like playing pipe tunes on a straw, but in fact some children at least seem to have had narrow escapes (see *T*27:172 note). *Haudin*: holding; *press*: cupboard; *wean*: child.

69b *(A Fairy Changeling)* SA 1981/34 B. Recorded from Nan MacKinnon, Vatersay, by Barbara McDermitt in English; published with a rather longer Gaelic text from the same tape in *T*38:20–23. This gives a credible ending for an island setting to what is basically the same story as the one above: the belief is apparently that fairies could not cross salt water (as they could not cross running water), and an earlier recording of the story in Gaelic makes it clear that the fairy man who had pretended to be the baby had to be taken off the rock by boat to exchange for the real baby, which the Gaelic explains had been taken when the woman left it alone in the house.

70a *(A Woman Saved from the Fairies)* SA 1966/16 B4–17 A1. Recorded from Angus MacLellan, South Uist, by DAM. *STT* No. 54a; *T*27:164–73 (with Gaelic text). This is a legend type (F53) which some might put into a couple of paragraphs, told by an expert teller of longer stories, who fills in the dialogue and descriptions and even gives the hero a name, though the scene is away on the mainland and the only place-name is Edinburgh. In other versions the hero merely has to throw his cap at an eddy of dust on the road to make the fairy abductors drop the woman, she recovers her speech gradually by herself, and the changeling (or 'Devil') left in her place is not mentioned – often an abducted woman is thought to be dead, the fairies having made a facsimile body out of wood. The woman's dilemma at the end, whether to go back to the husband she has hardly known or stay with the man who took so much trouble to bring her back to normal, is often more stressed than here, and either choice is possible. The theft of a cup from the fairies (ML 6045) is often a separate story.

70b *(A Dead Wife among the Fairies)* SA 1967/112 B3. Recorded from Sydney Scott, North Ronaldsay by AJB on 5th October 1967. *STT* No. 54b. Sydney Scott, stay-at-home youngest son of a remarkable family, crofter, piermaster, road foreman and general Mr Fix-It for the island, mostly recorded songs for me, but this story among others came up in a session of reminiscence with a returned native which was going on one evening when I called in. Sydney's sister Mary A. Scott published a version in her book *Island Saga* (Aberdeen n.d. [1968]):155–6). This is a memorate rather than a migratory legend, definitely a local if not a family tradition, but it underlines the fact that the survival of a pagan belief in the fairies as guardians of the dead, or some of them, extended beyond the Gaelic-speaking area. *Wardro* is evidently a version of *warto*, which according to Hugh Marwick's dictionary of *The Orkney Norn* is 'a stone pillar used by herd-boys for shelter in North Ronaldsay', a very bare, flat island. The 'new' lighthouse at the north end of the island was built in 1854. The combination of the Christian Bible, the pagan sacrifice of a black cat at the entrance to the underworld at full moon, and the staff to fight with the fairies, as local shamans in several parts of the Highlands including Orkney are said to have done, protecting their communities by night, in the last century (see *T*26:103) is a remarkable mixture of beliefs.

71 *(A Man Lifted by the* Sluagh*)* SA 1953/28/1. Recorded from Angus MacMillan, Griminish, Benbecula, by Calum Maclean. *T*39:146–9 (with Gaelic text). Angus MacMillan (known as 'Aonghus Barrach' because his ancestors came from Barra) a crofter and carter who had 'had little schooling and [had] forgotten it all but remembered every story he ever heard', told the longest stories Calum Maclean ever recorded (see *T*31:64) but hardly the most interesting: he specialised in prosy novellas with no magic in them, spun out to great lengths largely by carrying the technique Angus MacLellan uses in tale No. 70a above of reconstructing conversations between the characters to extremes. Most of Calum's recordings of him were recorded on Ediphone cylinders for the Irish Folklore Commission and erased after transcription, and this unusually brief legend (F34) is one of very few tape-recorded from him for the University of Edinburgh's School of Scottish Studies. The *sluagh* or fairy host was believed to carry people off through the air for great distances, and those who told their own stories often said they had been made to throw fairy arrows or elfshots (identified as prehistoric flint arrowheads) and kill or injure people or animals: this was evidently most effective from a mortal's hand, though as here the narrators of such stories often claimed to have deliberately missed the target (*SSH*:27, 68–70, 88–9; *FTFL*:120–25).

72 *(A Man with a Fairy Lover)* SA 1965/6 B9. Recorded from Nan MacKinnon, Vatersay, by DAM and Lisa Sinclair. *T*28:204–7 (with Gaelic text). The fairy lover (*leannan sìdhe*) of aristocratic men appears in Gaelic literature from early times. This story crams in a cocktail of motifs from all sorts of sources. The boat caught with a line was in tale No. 18 above and goes back ultimately to one of the oldest Irish tales, 'The Voyage of Bran'; the name from tale No. 61 above floats in for no apparent reason (unless the hero is the MacPhee from Mingulay who was one of Nan's ancestors); the birth delayed by witchcraft also appears in tale No. 79 below; the solution got by asking about an animal instead of a woman is in tale No. 73b below; and the belt put on a stone instead of a woman appears in a witch story (*SS* 11:22) which has parallels both in legends from the Alps and Old Irish myth. The pearlwort (*mungan*), like the bog-violet (*mòthan*) was valued as protection against fairy charms.

73a *(The Fairy Suitor Foiled)* SA 1968/184 B6. Recorded from Mrs Kate Dix, Berneray, Harris and transcribed by Ian Paterson. *STT* No. 55a; *T*20:128–9 (with Gaelic text). While men could have fairy lovers and still live in the ordinary world, women risked being carried off to the fairy hill by their fairy suitors – as they would leave home with a mortal husband, but in this case their families would never see them again, and they would lose any hope of salvation as Christians. This story follows a pattern more usual in stories of witchcraft, where a charm intended for a human is given to an animal. See *T*1:11–13 for a very similar North Uist tale where hairs from a goat's beard replace a lock of a girl's hair and a Shetland variant with quite different details: the story can be traced back to 1591 when the London pamphlet *Newes from Scotland* recorded that 'Dr Fian', the schoolmaster accused with the North Berwick witches, was said to have been followed by a cow whose hairs he had been given instead of a girl's.

73b *(Keeping Out the Sea Man)* SA 1971/262 A2. Recorded from James Henderson, South Ronaldsay/Burray, Orkney by AJB. *STT* No. 55b; *T*26:100–101. As in the story above, here too a cow's tail hair and a girl's hair replace each other, but in the reverse order: the story can be assigned to *ML* 6000, 'Tricking the Fairy Suitor', which in Norway involves a land fairy and a herbal cure to keep away a fairy bull. This one Orkney version, versions collected from two storytellers in Co. Mayo, Ireland, and the many Norwegian and Swedish parallels are discussed in a paper by Séamas Ó Catháin, *Béaloideas* 59:145–59. 'Sea people' in Orkney were under-sea dwellers who did not necessarily take the form of seals in the sea: see another story from the south end of South Ronaldsay, *T*26.96–7, where a sea man suitor with a 'sea skin' is killed with the iron coulter of a plough, and discussion in *TGP*:120–23.

74 *MacCodrum's (Seal) Wife* SA 1968/212 B1. Recorded from Donald MacDougall, North Uist, by Angus John MacDonald. *T*8:258–63 (with Gaelic text); *STT* No. 56. For the importance of beach-combing cf. tales No. 3a and 29 above. The basic idea of the legend appears in various forms throughout the world, notably in the 'swan-maiden' form incorporated in tale No. 10 above, 'The Green Man of Knowledge'. On the east coasts of Ireland and Scotland the type (F75) may be told of a mermaid whose fish-tail (English 'slough', Gaelic *cochull*) the man steals, as in Betsy Whyte's version, *T*23:273–4. On the west coasts and in the islands from Ireland to Iceland the story is about a seal-skin: though Christiansen gave it a type number (ML 4080) he can only cite one Norwegian version, and the distribution suggests an origin for this form in the British Isles, but we await publication of a definitive study from Dublin, probably in *Béaloideas* 60. The story is associated with the family to which the North Uist bard John MacCodrum belonged in Uist, with the Conneely family and others in Ireland (*FLI* No. 21), but not with any particular family in Orkney and Shetland, though the legend, including the hiding-place in the corn-stack, was well-known there.

75 *(Rescued by a Seal)* SA 1970/244 B7. Recorded from Mrs D. Anderson, Fetlar, Shetland by AJB. *STT* No. 57. Mrs Anderson, who asked for her name not to be used while she was alive, was a charming, dignified lady of eighty-four, and told fine stories as well as singing some of her father's sea songs. Versions of this story since Hibbert's *Description of the Shetland Islands* (1822) all say the seal hunters were from the island of Papa Stour (or occasionally Scalloway) and went to the Ve Skerries off the west coast of Shetland: the story probably came to Fetlar with Papa Stour families cleared in the last century from one island to the other by the Nicolson lairds who held land in both. Descendants of one of these families, the Hunters, gave me some words of seal language – possibly Norse – which the seal mother said; Hibbert's names for her and her son, Gioga and Ollavitinus, seem to be Latinised Norse; another version gives the marooned seal hunter the Nordic-sounding name of Herman Perk, and overall the story seems to date from a time when Norn was still spoken in Papa Stour, 250 years or more ago.

76 *(The Limpet Pick)* SA 1975/163 A2. Recorded from Andrew Hunter, South Nesting, Shetland by AJB. First published in *T*34:274 as part of a short feature on this retired

seaman from the east side of the Shetland Mainland. I first heard of Andrew Hunter as a maker of kishies, baskets of straw and rushes once used to carry almost anything on these treeless islands, but soon found he carried almost anything about his home area in his own memory, including historical and supernatural legends. He was eighty-seven when this was recorded and still as clear-headed at ninety: the paragraph at the end of the story could speak for most of the storytellers in this book. This legend is a migratory type (F29) well-known in Shetland, but with several close variants in the Hebrides (cf. *SSH*:284–5; *Arv* 37:120–21) and Ireland (cf. *FLI* No. 23). It should be explained that 'went to get a boat' means 'from Norway': Andrew had just said in another story (No. 83a below) that in the days of the haaf fishing (see note 10 to the Introduction) all the boats in Shetland came from Norway in kit form, and the seal was probably a 'Norway Finn' or Lappish witch rather than a sea fairy. Limpets were gathered for ground-bait for fishing from the rocks. *Bassel*: a struggle. The fishermen's taboo-name *skjön* ('j' pronounced as 'y'), used at sea, when you were not supposed to say 'knife', is said to be from a Norse word related to 'shiny', but it is remarkably like Gaelic *sgian*, 'knife'.

77 *(The Magic Island)* SA 1971/262 A2. Recorded from James Henderson, South Ronaldsay by AJB. *T*26:95–6; *GMK*:93–4. Such tales (F14) are apparently related to early Gaelic accounts of a fairy 'earthly paradise' on an island overseas, as well as to accounts of vanishing islands off Orkney (*FOS*:26) and the Hebrides ('Rocabarraigh', now used to translate Rockall). Christiansen has a type ML 4075, 'Visits to the Blessed Islands', but says they are 'told as actual experience'. This story, however, has parallels in the plot of a Caithness tale (' 'E Silkie Man', serialised in *OLM* parts II–III, about a woman abducted by a seal to a chasm on the coast of Stroma) and Gaelic stories of seemingly dead cows taken by the fairies (e.g. *MWHT* No. 58). The father's refusal to rescue his daughter is a nicely cynical touch which gives this story a character all its own. *Ower weel* means just 'very well'.

78 *(The Last Trow in Yell)* SA 1978/63 B6. Recorded from Tom Tulloch, North Yell by AJB. *T*30:370; *GMK*:97. Stories of the fairies' final departure overseas (F31) are well-known in Northern Ireland (whence they go to Britain!) and Kipling put a Sussex version into his *Rewards and Fairies*, where they take a boat to France. There are occasional tales from mainland Scotland in which they have left for an unspecified destination (*AFH*:122), or shipped from Caithness to Orkney, for instance – and drowned in the Pentland Firth (see *T*28:226). A brief reference from Jamesie Laurenson on the same page in *T*28 shows that Fetlar had the same story of the old woman saying the 'Picts' had gone to the Faeroes, naming the same famous minister of the joint parish of Fetlar and North Yell, James Ingram, who moved to Unst in 1821 and 'came out' at the Disruption, still preaching after his son succeeded him as Free Church minister of Unst and dying there at the age of 103. The Yell version, however, adds the fiddler, who did not touch fairy food, but for whom time passed normally, not as in tale No. 64b above, perhaps because these were trows (the same word as trolls), in some parts of Shetland taken as equivalent to fairies, but not in North Yell, as Tom explains. Their *hadd* is the word for a wild beast's lair. Other

words and phrases: *aless*: except; *asaed*: beside; *Collyifa*: Cullivoe; *hidmast*: hindmost, last; *ipö owld Yül E'ën*: on Old Christmas Eve (5th January); *leem*: crockery; *on a doil-hoit*: in a depressed state; *t'owt*: thought.

Legends of Witchcraft

79 *The Brownie* SA 1978/61. Recorded from Mrs Betsy Whyte, Montrose, by AJB as she told the story to a Scottish Ethnology 1 class in the University of Edinburgh's School of Scottish Studies on 30th April 1987. T44·125 9, with some comments on the value of storytelling to cairds. The basis of this is a witch legend perhaps best known in the ballad 'Willie's Lady' (Child 6) but also told of various Highland chiefs' sons and others (*SS* 11:24; W8). The Brownie here advises the father as the 'Belly Blind', a similar helpful household spirit ('Belly' is usually 'Billie', i.e. brother), does in the ballad, but also takes an active part. The Brownie going for the midwife is usually a separate legend of which Allan Cunningham gave a Nithsdale version to Cromek (*AFH*:36). Travellers naturally feel an affinity for this spirit, which is shunned by most people, but if well treated does much good for little reward.

80 (*'London Again!'*) SA 1960/10 A4. Recorded from Angus MacLellan, South Uist, by Calum Maclean. *STT* No. 58. This type (W21; *SS* 11:27–30) is very popular in Gaelic, but the majority of versions have the words of command (typically 'Off to London!' and 'Kintail Again!') in English; there are Lowland Scots, English and Irish versions, and there is a reference to another in the 1591 pamphlet *News from Scotland* (*SS* 14:189–90). Burns collected a version set at Alloway Kirk (*ibid*: 190–91) which is half way to the alternative version involving invisible fairies (in Burns' story they are visible and possibly human witches) whose cry of 'Horse and Hattock' someone imitates, and this can be traced back to the seventeenth century (Robert Pitcairn, *Ancient Criminal Trials in Scotland* 3:604 note). In this form the story is known from Ireland to Norway (ML 6050, 'The Fairy Hat'). For both witches and fairies in Scotland the hat ('hattock' means a little hat) is usually more important than a broomstick or ragwort stalk to ride on. The majority of Gaelic versions are set in Kintail, and the search for a keel which at the end is provided by the gallows frames the story very neatly.

81 *The Tailor and the Fishing Wives* SA 1964/66 A2. Recorded from Peter Morrison, Grimsay, North Uist by DAM. T16:312–7 (with Gaelic text); *UAB*:59–62 (Gaelic only). This type too (W5; *SS* 11:21), depicting a witches' meeting as something like a Women's Guild trip to the seaside, seems to be a Lowland type taken less than seriously by Gaels. In other versions, however, the witches are actually drowned, and an early variant from the Tomintoul area in the east Highlands (*PSFA*:171–8) gives quite a lurid account of a witches' sabbat on a pool in the river Avon.

82 (*Duart's Daughter*) SA 1965/18 A3. Recorded from Nan MacKinnon, Vatersay by Lisa Sinclair. *STT* No. 60. This type takes the morality of the witch trials more seriously: the chief burns his own daughter for a sorcerer's apprentice fault of being

unable to stop what she has begun, and for what she has learned at the school (no doubt in the Lowlands) that he himself sent her to. The type (W7A; *SS* 11:22–3) is related to ML 3035, 'The Daughter of the Witch' (in most versions the girl learns witchcraft from her mother), and again there is an inland variant from further east (near Forres, *PSFA*:210–14), where instead of sinking a ship the girl merely stops ploughs in their tracks, a feat which (unlike sinking the ship) appears in Norwegian versions.

83a *(The Three Knots)* SA 1962/53 A4. Recorded from Donald MacLellan, Tigharry, North Uist by DAM. *STT* No. 59. Donald MacLellan (Domhnall Aonghuis Mhóir) was a piper and a good tradition bearer. His telling of this story shows a well-practised style more usual in fictional folktales, but this is definitely a local tradition: he heard it from the late Alexander MacQueen, whose grandfather was said to have been one of the crew involved. This legend type (W31; *SS* 11:31–33) is not in Christiansen's catalogue (ML), but it is well known in parts of Scandinavia (see *Béaloideas* 19:34), and a recent study has uncovered a handful of Irish versions: it was certainly localised in many parts of Northern Scotland. Witches in Orkney would still sell a favourable wind to becalmed whaling ships about 1800 (see Preface to Walter Scott's novel *The Pirate*, and cf. *FOS*:53). The basis of the plot is the same idea as in the story of Aeolus and his bag of winds, which drive Odysseus' ship back the way it came when the curious sailors open the bag, in Book 10 of the *Odyssey*, so it is over 2500 years old. Gaelic versions may have the witch who causes the harmful weather at home and the helpful one at the other end of the voyage, so it is not always a matter of accusing people in another island of being witches, but the story is told of Barra men going to Tiree, Tiree men going to Barra (*T*32:77), and similarly between Sutherland and Lewis, Caithness and Orkney and so on. The end may be the loss of boat and crew, boat only, or the crew being driven back to where they started from: in this version and the next they get off lightly.

83b *(The Three Knots)* SA 1975/163 A1. Recorded from Andrew Hunter, Nesting, Shetland by AJB. *T*34:273–4. Shetland versions see the witch as living in Norway, perhaps a Lapp or 'Norway Finn': there was a regular trade, mainly bringing in wooden material such as boat kits, between Shetland and the west of Norway until the First World War, and it is often pointed out that Lerwick is nearer to Bergen than to Aberdeen.

84 *(Dark Lachlan and the Witches)* SA 1981/1 A1. Recorded from William Matheson, North Uist/Edinburgh by himself. *T*35:308–9 (with Gaelic text), part of a full issue devoted to this notable tradition-bearer, collector and expert on Gaelic songs, genealogy and many other aspects of his native culture, on his retirement from university teaching. The type, W40B, 'Witches Fail to Sink a Ship' (*SS* 11:35) is a reversal of W40A, 'Witches Sink a Ship', where they likewise settle on the mast in the form of crows or black cats until there are enough of them to overcome the magic powers of the helmsman, and the boat goes down. That is mainly associated with one famous loss of a ship within sight of land, when Iain Garbh MacLeod of Raasay was drowned in 1671, and this story has only been collected from South

Uist, possibly referring to an actual occasion in the eighteenth century, when 'Alasdair nam Mart' MacDonald of Boisdale, whose epithet 'of the cows' testifies to his success as a cattle-breeder and salesman, and Lachlan MacMhuirich of the hereditary line of poets to his chief, MacDonald of Clanranald both flourished. William Matheson heard the story from Duncan MacDonald and others in South Uist. The MacMhuirichs, and especially this 'Lachlann Dubh', may have got the reputation of being magicians, which they enjoy in tradition, simply because they could read and write and had a collection of manuscripts in classical Gaelic.

85 *(John MacLachlan and the Girl)* SA 1968/245 B. Recorded from Donald Sinclair, Bailephuill, Tiree by Eric Cregeen. SIT No. 62b Told in Gaelic, but the opening paragraph is from a conversation in English. Donald Sinclair (Dòmhnall Chaluim Bàin, 1885–1975) was Tiree's best-known tradition-bearer, whose father had told many stories to the minister collector John Gregorson Campbell who died in 1891 (see e.g. *SSH and WSS*). See T18:41 ff. for Eric Cregeen's appreciation of this small bachelor crofter and shoemaker with an endless knowledge of everything from Fenian lays to Tiree families and locally composed songs. In this case he was getting a little vague in his old age about the hero of this story, which at different times he told of the nineteenth-century doctor and bard from Morvern named here, of Dr MacLaurine who became factor of Tiree in 1800 and was credited with having the Black Art, and with the 'Ollamh Muileach', the Mull Doctor – one or other of the local branch of the Beaton family who had been physicians to the Lords of the Isles and also had a reputation as magicians. The last is the most usual hero for this type, which has been classified as an international folktale (AT 285B*, 'Snake Enticed out of Man's Stomach'), but is more like a migratory legend – in Scotland more usually about a toad or frog, in Ireland a newt or lizard or a 'demon of hunger' (*Ion-chraois*) in the earliest version, which is the basis of the Middle Irish satirical tale 'The Vision of Mac Con Glinne', written in the twelfth century. Moreover, here the creature, generally said to cause insatiable hunger, is nearly always tempted out with the smell of meat rather than the sound of running water after a salty diet, as in the catalogue description (cf. *PTWH* 2:382).

86 *(The Dancing Reapers)* SA 1954/57 A15. Recorded from William MacDonald, Cùl na Ceapaich, Arisaig, by Calum Maclean. T15:256–61 (with Gaelic text and tune). William MacDonald, a retired crofter from a family of noted tradition-bearers, was described by Calum as 'a splendid storyteller [who] *stands* when reciting stories'. You can still hear him thump the floor with his stick (or the table with his fist?) on the recording of some fine hero tales, as he emphasises the rhythm of one of the runs which he recited at high speed and with great enthusiasm. This story is told of Michael Scot in the Borders (*AFH*:52–3) and MacDonell of Keppoch (*GAB*:92–5), one of several seventeenth-century chiefs credited with magic powers, in the Highlands, as well as less well-known characters like this MacGregor, or in Betsy Whyte's version a 'Black Laird' called MacCallum. Sometimes it is a drink that is refused, sometimes the dancers die of their exertions, but the setting is always harvest time.

87a *(The Borrowed Peats)* SA 1970/231 B2. Recorded from Tom Moncrieff, North

Roe/Virkie, Shetland by AJB on 12th September 1970. *STT* No. 61a. Most memorates and some migratory legends of witchcraft in recent times are concerned with the belief that witches could 'take the profit' of milk and butter, either by being able to milk other people's cows or by extracting the goodness which made butter from it, so that the witch got a churn full of butter and her victims got none. Since there are many reasons why butter may not form, especially when as in the Northern Isles whole milk rather than cream was churned, because of the by-products the storyteller mentions, there were many accusations of this sort of witchcraft, and indeed there is good evidence that women in Shetland still tried to practise it up to the 1930s. The quotation from Burns' 'Address to the Deil' shows that the belief had long been known in mainland Scotland too. There were also many stories of how the spell had been broken, and this is one known in both Gaelic and Shetland variants. Tom Moncrieff got this story from the same old woman born in Lunnasting in 1830 who was the source for his tale No. 42 above. 'Twa colls' means two or three burning peats, rather than bits of coal: it was thought unlucky both to have to ask for them to light a fire that had gone out or to be asked.

87b *(The Borrowed Peats)* SA 1965/18 A6. Recorded from Nan MacKinnon, Vatersay, by Lisa Sinclair in April 1965. *STT* No. 61b. It is not clear in this text, but in other Gaelic versions the butter does not appear in the housewife's churn but in the water the tailor put the peats into.

88 *(Milk in a Tangle)* SA 1965/18 A10. Recorded from Nan MacKinnon, Vatersay, by Lisa Sinclair. *T*38:42–3 (with Gaelic text). This looks like a local memorate, but is migratory: there is a Tiree version in *WSS*:9.

Robbers, Archers and Clan Feuds

89 *(The Girl Who Killed the Raiders)* SA 1968/47 A2. Recorded from Malcolm Robertson, Baleshare, North Uist and transcribed by Angus John MacDonald. *STT* No. 19. Malcolm Robertson (Calum 'Illeasbui' Nèill) belonged to a family noted as story-tellers and tradition-bearers. Like No. 56 above, this story uses the historical background of cattle-raiding by sea, and adds some North Uist place-names, but no family or even clan names: the rest is pure international folk-tale, AT 956B, 'The Clever Maiden Alone at Home Kills the Robbers' – though in this case she is alone in their own tent. The sequel of the surviving robber coming to court the girl is part of the type, which may be familiar from Morgiana in the story of Ali Baba. Bent or marram grass, on the other hand, is something which grows plentifully in Uist and is traditionally used to make horses' harness, though it seems unlikely that if this very hard grass had been used as its bridle a horse would be tempted to eat a knotted rope of it.

90 *Spòg Bhuidhe* SA 1971/5 B6. Recorded from Donald MacDougall, North Uist, transcribed and translated by Angus John MacDonald. *T*7:210–15 (with Gaelic text). Like the previous tale, this is an international novella of robbery, AT 952*, 'A

Sausage and a Revolver', though the type-index only lists versions from Finland and Lithuania: we have another version recorded in South Uist. The historical background of Highland harvesters coming home with their wages from the Lowlands, or more often Highland drovers returning from the Falkirk Tryst with the price of the cattle they had sold (e.g. *T24*:316–9), often provides a plausible setting for such tales of outwitted robbers. The robber's nickname may owe something to the legend of a supernatural robber, the 'yellow-footed weaver' of Gairloch who attacked travellers in the form of a goat (hence the word for an animal's foot rather than a human one: see *PTWH* 2:110–12 and *SS* 11:17–18 for the type, W2)

91 *Dark Finlay of the Deer* SA 1955/168 A11. Recorded from John Finlayson, Druimbuie, Lochalsh by Calum Maclean. *T39*:158–61 (with Gaelic text). John Finlayson ('Iain Smoc') was one of Calum Maclean's favourite storytellers: he describes him in *The Highlands* Chapter VII as 'absolutely steeped in the traditions of Lochalsh and Kintail. It was enchanting to listen to him, for with him the past seemed as living as the present.' His slightly formal style, aware of his audience, includes some stumbles and hesitations that have not been shown in the translation. This clan legend, set here in the context of the sixteenth-century feud between the MacKenzies of Kintail and the MacDonalds of Glengarry and Sleat, is one of several migratory types about archers. The bow is not generally thought of as a Highland weapon, but until guns became more available towards the end of the seventeenth century Highlanders going as mercenaries to the Thirty Years' War in Germany, for instance, were still carrying bows. This story is most often associated with Iain Beag MacAnndra, 'Little John MacAndrew' in Strathspey, who was really so small that the MacDonald raiders, from Keppoch in this case, raiding the cattle of the Grants, easily took him for just a herd-boy: it is not made clear how Finlay warned his wife to treat him as a herdsman, but perhaps it was a prearranged plan.

92 *Gille-Pàdruig Dubh* Donald John MacDonald MS 1:53–7. Recorded from his father Duncan MacDonald, South Uist (see above, note to tale No. 18). Translated by Peggy McClements. *T25*:26–9 (with Gaelic text). This is obviously a variant of the William Tell legend type, too well established in South Uist to be derived from published translations of the Swiss crossbowman's story in the past 200 years. The striking beginning is in any case quite different, though some people now substitute an apple for the more native egg; Angus MacLellan (*SSU*:78–81) gives details of how the egg was tied on to the son Iain Dubh's head with his own long hair and a pit dug so that only the top of his head showed above the ground. Gille-Pàdruig (or Gille Padara) Dubh ('Black Gilpatrick') can be identified as a seventeenth-century MacIntyre in South Uist whose descendants are still there. A 'graddaning hearth' was the place where grain was threshed and dried by burning off the straw and husks.

93 *Gaun Tait and the Bear* SA 1978/63 B1. Recorded from Tom Tulloch, North Yell, by AJB. *T30*:356–7. This is one of the very few Shetland legends which go back to the times when the islands were still ruled from Norway. In this Yell version the hero has the Scots name Gaun (Gavin) rather than the Dutch one Jan as in versions from Fetlar itself (*FOS*:175–8), but they are equally close to early Norse Jón, and

the surname Tait derives from the Old Norse nickname *teitr*, 'cheerful'. Moreover, rents from Orkney and Shetland were largely paid in butter since Norse times, and it was weighed using a heavy beam called a *bismar*. The opening probably started as a piece of wish-fulfilment like that of the last story, but like the hero's proof of courage in cutting off lumps from his toes, and strength in carrying the bear over his shoulder, it has much of the flavour of the Sagas of Icelanders. The capture of the sleeping bear, full of butter, on the advice of a typical donor figure, is more like international wonder-tale; and the end with the bear tied up on Lingey (Linga on the Ordnance Survey map) seems to be origin legend – Tom had seen the circle that he described, whatever the real explanation! *Band*: bound, tied (it up); *braa twa'r three year fae syne noo*: a good few years ago now; *shün*: soon; most other forms here are just pronunciations which it should be possible to decipher.

94 *(The Earl of Mar a Fugitive)* SA 1952/125/4. Recorded from John MacDonald, Highbridge, Lochaber by Calum Maclean. *STT* 65. John MacDonald (1876–1964, known as 'Iain Beag' or more often simply 'The Bard'), crofter, roadman, song-maker, and a very learned man though he only went to school for two or three years, provided most of the stories Calum Maclean recorded in his first field trip for the University of Edinburgh's School of Scottish Studies, starting in January 1951, and he describes their first meeting in Chapter 1 of *The Highlands*. John recorded hundreds of local historical and supernatural legends and other traditions and songs for Calum, mostly unfortunately erased after transcription. This story is apparently an old local tradition: Irish names such as O'Brien did come to the West Highlands with the retainers of chiefs who married Irishwomen, and see tale No. 95c below for another case – but nobody would put something so unlikely-seeming into an invented story. Killing the only cow, however, is a cliché that recurs in the next story, and the rhyme about the cold barley gruel (Scots 'crowdie', Gaelic *fuarag*) mixed in a shoe is elsewhere attributed to Robert the Bruce after his defeat in 1306 (*W&S* 1:76–7).

95a *Paul of the Thong* SA 1971/175 B11. Recorded from Angus MacLellan, Tigharry, North Uist, by Angus John MacDonald. *STT* No. 64. This Angus MacLellan (Aonghus Lachlainn Bhig), a crofter, former lighthouseman and shopkeeper, is perhaps the last person in the Hebrides who can tell a Fenian hero tale, as well as a bard who has composed a number of popular 'homeland' songs. Most of his stories were learned from the famous Alasdair MacCuidhein (MacQueen), who was a regular visitor at the MacLellan home when Angus was young (cf. *Arv* 37:120–23). This is a classic clan legend of the type defined a hundred years ago as the 'Celtic Expulsion-and-Return Myth'. Its historical basis is the murder of the two elder sons of Uisdean (Hugh), the first MacDonald of Sleat, by their brother Gilleasbaig Dubh ('Black Archibald'), who then took the chiefship – this seems to be fact, though the legendary methods of the murders, especially this one, seem less likely. Gilleasbaig was unwise enough to let his nephews live, and come with him on a hunting trip when they were old enough to kill him. In this very local legend, however, he and the chiefship of the clan are ignored, and the second brother (called Dòmhnall

Hearach, 'Harris Donald', because his mother was a daughter of MacLeod of Harris – all the brothers had different mothers) who inherited North Uist is treated as a chief in his own right. The son's posthumous birth and upbringing in exile, his recognition by the old woman who kills her wether for him, and the detailed itinerary of the avenging party are all typical of such tales. The arrow in the foot looks like a version of the Achilles heel motif, but perhaps is just a device so that he can be captured and put to a death befitting a traitor and tyrant. Paul of the Thong (Pàl na hÈille) seems to be a historical character, a MacIntosh, though probably a deputy for Gilleasbaig Dubh rather than a usurper in his own right.

95b *(Murchadh Gearr's Birth)* SA 1973/67 A5. Recorded from Donald Morrison, Ardtun, Bunessan, Isle of Mull, transcribed and translated by AJB. *T*24:296–7 (with Gaelic text), part of a feature by Eric Cregeen on this notable tradition-bearer from the Ross of Mull, a stylish storyteller and singer with a prodigious knowledge of local history and Gaelic poetry well into his nineties. The story of the posthumous birth here is turned into a story of a prisoner with little chance to beget a son. There may have been a real feud at this time (the mid-sixteenth century) between the two lines of the MacLeans in Mull, Lochbuie and Duart, but the facts seem to be totally different: Murchadh was not a baby when his father (presumably) died in captivity, but an illegitimate son of Lochbuie, legitimated after the death of his two elder brothers, who inherited in middle age and was kept from his inheritance not by Duart but by his own uncle Murdoch MacLean of Scallastle (*T*24:295). However, the pattern of posthumous birth and return from overseas (in the next piece) is so well established that it was imposed on the story in oral tradition, though some local antiquaries always knew it was untrue. See note to tale No. 85 above for the Mull Doctor.

95c *(Murchadh Gearr's Return)* SA 1976/54B. Recorded from Donald Morrison in English by Eric Cregeen. *T*24:293–4 (with Gaelic text of the same story from SA 1971/79B, recorded by Eric Cregeen and Donald William Mackenzie, and historical note). This part of the story brings in Donald's own family, and was told separately. The earls of Antrim (the title was not created until over fifty years after this) were in fact descended from a younger son of the MacDonalds of Islay (compare the account in the next story), and are always credited with helping their Scottish cousins, though in this case there is reason to suppose that Murchadh Gearr later married a sister of the future earl of Antrim. The Gaelic text says that the thirteen men were recruited from the teams at the traditional New Year shinty match. Donald's family of Morrisons may actually descend from the Irish bardic family of Ó Muirgheasáin, which also used the name Mac na h-Oidhche, 'Son of the Night', and supplied *seanchaidhs* or historians to the MacLeans of Duart before 1660 (*SS* 12:71, 73).

96 *The Battle of Tràigh Ghruinneart* SA 1968/98. Recorded from Gilbert Clark, Port Charlotte, Islay by Ian A. Fraser. *STT* No. 68; *T*44:110–17 (with Gaelic text and historical note). Gilbert (Gibi) Clark, a joiner and occasional boat-builder in Port Charlotte, was a great enthusiast for the waning Gaelic traditions of the Rhinns of Islay and indeed the whole island. When AJB first met him in 1966, and on later

visits with DAM and Ian Fraser and by Mary MacDonald and John MacInnes, he was too self-effacing to tell what he knew himself, but eagerly guided us to record slightly older tradition-bearers, though if he came in he might often prompt them when their memories failed. This is one of the very few recordings made of a story from Gilbert himself – a story that every Islay Gael knew, but Gilbert knew in more detail. The battle of Gruinart was fought in 1598 between Sir Lachlan MacLean of Duart (Lachainn Mór, originally perhaps physically big rather than 'the Great') and Sir James MacDonald of Islay, who had recently imprisoned his own father Angus and taken his place as chief. Sir James was in fact the son of Sir Lachlan's sister, whom Angus had married as part of an attempted settlement of a long-standing MacLean–MacDonald feud. Sir Lachlan actually came to Islay some time before the battle to claim the Rhinns of Islay, for which he had secured a charter direct from the Crown, though the MacDonalds claimed he held the district from them, and it was only after attempts to discuss the issue had broken down that they came to blows.

In the story, as recorded within a few years of the battle by Sir Robert Gordon (*FOC*:134–5) and as still told, the witch's warnings replace the taboos (*geasa*) of a pattern common in Old Irish tales such as the death of Cú Chulainn – once these taboos (acquired in youth) are broken the hero's death follows inevitably, and even in this story as told in Islay Sir Lachlan is clearly a great hero. An arrow under a raised breastplate or visor (neither used in the old-fashioned Highland armour shown on gravestones of the period) is often how a chief is killed in clan legends. The killer's name Dubh-Sidh, 'Black Fairy', shows he is no common man, and MacLean should not have turned him down. The MacDonalds have the makings of a heroic band of gifted retainers (warrior, doctor, prophet) as well as a totally imaginary contingent of helpers from Arran, which was never MacDonald territory. Various place-names and family origins are accounted for in the course of the story, again in the early Irish manner, there is a church-burning – all too frequent at this period – and even after Sir Lachlan's death his greatness is emphasised by the episode of the foster-mother killing her own son for mocking the body, and the gravestone with the two hearts, implying double courage (the 'hourglass' symbol is probably a chalice carved on a priest's grave). The ending, however, cannot be happy for Islaymen, since Sir James was imprisoned a few years after he won the battle, and the Campbell earls of Argyll began to move in.

INDEX OF STORYTELLERS